Magic in the Storm

What Others Have Said About The Other Books In The Storm Series

Storm on the Horizon

Usually with novellas I find myself anticipating the end almost as soon as I begin to read but I became so lost in this one I was disappointed when the end happened.— *Fiftysgirl2012*

This is one sweet, enjoyable, romantic read.— *Tamara*

Magic in the Storm

This book is a fantastic mix of the paranormal and a regency romance! It has action, excitement, magic, love, hate, social climbing, power grabbing and even a part in the story for Lord Byron the poet. The mix of magic and regency blend into a beautiful story—*Carin, 4myreadingobsession blog*

Magic In The Storm was an edge of the seat read.— *Martha A. Cheves*

Books By Meredith Bond

THE MERRY MEN SERIES

An Exotic Heir
A Merry Marquis
A Rake's Reward
A Dandy in Disguise
My Lord Ghost
My Gentleman Thief
Under the Mango Tree
When Hearts Rebel
A Spanish Dilemma

THE STORM SERIES

Storm on the Horizon
Bridging the Storm
Magic in the Storm
Through the Storm

THE LADIES' WAGERING WHIST SOCIETY

A Hand for the Duke
Jack of Diamonds
The Games She Played

Chapter One: A Fast, Fun Way to Write Fiction
Self-Publishing: Easy as ABC
"*In A Beginning*", a short story featuring Lilith

Magic in the Storm

MEREDITH BOND

THE STORM SERIES
BOOK THREE

ISBN-10: 0615598048

ISBN-13: 978-0615598048

Cover Art by QuarterbackTB, https://qtbdesign.wixsite.com/qtbdesign

Edited by The Editing Hall, http://theeditinghall.com

Published by Anessa Books

Dedication

As always to my husband for his unfailing love and support. And to the memory of Kate Duffy who said that this would definitely be my breakout book, but there was no way she was going to buy it—always honest and yet oddly supportive.

Prologue

June 21, 1794

The wind whipped through Tatiana's hair, prying it free from her forehead where it had been plastered with sweat. Heat swirled around them threatening to burst into flames. Vallentyn jumped as a bolt of lightning shot into the ground just feet from where he stood coddling that infant in his arms.

"Tatiana, stop this! Stop it right now. You cannot kill our son."

"Our son?" she repeated, fury burning through her. "And what of my daughter?" she shouted over the gale of hot wind that wove around them. "What of the prophecy? What..." her voice faltered.

She was tired. Too tired. Although the birth had been easier than many of the others, she was getting old. Only her fury at this injustice kept her awake now.

How could this have happened? Her child, her beloved, her daughter. Seventh child of the seventh child in the seventh generation—a boy!

Tatiana shoved down the pain that threatened to overwhelm her and instead burst forth with another bolt of anger, coming even closer to Vallentyn this time.

"I don't know, Tatiana. Truly, I don't know. But you cannot kill him!" Her husband stood his ground and pleaded with her even as the sweat poured down his forehead.

In a very brief moment of weakness, Tatiana almost felt for him. But then she caught sight of the abomination in his arms and the hot wind picked up once more.

"I can and I will," she shouted. "He was not meant to be. I was to have a girl. She was to be the most powerful Vallen in generations. As powerful as Morgan Le Fey." Tatiana could barely keep the tears from her voice. "My Morgan. She was to be..."

"I know, Tatiana," Vallentyn's voice filled with soothing magic. "But he is still our seventh child. Perhaps he will be powerful. Perhaps the prophecy will still hold..."

"Perhaps? Perhaps nothing! Perhaps he will burn in hell!" The temperature around them rose even hotter.

"Perhaps we all will, but you cannot kill him. Swear to me that you will not." Vallentyn's pale blue eyes looked deeply into her own and she could feel herself crack and cool. How could he do this to her? He was not nearly so powerful as she, and yet... "I swear." The words burned through her. They scorched the air and hung there dripping sweat and then were blown away on his cooling breeze.

The child peered at her from within the protective cocoon of his father's arms, his large dark eyes framed with black lashes so like her own. He reached out a small fisted hand toward her, but Tatiana turned away. She hated him as she had never hated before.

Chapter 1

May, 1815

Adriana Hayden didn't even have to turn around. The quiet click of the door closing and the sigh of the sofa were all that she needed to hear to know that her dearest friend and companion, Henrietta, had come into the room.

She finished dabbing the black paint onto her canvas before stepping back and deciding that she had probably put too much. Well, she didn't care. It was perfect and it reflected her mood so precisely Adriana imagined she wouldn't even need to say a word to Henrietta.

She would paint the whole thing black if it wouldn't ruin what was turning out to be a rather nice depiction of a stormy sea. The water thundered, crashing with violence onto the rocks at the base of a sheer cliff. Menacing clouds hung overhead within moments of letting loose a torrent of rain.

"Oh dear," her companion said quietly, over the roar of the sea in Adriana's mind.

Adriana closed her eyes for a moment to stop them from stinging and then swallowed down the anger that had risen to the top of her throat again. "They wouldn't even let me see him," she said, without preamble.

"Who wouldn't?" Henrietta asked.

Adriana turned around into the quiet of the room. Henrietta was sitting, as always, with her back perfectly straight and her legs crossed at the ankle and tucked ever so slightly under the worn, comfortable sofa. Her brown hair was pulled up so tightly Adriana wondered that it didn't hurt, but her hazel eyes spoke volumes of sympathy, for which Adriana was grateful. Adriana resisted the urge to run up to her dear friend and throw her arms around her.

Instead, she lifted her chin and replied, "The clerk at Sir William's establishment."

"So you didn't even get to see Sir William? You didn't show him your work?"

Adriana shook her head and turned back to her painting. Carelessly, she dabbed more black paint on where it wasn't needed, darkening the sky even further.

"But that's not right!" Henrietta said, full of indignation for Adriana. "What reason did he give?"

Adriana couldn't even bear to turn around to face Henrietta again; the hurt was still too painful. She bit her lip to keep herself from either screaming in rage or crying like a thwarted child. She swallowed hard, again. "The clerk told me that he was certain that my watercolors were very pretty, but Sir William Agnew did not deal in a young lady's dabbling. He only sold the work of true artists." She paused at Henrietta's gasp, but then continued. "He suggested that I give my work to some handsome young gentleman in the hope that he will marry me."

"No, he didn't!"

"Oh, yes."

"Why, the nerve! The gall! The temerity of such... such..."

"A man," Adriana finished for her.

"An imbecile is what I was going to say."

"Perhaps they are one and the same," Adriana said, allowing her mouth to quirk up in a little smile.

Henrietta just harrumphed.

Adriana turned around and attempted to put a real smile onto her face. How was it that Henrietta always made her feel better? No matter what had upset her, Henrietta always slipped herself right up under Adriana's hurt and pried it away.

"It's all right, Henrietta. I'll just try someone else. I don't have to sell my paintings through Sir William. I'm certain there are plenty of other art dealers who will take a look at my work."

"But Sir William is the best," her friend argued.

"Yes, but another dealer will be able to sell my work just as well. He may not get the prices Sir William could command, but at least we'll get the money we need."

"Oh, Adriana, it's such a shame to have to sell your beautiful work..."

"But necessary. Absolutely necessary," she said with all of the conviction and certainty she felt, and that was substantial.

"You wouldn't have to sell so many or worry so much about price if you just left me..."

"I will not! How could you even suggest that I leave you here to deal with Lord Devaux yourself?" She took the few steps that separated them and knelt down on the floor at Henrietta's feet. "We will wait until I have enough money for both of us to survive. I will never leave you."

Henrietta squeezed Adriana's shoulder gratefully. "But..."

There was a knock at the door. Before Adriana could respond, Lord Devaux himself walked into the room.

Adriana stood up. "Cousin!"

It was as if the rainclouds from her painting had just entered the room. Suddenly it felt cold and dark, despite the sun that still shone through the tall windows.

Next to her, Henrietta popped up from the sofa. "I... I'll... Excuse me," she slipped past Lord Devaux as quickly and unobtrusively as she could.

Lord Devaux didn't even acknowledge Henrietta's fast-retreating back. He just allowed his eyes to rove slowly over the small, bright room, taking in all of her paintings piled two, three, sometimes even four canvases deep along the walls.

Adriana's arms slowly wrapped themselves around her middle as she felt, in the pit of her stomach, the disgust that covered her cousin's face. His eyes slowly came to rest on her and his lip finally raised in a sneer.

"What a waste of money and time," he drawled.

Adriana closed her eyes for a moment. "What is it that you want, my lord?" To her own amazement, her voice came out calm and even.

"I want to be rid of all this..." he waved his arm around to indicate all of her hard work, "...this garbage. For once and for all, Adriana, I am finally going to get this trash out of my house."

Adriana found herself having to work hard to keep breathing, but it was becoming increasingly difficult. He couldn't! He couldn't get rid of her paintings. They were her life. They were the only thing that she truly cared about, and her only way out from under his thumb. "You promised me I could keep my work and my studio if I acted as hostess at your political dinner parties..."

"...And kept my house. Yes, I know. But you won't be doing that for much longer." Lord Devaux sighed and walked around the studio slowly, the look of disgust never far from his pinched lips.

"I had hoped to get more years of service out of you when I agreed to take you in." He turned and looked at her, his beady blue eyes glittering with malice. "No one else would, you know. No one else in the family was willing to take Hayden's daughter. He was... odd, what with his experiments and strange notions. But then, so was my cousin, your mother. I suppose that's why they got along so well.

"And you were such a scrawny little thing—you were what, five when they perished?"

Adriana gritted her teeth. "Six." She took a deep breath to dispel the anger that was growing inside of her. "You know I've always been grateful for your... charity," she said. She had thought to say 'kindness', but there was nothing kind in the way Lord Devaux treated her. There never had been.

"Yes, naturally." He made his way back slowly toward the door. "I just hope Henrietta will be as useful as you've been," he said. "I'll need someone to arrange my parties for me and to be my housekeeper. Although she was never very good at it before you took over, perhaps she has learned something from watching you do it for these past five years."

"Why would Henrietta..."

"My cousin has turned out to be an excellent nanny for you, but she is worthless when it comes to dealing with adults," Lord Devaux interrupted her. "We all have our talents, I suppose." He then turned and looked at her with something that could be construed as grudging respect. "You have a natural talent—for housekeeping at least. If not for this." He waved his stubby fingers vaguely around the room.

"Your talents have brought you a husband, Adriana. Er, your talents as hostess and housekeeper, that is."

Adriana's stomach lurched. "A husband? I don't want..."

"If you think I care for a moment what you want..." her guardian began. He didn't need to finish the sentence. Adriana knew he didn't care one whit for her or for what she wanted. She took a deep breath, letting the familiar smell of her paints and turpentine soothe her.

"You cannot force me to marry!" she finally said, trying to keep the triumphant tone from her voice.

"Your father may have stipulated that you had the right to choose your own husband in his will, but that doesn't mean that I can't, er, help you decide." A little smile flickered on his lips. "Either you marry the man I have chosen for you, or this, all of this," he indicated everything in the room with a sweep of his eyes once more, "goes. I will never allow you to draw again."

Spots began to dance in front of Adriana's eyes and the tightness in her stomach made its way up to her throat. "You can't do that," she whispered.

A smile slowly grew on Lord Devaux's face as he looked around the room. "Oh, yes, I can."

And this is the northwest field." Jonathan, the sixth Viscount Vallentyn held his horse steady, proudly looking over a large field filled with tall, green leafy plants.

For the life of her, Adriana couldn't have told the difference between the northwest field and the southwest field, they all looked the same. Idly, she wondered if it was possible to actually die of boredom. If it was, her life was definitely in danger.

"Here we have another crop of barley. Last year it was wheat and next year it will lay fallow in preparation for another..."

Adriana let Lord Vallentyn's voice fade away as she looked out over the rich, green and gold field.

She couldn't decide whether she liked Lord Vallentyn better nervous and nearly silent as he had been when she had first met him the day before, or more relaxed and talkative as he was today.

Yesterday, every time he opened his mouth to say anything his mother had cut him off or immediately contradicted him. Today, without the terrifyingly formidable Lady Tatiana Vallentyn next to him, he was clearly much more at ease, freely describing all of the workings of his estate—in painstaking detail. Adriana nearly groaned in frustration.

No, she had to do this, she reminded herself unhappily. And just to be good, she occasionally truly did listen to Lord Vallentyn's patter, so that she could make an appropriate comment, or ask a relevant question. After over thirty minutes of this, however, her patience was at an end.

This was such a waste of time. There was so much else that she needed to learn about Lord Vallentyn—not because she wanted to, necessarily, but because she had to. She had to find a good argument as to why her guardian should *not* force her to marry this man.

She was certain that if she could just find one thing that would convince Lord Devaux that her marriage to Lord Vallentyn would not be in his best interests, he would call off the whole thing. But what? What was it about Lord Vallentyn that her guardian would not like? Surely, there was something.

"My lord, yesterday you mentioned briefly that you do not actually like visiting London," Adriana said, finally getting desperate enough to set aside good manners and take the plunge into changing the subject.

Lord Vallentyn stared at her with his mouth gaping open for a moment, completely flummoxed by her interruption. A lock of his dark brown hair blew into his eyes. With a careless hand, he brushed it back. "Oh, er, did I? Didn't mean to. Let's continue on to the Northeast field, shall we?" Without waiting for her, he spurred his horse forward.

Adriana would not be put off so easily. "What are your views on the new enclosure laws, my lord?" Perhaps if he held opposing political views to Lord Devaux, then her guardian wouldn't be able to sponsor him in Parliament and, in fact, wouldn't want him there at all.

Lord Vallentyn paused, but only for a moment, before completely ignoring her question and going on with a detailed description of his plan for slowly moving more of his crops over to wheat. They had arrived at the next field, and Lord Vallentyn pulled his horse up so that Adriana could admire it while he went on with his monologue. As soon as they stopped, a large raven swooped down and landed on the ground next to them.

"Shoo!" Lord Vallentyn waved his arm at the bird. "Don't understand why we are suddenly overrun with these creatures," he said, as the bird flew off.

With a frown, Adriana watched the bird as it circled above them, and then turned her attention back to Lord Vallentyn. There had to be something he and her guardian would disagree on. "What about the corn laws, my lord? Surely that will impact your plans for what to plant in the future?"

"I leave that up to those who have more knowledge than I," he answered shortly, and then kicked his horse into motion once more. "I am sorry to hurry you, Miss Hayden, but I don't like the look of those clouds," he called back to her.

Adriana glanced up and had to agree that they did look menacing, but clearly not enough to deter either of them.

She and Lord Vallentyn were coming to the end of the fields, and she still hadn't received any information she could actually use to get herself out of this marriage. Frustration began to simmer inside her.

She had to find out something or else this whole excursion would have just been a waste of time. She didn't know when she would have another chance to be alone with Lord Vallentyn, and to speak with him candidly. Somehow, she was certain that he wanted to marry her as little as she wanted to marry him. If only he would admit it!

In desperation, she pulled her horse in front of Lord Vallentyn's so that he was forced to stop.

She looked directly into his large pale blue eyes, which were now wide with surprise. His heavy brow drew down in concern, but she would not be stopped. "Please, my lord, be honest with me." Adriana leaned toward him and held onto his gaze with her own. "Do you want this marriage as little as I do? If so, you must help me to find a way out of it."

"I do not want this marriage, but it is useless to even try to get out of it. My mother has decided that we should marry, and so we shall." Lord Vallentyn snapped his mouth shut, his eyes suddenly narrowing with suspicion.

Adriana shook her head in frustration. "I cannot simply let Lord Devaux blackmail me into marrying you, my lord. I am sorry."

"Miss Hayden, are you...? Can you...?"

A flash of lightning pulled Adriana's attention away. Only now did she notice that while they had been talking the wind had picked up. Lord Vallentyn had been right to worry. The gray clouds above had begun stirring themselves up into what looked like a significant storm. Luckily, the accompanying thunder took a few minutes to reach them. The rain was still some way off.

Lord Vallentyn's voice had fallen to nearly a whisper, but the wind seemed to blow the word "magic" into her ear.

She didn't know what he was referring to, but it didn't matter. All that mattered now was finding some way out of this marriage. "My lord..."

He shook his head. "Miss Hayden, I am sorry that you, too, do not wish to marry, but you simply must accept it as I have. This is the way of the world. You are from a good family, have been trained..."

"I don't care about any of that. I will not..."

The pounding of hooves interrupted her. A man rode toward them so quickly that, for a moment, she was afraid he would crash straight into them.

The rider stopped just short of where they stood. "My lord, there's... a fire... the Drummond's cottage... afraid it will spread... with this wind..." the man panted.

Adriana was surprised to see Lord Vallentyn immediately sit up straighter in his saddle and take charge of the situation. It was a completely different man who turned his horse in the direction the man had come. He paused for a moment and turned back to Adriana. "Miss Hayden, you must forgive me, I need to go. In any case, our conversation is at an end. There is no more to be said on this subject. Can you find your way back to the abbey?"

"Yes, but..." Another burst of thunder drowned out what she was about to say and Lord Vallentyn did not wait to hear any more. With a quick nod, he and the man rode off in the other direction, disappearing from view within moments.

Adriana sighed. She would not give up this fight just because Lord Vallentyn had. Slowly walking her mare along the border of the forest that edged the last field they had visited, she tried to think of some way out of her difficult situation. It just wasn't right. She was an adult and, as such, should be allowed to decide who, and if, she wanted to marry. Men had this right—well, most men. It seemed as if Lord Vallentyn was as bound to his mother's will as she was to Lord Devaux's.

The raven that had bothered Lord Vallentyn earlier landed in front of her horse, startling her. It took a few hops off to one side, seemed to look directly at her, and then flew up and away.

As she watched it go, she noticed the beauty of the wood next to her. What a good thing it was that she had thought to bring her sketch book along—that was just what she needed to make herself feel better and get her mind off of her problems, at least for a little while.

A glance up at the sky had her praying that the storm would hold off for just a little bit longer. If it didn't, Adriana considered, well then, she would get wet. A few more minutes of freedom was worth a soaking any day.

A well–worn path leading into the dense woods teased her with its enticing twist around a large oak tree before disappearing immediately afterward. She longed to see where it led. She hesitated for only the briefest moment before giving a little click of her tongue and turning her horse onto the path.

The forest gloom could not block out her thoughts as they wandered back to her problems. Even here in the silence of the woods, she found herself desperately wishing she could find some respite from all the horrible twists her life had suddenly taken.

She stopped her horse, and closed her eyes for a moment. Her problems would sort themselves out. She had to have faith that they would.

Taking a deep breath, she let the wind gently caress her. It blew over her eyes and her forehead, smoothing away the troubles that were causing her so much tension. It filled her nose with its fresh scent and allowed her mind to relax and empty.

She opened her eyes to a flash of lightning feeling wonderfully refreshed. Darkness had moved into the forest, deepening the colors all around her, but she could still see clearly ahead of her. It was so pleasant here in the woods with only the sound of the wind in the trees to disturb the absolute quiet. She would explore only a little bit further before turning back.

Chapter 2

Heart pounding, blood racing—he was free. Crouching down against the neck of his horse, Apollo, they moved as one. Skirting low branches, leaping over fallen trees, they flew through the forest, taking the sharp turns that threaded them through the closely growing trees.

The wind was hard in Morgan's face, making his eyes water and his hair fly behind him. This was magic. This was true magic, and nothing could compare. If he closed his eyes, he could almost imagine himself speeding across open fields, down long straight roads, through towns and villages—riding away, far, far away.

Ah, they were approaching the stretch where there was an arrow—straight path through the trees—that beautiful straight—away where they could really run, at least for a short distance. Apollo increased his speed. Morgan knew that the horse was looking forward to this part where he could really stretch out his legs and gallop at full force. Morgan, himself, loved it because he could almost imagine himself free of these towering trees that pressed down on him constantly, never letting him go.

Morgan whispered into Apollo's ear, "Yes! Go, boy, go." He encouraged the horse, praising him as they approached the last tree that held them back.

A burst of fire exploded directly in front of them, the sound echoing in his ears.

Morgan's arm shot up to protect his eyes and face. The horse reared and twisted under him, but instinct kept Morgan seated. He held on as tightly as he could as Apollo fell back onto his forelegs.

Within moments, Morgan was down, off the horse's back trying to figure out what had just happened. His heart pounded in his chest.

The ground beneath his feet began to rumble with thunder, before the sound could even reach his ears. Morgan had never felt anything like this before—it was the strength of the earth, just barely contained.

But there was more. There was something... As the thunder rolled away, he heard it, like a voice in the rumbling of sound. *It's coming, be ready!*

Morgan spun around, looking everywhere, but there was nothing out of the ordinary. Nothing but the forest surrounding him and the tree in front of him, from which smoke lazily snaked up into air. Following the trail of smoke through the thick canopy of trees, Morgan noticed whisps of grey clouds overhead.

A storm.

The tree had been hit by lightning. But there was more. The message had been clear, but he still didn't understand it. What was coming?

Whatever it was, Morgan was ready. He had been ready for years. A sudden chill made him shudder for a moment, but it passed quickly. Could this be it? Could this be what he had been waiting for his whole life?

No matter what, he would be ready.

He turned back to Apollo. The horse was still shaken, so Morgan reached down inside of himself for calm.

Yes, that would help Morgan too. It would help him be ready for whatever it was that was coming.

Slowly, gently, he stroked the horse's soft muzzle, letting the calm flow from his hand into the animal. The horse settled down, but Morgan didn't. Another flash of lightning lit the deepening gloom that was spreading through the forest in anticipation of the storm. The wind ruffled his hair.

He had work to do. If there was going to be a major storm, he would have visitors seeking his protection—many, many of them.

Another deep roll of thunder shook the walls of the old barn, while the wind outside howled with fury as it picked up strength. The door to the barn smashed open and closed behind Morgan. The wooden building groaned at the onslaught.

Apollo whinnied and stomped his hooves in agitation. Morgan turned toward the horse, following his line of vision, but there was nothing—nothing other than a barn full of creatures of every sort.

There had better not be any fighting. Prey and predator were jammed into this too small space, but it would just be for a short time. Surely, they could control their instincts until the storm was over—they had before. But Apollo was clearly agitated.

"What...?" Morgan began, when from somewhere deep within the forest, he heard another horse shriek out in fright. This was followed by a loud crash, and an agonized scream.

This one sounded almost... human.

Morgan froze. How could that be? There was no one in this forest besides him. Neither his cousin nor his old nanny, who sometimes came to visit him, would ride out on a day like today. It must have been an animal.

Still, it was an animal in need. Morgan could almost feel the creature's pain radiating out, calling to him for help.

And there was something else entwined with the need. Deep within him, he felt the same sensation he had had earlier—a sense of anticipation, of beckoning, of portent.

He looked down at the tiny foal in his arms. The poor thing was shaking with fright, and his mother was gently nipping at Morgan's shirtsleeve—reminding him that he had been in the middle of doing something when the scream had distracted him.

Looking quickly around the barn filled with the animals he had brought with him and those which had come there on their own, Morgan swallowed a moment of panicked frustration. How were they all going to fit? If any more came... but there would be more, at least two—the horse he had heard and... whatever else had made that scream.

But there just wasn't space!

Morgan squeezed into Apollo's stall. The small pile of hay in the front corner would have to do for now. Gently settling the foal in the soft hay, he turned back to his horse. "Sorry about this, but you'll just have share."

The horse whinnied resignedly.

With the foal settled, Morgan turned to look for Oberon, his black Labrador.

"Oberon!" Morgan called out. His loud, deep voice caused some of the smaller animals to scurry for cover.

The dog trotted out of the last stall, where Morgan supposed he had been settling in the new litter of pups that a vixen had just brought in.

"I need you to watch over the animals. I'll be back soon." The dog barked his assent, and Morgan knew that he was leaving the creatures well cared for.

As soon as he stepped out of the door, Morgan was buffeted by the strong wind. Despite the urgency of the situation, he stopped and took a deep breath of the fresh air basking for a moment in the wonderful anticipation of the storm.

The expectant feeling he had sensed earlier overcame him once again. It was so close. He reached out with his mind— what was it? Then a thought stopped him.

Could it be? Could it be the destiny his nanny had whispered about as she had soothed him to sleep when he was a child? Could it possibly be exactly what he'd been waiting for all these years?

A flash of lightning arched overhead, sending a shiver of anticipation shooting through him. He loved a brilliant storm. It made him feel vibrantly, joyously alive. This new sensation just added fuel to his exhilaration.

Whatever it was that was coming, he would meet it head on.

He set off, running through the forest, weaving in and out of trees, avoiding the branches trying to reach out and grab hold of him. As a clap of thunder shook the ground, he exulted at the sensation. It was incredible to be out and a part of the storm.

His muscles flexed and flowed like the wind, as he skipped over fallen debris, ducked under low branches, and moved rapidly through the closely grown forest. Flashes of waving branches caught his peripheral vision, but he kept moving forward toward whatever it was that had called out to him. He was moving toward his destiny—he knew it deep in his heart.

He ran faster, eager to get there—until a large half–fallen tree brought him up short. Morgan urgently shoved his shoulder against the trunk, frustrated at the delay. He needed to get through—now.

Amidst the rustling of the leaves and his own heavy breathing, he heard the horse's agonized whinny again from somewhere to his left. The tree was wedged in tight. It wouldn't budge. He would have to find another route, and quickly; the cries were becoming more distinct, urgent. His heart pounded in his ears as he doubled back, looking desperately around for a break in the growth. Within a minute, he found another path, and ran along it as fast as he could.

The sounds were closer. They almost seemed to be grunts or groans rather than cries, but he knew of no animal that would make such sounds. He was nearly there!

Finally, shielding his face with his arms, he leapt through the undergrowth into a newly made clearing. A flash of lightning illuminated the scene before him, but as he stood there panting, he could barely believe his eyes.

A sense of brilliant auburn hair glinting in the lightning—red and a touch of gold mixed in with the soft brown. Deep blue clothed arms reaching out from a slender form.

A girl?

Disappointment dropped in Morgan's stomach. It wasn't his destiny that had been calling out to him. His destiny didn't lie with a girl.

It had been a trick, a cruel trick. He wanted to shout out his frustration. To scream down the heavens. How could this happen? He'd been so sure...

He took a deep breath and pushed aside his disappointment. The woman needed his help. She had called out to him and he, as always, would do everything he could in response.

Morgan took a step closer to her, his eyes flitting around the open space all around her. How odd it was that the trees held back, away from her.

She looked up at him then—and Morgan's breath caught in his throat. A vibration hummed through his body. Through her pain–filled eyes there was something there—something familiar. It was as if he knew her. Surely he'd never met her before. He certainly would have remembered meeting such a beautiful girl.

Her face was framed on one side by a lock of hair that had fallen from the loose knot at the top of her head. If it were not for the contortion of pain on her face, she would have been the most beautiful woman he'd ever seen. Tears slid over high cheekbones and down creamy white cheeks, falling toward pink lips.

A rush of heat rose within him, and he pulled his eyes away from her face with difficulty.

Pushing aside these peculiar feelings, he focused his mind instead on rescuing her. He instantly saw her problem—a tree had fallen onto her leg, pinning her down. She was trying to push it off, but it was an impossible task, and she moaned and cried with the effort and pain.

She looked up at him again as he approached her, a gust of wind blowing her radiant hair from her face.

He was struck by the allure of her shining green eyes, her tears magnifying the brilliance of their color. The exact color of new leaves in spring, they were filled with a pain that touched his heart.

Squatting down next to the young woman, he stroked away the tension in her face. As he did so, however, heat surged again into his hands and down his body. He swallowed hard, looking deeply into her eyes. They were as familiar to him as his own, and their depths pulled him in. These were eyes he could drown in.

But not now. Now he could feel her pain as if it were his own. He had to help her.

Running his thumbs across her forehead, he wiped away her fears, all the while holding her gaze. Making his voice as soft and soothing as possible, he said, "Be calm. It is all right. I am here."

He felt her give a deep, shuddering sigh as she quieted, as every animal did at his touch. He then moved to the tree. It was a good–sized one, and had probably been standing in this forest for more than fifty years. Straddling it just next to her, he fitted his hands underneath as far as they would go, and bent his knees.

His eyes still fixed on hers, he said quietly, "When I lift, pull your leg out."

She nodded her understanding, tears still streaming down her face as a testament to her pain. He took a deep breath, focusing his energies—and then, muscles knotting at the effort, lifted the enormous tree trunk.

It was not much, merely a few inches, but it was enough.

The woman quickly backed away so her leg came out from underneath. As soon as she was clear, he let go, and the tree fell once again with a thump and a rustle of leaves.

Morgan knelt next to her as she sat crying softly. He admired her for her forbearance. Still, he did what was natural to him, calming her once again with a stroke of his hands down soft pale cheeks. He knew just how to calm her, how to make her feel better—and it thrilled him that he knew this.

"Calm, now. It is all right," he said, looking deeply into her eyes and willing his voice to soothe her and ease her fears.

Her breathing slowed, but he could sense that she was still in a great deal of pain.

He moved back to her injured leg and lifted her skirt away just enough to bare her calf. Luckily, the bone had not broken through the skin. All he needed to do was to lay her leg straight once more, the bones aligned with each other.

He wrapped his hands around her delicate leg, to ease away the pain and mend the hurt. He could already feel the tattered tendons, nerves and bone obeying the heat of his touch as they moved together...

And then he stopped, snatching his hands away as if they were burned by her skin.

Chapter 3

Fury flared in Lady Tatiana Vallentyn's breast.

"Vallentyn! What are you doing here looking like a chimney sweep? Where is Miss Hayden? Where have you been?" Tatiana wanted answers, now.

Jonathan turned around and slowly descended the two steps he had just taken up the broad staircase. His face was streaked with soot, as were his hands and clothes.

"I beg your pardon, Mother. I was just on my way upstairs to get cleaned up. There was a fire and I was forced to leave Miss Hayden in order to attend to it."

He stopped speaking abruptly, his eyes widening. "Is she not here? She said she would return to the abbey when I left her."

Tatiana gritted her teeth together in a vain attempt to control her anger. "Fool!" she spat. She turned from him and accosted the footman who was standing at attention just inside the front door.

"Has Miss Hayden returned yet?" she asked.

He clasped his hands together in front of him to stop them from shaking so obviously. "No. No, my lady. I have not seen her."

Tatiana turned once more, rounding on her son, who was looking like an idiot with his mouth hanging partially open.

"I don't understand," he said helplessly. "She said she knew her way back. We were just about to return when I was informed of the fire. She said she would continue on by herself."

"And why were you on your way back so early? Why were you not courting her like I told you?"

"I took her on a tour of the estate and we, um, conversed. She seemed to be getting a bit tired, however..."

"Conversed? I sincerely hope you didn't bore her to tears by prattling on about your farm?"

"No! We spoke of other subjects as well. Of, er, my plans to enter parliament, the new enclosure laws and the Corn Laws. I believe she is quite interested in such things."

Tatiana didn't believe her son for a minute. He clearly believed he was telling the truth, however—either that or he had suddenly attained the ability to hide his true feelings from her. She decided to let him go on this point.

"Then you should have seen her safely into the house before going off on your foolish errand."

"It..." Jonathan wisely stopped before attempting to defend himself. He had learned well not to antagonize her any more than was necessary, she thought with satisfaction. All but one of her children had learned that valuable lesson when they were young, and that one child had been banned from the family home, never to be spoken of.

"Yes, Mother. I am sorry. I did not stop to think," Jonathan said, hanging his head, both to show his guilt and to avoid looking into her eyes.

She knew his tricks, but this time she was not going to allow him to get away with them. Too much was at stake here.

"You are an imbecile, Jonathan. A worthless idiot. I give you one simple task, and you cannot even handle that," she hissed. He flinched and held his arms protectively over his chest as her words cut into him. "This girl needs soft words, not talk of enclosure laws. You must court her. If you don't, it will be that much more difficult to convince her to marry you. Need I remind you that you must marry someone with clout in order to make your mark in Parliament?"

Tatiana allowed her voice to soften. "You will be great, Jonathan. You will be powerful. But you need the contacts that Devaux and this girl can give you. There is no one who can ease your way into the upper echelons of Parliament better than Devaux."

"Yes, Mother." Jonathan stared down at the floor. She knew what he was thinking. She could sense his dissatisfaction, his unhappiness. Eventually, he would be grateful. Once he became powerful among men, he would thank her for making it possible. He would understand.

She softened her tone even further, stroking him gently with her words. "Go then. Get changed and cleaned up. You will need to look your best this evening in order to continue your wooing of Miss Hayden."

He sighed softly and dropped his arms back down to his sides. "Yes, Mother." With a small bow, he left her presence and went up to his room.

"You," she said to the footman, "I will take care of you now. Join me in the solarium." He bowed low and, quaking, followed her as she continued on her way toward the back of the house.

He couldn't. He couldn't heal her.

Morgan sat back. If he healed her, he would be putting his life at risk.

This woman was a stranger, even though he felt as if he knew her. But what if she told someone that he had healed her leg with his hands? They would come and find him—they could even put him to death. His entire family would be in danger then.

He looked once again at the girl who sat crying quietly. She was being so brave, but her agony tore at his heart. He could sense how much effort she was using to control herself, and deal with the pain. Never had he seen a girl behave with such strength in a situation like this. Surely, she wouldn't tell anyone?

The wind whipped around both of them, swirling around the small clearing. The storm was approaching quickly.

The young woman raised her face to him, her green eyes overflowing pools of pain. Reflecting the green of the thrashing branches overhead, they somehow pulled Morgan deep into them. They pleaded with him to do something, to help her. He could not bear to see her hurting in this way—but the fire that raced through his veins was not just one of compassion. He was drawn to her as he had never been drawn to anyone before. She sparked feelings in him—feelings he didn't quite understand, but without a doubt, he knew he had to help her. He had to heal her—no matter what the consequences.

He ran a hand down her soft cheek once more, this time reveling in the flames that surged through him as he did so. "It will be all right," he said softly.

Then, placing his hands once again around her leg, he focused his eyes on the broken bone and concentrated. Slowly, his magic began to build again. It moved from all parts of his body, like a tingling sensation, to converge in his hands. His palms grew hot with magical heat binding the bone back together.

The girl gasped as her leg heated and healed. He saw her eyes come back into focus as she relaxed now that the pain was gone. He watched, fascinated, as she wiped away the tears from her face, leaving muddy streaks down her soft, white cheeks.

With his eyes still fixed on her face, Morgan ran his hands a little further up her leg and then along the other. His hands still tingled as he felt her slender, shapely limbs. Never before had his hands felt like this after mending bones – usually the magic went away immediately, but he had never mended a stranger's bones before—perhaps there was something different in that.

Or perhaps it was her.

With a gasp, she quickly freed herself from his touch, curling her legs underneath her and moving her skirt down to cover herself again.

"I am checking for other breaks," Morgan said, sitting back. It was the truth, but it had also been extremely pleasant feeling her legs. He could not deny that.

"There are none, thank you," she said gently, but firmly. Then she paused as if about to say more. "How, how did you...?"

The wind whipped her hair into her face, and she had to stop speaking to remove it from her mouth.

Morgan looked up at the sky and silently thanked the wind for coming to his aid. He could not risk her learning any more about him—already he had done too much. There was no doubt that there would be repercussions from his actions.

"There is no time for that," he said, standing up and moving away from her. "You must return, quickly—before the rain comes," he said, fervently wishing that he could ask her to stay. But there were too many reasons why she couldn't.

He moved to her horse and stroked the animal's nose, looking into its eyes to calm its fright. Then, with practiced ease, he felt down each of its legs, checking for injuries.

When he turned around, he saw that the young woman had managed to stand up, if a bit unsteadily. He noted the confusion clearly mirrored in her face as she realized that her leg would take her weight.

"Who are you? Why do I feel as if I know you? Have we met?" she asked, approaching him slowly and trying to secure her long hair back at the same time.

Morgan nearly dropped the reins in his hand. She felt it too?

"Have you ever been to these parts before?" he asked.

"No, never."

"Then we could not have met. But," he paused and took a few steps closer to her, "I feel it too—as if I know you, but I don't. I couldn't."

She reached out and put a hand on his arm. Looking up into his eyes, she held his gaze for a moment and then said softly, "Please, tell me who you are."

"My name is Morgan, but..." another flash of lightning arced overhead, catching his attention.

That was odd. He had told her his name without intending to do so.

The roll of thunder immediately followed the lightening. He shook his head and pushed aside his confusion. There wasn't time for this—the storm was nearly upon them. "You really must go."

He reached out and wrapped his hands around her slender waist, lifting her easily. As if they'd done this a hundred times before, she rested her hands comfortably on his shoulders. Her skin felt warm through the thin material of her dress, and he was tantalized by her sweet smell... elusive, unidentifiable, but reminding him of the first wildflowers of spring. A fierce desire to hold her close to his own body overwhelmed him.

A strong gust of wind blew directly in his face. Yes, he agreed silently with it, he had to resist these traitorous urges. Already he had placed himself in jeopardy by healing her. How much more stupid could he be?

He placed her gently on the saddle. Whispering softly in the mare's ear, he gave it a slap on the rump and then watched as the horse took off in the direction of the stables.

Morgan stayed where he was, concentrating on the sky, willing the storm to wait until the girl reached the abbey. Yes, he had recognized the horse as one belonging to his brother, Jonathan, Lord Vallentyn.

He turned in the direction the girl had gone and found her straining to look back at him. She was... enthralling, but he did not have the time to wonder who she was or why she was visiting his family.

He took a deep breath, savoring the prelude of the rain in the air. He could still sense the lingering anticipation of his destiny—or whatever it was. But now, it had changed. There was still tension charging the air, but no longer did he feel as if something was coming. In fact, that sensation was almost entirely gone.

Had he missed it? Had his chance come and gone? Was he doomed to live in this forest forever?

No, he couldn't, he wouldn't, believe that to be true.

Chapter 4

The wind lashed around Adriana as she rode to the stables. She wasn't sure if she was directing the horse or if it was following orders from the mysterious man she had met in the woods. He had certainly said something to the horse. Was it possible that he could communicate with animals as well as heal bones?

Adriana nearly laughed at her fanciful thoughts. Men could not heal bones with a touch. Nor could she know a man she'd never met. But she *did* know him. Everything about him had been familiar and comforting. How could this be? She needed to think this through, but of much more immediate concern was the storm overhead, and the slate–colored clouds looming ominously. She needed to get back to the abbey quickly.

Much to her amazement, she made it to the house just before the storm broke. The moment she was inside, there was a great crack of lightning followed immediately by a booming of thunder that shook the old stones of Vallentyn Abbey. Rain pelted down from the sky in relief.

Adriana looked out from the doorway and took a deep breath, smelling the wonderful, fresh smell of the first raindrops hitting the ground. She was tempted to go back out into the storm—to be a part of it, to feel the cool water against her warm skin. She took a small step forward, wondering if she actually dared to go back out.

A large dog came and stood very close to her. He looked as undecided as she felt, only he stood with one paw in front of her. It was as if he was intending to block her from leaving the house.

"Adriana! What do you think you are doing? Where have you been?"

With a start, she turned around and saw her guardian, Lord Devaux, bearing down on her from across the great hall. She stood up taller and moved away from the door, toward the staircase in the center of the hall. All thoughts of going out into the storm disintegrated like dust at her feet. Her guardian, worse than the harshest governess, was here to see that she did not do anything daring or fun.

"I was out riding. If you will excuse me, sir."

He stopped her at the bottom of the stairs and narrowed his little blue eyes at her as he did every time she returned from being out. What he was thinking when he did that? Was he looking for some evidence of misconduct?

If so, then he was, once again, to be sorely disappointed. She smiled at him, secure in her innocence.

"Lord Vallentyn returned nearly an hour ago and was concerned that you had not returned before him. Where have you been?" he said, his voice high with annoyance.

The large oak door closed behind them with a boom that echoed through the medieval hall—shutting out the storm, shutting out her freedom.

Adriana flinched. Her precious moments of liberty were gone, but she would hold onto whatever she could—she had to.

"I was enjoying the fresh country air," she said in a firm, but quiet voice. "Now, if you will excuse me, I need to change and put away my sketchbook."

He took a step back, eyeing her sketchbook with distaste. "See that you hide it well. We do not want anyone seeing that rubbish."

Her guardian knew so well how to hurt her. She would not give him the satisfaction of showing it, however. She turned away from him and began up the stairs, her pace slow and dignified.

Her steps quickened after she reached the top of the stairs. By the time she reached her room at the end of the long corridor, she was nearly running.

Throwing open the double doors that led from her room out onto the balcony facing the back of the house, she allowed the storm to blow the hurt and tension from her mind and body. The curtains framing the door flew out behind her as the wind and rain gusted in.

Adriana did not mind. She stood just inside the door watching the magnificent storm play out as if solely for her own enjoyment.

Taking a deep breath of the cool air, she closed her eyes and allowed the wind and rain to wash over her.

Freedom. This is what it would feel like. Like the wind and the rain going wherever it willed, like a bird soaring over the land, like the waves of a briny ocean. Freedom was the knowledge that she could leave any time, or stay and do whatever she wanted. Freedom, however, was not something that Adriana had—only something she longed for with every ounce of her being.

Enjoying the feel of the storm, she could pretend that, for the moment at least, it was hers.

In her mind's eye, she saw again the black, piercing eyes of the man in the wood. Morgan. She shivered at the memory of the fire in those eyes when he had held her leg and mended the bone.

Quickly, she spun around and grabbed up her sketchbook. With a few quick strokes of her pencil, she captured those eyes before they faded from her memory. Filling in the dark pupils, she stared at them as they stared back at her.

The fire was there. His eyes looked at her with an intensity that sent a rush of heat through her.

That same fascination, and the deep feeling as if she knew him, overcame her as she stared into his black eyes in the center of her white sheet of paper.

The eyes needed a face.

She sketched in Morgan's features around his eyes. His slightly curving eyebrows, his long straight nose and his mouth. She drew his mouth very slowly and carefully, making his bottom lip full and his top lip thin.

She imagined what it would be like to kiss those lips. They would be warm and gentle. She looked again at what she had drawn, and noticed a slight smile to his lips. Yes, he was a kind man. And set now in his face, his eyes showed him to be thoughtful as well.

She drew the outline of his face, shading in his high cheekbones and strong chin. And then his hair. He had long, wavy black hair. Adriana's pencil took many long curving strokes in drawing his hair, reveling in its thick softness.

She added the lines of his neck and the top of his shoulders. They were broad shoulders. Strong shoulders. Perfect for relying on. She knew he would care for her and make her happy.

She sat back and studied her drawing. Yes. She had captured the man with her pencil. In careful lettering she added his name, "Morgan" to the bottom of the page and then the date, 5 May, 1815.

She was very pleased. She had never drawn a person before, only inanimate objects and nature. Storms were a passion of hers, as were sunsets, violent seas and swift rivers.

It depended on her mood what she drew or painted. When she was happy, which was not too often, she painted sunrises and sunsets with a beautiful blending of all the muted colors. When she was angry, it was a storm or a violent sea that flowed onto her canvas with its grays, blues and black. When she was feeling trapped in her London prison, she drew large open spaces—fields to run free in, beaches to splash through the cool water, rolling meadows and hills.

Painting freed her. Only in her paintings did she truly live. She did not care if her guardian was right and she had no talent. When she looked at her paintings or drawings, she felt the same feelings she had when she created them. Somehow, she felt as if she were there, wherever it was that she had painted.

Never before had she drawn a person. She looked at the man in her drawing. That he had known just what to do to make her calm unnerved her, but she had known somehow, from the minute she had seen him, that he would.

And there was something more. She was attracted to him in a way she'd never felt towards any other man. He was so large, with a raw strength that emanated from his very being, and yet he had been kind, gentle and soothing when she had been in pain.

He had healed her.

But that was impossible.

Men, no matter how strong or calming, could not heal broken bones. Yet he had. He had placed his hands around her leg and...

Adriana touched her leg where Morgan had touched it with his large, warm hands. It was bruised, but that was all. A shiver ran up her spine.

She had to find out more about him. Knowing his name was not enough.

The thought of asking her sent a chill through her, but Lady Vallentyn was the only one who would know.

Chapter 5

There were only a few candles lit in the long, dark solarium, creating a small pool of light at the table where Lady Vallentyn and her niece, Miss Havelock, were working. Every so often, flashes of lightning from outside the large windows dispelled the shadows. The women paid no attention to the storm, however, speaking quietly and intently as they tended to their plants. Adriana hesitated at the door, unsure of whether she should interrupt them.

It seemed as if a lesson was going on. Lady Vallentyn, who had her back to Adriana, was explaining something to Miss Havelock about the particular plant in front of her. Miss Havelock nodded her understanding, but before she could say anything, Lady Vallentyn held up her hand to quiet her.

"What is it, my dear?" Lady Vallentyn asked sweetly, turning around and looking over at Adriana. "I do hope that you had no trouble finding your way back to the abbey after my son so rudely abandoned you."

How had Lady Vallentyn known she was there? The question flitted ever so briefly through Adriana's mind, but she the sickly sweetness in her hostess's voice distracted her. There was something about this woman that made Adriana very uneasy. She was so cold and serious. Adriana suppressed a shudder.

"It was not a problem, my lady. I didn't get lost. I merely continued my ride alone."

"And where did you go, alone?" Lady Vallentyn asked, sending shivers up Adriana's spine.

"To, to the forest," Adriana began hesitantly. She then shook off her irrational fear, told herself she was being ridiculous. Lady Vallentyn was clearly mistress of this estate; if anyone knew who this man was, it would be her. Adriana then succinctly told Lady Vallentyn all that had happened—including how Morgan had healed her with his touch. As she finished her tale, a bolt of lightning illuminated the look on Lady Vallentyn's face and Adriana knew that she had just made a mistake. Possibly a very serious mistake. She took a step backwards toward the door.

Even now in the bleak candlelight, she could see that Lady Vallentyn's face had gone quite pale. Her deep red lips were pressed together to form a thin line. Suddenly Adriana was very scared—but still, she had to know.

"Do you... do you know who he is, this man?" Adriana asked, gathering her courage.

Lady Vallentyn's mouth turned up into an unpleasant smile. She took a few steps toward her, and, with some effort, Adriana held her ground.

Putting her hands on Adriana's shoulders, Lady Vallentyn looked into her eyes. When she spoke her voice was oozing with so much sweetness that Adriana almost shook with fear.

"My poor dear. Obviously you hit your head when you fell." Her voice became deeper and more resonant as she said firmly, "There is no man who can heal bones with a touch. That is patently ridiculous, as I am sure you would agree."

Adriana shook her head. That was an odd sensation—it was almost as if she had heard the words inside her head. Had she said them, or had Lady Vallentyn? She couldn't be sure.

Lady Vallentyn turned Adriana toward the door and walked her to it with her arm across her shoulders. When they reached the entrance, she faced Adriana again. "You must go directly up to your room, my dear Miss Hayden. You have had a terrible shock. You are clearly imagining things."

"But what about the man? He said his name was Morgan. Do you know of him?" Adriana was unsure of why she kept asking questions. She wanted nothing more than to get away from this woman. There was something odd happening. It frightened her.

She felt very confused. She should just go back to her room. But then it happened again.

"There is no man. It was all in your imagination."

Adriana saw Lady Vallentyn's lips move, but the voice she heard was in her mind.

Lady Vallentyn looked at her with some concern. "Go now and lie down, Miss Hayden. You do not look well. I will send a maid up with a draught that will calm you down and make you feel better."

Adriana paused just inside the door and looked up once more into Lady Vallentyn's eyes. They were black, shuttered and cold. Adriana suppressed another shudder and then did as she was told.

"Oh, and Miss Hayden..." Lady Vallentyn called after her.

Adriana stopped and turned around.

"Please do not ride in the forest any more. It is an old wood and clearly there are many unstable trees. I would not want you to chance getting seriously hurt."

Adriana gave a little nod, and then turned and went up to her room.

Once again she had heard that voice in her mind. As she climbed the steps to her room, Adriana tried to shake off the creepy feeling this left her with. She had the impulse to shake her head, as if she could shake the voice out of it. Instead, she felt the words interweaving through her mind, entwining with her own thoughts and ideas. They began to mesh and blend so that it was getting to be more and more difficult to remember what Lady Vallentyn had said to her and what she had thought on her own.

Did the man Morgan really exist or had she just imagined him? What would happen if she went riding in the woods? Would a tree fall on her again? Or perhaps she would become seriously hurt in another way? She could not take that chance, it was too dangerous—or was it?

Adriana's head began to ache from trying to figure out what was real, and what she had imagined; what she had said or thought, and what had come from Lady Vallentyn. Hopefully, the draught would not only help her sleep, but would make her head stop aching as well.

"Morgan, I would speak with you," a voice called from outside.

All of the animals in the barn suddenly became very quiet. Morgan finished cutting the apple in his hand and distributed it to a few animals. Sheathing his knife, he gave Apollo a gentle pat on his nose and then went out into the pouring rain.

His mother sat on her large black stallion, waiting impatiently for him. The rain fell in sheets all around her, but not one drop dared to fall directly on the lady or her horse.

As he moved closer to her, the rain bent to avoid him as well. Within her protective circle, it was as if there was no storm. No rain, no wind. Just tension. While all around them mother nature gave vent to all of her feelings, within Lady Vallentyn's world there was nothing.

"Good afternoon, Mother," Morgan said, giving her a slight bow, and ignoring the cold rain water that dripped from his hair.

"You met a girl today and healed her broken leg," she began without preamble.

"Yes." Dare he ask about her? He had hardly been able to focus on caring for the animals in his barn for thinking about her. He *had* to find out who that girl was.

"You imbecile!"

Morgan flinched and automatically turned his shoulder toward her as her harsh words cut him. "You know very well what would happen if she were to tell anyone of the man who could heal broken bones with a touch. We would all be discovered."

"I was aware of the consequences of my actions," he said. He stood tall, all of his muscles tense, ready for the scolding she was about to unleash upon him.

"But that did not stop you?"

"No. She was in pain and needed immediate care." He didn't mention the fact that he couldn't stand to have anyone that beautiful in such pain, nor how brave and strong she had been in light of the situation.

Do you worst, Mother, he said in his mind, knowing she could read his emotions if not his very thoughts. *I would do it again in a moment were I given the chance.*

His mother let out a sound like the hissing of a cat. "You spineless little boy. Such weakness will be your downfall. Just be sure that it is not mine as well."

There was nothing for him to say. He had known when he healed the young woman that he was doing something dangerous, something that he would pay for. He did wonder how his mother had found out, but then, she always seemed to know whenever he had done anything wrong, no matter what it was.

"Is she all right? Who is she?" Morgan bit his tongue, and wished the words back into his mouth.

"You are not to seek her out," his mother said, in her deep commanding voice. Her words resonated in his mind.

Morgan knew what she was doing—she was using her powers of persuasion to make sure he did her will. He had experienced her powers enough times in his life to know that he would not be able to stop them from taking hold of him.

That didn't stop him from trying to fight them. He stared into her bottomless black eyes and tried to block her words with his mind. Even as he did so, however, he felt the coils of her power insinuate themselves into the niches and crevices of his will, and he knew he could never win. His mother's words bound him, and forced him to obey.

His hands balled up into fists as he stared harder at his mother, fighting her power over him with everything he had.

He would not obey. He would seek out this girl. He would find out who she was. He would not obey his mother. He would do as he willed.

A sharp pain caught him directly between his eyes. Thrown backwards, he had to break eye contact, and ended up on the ground.

Frustration seethed from within him. He was destined to be the most powerful Vallen of all time! And yet, he could not even protect himself from his own mother's powers. How was he to attain his destiny if he were so helpless? He knew his mother was strong, but he should be even stronger.

His mother laughed. "What a fool you are, Morgan. You think you can best me? I am the most powerful Vallen in Great Britain, and you..." She moved her horse forward so that it was only inches from him. "You are nothing but a man."

Morgan held himself stiff, refusing to let her see the pain she was causing as her words cut deeply into him. She leaned down and whispered, as if telling him a great secret, "Never shall you know your full powers, Morgan. Never."

She sat straight again and looked down at him with contempt. "You are nothing, and you never will be anything because you are male. It is your own doing. Had you been born a girl, as was destined, you would not be in this position now."

It wasn't his fault! He wanted to scream at her, to shout and fight against her for taunting him as she always did. But it was of no use. Not only wouldn't she listen to him, but she would laugh. She would laugh at his impotence just as she always had—and that would hurt more than anything else.

Her cutting words had already reopened all of his old wounds, the lashes that criss–crossed his back. Soon his shirt would be soaked with his blood, but he ignored the pain. He would not give her the satisfaction of seeing how she hurt him, nor would he back down. He would never...

"Give up, Morgan."

He seethed, his heart pounding with anger.

"No! Never! I will be powerful. I will attain my destiny!" Morgan's shouts echoed through the woods as he leaped to his feet.

"You are nothing!" she said quietly, interrupting his rant. She had no need to shout. She could make her herself heard with a mere whisper. "You are nothing, and soon you will be even less."

That stopped him. "What do you mean, I will be less?"

"You shall see. It is almost time," she said cryptically, but it was the true happiness on her face that terrified Morgan. "No longer will I have to worry about you stupidly misusing your meager little powers. Soon, Morgan, very soon."

"I did what I had to do," he ground out from between his teeth.

His mother's eyes narrowed in anger. "Then you will pay for it." She raised her hand, palm facing outward and focused her eyes on the barn.

"A pox on all that dwells in this place!" Her voice resonated throughout the clearing, permeating the air and was carried, swirling into the barn.

"No!" Morgan bent his mind to retrieve the words, to pull them to him instead, but it was too late.

With a laugh, his mother turned her horse, and rode away into the dark woods.

Morgan dropped to his knees, his heart pounding hard in his chest, as he watched her ride off. Slamming his fist into the soft, wet ground beneath him didn't do anything, but his frustration and anger demanded some action.

Morgan looked up, thankful that the rain was falling on him once again. He needed to feel it on his heated face and body. He needed it to cleanse him of his anger.

As his heart slowed, he realized that there was something missing. He had felt something leave him earlier when he was working in the barn, but now he felt it more acutely. It was like a hollow in the pit of his stomach. Something had been taken from him.

Had his mother taken it? She had extracted no promises from him, and he had given none. He didn't quite understand it, but somehow some small piece of him was gone.

Slowly, he got up and wiped the dirt from his hands on his breeches. He paused to remove his shirt and vest—he would reopen his wounds if he took them off later, once his cuts had begun to heal. Tossing his ruined clothing towards the door of his cottage, he went back to the barn.

How many animals would he have to cure of the pox? How many hours of sitting and making the needed potion and then feeding it to the innocents his mother had harmed due to his own stupidity?

No, not stupidity. He had known he would pay for healing the girl.

Chapter 6

Adriana was finally able to escape her duties later the following afternoon. She had to search for Morgan—had to find out if he was real or not.

She immediately changed into her riding habit and, armed with her sketchbook, went out riding towards the forest.

It was a perfect day for a ride. The sun was shining, and the storm of the day before had moved off in the night, leaving the world looking bright, and smelling refreshed.

She enjoyed a brisk trot, moving with her horse and relishing the feel of the warm air brushing against her face. She felt good just knowing she was taking steps towards solving the mystery that had been plaguing her.

She would find out the truth. She was determined to scour the woods for any sign of this man—for anything to clear up her uncertainty.

As she neared the forest, however, a strong feeling of foreboding overcame her. She did not know why, but suddenly riding through the forest was a terrifying proposition. She jumped as a large black bird swooped over her head and landed just in front of her horse. It was the same raven she'd seen the other day. She didn't know if this was a good omen or not. She nearly laughed at herself—it probably lived in the woods, that was all.

Still, her stomach muscles tensed as she looked at the thick stand of tall trees. Why, anything could happen if she rode through the forest. The trees were old and set so close together. She had been extremely lucky the day before when the tree had only fallen on her leg. She might not be so lucky this time.

Adriana stopped short of the line of trees. No, it would not be a good idea to ride into the woods. Not today. Possibly not ever.

But she had to find out if Morgan existed!

Adriana sat on her horse in indecision for a few minutes, trying to figure out how she was to do this. Slowly, she dismounted, keeping her eye on the forest. If she was going to have any chance of finding this man, it would be here, in the woods.

Just as her foot touched the ground, she realized what she could do.

What if she walked through the forest? Surely there was nothing wrong in that. She couldn't fall from her horse, and if a tree began to fall, she could run for safety.

She loosely tied her horse to a tree. Tucking her sketchbook under her arm, she took a few hesitant steps into the wood.

This felt right.

She took a few steps more and decided this was indeed the answer. She could most certainly walk through the woods, but never, ever ride. Riding was simply too dangerous. She had realized that yesterday—or had Lady Vallentyn told her this?

She couldn't quite remember who had said it, but then, there were a few things she was uncertain of after her conversation with Lady Vallentyn. It was very odd.

Now, however, she would find out whether Morgan was just a figment of her imagination. For once and for all, she would solve this mystery.

She focused her mind on her search and, with growing confidence, followed the path her horse had taken the day before.

She found the tree that had fallen and pinned her down quite easily. It lay just where she remembered it. Was there any sign that it had been lifted and put back down or that her leg had been caught under it?

No. There was nothing to show that any of that had happened.

Perhaps when she found Morgan again—if she found him—she would be able to find out what had really happened. But where could he be? Did he live in the forest, or had he just been passing through when he had heard her scream?

Adriana spent nearly an hour wandering the paths around the forest, searching for any trace of her rescuer. The more she looked, though, the more certain she was that it had not, after all, been real.

Only one thing was certain—there was no man in these woods and nothing to indicate there ever had been. She could find no trace of him, or of anyone at all.

It was just a lovely old forest. A perfect place to lose oneself.

The cool, quiet of the woods soothed away the pain that had been throbbing in Adriana's head all day. Although she was horribly disappointed, the peace of the forest enveloped and comforted her. It rather reminded her of her painting studio—only good feelings pervaded here. Adriana felt almost lulled by the tranquility she found in walking through such majestic trees.

If only there was not that nagging feeling that she was missing something. But there really was no sign at all of Morgan.

Finally, and very reluctantly, Adriana decided to turn back. Running her hand over the rough bark of a tree, she grasped hold of it and slowly swung herself around so that she continued walking back the way she had come.

Her steps homeward were soon halted by a dog's bark. Its sound was clear, as if it were somewhere very nearby. Adriana stopped walking and strained her ears to try to tell the direction from which the sound had come.

The dog barked again, but this time a loud splashing sound followed it. There had to be a stream where a dog, or dogs, were playing. Without a moment's hesitation, Adriana turned toward the sounds. Perhaps, at the very least, she would take a moment to sketch the flowing water of the stream.

She turned off the path, and picked her way through the wood toward the sounds. There was a clearing not too far ahead, but Adriana was stopped by the sound of a voice—a man's voice. More carefully and quietly now, she made her way to the edge of the clearing and peeked out from the trees.

Adriana's breath caught as she watched a dark head emerge from under the water.

It was him! He hadn't been a dream, or her imagination. He was real!

Morgan flipped his long black hair back out of his face, sending a spray of water flying toward Adriana. As he did so, he turned around to face her. She very nearly took a step forward to let him know that she was there. Her hand was half−way raised, her foot in mid−air about to step out from the trees when she noticed that he wasn't wearing anything—at all. .

Chapter 7

S he will do," Tatiana answered with a nonchalant wave of her hand when Lord Devaux asked her what she thought of his ward.

If truth be told, she had been quite pleased with Adriana's conversation when the girl had put in some effort. But she wasn't consistent. It was clear Adriana was still unsure about this marriage.

Lord Devaux sputtered. "She will do?" He sat down on the chair opposite Tatiana without waiting to be asked. Narrowing his little eyes at her, he said, "That girl is brilliant. She can converse on any subject you'd care to name, including all of the bills currently up for discussion in the House of Lords."

"Perhaps. But my neighbor, Lady Hepplewhit, doesn't care for politics, and Miss Hayden looked particularly lost when asked about the current styles in London. And she had nothing at all to say about Countess Lieven's ball. Did she even attend?"

Lord Devaux pursed his lips repeatedly, clearly at a loss. "Er, well..." he began. He cleared his throat and then tried again. "I am certain she received an invitation. Whether she attended or not..."

"In other words, no," Tatiana said, losing her patience with the little man.

"Perhaps not. I assure you, though, Adriana is an excellent political hostess. She can converse with any guest on the issue at hand, and that is just what Vallentyn needs—

someone to promote and garner support for the issues he is working on."

His face brightened perceptively as a thought overtook him. "You don't need someone who follows every fashion, and spends too much money on her wardrobe," he said, voicing his idea. "If she is overly concerned with her own social position among the beau monde, how could she possibly help your son? No, you don't want some flighty society miss, you need a political hostess. You need someone who will help support Vallentyn's career in Parliament—and that is just what Adriana will do." He paused for a moment and then quickly added, "With my help, of course."

Tatiana thought about this for a moment. He was right. It was still important for the girl to be involved with society to some degree, however. "You will see to it that she becomes more a part of proper society. And I will see to it that she does not become so involved she forgets her duty to her husband. Moreover, I don't care what she spends on dressing herself. I want a daughter–in–law with an excellent reputation in every part of society—and with the best connections."

"Yes, of course," Lord Devaux said meekly.

"And you *will* ensure she marries my son, won't you?"

"Oh, yes. Of course she will. There is no question..."

"There still is the question. That is why I am telling you this." Tatiana infused her voice with just a touch of magic. "You *will* make sure that she marries Vallentyn."

Devaux's Adam's apple bobbed in his throat as he swallowed hard. "She will marry him. I will see that she does."

"Good." Tatiana sat back in her chair. She herself could easily ensure that the girl did marry her son, but she would really rather not have to resort to such... force.

Adriana stopped and caught her balance on a tree. How embarrassing!

She couldn't allow Morgan to see she was there, not when he... she could feel her face heat and was sure she was blushing furiously.

She resolutely tried to keep her eyes on his face, but they disobediently darted down his exposed body. Strong muscles defined his bare shoulders and chest. Below that Adriana couldn't see anything because of the water, and she was extremely grateful. She had never seen a naked man before, and was certain that she never should—at least not until after she was married.

In her mind, Henrietta's stern voice told her in no uncertain terms she was to leave immediately. Adriana knew the voice was right—she shouldn't be here at all. She started to turn away, but Morgan gave another bright shout of laughter. She looked over at him playing in the water and knew she just couldn't go.

The thought of leaving without drawing even one little sketch of Morgan and the river was unthinkable. Surely it was alright from an artistic point of view. Men painted naked women, so why couldn't she draw a naked man?

No, neither Henrietta's voice in the back of her head, nor the threat of being caught in so compromising a position could force her to leave. She would stay, but only for a very short time. Just long enough to do one quick sketch, she told herself sternly.

She opened her sketchbook, took out her pencil and watched in fascination as Morgan reached out and grabbed a long stick floating on the water in front of him. He threw it further downstream and, with a bark of excitement, a great black Labrador went swimming after it.

Morgan dove for it as well, with a jump that gave Adriana a glimpse of a sleek, sculpted back and buttocks. His legs kicked powerfully at the water. He reached the stick just before the dog. Laughing, he came up for air as the dog barked again.

Adriana watched transfixed as Morgan and his dog played together in the water, throwing the stick back and forth. Morgan was so happy and carefree, so strong and handsome.

Adriana stopped. Where had that thought come from? She silently reprimanded herself.

But it was true.

Even as she watched, she could feel herself become as relaxed and happy as he was. But there was something more. There was another feeling deep inside her. Desire.

Heat was building up in Adriana's blood, she could feel it churning within her. The heat and tingles of desire and happiness, like laughter, bubbled through her veins. Overcome with her emotions, Adriana put her crayon to paper and let the heat flow through her body and out through the crayon. Her hand carefully, but quickly, sketched Morgan, his dog and the flowing water.

But there was more. There was the bright sun in the heat of the day, Morgan's laughter, the dog's joyful barking, and the splashing of water. She captured it all in her drawing so she could experience it again another day.

On another lonely day, Adriana thought, looking at her sketch. When she was back in London, she would want to remember this day and this time. These feelings would come back to her when she looked at her sketch, and she would be able to live these happy moments all over again. She was glad—these were good feelings.

A shout of laughter interrupted her thoughts, and she looked up to see Morgan holding the stick up triumphantly once more. Suddenly, Adriana noticed Morgan's back, which was turned towards her. Long red welts stripped it, as if someone had whipped him. Her crayon hung suspended in mid–air as she stared at his back.

How could someone do that to him? How could he allow it? He was such a large, strong man—and someone had whipped him?

Adriana's hand came to life once more, adding in the long welts down his strongly muscled back. A tear dropped onto her paper.

As she smoothed the black lines running down Morgan's back in her drawing, her hands tingled with an overwhelming desire to run her fingers down his real back and sooth away the hurt. Suddenly, she wanted desperately to touch him. To run her hands over his back and his chest and along the strong muscles of his arms. To trace the contours of his muscles with her fingers. To feel his soft skin and its warmth. To hold him close and feel the strength in his arms as he wrapped them around her and...

She put her hand up to her heated cheek, unable to even continue with the thought.

Directly in front of her, Morgan came up from under the water, having once again beaten his dog to the stick. This time, the dog grabbed hold of one end of the stick and began to pull. Morgan laughed and held on to the other end with both hands. Slowly, he began to back out of the water, dragging the dog, who still clung with determination to the stick.

Adriana watched with fascination, flipped to a clean page and sketched a new drawing rapidly as, step by step, Morgan slowly revealed more and more of his naked body.

Her conscience pricked her. She should leave. But she just could not tear her eyes away from the sight of this amazingly attractive man.

Quickly, she worked on her drawing, copying his lines down to his bare ankles, trying to see him purely as an object to be sketched rather than an incredibly handsome, and disturbingly desirable man.

When Morgan was standing at the very edge with only his feet still covered by the lapping water, the dog suddenly stopped tugging on the stick and let go.

Morgan took a step backward to regain his balance and laughed, "Ah ha, you finally give up, do you, Oberon?"

The dog had not given up, however—he had been distracted by the sight of Adriana. He gave a bark and took a few tentative steps in her direction. Morgan stopped laughing, and began to turn inquiringly toward the wood where she stood.

With a gasp of fright, Adriana dropped her sketchbook, turned, and ran.

Chapter 8

Oberon took a step or two towards the trees, and barked. He had seen something or someone in the woods.

Morgan turned around in time to see a woman's fleeing back. *It was her!* He knew it instinctively. It was the woman he'd saved in the forest the day before.

He ran to the edge of the trees and tried to call out to her. He wanted her to stop running away, he wanted to talk with her. But his voice wouldn't come. No matter how hard he tried, he could not get a sound out. Morgan's throat was closed. There was nothing he could do.

His mother's command! It was her command stopping his voice!

He hit a tree in frustration, and hurt his hand.

He hadn't sought her out. She had found him. Didn't that count? Morgan supposed not, since she was running away from him.

But why was she running away? Why hadn't she come and spoken with him? If she had come all this way, why hadn't she... Oberon gave another bark to draw his attention to something on the ground.

It was a book, a sketchbook. Morgan picked it up and turned it over. His skin prickled at the drawing of a naked man pulling on one end of a stick while the other end was held firmly by a large black Labrador. He could almost hear the sound of the man laughing in his game of tug–of–war with the dog. He knew immediately this was a picture of himself and Oberon as they were just moments ago.

She had been watching!

He continued to look at the picture, even as this knowledge sent an excited chill down his body. But there was something more here. There was something else in the picture, beyond the simple representation of him and Oberon, which, admittedly, was excellent.

A feeling came over him as he stood staring at the picture. It was a feeling of happiness—no, not just happiness, but contentment and joy. He felt like laughing once again at the good feelings embodied in the sketch. And he felt... he felt a stirring in his nether regions as heat rushed to that part of his body. Yes, he felt desire. But it wasn't desire for the woman who had drawn the picture—although he couldn't help but admit to some of that as well.

It was more that she had been feeling desire for him when she'd drawn the picture.

He didn't know how he knew that, but somehow underneath the lines and smudges that made up the picture were these feelings. He felt all of her feelings as he looked at her sketch.

It made absolutely no sense. He had never felt emotions and feelings when looking at pictures before. Why would he do so now?

Morgan walked toward the river bank and sat down on the soft grass, still examining the drawing.

The scars on his back caught his eye. He had never seen them before, but naturally, he knew they were there. His mother had lashed out at him, scolding him and berating him so many times the marks were now permanent. He had never allowed her words to hurt him emotionally, but looking at the drawing, he knew that just seeing his scars had hurt the young woman.

He felt bad, and wished he could have soothed her, told her that it was all right, really. But she was gone. An empty feeling of frustration settled in his gut.

Out of curiosity, he turned the book over and turned back a page.

There was another picture of him and Oberon playing. This time they were in the water. His hand was reaching out for the stick while Oberon's mouth was nearly on it. Morgan knew that he would snatch that stick right out from under Oberon's nose and laugh heartily over the dog just missing it. But that knowledge was not because he had just experienced it, it was because the drawing told him so.

He shook his head in disbelief. It was a drawing, a sketch. And yet, he felt as if he were there watching this happen. He could feel the warmth of the day, hear the sound of the splashing water as he and Oberon swam about.

Morgan looked around to see if he could possibly be experiencing something that was really happening. But the river was quietly rushing past as always, and the sun had hidden itself behind a cloud.

He looked back at the drawing, and heard the splashing sound again. He could almost see the water in the picture undulating with his movements and Oberon's. And once again, he could feel the happiness the woman had felt as she had watched them play. But there was another feeling in this picture as well. Not so much desire, as there had been in the first drawing, but something more akin to embarrassment. Yes, she had been embarrassed at seeing him naked.

That was why she hadn't come and spoken to him! She had been embarrassed by his nudity! Morgan nearly laughed.

He turned back another page in the book and stared directly into his own face. Suddenly the hollowness he had felt the other day was filled. It was an amazing likeness.

This drawing too was filled with emotions—wonderment, curiosity, interest, and the same feeling of familiarity he had felt when he'd first seen her in the woods the day before. He longed to find out how they both had this feeling, and where it was coming from. He knew they'd never met before, and yet, he'd felt so right being with her. He'd felt...complete and happy. He needed to feel that again.

But there was nothing he could do until she came and actually spoke to him instead of just drawing pictures of him.

And then he noticed at the bottom of the drawing, in one corner, she had written her name, Adriana Hayden.

Adriana. What a beautiful name for such a very beautiful and talented artist.

Adriana, if only you had not been so embarrassed and had spoken with me, he thought. Morgan closed the book with a sigh. I will meet you, Adriana Hayden. And I will find out who you are, because, clearly, you are a very special person.

The knock on his cabin door later that afternoon interrupted Morgan's musings. He had gone back to staring at Adriana's sketches. He couldn't stay away from them—looking at them made him feel close to her. It was almost like being with her—only that, he knew, would be much, much better.

Reluctantly, he slid the sketchbook under the mattress of his bed and then went to open the door. As he had expected, it was his cousin, Kat.

She came to visit him nearly every day. Usually, she was filled with good cheer as she laughed and told him all the gossip from the abbey. Today, however, she looked odd, as if she didn't know whether to smile or be upset.

Morgan had always been very sensitive to Kat's moods, ever since she had moved into their home when they were only six years old. Born on the same day, their mothers as close as two sisters could be, Morgan and Kat had a bond even stronger than most siblings. They understood each other, and had done so ever since the first day Kat was at Vallentyn, and they had banded together in the fight against his older sisters' attempt to rule over them both.

He moved to his table where, earlier, he had been grinding some herbs for the potion to cure the animals. He was fully confident she would tell him what had happened without him having to ask—she always did.

She followed him, and began to absent–mindedly separate some dried flowers from their stems. Morgan looked over at her, but she remained silent, lost in her own thoughts and her mindless task.

He wondered if he dared to ask Kat about Adriana. His cousin would surely know who she was. If Kat hadn't seemed so very upset about something, he would have. And he still might, but first he had to be patient and allow her to tell him what was on her mind.

Just as the silence was beginning to become awkward, she said, "I heard about your meeting with your mother."

"It is my own fault," he acknowledged.

She stopped her work and looked up at him. "You did the right thing, Morgan. No matter what your mother may think."

Morgan gave her a little smile. He knew he could always count on Kat to take his side. "Thank you. I believe so too. You should have seen her, Kat. She looked so beautiful, even though she was in such pain. And she was brave—she didn't scream or cry hysterically or carry on. She just sat there crying softly. But I could feel her pain. I just couldn't have left and not helped her."

Kat was looking at him with a very worried look on her face as he spoke. She didn't say anything, but only looked more and more upset.

Morgan leaned toward his cousin and spoke more gently. "What is it? Why are you looking that way? I know I shouldn't have healed her, but..."

"No, that's not it. As I said, I'm glad you healed her, it's just..."

"Just what?"

Kat shook her head, but didn't say anything.

Morgan had never seen her so upset before.

A flower crumbled to dust in Kat's trembling fingers. She pulled her hands away from the delicate herbs and wiped them on her dress while turning away from him.

"It's what I came to tell you about." She crossed her arms protectively over her body.

Morgan stopped grinding the herbs. He touched her arm gently, and was shocked to see a tear making its way down her cheek.

"It can't be that bad," he said, trying to give her an encouraging smile.

"Oh, Morgan, it is! And it is all my fault." She hastily wiped away her tear, and took a deep breath.

Turning to him fully, she said, "Your mother was... was so angry yesterday after she returned from speaking with you. I've never seen her like that. She, she said things..." Kat paused, and took another deep breath.

Lowering her voice to a near whisper, as she did anytime she spoke of magic, she continued. "She said that very soon you would no longer be a threat to me, or to anyone. That in a little over a month, you would lose any powers you have and become just an ordinary man, and then the time would be ripe for me to take my rightful place. Your destiny would be mine for certain."

Morgan felt a tightness developing in his chest, and anger beginning a slow burn in the pit of his stomach. He tried to think clearly, but with Kat's words echoing in his mind, he just could not seem to form any coherent thoughts.

"Are you certain?"

"Yes," she said in a whisper that left a taste of anguish in his mouth.

He turned and walked away from her, facing the empty wall next to the door.

He would lose his powers? But what about the prophecy that had proclaimed his greatness? The seventh child of the seventh generation... he was that child! That destiny, those powers, they were his. How could this be taken away from him?

He spun around to face Kat. "In a little over a month? My twenty-first birthday is in a little over a month." In two strides he was back at her side. He grasped hold of her arms, anger still flaming inside of him. "What happens when I turn twenty-one?"

She looked up at him, her normally soothing hazel eyes now wide with fear and worry. "I... I don't know. She didn't say."

"She must have said something. You'll be turning twenty–one on the same day. She must have told you what to expect." He gave her a shake. He *needed*to know. Now!

"Morgan, please, you're hurting me!" Kat cried, twisting her body and trying to reach his hands.

His anger deflated immediately. He would never hurt Kat, he loved her with all of his heart. He didn't want to hurt anyone—he just needed the truth. He let go of her arms, and instead wrapped his own around her body. "I'm sorry. I'm so sorry, Kat."

Morgan could feel his heart pounding in his ears. He wanted answers so desperately that he was capable of hurting one of the few people in his life who had ever really cared for him. Kat, who had always been there for him, who had defended him against his sisters, and even, at times, his mother. How could he hurt her?

But still, he had to know.

She pulled away from him. "I wish I knew the answers, I really do. But she said nothing, honestly. I don't know what will happen, but I'm afraid that if you don't have your powers by then, you will lose what you have for sure."

Morgan dropped his arms to his sides. "But how do I get them? I've been trying, practicing, and working on my magic for practically my entire life..."

Kat winced as he said the words out loud. He knew he shouldn't speak of such things outside of a whisper, but there was no one here and no one nearby. To hell with hiding— Morgan had nothing to hide, or, well, nearly nothing. His powers were so limited.

"I know. I've been the one encouraging you, but... but maybe I shouldn't have. Maybe you'll never..."

"No! I can't believe that. I can't allow myself to give up." Morgan's answer was swift and sure. He may not have powers now, but he would—it was destined! "You have always supported me, Kat, ever since we were young."

She shook her head slowly. "You know I admire you a great deal. I mean, the fact that you have continually tried... and what you've done here in the forest, with the animals and the herbs—it's just amazing. This is the most vibrant, safe forest anywhere. Are you certain it isn't enough for you? Are you sure..."

"Don't even say it, Kat!" Morgan's voice was a low growl, but he couldn't control it. What his cousin was saying went against everything he had ever lived for, everything he had ever strived for. Yes, he had worked hard to make this forest a good home for all of the creatures, but he did it knowing that his great destiny was waiting for him. *His* destiny, not Kat's.

"You know that I don't want it, Morgan," Kat said, able as always to read his emotions before he was hardly aware of them himself. "I want that prophecy to come true even more than you do, but... the more I think about it, the more I wonder if what I've been doing, encouraging you in this way, hasn't actually been... well, cruel."

"What do you mean?"

"Well, if you are never to going to gain any powers, no matter what you do..."

Morgan stood away from his cousin, straightened his back and held up his hand for her to stop speaking. "I am. The prophecy *is* going to come true, Kat. I *will* be the most powerful Vallen of my time and I *will* attain the destiny that has been laid out for me."

Chapter 9

Adriana stepped out into the clearing by the stream. She had walked straight through the woods, once again searching for Morgan. But she saw no signs of him.

He was not here at the stream either. She looked around. Was there anything that might point her toward where he had gone? Standing by the water, she scanned the trees for some sign of a path, of anything at all.

She couldn't bear yet another sleepless night filled not only with visions of Morgan's eyes, but of the rest of his body as well. She had to find him. She had to speak with him. She could not rest until she knew more about this mysterious man. She also needed to get her sketchbook back, and that, she recognized, was her best excuse to seek him out.

As she wandered about the river bank, a sudden shout and a crash caught Adriana's attention. It sounded as if someone or something large had fallen. But that was not the end of it. Things continued to fall with loud bangs, clangs and crashes.

Following the sounds as quickly as she could, she moved through the thick undergrowth and between narrowly spaced trees. As she was about to step out from between the closely growing trees into a clearing, she brought herself up short.

She had found him! Morgan stood in the middle of the clearing, in front of a pile of wood with a black metal pot hanging above it.

Her heart was suddenly light. Happiness tingled through her just at the sight of him. He was so very handsome. Although the men she knew and admired dressed in the latest styles and Morgan didn't even have a coat on, he still made her heart pound in the most awkward manner. It didn't make sense, she thought merrily, nearly laughing at her own foolishness. Suddenly, now that she had found him, she felt utterly, unreasonably giddy with joy.

He looked so strong and commanding as he stood there with his arm outstretched, palm facing the pile of wood in front of him.

"Fire!" he commanded.

Adriana looked at the wood, but there was no fire there. What was he doing?

She watched with growing confusion as he now pointed at the wood with his finger. He shifted his weight on his booted feet, firmly planting them on the ground, and then said again in a voice that sent a shiver down Adriana's spine, "Fire!"

An odd sensation came over Adriana, as if there was a memory just on the edge of her consciousness—but she could bring it no closer. Somehow, what Morgan was doing resonated deep within her. A shiver ran across her skin, and she rubbed at her arms.

She shook her head, dispelling the thought. Did he really believe he could start a fire just by pointing at a pile of wood? The ridiculousness of the situation caught up with her and she covered her mouth to hold back her giggles.

Morgan, however, only seemed to have become angry. He picked up a piece of wood from in front of him and threw it at the pile, just barely missing the pot that hung suspended above it.

"I said, fire!" he shouted at the wood.

Now he was really being silly, and Adriana could no longer hold back her laughter.

He started, and turned at the sound. "Adriana!"

"Perhaps it would be easier if you used a tinder box," she giggled, walking over to him.

He looked at the heap of wood, pausing for only the briefest moment before he laughed. "Yes. I wasn't, er, I mean..." he stopped and laughed again. "You must think me completely insane."

"Well, I did wonder for a moment," she said, moving closer.

"I'm not, really. But I am very happy you've come." He stopped suddenly. "How did you find me?"

"It was quite easy, actually," she said. "I just followed all the yelling and noise." She stopped a few steps away from him, but he continued moving closer.

"I'm sorry if I was being too loud," he said, the smile growing on his face. "But I'm very glad you were able to find me. I shall have to try throwing wood more often if that draws you to me. I may not have started the fire, but I got something much better..." The 'you' was unspoken, but Adriana could hear it in her mind, nonetheless.

His voice had become quieter, and held a deep, rich timbre that made Adriana want to reach out to him. She held herself back, however, and contented herself with just looking up at him, and trying to keep her breathing slow and steady.

He was much taller than she remembered, but even more impressive than that was the mere presence of him. He radiated masculinity and virility. His simple white shirt, open at the collar, did nothing but accentuate what Adriana now knew lay beneath it. And the muscles of his strong legs were barely hidden by his tight buckskin breeches.

He stood so close, she could smell the fresh clean scent of his soap, tinged with the not–so–pleasant smell of the stable that lingered about him. She was near enough to him that she could have easily reached out and placed her hand flat against his chest just like...

And then she saw she had. How had that happened? There was something about him that she just could not resist. She *had* to touch him, to be close to him.

"Who are you?" she whispered.

"I am yours." The words echoed in her head and touched her soul, and she knew deep down that indeed he was.

"Yes, but, I don't understand. I know you, but..."

"I don't understand it either, I only know what I feel." He placed his warm hand on her cheek. "And with you, I feel happy."

"Yes! No one I've ever met before has made me feel this way."

He smiled, and traced his thumb along her cheek bone. "I want to know everything about you."

"And I want the same—to know you and to be with you."

He gave a laugh. "Well, you've already seen me, all of me."

Adriana gasped and took a step back, feeling her face burn with embarrassment. She'd almost forgotten—her sketchbook!

He laughed again. "It's all right. I just wish I knew how you put your emotions into your drawings. And the feel of the sun and the sounds, and... they are the most incredible pictures I've ever seen. How did you..."

"I didn't!" she said, interrupting his silliness. "It's just your imagination. My companion says the same thing, but really, those feelings are not in the picture. How could they be?"

Morgan frowned, making his eyes look even deeper than they were naturally. "But I felt..."

"Do you have my sketchbook? May I have it back, please?"

"You truly want it?" he asked, his lips quirking up a little on one side of his mouth.

"Yes!" He was teasing her now, she could tell. Silently she pleaded with him. She was already embarrassed enough that she had been caught having drawn pictures of him naked.

After a moment, he took pity on her and turned toward his house.

As he was about to disappear into the neat little cottage, she called out, "You might want to get the tinder too while you are in there." If he could tease her, she could do the same, she thought with satisfaction as he flushed before giving a little laugh.

She wished she could have followed him so that she could peek into his home and find out how he lived. She burned with a curiosity to know all she could about this confusing, fascinating man. But the voice of propriety inside her stopped her with "a lady never enters a gentleman's home, and certainly not alone!"

She contented herself with looking around the outside, taking a turn around the clearing between the cottage and the barn. Morgan's home looked very much like him—a little rough, but beautifully built, very masculine and spare. The one window of the well–proportioned cottage had no curtains, only plain wooden shutters that had been left carelessly open. There were no flowers growing by the door, but the area was clean and well–kept. It looked very comfortable, lived in and home–like.

Morgan reappeared, carefully closing his door behind him. Walking back to where she stood near the pile of wood, he took a moment to look down at her sketchbook in his hand. "May I... do you think I could have one of your sketches?"

"You want one?" she asked, amazed someone would. Her guardian had always told her they were awful, emotional hogwash. But Morgan actually liked them enough to want to keep one?

He gave a shrug and a little smile. "It allows me to feel close to you, even when you're not here. I can feel you in the picture."

Adriana caught her breath as she was engulfed by emotion. That was the sweetest thing anyone had ever said to her! She blinked back the tears that came to her eyes.

"Of course," she said, her voice rough with emotion. She cleared her throat and tried again. "If you truly want one."

"I do."

She opened her book to the first sketch she'd made of him by the stream. It was the happy picture showing Morgan and his dog playing. She had wanted to keep it to remember seeing him having fun. The second sketch was much more intimate and full of desire. He was in all of his naked glory. Yes, perhaps she had better give him this one. It wouldn't be right if anyone were to see that she'd even drawn such a picture.

She felt her face heat—she still couldn't believe he knew that she'd seen him this way. She took a deep breath to dispel her embarrassment and even managed to look up into his eyes. They were filled with something Adriana couldn't quite... oh, but she could—they were filled with desire. She was shocked to admit it, even silently to herself.

"Yes, that one," he said, his voice deepened with emotion.

Adriana swallowed hard, and felt awkwardly warm all of a sudden. She didn't dare to say a word, just gave a nod and then carefully ripped it out of her book.

"Thank you," he said, as she handed it to him. "I shall always treasure it."

Her eyes met his. She tried to look away, to act like the demure young lady she was supposed to be, but she just couldn't. He drew her to him, like a moth to the flame.

He was the first to break the spell, taking a step away from her as if it were the most difficult thing to do. "I'll keep this carefully."

He turned and ran back to his house. He slipped in and out quickly this time, returning to squat by the wood and set it alight. Not meeting her eyes, he gave a stir to whatever was in the pot with a large spoon.

"What are you making?" she asked, moving closer, unable to even stay two feet away from him.

"A potion to heal the animals," he answered.

"A potion? You mean medicine?"

He paused for a moment then replied, "Yes."

He kept his back toward her, and seemed to be muttering some words as he stirred the pot. He sprinkled in a powder from a wooden bowl sitting next to him and continued stirring and mumbling.

She watched, fascinated. "What is wrong with the animals?"

"They have the pox."

Adriana gasped and took a step backward away from Morgan. The pox was very dangerous. She had heard that even being near someone with it could cause you to become ill as well.

He looked up at her then and narrowed his eyes. "Is there something you fear?"

"It... it is just that, well—wouldn't it be better to simply put the animals out of their misery rather than try to heal them? You might catch it yourself if you get too close."

Morgan turned back to his cooking. "No. I will not get it. It only affects the animals in my barn. This potion will cure them."

"You know a great deal about healing?" Adriana asked, wondering if she dare ask about her leg and how he had healed it.

Morgan stopped stirring the pot. "I know about healing animals," he said.

"What sort of healing do you do, aside from making medicine?"

"What other kind of healing is there?" he said, keeping his faced turned away while sprinkling in more herbs.

Adriana swallowed hard. "The other day, you—you touched my leg."

Morgan abruptly stopped what he was doing and stood up to his full height before her. Looking deeply into her eyes, he said intensely, "You imagined that."

Adriana looked back, not able to break eye contact. His black eyes glittered with something indefinable that sent chills down her spine. He didn't look angry. He stared into her eyes so hard that his gaze seemed to penetrate her mind.

He said once again, "You imagined I touched you, Adriana. I did not do so."

His voice was deep and resonant, but Adriana somehow knew he was not speaking the truth. Having him this close to her, feeling the warmth of his body at arms' distance, she knew she had not imagined the experience. No matter what, nothing he nor Lady Vallentyn said would convince her that he had not healed her leg.

Slowly she shook her head. "No. I know what I saw. What I felt."

Morgan looked away quickly. "You are wrong. How could I have healed your leg? It's impossible, Adriana, you know that."

"I do, but..."

"It must have been your imagination," he said, sitting back down on the ground and tending to his pot again.

That's what Lady Vallentyn had said, Adriana thought to herself, or was it what she had thought? She couldn't remember. She just remembered beginning to doubt her memories after she had met with her hostess to try to find out more about Morgan.

"Who are you, really? Why do you live here? Are you Lord Vallentyn's gamekeeper?" The words tumbled out of her before she could stop them.

He looked up at her, uncertainty wrinkling his forehead.

Adriana knelt down on the grass next to him. Gently placing a hand on his forearm, she said, "I simply want to get to know you."

Morgan softened at her touch, and she saw the tension leaving his shoulders. He gave a little shrug. "I am no one you should know. No one you should care to know."

"But I do care." And indeed she did, too much, for someone she didn't even know. But they shared something.

Morgan turned his head to look at her hand still resting on his arm. Looking into her eyes, he asked, "Who are *you*? What brought you here to Vallentyn?"

Adriana removed her hand, but settled herself next to him on the ground. She wanted to be close to him. Perhaps if she told him about herself, he would open up to her as well.

She gave a little shrug. "My guardian, Lord Devaux, brought me here. He and Lady Vallentyn are trying to arrange a match between me and Lord Vallentyn."

"You're going to marry Vallentyn?"

Once again she shrugged. "I haven't made up my mind yet."

"But that's why you're here," he said, sitting back.

Adriana gave a nod.

"You don't want to marry him," he said, more as a statement than as a question.

Adriana almost felt as if he could read her mind, or her feelings—it unnerved her. She stood up and took a step away from him, looking blindly at the trees that closely surrounded his home.

"No. But I may not have a choice. My guardian is trying to force my hand. So far, though, I haven't given in. I'm going to find a way to convince either him or Lady Vallentyn that Lord Vallentyn and I shouldn't marry. I've got to."

"You can't just tell your guardian that you don't wish to marry?"

Adriana gave a little laugh at that. "Oh, no. He could care less about what I want. He's only concerned with what's best for himself, and somehow he's become convinced that this marriage would be to his advantage."

Morgan stared at the ground, deep in thought for a moment. "I know what it's like to have no one care for you or what you want," he said, almost in a whisper.

Adriana's breath caught in her throat; her eyes stung with tears. The emotion, the sadness with which he said this—it touched her deep inside.

Without a thought, she moved back and sat down on the ground next to him, wishing she could take him into her arms. In his deep, black eyes, he looked so sad and lost. His long hair hung loose about his shoulders—one side tucked behind his ear, the other brushing his cheek, the length of it grazing his collar bone. Somehow it just added to his beauty, and his sorrow.

Once again, she found her hand in his as she looked deeply into his eyes. "You're all alone here," she said quietly, knowing that this was true.

He nodded, "And you?"

She tilted her head slightly without breaking their eye contact, to indicate that she was.

She gave a little shrug. "But I have my painting."

"I take care of the animals," he said, giving her a little smile. And just like that, she didn't feel so lonely anymore.

Moving away from the fire, he positioned himself so close to her their knees touched, but she didn't move away—she didn't want to.

Gently, he brushed his rough fingers down her cheek. "You are so beautiful."

Adriana felt her face heat with embarrassment. No one had ever called her beautiful before, and never with such softness and truth in his voice. Her cheek burned at the spot where his fingers had grazed it.

"You make me feel beautiful," she whispered.

He smiled. "You make me feel good."

"Why is it that, with you, I'm happy?"

He laughed quietly. "I don't know. I wish I understood how or why this is, but I can't explain it any more than you."

I only know this is right," he added, leaning forward. Very slowly, with a touch as light as the wings of a butterfly, Morgan brushed his lips against hers, sending shocks throughout her body.

He withdrew for a moment, and then slowly he pressed his lips more firmly to hers. Warmth, connection, completeness: they all flooded through Adriana. She closed her eyes, and for the first time, allowed all of her other senses and feelings to explore this wonderful new sensation. It was as if something deep within the two of them was holding them together—and would keep them there for all eternity.

Too soon, he sat back. Adriana opened her eyes. She wished she hadn't, because her gaze was immediately caught by the lengthening of the shadows.

She jumped up. "It's so late! I must get back to the abbey before I'm missed."

Morgan stood too, all softness and joy abruptly gone from his face. "Adriana, no one is allowed to speak of me. You must not either," he said quietly, but in a voice that resonated in her mind. His eyes bore into hers for a moment as he ran his fingers down her cheek, giving her a sad smile.

Slowly, Adriana nodded, her mind feeling as if it were in a fog.

Then she watched as Morgan turned away from her and lifted the pot off the fire. He carried it into the barn, disappearing inside. She, too, turned away and slowly headed back to the abbey—still feeling the heat of his lips upon hers and hoping the happiness she had felt with him would not be leaving her too soon.

Chapter 10

Adriana ignored the clatter behind her as the tea tray arrived after dinner that night. Pushing aside the deep red drawing–room drapes, she sat down on the window seat and looked out at the black night, but saw only reflections in the glass. Shadows moved behind her in the flickering candlelight, but she kept her face turned toward the window as if she could see outside.

Odd events from the day kept replaying in her mind like the shadows in the glass: Morgan trying to start a fire by pointing at a pile of wood, and his sweet kiss that made her feel so connected to him; Lord Vallentyn's blank stare after she told him at dinner to finally stand up to his mother, after they had discussed that he was only marrying her because his mother had told him to do so.

Lord Vallentyn seemed to have no mind of his own, except when it came to his estate. Then he truly shone—and almost literally shone too, she thought with amusement. His eyes sparkled and his whole face lit up when he spoke of his estates.

But in everything else, his mother's rule was law. Adriana wondered if he would ever find the courage to stand up to her. And if he didn't, what would she do? Perhaps when Lord Devaux found out that Lord Vallentyn really had no interest in Parliament, he would no longer be interested in this marriage.

She rather doubted that getting out of marrying Lord Vallentyn would be that easy, but it was worth a try. And it was better than being married to a man she didn't even know. The alternative was unthinkable—when Lord Devaux said he would destroy all of her work if she didn't agree to the match, she knew he would not hesitate to carry out his threat.

No, she could not sit idly by while her life was destroyed.

A hand gently placed on her shoulder made her jump. Adriana hadn't even noticed the shadow coming closer to her. She looked up into Miss Havelock's kind face.

"I'm sorry, I didn't mean to startle you."

"Oh, no, it's all right. I was just woolgathering, I'm afraid." Adriana tried her best to sound lighthearted.

Miss Havelock sat down next to her. "I was sent to ask if you would you care for some tea, but perhaps a friendly ear would be more welcome."

Adriana gave a little laugh, but seriously began to think that Miss Havelock was right—a friend was exactly what she needed right now. They had spent a bit of time getting to know each other already, so Adriana was very pleased to have Miss Havelock's company, and her friendship.

"Did you have a pleasant dinner with my cousin?" Miss Havelock asked. Her pretty hazel eyes smiled at Adriana, and Adriana knew that she could trust her completely.

"It was certainly enlightening," Adriana admitted.

"In what way?"

"Well, I learned your cousin wants to marry me as little as I want to marry him. Only he is much more willing to fall in line with his mother's wishes than I."

Miss Havelock's face lost its smile. Putting her hand on Adriana's arm, she said earnestly, "You must not think less of Vallentyn just because he won't stand up to his mother in this. It... it is difficult. Aunt Vallentyn is..."

"Used to getting her way?"

Miss Havelock stole a scared glance in the direction of her aunt. "Well, let's just say, no one dares to go against her. It would not be wise."

"That is very much like what Lord Vallentyn said to me at dinner," Adriana said, suppressing the slight shiver that came over her. What silliness! There was surely a rational explanation for this. It was clear that everyone did as Lady Vallentyn said, but there had to be something reason why Lord Vallentyn, not only a man, but a viscount, still listened to his mother. Adriana couldn't help but think of her own situation. "I presume she is holding something over him to force him to marry me?" Adriana asked.

"Why do you say that?"

"Well, he clearly doesn't take orders from anyone when it comes to his estates," Adriana said, watching Lord Vallentyn idly play a tune on the pianoforte on the other side of the room.

"No, but my aunt has no interest in the estate. Vallentyn may do as he pleases with it—and he does so love his land."

"That much is clear," Adriana laughed.

"Vallentyn," Lady Vallentyn called out above the sound of the piano. Her son immediately jumped up and was at her side in three long strides.

"But when it comes to his mother..." Adriana said, not taking her eyes off of him.

"Exactly," Miss Havelock said, not even waiting for Adriana to finish her sentence.

How odd that she knew just what she was thinking, Adriana mused. It was lovely in a way. It made her feel close to Miss Havelock, even though they had only known each other about a week.

"But she holds nothing over him. She has no need to, I assure you," Miss Havelock finished. She paused for a moment and then asked gently, "Do you ask that from experience? Are you being forced into marriage with my cousin?"

Adriana dropped her gaze to her own hands clasped tightly in her lap. "My guardian has told me if I don't marry Lord Vallentyn, he will destroy all of my paintings and never allow me to paint again." A tightness began to well up in the base of her throat, but she swallowed it and went on, "Painting is my one joy in life, it is the only thing that makes me happy. He knows this and uses it to control me. He always has." She was unable to keep her mind from straying to the only other thing that had ever made her truly happy—Morgan. "I thought perhaps your aunt had some sort of similar hold over Lord Vallentyn," she finished.

Miss Havelock's grip on Adriana's arm tightened consolingly and Adriana was surprised to see tears well up in her new friend's eyes. She blinked them away. "No, Aunt Vallentyn does not need to resort to such tactics. I am so sorry your guardian threatens you in this way."

Adriana could only nod. Her throat was beginning to constrict, even as she held her own tears in check.

Miss Havelock sat in quiet sympathy while Adriana gathered her emotions together. Then she asked, "Were you successful yesterday afternoon with your search?"

A rush of heat and good feelings suffused Adriana as she allowed her mind to dwell on Morgan and remember their encounter earlier that day.

Adriana had built up the courage to ask Miss Havelock about Morgan the day before, but all she had said was that Adriana must find out for herself. Now she was very glad she had followed that advice. She smiled and opened her mouth to tell Miss Havelock that she had, in fact, met Morgan when suddenly she found she could not call forth her voice. She did not know what was wrong.

She tried again, and then thought to move her hand to her throat.

She could not move! She couldn't even nod her head to indicate she had found him. She couldn't do anything.

Her heart began to pound in her chest and she thought her head would explode from the tension building up. She was frozen with fear and... and she did not know what.

Help! She screamed out in her mind. *Oh God, help me!*

Her eyes must have shown her distress, for immediately Miss Havelock grasped tightly on to her hands. "It is all right, Adriana. Do not fight it. Be calm. Just take a deep breath and relax." Miss Havelock's hazel eyes looked directly into Adriana's as she said the words again more softly.

Adriana did not break the eye contact. She was not sure she could if she wanted to, but she did *not* want to because what she saw in Miss Havelock's eyes was kindness and concern. Like someone who was drowning, Adriana held on to Miss Havelock's gaze as a life support. A calming heat from her hands slipped up Adriana's arms and filled her chest and throat. She could feel her heartbeat slow, and the pain in her head reduced to a dull throb.

Adriana felt the invisible force fade away. Tentatively, she opened her mouth. "What...what happened?" she whispered, but couldn't keep the tremors from it. "I couldn't move, I couldn't speak!"

"It is all right. Did someone, my aunt perhaps, tell you not to speak of him?"

Adriana's throat tightened again as if it were about to make it so she couldn't speak again. But before she lost her voice altogether, she quickly whispered, "Not Lady Vallentyn."

Miss Havelock's eyes went wide. "Was it Morgan then?"

Adriana tried to nod, but her muscles had formed knots in her neck and again she couldn't move. She tried hard not to panic a second time, forcing herself to take deep breaths and pushing down her fear.

Miss Havelock smiled and gave her hands a reassuring squeeze. "I will take that for a yes. It is all right, I understand. Do not even try to speak of him. And I promise not to ask you any more questions." She paused and drew her eyebrows down, a look of worry coming into her eyes. "How did he manage to put a suggestion into your mind? I shall have to ask him how he did it."

"Do you know...?" Adriana couldn't believe that Miss Havelock knew Morgan. Why hadn't she said anything when Adriana had asked?

"I am so sorry that I couldn't say anything yesterday," Miss Havelock said quickly. "I did so want to, but it is forbidden to tell anyone about him who doesn't know him. The same thing would have happened to me that just happened to you. But the two of you have met now, so I can..." She stopped, her eyes darting over to Lady Vallentyn, who had now moved over to the table and was helping Lord Devaux and Lord Vallentyn to more tea.

"It is still unwise to speak of him within my aunt's hearing," she said, her voice barely audible . She let go of Adriana's hands just as Lady Vallentyn looked over toward them.

"Would you care for some tea, Miss Hayden?" Lady Vallentyn asked in her overly sweet, unctuous voice.

Adriana took another deep calming breath before she could trust her voice not to give away any of her inner turmoil of just a moment ago. Oh, how she would love a cup to quiet her nerves! "No, thank you very much, ma'am," She replied, not trusting her hands not to shake and spill it.

"Katrina?"

"No, thank you, Aunt Vallentyn."

As Lady Vallentyn turned back to the gentlemen, each sitting straight–backed in one of the matching chairs formally arranged around the tea table, Miss Havelock gave Adriana's hands one more quick, reassuring squeeze. But Adriana's mind could not be soothed so easily. Something had happened, something Miss Havelock knew about and understood, but Adriana did not.

And that frightened her nearly as much.

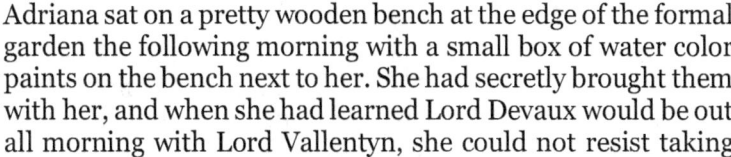

Adriana sat on a pretty wooden bench at the edge of the formal garden the following morning with a small box of water color paints on the bench next to her. She had secretly brought them with her, and when she had learned Lord Devaux would be out all morning with Lord Vallentyn, she could not resist taking them out. In her lap was her sketchbook.

Very carefully, she added the final touches to the painting she had been working on—a single pink rose, glistening with moisture and hope.

The person for whom the painting had been intended slowly walked up the path toward her. Miss Havelock looked particularly pretty this morning, wearing a peach–colored dress that brought out the natural pink of her cheeks and accented the beauty of her chestnut colored hair.

She stopped and closed her parasol as she approached Adriana, who sat in the shade of a large elm tree. "Good morning, Miss Hayden. What are you working on?"

"A present for a friend," Adriana said, smiling up at her. She then put the final touch on the rose and signed her name to the bottom of the page.

Miss Havelock bent her head to see. She gasped with pleasure. "Oh, how beautiful! Oh, Miss Hayden, that is…" She stopped speaking, her mouth open just a little, as if at a loss for words.

She then looked to Adriana curiously. "How…? Is that for me?"

"Yes! How did you know?" Adriana laughed.

"I… I don't know…" Her new friend was finally at a loss. She looked just like Adriana imagined herself to look when Miss Havelock sensed how she was feeling or knew what she was thinking.

"You are sounding very much like me, Miss Havelock," Adriana giggled.

"Oh, please call me Kat, and I shall call you by your given name as well."

Adriana smiled. "Of course, I am very happy to. Now will you tell me how you knew this was for you, or is that another one of those questions I should not ask?"

Kat looked perplexed for a minute, clearly trying to figure out the puzzle. "Well, I… I could feel it. Is that right? I could feel you had painted it for me. And you have painted in such beauty and—and hope and happiness!"

Had she painted in happiness? Adriana supposed that she had, since she had felt that way while she had painted the picture. Or perhaps Kat could just feel it now that they were together.

"It is to thank you for being so kind to me last night, and yesterday morning as well. Late last night, when I couldn't sleep for thinking about what had happened to me in the evening, I realized that if you had not been there, if I had been trying to speak with anyone else, I would have been in terrible trouble. You were so good and kind. You calmed my fears and helped me. This painting is just a small way for me to thank you."

Kat impulsively reached out and grasped Adriana's hand. "I am so glad I was able to help. And I would be happy to do so again, in any way you need me."

Adriana gave Kat's hand a squeeze. "Thank you. I can't tell you how much that means to me. The only friend I've ever had is my companion, Henrietta. Now, I would be honored if I could call you friend as well."

"Of course! Morgan is my only friend, and as you know, he cannot be spoken of. It can be difficult for me to see him at times, since my aunt usually keeps me very busy here. I do try to visit him as often as I can, though."

"You, you are very close?" A slice of pain bit into her heart. The thought of Morgan looking at anyone else the way he looked at her the previous day made her sick to her stomach. He had said she was special, but perhaps he said that to every woman...

"We are good friends only," Kat said quickly. "I assure you. We grew up together. He's like a brother to me."

The pain eased, and Adriana's stomach muscles relaxed. Adriana even managed to smile and nod her head. "Thank you for explaining." She couldn't believe the sudden anger that had assailed her. She had never felt such a thing about anyone before. She paused to calm herself down and then asked, "Are not you and Lord Vallentyn close friends?"

Kat thought about that for a moment, and then said, "Vallentyn is much older than I am, and he's always been so busy with his estates. Caroline and Susan are closest in age to me, but both are rather empty headed, I'm afraid."

Adriana looked questioning at Kat. "Caroline and Susan?"

Kat laughed for a moment. "Vallentyn's sisters. Did you not know? He has five sisters."

"Oh, no, I didn't know!" Adriana said, rather grateful for the change in topic.

Kat nodded absently, "They're all married now." She was looked intently at the painting sitting on Adriana's lap, and then up at the house as if expecting someone to be there.

The beauty of the ancient abbey was certainly not lost on Adriana, but somehow she didn't feel compelled to sketch it. It was too... heavy, she decided, too closed and too cold. While still formal, at least the gardens held some feeling of warmth and openness to them.

"May I take the painting? I am very selfish and do not wish to share it with anyone!"

Adriana laughed. "Of course. Just be careful, the paint is not fully dry yet. And I really must put away my paints before Lord Devaux comes back and finds out that you have seen my work."

"Is no one allowed to even see your paintings?" Kat asked a little incredulously.

"No. Lord Devaux doesn't like my work. I'm afraid he is embarrassed by it because it is too emotional."

"Oh. Well, I will take this upstairs before anyone sees it, then," she said, indicating the picture resting delicately on her hand.

They walked together back to the abbey, but stopped short as soon as they entered the rear of the great hall. Standing directly in front of the grand staircase were Lord Devaux and Lady Vallentyn.

Adriana began to back away. The last thing she wanted was to be caught by her guardian with her paint box in her hands, but his words stopped her.

"My dear Lady Vallentyn, I would be honored if you would join me for a walk in the garden this evening—after dinner perhaps?" Lord Devaux was asking, looking up into Lady Vallentyn's face with a smile that made Adriana's skin crawl. What could he possibly be up to?

The lady looked at the diminutive man with a look of contempt. "I thought I had made it clear that I am not interested in your puny aspirations."

Lord Devaux lost his smile. "Puny... I will have you know, my lady, that I am a major player in Parliamentary politics. A major player! Why, I might very well end up as Prime Minister one day..."

"Which is why I am allowing my son to marry your ward," Lady Vallentyn interrupted Lord Devaux's rant, her voice quiet, but filled with contempt. "But that does not mean I will subject myself to suffering *your* attentions."

Kat's mouth dropped open, but she quickly covered it, hiding her smile.

"Well, you will have to suffer my attentions if you wish for your son to marry Adriana! I can put a stop to this marriage without a moment's hesitation," Lord Devaux threatened.

His face began to turn a rather alarming shade of red, but he snapped his fingers to show just how quickly he could put an end to the engagement. Silently, Adriana applauded him. Oh, if only he would carry out his threat!

Lady Vallentyn exuded menace and anger, then took a step closer to Lord Devaux. Locking her eyes onto his, she said in a deep penetrating voice, "Adriana will marry Vallentyn. You will ensure that she does. No matter what you have to do, you will see to it that this marriage takes place."

Lord Devaux's eyes widened as he looked directly into Lady Vallentyn's eyes. Slowly he began to nod his head. "Adriana will marry Vallentyn. I will see that she does," he repeated.

"And you will forget this nonsense about being fascinated with me. I am a very attractive woman, but not one with whom you would want to become more intimate, I assure you."

Lord Devaux took a step backward away from Lady Vallentyn, shaking his head. "No, no, of course not. Whatever put that idea into my head? How ridiculous! Well, I suppose not so ridiculous, as you are an extremely attractive woman, but... no!"

Lord Devaux blinked his eyes a few times and then laughed awkwardly. "Of course, it is the children who will marry, not us! And it is certain that they *will* marry. I will see to that. You should have no fear on that head. Adriana and Vallentyn will marry, and the sooner the better." Nervous sweat rolled down Lord Devaux's face.

Adriana nearly gasped. What had just happened? One moment things were looking up, and the next her fate was sealed. She did not understand this. Kat's eyes met hers, but there was something—could it be fear?— Adriana saw in her friend's eyes.

Lady Vallentyn looked with obvious disgust at Lord Devaux, but then suddenly spun toward Adriana and Kat. "What is this?" she hissed.

"Good afternoon, Aunt Vallentyn," Kat said quickly, clearing her face of all expression. "Lord Devaux." She nodded in his direction.

Lady Vallentyn narrowed her eyes at them. "Good afternoon."

"Adriana and I have just come in from the garden to see about luncheon. I thought Thomas would know. Have you seen him?"

The large dog Adriana had seen once before was by the front door. He stood and gave a hearty bark.

"The footman? No," Lady Vallentyn said, not even looking over at the dog. "You *just* came in?"

"Yes," Adriana said, matching her tone to Kat's carefree one and curving her lips up into a smile. "Just this minute. I suppose you and Lord Devaux were talking, so you did not see us come in."

"We were just discussing the fact that I need to send an announcement to the Times regarding your betrothal," Lord Devaux said smoothly.

Adriana looked at him, trying to hide her shock and dismay. "I thought you were going to wait until I have had a chance to consider Lord Vallentyn's proposal."

"There is nothing for you to consider, Adriana. You will marry Vallentyn." Lord Devaux took a few menacing steps toward Adriana.

"But..."

"Adriana, what is that in your hand?" His voice came out high with annoyance.

Belatedly, Adriana remembered the box of paints she was still carrying.

"They are mine! Those are my paints." Kat said quickly, dropping her hand which was carrying the painting to her side and a little behind her. "She was just carrying them inside for me."

"You do not paint, Katrina," Lady Vallentyn said, her voice gliding through the words.

"I... I wished to try it," she said, trying to cover her lies.

"And I had promised to give her a lesson. That is what we've been doing in the garden," Adriana added.

"Yes. Adriana is an excellent artist. And she has been very kind and patient in teaching me how to paint."

"Excellence is subjective. If you like emotional hogwash, then yes, her painting is excellent. If you prefer good solid representations of nature, then they are disgustingly bold and often quite bizarre. I would suggest, Miss Havelock, that you find a lady who knows how to paint properly if you wish to learn the art."

Lord Devaux paused for effect and narrowed his gaze on Adriana. "I believe I made myself clear when I told you that you were not to show your art to anyone. Now, if I learn you have been doing anything other than just teaching Miss Havelock how to paint, Adriana, I will be forced to search your room and have all of your materials disposed of immediately. Is that clear?"

Adriana took a deep, shaky breath and nodded her head.

Lord Devaux lowered his voice, "Any more transgressions on my good will, and I will not hesitate to carry out this threat."

"Katrina, you will please attend me in the solarium. We have matters to discuss," Lady Vallentyn added, in as threatening a tone as Lord Devaux's.

Kat blanched noticeably. "Oh?"

Lady Vallentyn gave her a falsely sweet smile. "I want to hear what you learned regarding our conversation at dinner last night."

"Oh, yes." Kat's eyes slid toward Adriana nervously. "I, er, just need to put away my paints and I will be there directly." She took the paint box from Adriana's hands, gave her a very brief little smile, and then ran past Lady Vallentyn and Lord Devaux and up the stairs.

There was definitely something odd going on here, but Adriana just couldn't figure out what it was. She just prayed that her friend hadn't just gotten herself into trouble on her account.

Chapter 11

"Come on now, just a bit more." Morgan tried to coax the foal into swallowing more of his potion. The poor animal was so weak it could barely lift its head to swallow.

"Have you given him milk?"

Morgan twisted around from his seat on the floor of the stall. His cousin, Kat, stood just at the door, watching him.

Relaxing a bit, he turned back to the foal. "He's too weak to stand on his own to nurse."

Kat came over and squatted down next to Morgan and the animal. Looking deeply into the foal's moist brown eyes, she stroked his head and then said, "He's hungry and he yearns for his mother's comfort."

Morgan nodded sadly. "I'll do what I can," he said, getting up and retrieving a small pail. He then stroked the doe's nuzzle and told her, "I need your milk for your foal."

The doe moved herself to allow Morgan to milk her. He squatted down next to her and set to work on his task as Kat continued caressing the foal and murmuring words of comfort.

Finally she said, "Morgan, how did you put a suggestion into Adriana's mind?"

Morgan stopped what he was doing and looked at Kat. "I did what?"

"You put a suggestion into her mind. Didn't you know?"

"No... are you certain?" A small fire sparked into life inside of Morgan's belly.

It only grew as Kat related to him the events of the previous evening—how Adriana hadn't been able to speak his name or mention that she'd met him.

He couldn't speak for the excitement, the thrill, that was welling inside of him. The doe shifted, reminding Morgan of what he had been doing. He set to work once again, but he hardly paid any attention.

He had put a suggestion into Adriana's mind! He had performed magic! But how? And how could he have done it unintentionally? It didn't make sense. He almost wished that he could just accept this as fated, but it was too important to not examine. He needed to know more. Did this mean that he now had his powers—the powers he should have had his whole life? It took all of his willpower not jump up and try something—anything!

"What were you doing when you put the suggestion into her mind? Where were you?" As always, Kat was thinking along the same lines. Yes, he thought with a sigh, this had to be explored before he could try anything new.

Morgan remembered the day before and the incredible time he had spent with Adriana—it didn't take much to think back to it since it had hardly left his mind. "We were sitting outside. I was making the potion to cure the animals."

He replayed the wonderful scene again in his mind, but this time tried to look for any magic that might have taken place, or for anything... different. There had certainly been sparks between them—that had been magic of a sort. But it was surely not the kind that could put a suggestion into Adriana's mind.

His hands paused their work, and he shifted uncomfortably on the ground before saying nonchalantly, "And I kissed her."

Kat jumped as if he had just touched a flame to her skirts. "You kissed her?" she nearly shouted.

The doe startled, nearly knocking over the pail of milk. Morgan calmed her, and then looked to see if there was enough milk. He could hardly see it. All he could see was Adriana's green eyes sparkling with unshed tears when he had told her he knew what it was like to have no one care for you. All he could feel was the burning of her hand in his and the knowledge that she, too, felt the deep loneliness that perpetually resided within him.

He shook his head to clear his mind, and then truly did look at the amount of milk he had collected. It would be enough. He set a cloth into the pail so that he could feed it to the foal.

Morgan could sense Kat watching him closely. Finally, he couldn't delay answering her any longer. "Yes, I kissed her," he said, straightening his back but not meeting his cousin's eyes. "She's very beautiful and I... I'm attracted to her. I told her she was very pretty and then I kissed her."

He tried to hide his smile as he remembered Adriana's soft lips and her sweet scent when he had leaned forward and pressed his lips to hers. She reminded him of a field of wild flowers on a warm summer's day. She had that same fresh smell and made him feel warm and happy.

"I hadn't intended to kiss her—it just happened," he admitted. "It was incredible," he added very softly. He didn't tell her how shaken up he'd been by the kiss. How she'd touched him something deep inside both his body and his mind. How heat had flooded his nether regions, but that it was the sparks in his mind that had really... There was no way to explain something like that to Kat, and even if there was, Morgan wasn't entirely sure he could, because he didn't even understand it himself. He just knew that being with Adriana made him happier than anything else ever had.

Kat sighed and sat back. "I hope someday a man might kiss me," she said, wistfully.

Morgan smiled and stole a peek at her. She was sitting staring blindly at the foal. "I would offer, but you don't make me feel the way Adriana does. You don't stir my blood."

That broke her out of her spell. She laughed and said, "Well, I should hope not! We are almost brother and sister."

Chuckling quietly to himself, Morgan took the cloth from the foal's mouth and set it back into the pail to soak up more milk.

"And I assure you, I was not asking *you* to kiss me, Morgan," Kat said seriously.

"No. I know that," Morgan said, letting the words fall through his laughter. But then, he too became more serious. "I must admit, I was a little surprised when I kissed Adriana. She is the first girl I have ever wanted to kiss."

"She is the first girl you have ever met aside from me and your sisters," Kat pointed out needlessly.

Morgan gave a little shrug of dismissal, and then added, "Well, if I could leave this forest..."

"Don't even try, Morgan! You remember what happened the last time you did."

Morgan stifled his sigh and turned back to the foal, placing the cloth back into his eager mouth. "Yes. If you hadn't been there to put out the fire, my leg—and perhaps more of me—would have been horribly burnt. My mother's spells can be very cruel."

He was quiet for a moment, but not even the thought of how he was held here in this forest against his will could dampen the inner joy that had begun singing inside of him.

He had done magic—powerful magic! And he had met Adriana.

She was so beautiful. And, oddly enough, as attracted to him as he was to her. They didn't even know each other, and yet he had felt such a deep connection with her. She was as lonely as he. She, too, was being held against her will. And the way they had recognized each other...

"Something's coming, Kat. Something is changing."

Kat's eyes jerked to meet his. She lifted herself onto her knees. "What is it? Did you hear something? Your mother, did she...?"

But Morgan could only shake his head. "No, my mother has nothing to do with this. I don't know... It's just a feeling," he shrugged, watching the foal suck greedily at the cloth.

Kat sank back down again, disappointed.

"But something's got to be changing," Morgan continued, dipping the cloth into the milk once again. "I did magic, Kat, real magic!" He could still hardly believe it. "And Adriana? There must be something special happening for her to come into my life."

Kat gave him a sad smile. "Adriana is here to become betrothed to your brother, Morgan. I'm sorry."

"Yes, I know. She told me. But she's being forced into this marriage against her will."

Kat nodded. "That's true. And so is Jonathan being forced, but that doesn't change things. Adriana's not here for you. You weren't supposed to meet her at all. It's just an accident that you did."

"I don't know…"

"Morgan," Kat said, and then reached over and put a consoling hand on his knee.

He was quiet for a moment as her magical touch warmed him and made him happier. "Well, one thing is certain—my magic is increasing, for whatever reason. And I plan on helping it. Working harder at it. I am going…."

"No! Morgan, you mustn't!"

"Why not?"

"You just said yourself, we don't know where this magic is coming from."

"No, but the more I think about it, the more certain I am that we'll never know—so I might as well use it, make it stronger."

"I don't think that's wise, Morgan. In fact, I think it could be dangerous."

"Dangerous?" Morgan started to laugh, but the seriousness of her expression stopped him. "Kat, you can't mean it!"

"I *do* mean it, Morgan. I don't think you should try using this magic until we know where it's coming from." Kat reached out toward him again. "I know you don't like it, but please,

Morgan, please. Promise me you won't use this magic until we know more about it."

Morgan hardly had to think this through before he shook his head. "I can't do that, Kat. I can't! For the first time in my life, my magic is working the way it's supposed to and you want me to just turn my back on it?"

At the thinning of her lips, he said, "And how would you propose that we find out where this power is coming from?"

That did stop her.

"What would you do?" he continued, "Ask my mother? She's the only one who might have some idea, the only one who might be able to figure it out. She is the High Priestess."

"I know that," Kat snapped, meeting his anger with some of her own.

Morgan sat back. "Are you going to tell her?"

"No! No, of course not. I'm not so stupid."

"I hadn't thought so," Morgan said. He didn't want to be angry with Kat, nor have her upset with him. "I'll be damned, and rightfully so, if I don't take this gift that is being offered to me, if I don't use this power. It is mine, Kat. It should have always been mine."

"Miss Hayden, I just cannot," the wicker chair creaked as Lord Vallentyn leaned forward.

Adriana shook her head, and put her hand on his arm to emphasize her words. She was not going to give up on this. She couldn't afford to. "I'm sorry, my lord, but you must. You must tell your mother you will not marry me. You will not let your mother and my guardian force us into marriage."

Lord Vallentyn just sat staring, unblinking, into her eyes. In the bright light of the solarium, his pupils were tiny pinpoints of black amidst the pale blue of his eyes, but the intensity of his stare unnerved her. She would not let it affect her—she refused break eye contact.

Finally, he blinked and shook his head. "But you don't understand..."

"I do. I understand very well. You are being forced to do something that is repugnant to you, but you must stand up for yourself. How do you expect to make a name for yourself in Parliament if you can't even stand up to your own mother?"

Lord Vallentyn winced at her brutal honesty, and indeed, Adriana could hardly believe it herself. Henrietta's voice echoed in her mind—scolding her and reminding her that a lady never spoke to a gentleman in such a way. And, indeed, she had never been so blunt with anyone before. But this was her future—her life—that was at stake here. She couldn't afford to be nice and polite. She blocked Henrietta's voice from her mind and concentrated instead on Lord Vallentyn.

But now he had risen, and was pacing back and forth in front of the open windows, muttering to himself. He seemed to be truly agitated by what she had said. "I can't!" he said, coming towards her but staring hard at the floor. He spun around on his heel. "But I must! I don't want this marriage." He spun around towards Adriana once again, "But Mother..."

"I don't understand why you must do as your mother says. My lord, you are a man! From all that I have ever learned and experienced, men are the ones who hold the upper hand. They answer to no woman."

Lord Vallentyn laughed, but there was no amusement in it. Indeed, it was a very sad laugh. Adriana looked, perplexed at Lord Vallentyn.

He only shook his head and said, "That may be so in ordinary society, but, well," he sighed heavily. "We are not in ordinary society, are we?"

"Aren't we?" Adriana asked. This made no sense to her. *Ordinary* society? What other type of society was there?

"Let me just say that you do not know my mother, Miss Hayden. If you did, you would understand, I assure you."

But Adriana wasn't going to allow him to misdirect her. Getting out of this marriage was too important. "No. I don't understand, and from all I've heard, I don't believe I want to." Adriana stood up to encourage him further and confront him. "My lord, please. You must be strong. You must stand up to her!"

"I can't!" His eyes locked on to hers for a moment, and then immediately he turned away again. "Oh, but I must!" With his fingers to his temples and one last agonized look at Adriana, he escaped out the door to the garden.

Adriana shook her head sadly. She hadn't meant to cause him so much distress. But just think how miserable we will both be if we are actually forced to marry , she reminded herself.

She reopened the book on her lap to a random page, and then stared out the window thinking over her situation. It couldn't have been more than five minutes later that Lord Devaux walked into the room and strode directly over to her.

"Adriana, it is time you stopped wasting my precious time and accepted Lord Vallentyn's proposal," he said, getting straight to the point.

Adriana sighed. Her guardian never was one for small talk. Then, just to be perverse, she pasted her social smile on to her face. "Good morning to you, my lord. It is a beautiful day, isn't it?"

Lord Devaux stopped and scowled at her. "We don't need any of that, young lady."

"No, of course not," she said brightly, and then added "Please do sit down."

"That is enough," he said, despite taking the offered seat. His voice was high with annoyance. "When are you going to accept Vallentyn's proposal so we can get back to London? I've got important business to attend to there, but we can't leave with this unresolved."

The light in the room dimmed considerably as a cloud moved to cover the sun. Adriana let the smile drop from her face. "I'm afraid I don't see the point in this marriage, my lord. Are you truly going to put your career at risk to help Lord Vallentyn, who doesn't seem to have any firm views on any subject, to attain a significant position in Parliament?"

Lord Devaux scowled. "The only thing you need to concern yourself with is that you will be able to keep that garbage you call art... and Lady Vallentyn will give me an advantageous marriage settlement," he added quietly.

Adriana's jaw began to drop, but she caught it before she gave herself away. So that was it. She was being sold.

The pain of hurt burned its way up into her chest.

Her father had tried to protect her from this. He had known that it was a common enough practice and didn't want his daughter to suffer from it. He had written into his will at Adriana's birth—a mere six years before his and his wife's untimely death—that she was never to be forced into a marriage. But Lord Devaux had found a way around it. Yes, Adriana would have to sign an affidavit saying that she was not being forced into this marriage, but in truth, she was and there was nothing she could do about it—unless Lord Vallentyn came through for her and did actually stand up to his mother.

"I hadn't realized you were so desperate for funds," Adriana said quietly.

"I'm not!" Lord Devaux paused and then continued more calmly, "This will simply put me on the same footing as some of the other more prominent members of Parliament."

Adriana nodded her head slowly. Now she understood. Everything her guardian did furthered his career in Parliament—this would be no exception.

"There is only one flaw in your plan, my lord," Adriana said, beginning to feel true hatred towards this man who thought nothing of using her for his own ends, regardless of the consequences.

Lord Devaux looked at her askance.

"Without me, your political dinner parties will be nothing. Henrietta, although I love her dearly and she is a sweet soul, does not have the knack that I have for these things. She can never be the hostess I am—you said so yourself," she added for good measure. If he wasn't going to play fair, well then, why should she?

Her guardian nodded his head in agreement. "You are correct. That is why you will continue to host political dinners. The only difference is they will have the added benefit of being in Vallentyn House on Grosvenor Square instead of my humble abode. And I, naturally, will always be invited."

"And why would I want to do that?"

"Because it is the reason Vallentyn is marrying you, you silly little girl. Without your dinners and my presence, Vallentyn will never gain the position his mother wants for him."

"And if I refuse to hold these parties?" Adriana asked, holding her head high.

Lord Devaux narrowed his eyes at her. "I wouldn't do that if I were you," he said very softly. "I may punish you by taking away your art, but I've heard that Lady Vallentyn's punishments are much, much worse."

A shiver ran down Adriana's arms as she remembered her conversation with Lord Vallentyn not ten minutes ago. If that were the case, then what choice did she have? She was being backed into a corner. Every road to her freedom, one by one, was being made impassable. If only... if only she had the means to run from this life—no, this was no life, this was servitude.

So long as she still had her painting, she could escape.

Morgan could hardly wait to try out his new powers. Finally, in the early afternoon, his patience wore out. He knew he still had chores to do, but what would it hurt to just try?

His eye landed on a small pile of hay sitting in a corner of the barn. The energy was swirling around inside him, surely there could be no harm in using it. In fact, it could only help him to use it. He knew that magic was like a muscle—the more you used it, the stronger it became. If he practiced, if he used his magic, it would become easier and easier.

He focused his eyes on the hay and thought, fire.

Nothing.

No, it couldn't be that easy. All right. He reached inside of himself, pulling his energy together and imagined the hay on fire. "Fire," he said aloud, this time.

Oberon, who was standing nearby watching him, slid down to the floor. Morgan looked over to him. "I can do this. I know I can."

The dog gave a small bark of encouragement.

Morgan nodded and tried again. This time he really concentrated. He imagined the energy swirling within him. He saw it move about his body and gathered it, directing it into his arm, just as Kat had told him. Pointing his hand at the hay, he released the energy like an arrow from a bow. "Fire!" he shouted.

The hay twitched, as if a light breeze had blown past.

"I am tied to the element of fire! I am one with it. It is mine to command!" His anger mixed with the magic and swept into his hand faster this time, but still there wasn't even the smallest spark.

Morgan slammed his hand against the wall in his anger. He heard the wood crack, but didn't care. Oberon gave a little whimper.

No, maybe I'm starting too big, he thought. Maybe I need to start with something smaller. Even his brother and sisters could move objects with just a thought, and he had heard his mother lamenting over how weak they were. Surely, he could make something move. Any Vallen could do that.

He looked around the barn for a likely object. A fox crept quietly out of the end stall and slinked up to the water trough. Morgan had yet to refill it that day and it was nearly empty. Still, the animal lapped up what little there was.

As soon as he was done, Morgan moved to the pail that sat ready for him to take to fetch the water. Holding his hand out over it, he willed it into his hand.

Come into my hand, he thought. Come, he projected. Up! But still the pail didn't move. Once again, Morgan, grasped at his magic, pulling it, cajoling it into his hand. Rise, he thought, focusing his energy on the pail at his feet.

"Rise!"

"Up!"

"Move!" he finally shouted.

And then kicked the pail with all of his frustration and anger. It went flying across the barn. The fox shot back into his stall, so fast that it was hardly a blur.

Why didn't this work! How could it not? He had put a suggestion into Adriana's mind! That was powerful magic – much more powerful that lifting a pail or starting a fire. Why couldn't he do this?

Was this why Kat hadn't wanted him even to try? Because she knew he would fail? Had she been trying to protect him?

It wasn't right. It wasn't fair! He was destined to be the greatest Vallen of his time and he couldn't even move an empty pail!

Leaving his heart and his anger spent on the floor, he went and retrieved the pail. He still had chores to do.

Chapter 12

As always, Oberon bounded on ahead. Morgan heard him give a little bark, warning him there was someone by the stream. But who could be there?

Morgan's heart gave a little leap at the thought that it might be Adriana. He had been hoping she would come back to visit him again.

He looked out from between the trees. It *was* her! All of the pent–up tension in his body disappeared at the sight of her. Morgan moved a step closer to her into the clearing.

Her auburn hair glinted in the sunlight as she sat on the ground facing the stream, a pretty straw bonnet on the ground to her left. Oberon was sniffing at something in the grass to her right.

"No, puppy," Adriana laughed, pushing Oberon's nose away. She gave his jaw a rub to move him away from whatever it was he'd been smelling, and then started massaging him between his ears. Oberon moved closer, enjoying her attentions, but nearly stepped on the thing she'd been pushing away from him.

"Oh, no! Please, do be careful!"

Morgan moved forward, eager to talk to her and be with her once again. "Oberon," he called, both to save whatever it was Adriana wanted him to move away from and to let her know he was there.

Adriana jumped at the sound of his voice, and twisted her body around to look at him.

"Oh, you startled me." Her cheeks turned a little pink and she tried to quickly gather up her things. Putting on her hat, she closed what Morgan could see now was a box of paints, and tried to stand up at the same time.

She stumbled as she stepped on the hem of her dress, but Morgan took a few quick steps forward and caught her elbow before she fell.

"There is no need for you to get up," he said soothingly. She seemed to be very agitated all of a sudden.

She gave a nervous little laugh, but then looked down and noticed that part of the hem of her dress had torn. "Oh dear!" she gave an exasperated sigh. "I wish I weren't so clumsy!"

Morgan smiled. "I just can't imagine anyone as graceful and beautiful as you could be uncoordinated."

Adriana shook her head, as color flooded her cheeks. She was clearly at a loss for words. But Morgan didn't think she needed to say a thing as he sank into the warm pool of her green eyes.

He could have just stood there, staring into her beautiful eyes, and maybe caressing her soft pink cheek. But then that wouldn't have been enough, he'd want to kiss her again...

Oberon gave a bark, abruptly recalling Morgan to his surroundings. When had his dog become so annoying and rude? He took a step back, away from Adriana, although he wanted nothing more than to get closer—much closer.

"What were you were painting?" he asked, in an effort to pull his mind away from where it had been heading.

"What? Oh!" she gave another nervous laugh and looked down at her sketchbook that was still lying on the ground where she had left it.

Morgan bent down and picked it up. The picture was that of the flowing stream. She had caught the flow of the water beautifully, its ebbs and eddies and the slightly turbulent nature of it as it moved briskly downstream. She had begun to paint the greenery surrounding it, but that was where she had stopped.

As with Adriana's drawings, she had somehow infused feelings into the painting as well as simply depicting what she saw. This one gave a sense of longing and sadness, as if she wished she could continue on with the flowing water instead of being trapped here on the bank. And there was something more... there was a feeling Morgan was more familiar with than, he thought, anyone.

He looked up at her questioningly.

Her eyes were unusually large as she watched him look at her painting. Their green depths were dark with anxiety.

"It's lovely," he said, reassuringly.

She released her breath, and gave him a little smile and a shrug. "Some people hate my work."

"Why? It's beautiful."

She bent down to pick up her paints, which had fallen when she'd lost her balance. "My guardian says they are too emotional. I believe he finds them disturbing."

Morgan nodded his head. He could understand some might find that to be so. The painting did carry a lot of emotion within it. But he wasn't disturbed by it, only intrigued. He'd never experienced anything like this before when looking at a painting—then, of course, he hadn't spent much time looking at paintings. The only ones he'd ever seen were those of his ancestors hanging in the abbey, but clearly none had ever made much of an impression on him. And they were nothing at all like Adriana's work.

Morgan marveled at the emotion in the painting he was holding. This time knew better than to ask her about it, but it was there—that desire, that need to escape that was sometimes so strong within him that he could barely contain himself. When he couldn't take it anymore, he would go riding through the forest—riding as fast as he could. Or sometimes he ran, feeling the blood pumping through his muscles as he zigzagged through the trees. It made his heart pound. And that was what was depicted here in the swiftly flowing stream—the desire, the need, for freedom.

But it couldn't be. Adriana *was* free. She wasn't caged in like he was. She was free to go wherever she wanted, while he could never leave these woods.

No, it must be a mistake. He must be misinterpreting her painting. But there was definitely something there. "What do you want?"

"I'm sorry?" she asked, straightening her hat and tying the ribbon underneath her chin.

"In the picture, it looks, er, feels, as if you want something."

Her cheeks turned pink once more and she shook her head, but didn't say anything. She turned to stare at the stream. Morgan allowed her a moment of silence to collect her thoughts. He had clearly hit on a nerve.

"It is nothing." She took her sketchbook from his hand and carefully closed the book.

Whatever it was, he supposed she wasn't ready to tell him about it. He let it go.

Remembering that he had come here to collect water for the animals, he walked down to the bank and bent down to fill the pail.

"How are the animals in your barn?" she asked, watching him.

"Most are better. There are still a few who have not yet fully recovered." He stood up, careful not to spill the water. He had managed to fill the pail very full. "Would you..." he stopped. He'd almost forgotten—girls generally didn't like animals. At least, none of his sisters had, although Kat had never seemed to mind them too much.

"Would I what?" she asked.

"I was going to ask if you'd like to see them, but I don't suppose you would."

"Well, yes, actually, I would very much. What sort of animals do you have?"

Morgan came closer to her again. "Squirrels, rabbits, hedgehogs, a vixen with her cubs. And there is a foal with his mother. Unfortunately, he's having the hardest time of it. Are you truly interested?" He could hardly believe she would be.

Her smile was like a ray of sunshine. "Yes, I am. I would love to see them. May I?"

Heat shot through him as he gave a nod before leading her back to his barn.

How did Adriana make him so happy? Did she just know that wanting to see the animals would make him feel this way? Did she do it on purpose, or was she actually interested? Morgan hadn't a clue, he just knew that his feet hardly touched the ground as he led her back to his barn.

Morgan propped open the barn door to let in some fresh air. It was getting rather ripe with so many animals all living together like this. He was almost embarrassed to have Adriana visiting when things weren't so clean.

He poured some of the water into a trough small enough to allow even the smallest animals to drink from it, while Adriana stood looking out of place in her pretty frock.

Many of the animals, upon smelling a stranger, had quickly run to hide, but Adriana, after carefully placing her painting materials on a shelf by the door, sat down in the middle of the floor, heedless of her dress. She put her hands out, palm up and waited.

Morgan stood off to the side to see what would happen. After a few minutes, a few of the rabbits and a squirrel ventured out of their hiding places. Slowly approaching her, they sniffed, taking in her scent. Clearly they liked it as much as Morgan had, for they came closer, and even, eventually, allowed her to gently touch them.

She turned and gave Morgan a brilliant smile. Heat burned through him, hotter than if he'd been hit by lightning.

He could no more resist her allure than the animals. He walked over and picked up a rabbit that was sniffing at her skirt. He settled himself next to her, gently petting the bunny in his hand.

He saw her eyes slide towards him briefly, but she kept her focus on the animals surrounding her.

"They are so sweet," she said, quietly.

"They trust you."

"Well, I would never hurt them."

"Neither would Kat, but they don't come so near to her."

"That's right, Kat told me she sometimes comes to visit you."

Morgan nodded. "She does, but very rarely does she interact with the animals. They usually keep their distance. But they can sense when someone is friendly and trustworthy."

She gave a little smile, and a comfortable silence fell between them. It was so wonderful, amazing really, to just sit here with her like this—to share these little details of his life with Adriana.

"Freedom," Adriana said quietly, while watching a fox cub smell around her foot.

"Freedom?" Morgan asked. He had been lost in his own thoughts, and wondered for a moment if he'd missed something.

"It was what I am longing for in the painting."

Morgan felt his throat clench and he swallowed hard. He had been right! But it still didn't make sense.

"How could that be? How do you not have freedom?" he asked, wishing desperately he could tell her that he had recognized the feeling—it was one he was all too familiar with.

"I told you I was here to become engaged to Lord Vallentyn."

"Yes, but you said you were going to find a way out of it."

"I had hoped I could find a way to do so, but Lord Devaux informed me today that I was going marry Lord Vallentyn no matter what and I should just get on with it and accept the proposal."

"What would happen if you refused?"

Adriana shook her head. "My guardian would destroy all of my paintings and never allow me to sketch or paint again. It's not something I could live with, and he knows it." She paused to wipe away the tear that was making its way down her cheek and to take a deep shaky breath. Morgan marveled at her restraint.

"Painting is my life," she continued. "It *is* my freedom. It's the only thing I have... in a world where I am not even allowed out of the house without Lord Devaux's express permission, painting allows me the freedom I desire— to roam the world. To visit places I long to go. To do what *I* want. If he takes that away from me..." She sniffed, taking in another deep breath. "He knows I would never give it up. I would rather marry a man I don't know than stop painting."

She turned her face to him. It was filled with such sadness, and yet she had the strength to endure her guardian's dictates in order to keep what was most important to her.

This time Morgan didn't pause, or even try to stop himself. He kissed her. Pressing his lips to hers, he let her know he understood exactly what she was feeling, and took all of her sadness, anger and frustration away. He knew—he knew so well—what it felt like to be imprisoned like this. To have your freedom denied to you. To want, no, to *need* to be free.

He longed to share with her what he had been going through. How he lived. Caged in these woods, he could no more escape his situation than she could escape hers. He too felt as trapped as she did—only she had her painting to free her. And he had... nothing.

Adriana pulled away. Everything rushing through her was disturbingly wonderful. She could hardly think—her mind was so full of Morgan, and how incredible he made her feel. But she had to think, she had to keep her wits about her, or else she would find herself in a situation that even Henrietta wouldn't be able to accept. She had already gone too far, she knew, just by allowing him to kiss her. She would not give any more fodder to Lord Devaux and his disdain of her.

But when she was so close to Morgan... it was impossible to say no.

She needed distance. That's what would allow her to regain control over her wayward emotions. Distance.

She carefully removed the fox cub that had crawled into her lap. Getting up, she tip–toed through the animals which surrounded them and moved toward the door.

She stared out at the seemingly unending forest of trees, trying to compose herself. Her lips were still tingling from their kiss, and her skin was hot where he had touched her. "How wonderful it must be to live here in the woods with the animals. You can do whatever you want." She shook her head. She didn't want to wallow in her problems any more than she already had. She wanted... she wanted what he had, the freedom to be carefree and to have fun.

She spun back towards him. "What do you do for fun— besides play with your dog in the river?" She took a few steps toward his horse, Apollo, who was watching her from his stall. "Do you ride?"

Morgan too stood up, and carefully moved away from the animals, which were wandering about now that they weren't the center of attention any more. "Yes. That's how I feel free. I ride or run through the forest."

"It can't be easy riding with all of the trees growing so closely together," she said, peering outside again.

"There are some straighter paths where the trees aren't so close. It is mainly around this area that the trees are so dense." He followed her out of the barn door.

She looked around at the trees that surrounded his home. A neat and very definite line seemed to have been drawn between the well–tended ground around Morgan's cottage, and the dense wild growth of the woods, making his home into a sort of haven amidst the forest.

"It must be a fun challenge to run as fast as you can without colliding into a tree," she laughed, daring to forget her troubles, even if it would just be for a short time.

Morgan stood next to her and looked around at the trees trying to see them as she did. "I used to do that when I was young. Kat and I would have races through the woods—the toughest one was always going from here to the stream."

An idea began to form itself in her mind. Adriana turned and gave him a sly little smile. "Ready?" She paused for the briefest moment and then said very quickly, "Steady. Go!" And took off running toward the stream.

She ran, wishing she could throw her arms out with abandon. She ran, taking the fresh air of the forest deep into her lungs and breathing in the freedom. She laughed as she weaved in and out of the trees, nearly colliding with one after another. She hoped she was running in the right direction—she thought that she was, but she wasn't entirely sure of the way. Because of that, too, she laughed.

Ducking under the low reaching branches and skirting low growing brush, she ran as quickly as she could. It wasn't easy, and she had to hold her skirt up indecently high, but she didn't care. She glanced behind her to see Morgan not too far back, his laughter lighting up his whole face. A branch whipped at her cheek, causing it to sting. She turned back to watch where she was going.

She burst out from the trees to the bit of green by the edge of the stream and straight into Morgan's arms.

He laughed as he caught her. Giggling and out of breath, she grasped on to his shirt to stop herself from falling, but he held her with a strength that was comforting and thrilling at the same time.

"How did you get here so fast? I thought you were behind me." she asked, still laughing, and hardly able to speak for her panting.

Morgan laughed at her, hardly even breathing hard. "I'm used to running through the forest. It wasn't a fair race to begin with."

She tilted her head back to look up at him. "Oh. Yes, I suppose you're right." She gave a little shrug. She didn't care. She had just wanted to have some fun, and she had. In fact, she couldn't remember the last time she had run like that. Or felt so free.

Morgan's face became serious for the briefest of moments, and then he leaned down toward her. Gently taking her face between his large hands, he pressed his lips to her cheek where it stung. When he pulled away, her cheek burned for just a moment where he had kissed it, but the stinging was gone.

She was still breathing hard, but now she didn't know if it was because of her run or his kiss.

The fire crackled warmly in the grate of the family sitting room as Tatiana stared into the flickering flames. She'd been summoned to another Vallen's assistance.

She would go, of course. It was her obligation, and it was her pleasure. Helping others who'd lost control of their magic, or stopping the abuse of the power—it was her duty as High Priestess to see to these sorts of problems, as it had been her mother's and her mother before that, and so on back for countless generations. Just as Merlin's chalice had been passed down from generation to generation—and now was in her care.

She looked up at the chalice as it sat in the special nook she'd had made for it above the fireplace. The entire sitting room had been designed around that cup. It was a futile attempt to reflect its magnificence. The plush white sofa and black chairs, all of the tables of white marble with black veining—they were nothing compared to the perfection of the white marble chalice. Nothing could possibly come close to mirroring its beauty, because its splendor came from within— from the power that the chalice exuded, not from the stone of which it was made.

Tatiana knew that she would never use the chalice. It was a bitter knowledge, but one she had come to terms with. Merlin's chalice was not for her—she was merely its keeper. Only the seventh child of the seventh generation was given the honor and the power to use the chalice. It sickened her that that child was Morgan.

Because Morgan was male, he would never attain the level of power necessary to wield the chalice. Never in all of the history of the Vallen had there been a male Seventh. It was unheard of. And Morgan's lack of powers only confirmed what a mistake it was.

No, the chalice would have to go to Katrina, the sixth of the sixth of the seventh generation. She was strong and worthy of it. Tatiana had decided this, and so it would be. It would have to be!

"Well, I'm off to bed," Kat said, standing up from her favorite chair and stretching like the cat she was so aptly named after. She had the honed senses of the animal. Tatiana had always found it very useful having the girl around.

She toyed with the idea of taking Kat on this little trip. Someday this obligation would be hers—if all went as Tatiana planned. But no, the girl wasn't quite ready yet—and Tatiana wasn't ready to give up what was still hers. It wouldn't be for too much longer—but for now, she would enjoy the duty that had been a part of her life since she had turned twenty–one.

"I need to leave early tomorrow morning," Tatiana said, stopping Kat from leaving the room so quickly.

"Oh?"

"There is some business in Bath which needs my attention."

"But what about Adriana and Lord Devaux?"

"They will have to excuse me, I'm afraid. This can't wait."

Kat just looked at her, clearly shocked that she would be leaving at this important time, and indeed, it surprised Tatiana as well. But duty was duty, and she couldn't shirk it just because her son was a fool who didn't know how to woo a girl.

"You will understand soon enough, Kat."

"Ma'am?"

"Soon you will attain your destiny. When that worthless son of mine turns twenty–one, we will prove he is not capable of taking up the destiny that should have belonged to him, and then it will be yours." Tatiana rose and stalked over to the fire. She paused for the briefest of moments to caress the chalice. Its heat and naked power tingled through her fingers. But it didn't soothe. Just the opposite, it made her even more infuriated as she thought about Morgan.

"But I don't want Morgan's destiny. Aunt, please..."

"You don't have a choice, Katrina," Tatiana said, as she picked up the poker leaning by the side of the fireplace. Despite the warmth of the room, she jabbed at the flaming coals, enticing even more heat to come from them. "If he had done as he should have and been born a girl, then you would not be in this position."

"But he is not to blame," Kat whispered, too embarrassed, or frightened, to say it out boldly.

Tatiana jabbed at the fire once more. "You think I should take the responsibility for this? I assure you I will not. I did all that I should have, all that was within my power," she said, knowing full well that the fault did in fact lie with her. But she wasn't about to admit to such weakness, nor would she ever.

Yes, she had been the one to create the monstrous disappointment that was Morgan. She still could not believe it. How could she, the most powerful, talented Vallen of the century, have given birth to such a pitiful, weak little boy? A boy! After five girls, the one that had to be a girl...

That would have been bad enough even if he had been powerful. If he had been a talented Vallen with natural abilities such as was the right of the seventh child in her family... But no! He had been pitiful and weak. From the moment he was born, he'd had almost no magical powers at all.

Tatiana could put up with that from her other children. It was even expected of them. Surely her body had been waiting, waiting until the seventh child, until the rightful heir was born to be imbued with all of the magical abilities she had and more.

But no! "No! He has nothing. He *is* nothing. I will not suffer that boy to live!" Tatiana threw the poker against the black marble of the fireplace and spun around, ready to destroy anything that got in her way.

Kat stood just behind her, her hazel eyes wide with fear and shock. "You cannot kill him," she said, clearly horrified at the thought.

Tatiana spun back around to face the fire once more. That was what her husband had said, only he had done so much more forcefully—and with magic. "No. I cannot," Tatiana admitted, "His father saw to that. Morgan has a protection spell over him that even I cannot break. I assure you, if I could, I would have many years ago."

"You can't mean that, ma'am."

"Do you question me, Katrina?"

"No, ma'am, it's just that... even though he isn't the girl he should have been, Morgan is still your child."

"And what of that? A mother was never more disappointed than I."

"Even so. You carried him in your womb for nine months. You do have some love for him?" The last was said more as a question, but with the certainty of a statement.

Tatiana though about what Kat said for a moment. Did she have *some* love for Morgan? She supposed she must. She hadn't killed him in all these years. She hadn't really even tried to break his father's protection spell, although she probably could if she truly wanted to. So perhaps there was some love in her for her son after all.

But she would rot in hell before admitting it.

Chapter 13

Adriana let out a startled scream as Oberon, Morgan's dog, grabbed her hat between his teeth and lifted it off her head. She was looking extremely pretty today. Her sunny yellow dress and straw bonnet adorned with yellow silk flowers blended perfectly with the bright sunshine of the day, and contrasted beautifully with the colors of the forest. She had been kneeling down on the soft earth, carefully plucking the pretty white flowers of a marsh–mellow plant, when Oberon had decided that it was time to play.

The dog stood just out of Adriana's reach. As she leaned forward to grab her hat, he jumped back. She moved forward very slowly, woman and dog staring eye to eye. Quickly she lunged for the hat, and just as quickly the dog leaped backward and avoided her grasping hand.

Morgan stifled a laugh.

But Adriana was laughing herself as she got up off the ground and dusted off her dress. "You want to play, do you? Well, that is all fine and good, sir, but I will not have you ruining my best chip straw bonnet," she addressed the dog with mock severity, placing her hands on her hips.

Oberon was clearly having a lot of fun teasing Adriana. Morgan almost wished he'd thought of it himself.

She took a menacing step toward the dog, watching carefully as he retreated, and then, without even trying to take back her hat, she turned around as if she no longer cared.

Oberon hesitantly moved closer. And then with a swift movement, Adriana spun around and reached for the hat.

But once again, Oberon was too fast for her.

This time Morgan could not contain his laughter as his dog outwitted her yet again.

Adriana spun around to face him. Her face was flushed with happiness, her eyes sparkling with laughter. Morgan's breath caught in his throat. Never had he even dreamed that a woman could be so incredibly beautiful. He thought his heart was ready to burst with joy.

"Well, are you going to just stand there and laugh at me, or are you going to help?" she said, rounding on him.

He gave a non-committal shrug and laughed once more.

Each and every day he and Adriana spent together, Morgan was happier than he had ever thought he could be. For long stretches of time, he had been able to forget his troubles. Each day they spent together was better than the day before— and so it had been for the past two weeks. The only thing marring his happiness was the time Adriana was away from him, and the fact that his powers did not seem to be increasing anymore—no matter how hard he worked and practiced his magic.

A yelp from Adriana broke Morgan out of his reverie, and he watched as she went running off toward the stream after the dog.

Morgan followed. He couldn't help but burst out laughing at the sight of Oberon standing in the stream up to his shoulders, still holding the hat just barely above the level of the water. The long yellow ribbons trailed in the gently flowing water.

"Why, you horrible thing, you! You wouldn't dare!" Adriana said, standing on the shore. But Morgan could see that she was desperately trying to hide her smile.

Then just to show that he would dare, Oberon slowly lowered the hat so that it skimmed the surface of the water.

"No! That is one of my best hats!" Adriana cried and laughed at the same time. Kicking off her shoes and quickly pulling off her stockings, she carefully tried to follow the dog into the water, holding her dress up so it wouldn't get wet. She displayed quite a bit of her enticingly long, shapely legs as she tried to coax the dog out of the water.

She had nearly come within a hand's reach of him when he turned with a great splash and leaped into the deeper water, heedless of the hat still in his mouth. Adriana let out another screech, but this one sounded less like a laugh than the others.

Morgan decided it was time he took matters into his own hands.

"Oberon, come!" he said in his most masterful voice.

The dog continued swimming across the river.

"Come, Oberon, now!" Morgan tried again.

"Oh, he is going to ruin my hat, Morgan. Can't you make him listen?" Adriana said, taking another hesitant step forward. The bottom few inches of her dress was now hanging into the water.

There didn't seem to be anything else for it. Morgan pulled off his own boots and stockings and ran past Adriana, heedless of his own clothing. Adriana gave another little shriek as he splashed past her.

Morgan dove into the cool, refreshing water, swimming up under his dog. In one swift movement, he had the dog on his shoulders, and turned around heading back to the shore.

Adriana's beautiful tinkling laugh greeted him as he sloshed to the shore. She reached up to take her hat from the dog's mouth, and at the same time waved a finger in his face. "That should teach you a lesson in manners."

Her laughing green eyes slid down to Morgan's and then her lovely smiling face turned bright pink as they moved lower—to take in his wet shirt and breeches.

Morgan, too, noticed that quite a bit more of Adriana's dress had become wet and was clinging to her shapely body. He felt a stirring as his blood heated.

He turned and knelt to the ground to put Oberon down. When he turned back around, Adriana had begun to rub her hands up and down her arms as if she were cold.

Morgan picked up his boots and stockings and placed his arm around her shoulders. "Let's go build a fire and dry off."

She nodded, but did not look his way. With a slight coloring of her cheeks, she picked up her ownstockings and rolled them up to keep them from his sight.

After slipping her bare feet back into her slippers, Adriana allowed Morgan to lead her back toward his cabin. Oberon followed at their heels, his head lowered slightly as if he were ashamed that he got too carried away by his game.

Morgan stacked a few dry pieces of wood in the clearing in front of his cottage, and lit the fire with his tinderbox—deliberately not even thinking about trying to light the fire magically.

Sitting on a log near the fire, Adriana reached out her hands to its growing warmth. Morgan settled himself on the ground next to her and stretched out his legs so that his breeches didn't become too tight as they dried on his body. Already he could feel the leather stiffening as it began to dry.

"Will you tell me some more about your home in London?" he asked, hoping to relieve some of the awkwardness that had suddenly sprung up between them.

Adriana shrugged. "What more is there to tell?"

"You said that you run your guardian's household. Is there much work in this?"

"Well, part of my duties include arranging parties for Lord Devaux so that he may meet and talk with other members of parliament," Adriana said, tucking a lock of her beautiful hair back into the knot on the back of her head. Morgan wished she would just open it so he could run his fingers through the silky tresses.

He forced his mind to stay focused on what she was telling him.

"Parties? That must be fun." Morgan couldn't help the touch of jealousy that crept into his voice. How wonderful it must be to live in a big city and have parties!

But oddly enough, it was a rather sad smile that came to Adriana's full pink lips. "I wouldn't go quite that far. They are not the sort of parties where one dances and talks to friends."

Morgan watched Adriana's beautiful eyes as she spoke. They kept straying down his body, and at the moment, were lingering on his shirt. A thrill ran through him as he looked down and noticed that it was nearly transparent and clinging to his body, since it was still soaking wet. She was as attracted to him as he was to her!

"These parties," she continued after a moment, "are for the sheer purpose of making political connections or pressing an idea onto other members of parliament." Her voice slowed, and she stopped speaking altogether. Then, abruptly, she turned her head away from him, and stared into the fire. "My guardian gives me a list of people he wants me to invite and I make all the proper arrangements."

"You don't get to invite your own friends as well?" he asked. He knew he should be feeling chilled in his wet clothes, but the heat inside of him was too intense.

Adriana shook her head and smiled, keeping her eyes trained on the fire. Morgan wondered at her not even daring to look back at him. He wished she would, just so he could see the desire in her eyes once more.

He too turned to the fire, determined to listen to her words and not to his heart.

"I don't have any friends. I don't attend society parties, and therefore don't know many people my own age. I only attend Lord Devaux's parties to act as hostess for him."

"Oh." Morgan was amazed. Even living in London, surrounded by people, she was as lonely as he.

But Adriana turned toward him with deliberate brightness. "It's not all boring and difficult work, however. There are a great many people whom we entertain who are quite amusing."

"In what way?" Morgan asked, marveling at how she could set aside her loneliness and still see the bright side of her life.

"Frequently, the gentlemen we invite are very important men—or men who want to be important. And they're often very huffy gentlemen." She spread out her arms to indicate a very large man and blew out her cheeks. Her eyes now twinkling with merriment, and speaking in a deep voice, she said, "Well, er, yes, my dear gel, of course a pretty little mite like you could never understand the intricacies of, er, social reform, eh? Heh, heh, heh, why don't you run along and, er, pour the tea or, er, work on your little sewing project like a good gel."

Morgan laughed. He could imagine a large gentleman, his face mostly covered with side burns, such as he'd seen illustrated in the papers Kat sometimes brought to him.

"And the ladies, their wives," Adriana continued to the fire, "many of them are quite in awe of their husbands. They twitter and giggle, and say things like," she switched to a high, tittery voice, "'Oh, my, how marvelous it is that my lord is doing such wonderful things for the little people.' And then they go on to discuss the latest fashions and how they have spent hundreds of pounds on their newest gowns—not even realizing that the work their husbands are doing will not help the 'little people' at all, but are solely for their own benefit so they can buy their expensive clothes."

Morgan shook his head, smiling.

Adriana shifted away from the heat of the fire, accidentally brushing her leg against his. Instantly, desire uncoiled itself inside him once again. She turned and looked at him, the smile slipping from her lips. As their eyes met, he was surprised at the open flame of yearning reflected in her deep green eyes.

He reached out and gently caressed her cheek, running his thumb along her cheekbone and down to her parted lips. Her eyes widened, and her chest began to rise and fall with her quickened breaths.

The fire in front of them let out a sizzle as a drop of rain fell into it. A large plop landed next to Morgan's foot, and then another on his shoulder, but neither of them paid it any heed.

"Part of my duties as hostess is being able to discuss everything that is currently under consideration in Parliament," she said, a little breathlessly.

"That is fascinating," Morgan said, pulling her head closer to his own. He could feel the heat emanating from her body and smell her distinctive scent of wildflowers.

His lips were nearly upon hers when she pulled back and added, "All of the ladies are not quite so silly. There are actually a few who are interested in what their husbands are doing and are not afraid to speak their minds."

"That's good," Morgan said, moving in closer again. Then, with hardly any warning at all, as Morgan was making another attempt at a kiss, a gust of wind blew into his face, and with it, rain began pelting down in earnest.

Morgan froze for a moment. He hadn't even seen the clouds moving in—he was so intent on Adriana and kissing her. But they couldn't sit here in the rain. Already they were both soaking wet. He jumped up, reaching for Adriana's hand. Just as he pulled her to her feet, a low rumble of thunder shook the ground. He ran with her to his cottage, as a flash of lightning briefly illuminated the ever darkening sky.

Morgan immediately moved to build a fire in the hearth, turning back to Adriana as soon as he had a blaze going. She was standing looking around, her arms wrapped around her slender body.

He, too, looked around his home and wondered how it looked to her. Of course, she was used to the grandeur of the abbey and probably had one of the nicer carpeted bedrooms there.

Morgan had no carpet, but rather a plain wood floor. This was matched by the rough–hewn table and lone chair that sat by it, both of which he had made himself. His bedstead stood off against the far wall, a small simple washstand next to it. The cottage was tidy, but then again there wasn't much to clutter it up.

Adriana hugged her shivering body and moved closer to the fire.

Morgan stood up, and on instinct, wrapped his arms around her.

Adriana started, but Morgan hushed her saying, "My heat will warm you."

She laughed. "Perhaps, but your clothes are cold and wet."

He quickly pulled away from her. "I'm sorry. I forgot." Quickly he pulled off his shirt and then pulled the blanket off his bed. "You would be warmer if you took off your wet clothes too."

Adriana took a step back toward the door, her eyes wide and her face turning pink.

"It is all right," he said, moving closer and looking deeply into her eyes. Gently placing his hand on her cheek, he gave her a little smile and said, "There is nothing to fear."

Chapter 14

Tatiana could feel her son Jonathan's presence just outside her bed chamber door long before he knocked. What was it he had to say to her that would keep him standing outside for so long before he gathered up his courage to knock? She had only been back from her trip to Bath for less than a day, so he must have something important to report to her.

She waited patiently for him to knock. "Come in, Vallentyn," she called, as soon as he had done so.

He shuffled into the room, his head bowed. He would not look her in the eye. This was another bad sign.

"Good afternoon, Mother," he said, and turned to look out the window, as if he were checking to make sure that it was still light enough to call it afternoon.

"Good afternoon. To what do I owe this pleasure?" she asked, as sweetly as she could, hoping to encourage him to drop his defensive stance.

"I, er..." he glanced quickly in her direction where she was sitting on the settee by the fire, but then just as quickly, turned his eyes away. "I wished to speak with you."

"So I assumed when you knocked at my door."

"Er, yes."

"What do you wish to speak to me about, Jonathan?" Tatiana asked, beginning to feel her patience ebb away.

"I, er, well," Jonathan took a deep breath and then said very quickly, "I do not wish to marry Miss Hayden. I am the viscount, I am the one in charge here and I say that I will not marry her. I will remain a bachelor." He released what was left of his breath.

He then turned and, much to Tatiana's surprise, began to leave without waiting for her to say, or do, anything—as if that were the end of the conversation.

If this were funny, Tatiana would have laughed. Unfortunately for her son, she did not find it amusing in the least.

As Jonathan began to open the door, it pulled from his hand, slamming itself shut. Jonathan jumped back, startled, but unharmed.

Tatiana could feel her anger rise. She did not want to hurt her first born, her only true son, but it seemed as if he was not going to give her much of a choice in the matter.

"You are the viscount? The lord of the manor? The one in charge?" Tatiana repeated very slowly to her son's back.

Silence.

"I thought that you had learned, Jonathan. You have never crossed me before. What has caused this extreme lack of judgment?" The air in the room began to get hot as Tatiana's anger grew.

"Is it Miss Hayden?" she continued, ignoring the fire in the hearth that had begun to burn larger and brighter. "Surely she could not have put you up to this. You know better than to listen to a girl who does not know me or what I am capable of doing." The last she was careful to say slowly and deliberately.

Sweat began to drip down Jonathan's face. He ran a finger underneath his neck cloth, pulling it away from his burning skin even as his face went from pink to red. "I... I did not mean..."

"What did you not mean?" Tatiana said quietly. "Did you not mean to tell me that you are the one who makes the rules in this house, in this family? Did you not mean to put me in my place?"

"No! No, I..." Jonathan had begun to breath more heavily as if he couldn't get enough oxygen through the dense heat that now coated the room. The overstuffed furniture—the bed, the chair, even the tables that crowded the room, they all seemed to bleed warmth into the air.

"You what, Jonathan?" Tatiana lowered her voice to a mere whisper.

"I will marry her, but..."

"But?" Tatiana focused her eyes on her son's bright red face. Still, he refused to meet her eyes.

"But I don't want to join parliament. I have no interest in politics." The words seemed forced out of him, as if he wished he could hold them back, but he could do nothing to stop them.

Jonathan stepped to the door and leaned his head against it, panting as if he had just run a mile. "I am sorry, Mother," he whimpered.

At the sight of her weak, worthless child, everything within her went ice cold. Tatiana's rage could no longer be contained. Jonathan would learn for once and for all not to cross his mother.

The sound of the rain pounded in Adriana's ears, the noise from the roof reverberating throughout Morgan's little cottage.

She was chilled to the bone—first from the splashing about in the river, and now by the rainstorm that had taken them by surprise. She knew Morgan was right. The only way she'd get warm was if she took off her dress. It certainly wasn't drying on her.

She gave a little nod, and then moved closer to the fire and turned her back. He did the gentlemanly thing and moved away to his bed while she struggled with a dress that was not designed to be put on or taken off without the help of a maid. She had gotten it half way over her head when strong hands appeared to help her pull the clinging material off. Her face burned as she prayed that she was still covered decently enough, but still could not resist covering herself with her hands as well.

Morgan was not paying attention. He was carefully laying out her dress over the chair in front of the fire so that it could dry. Adriana could not help but notice how his bare chest glowed golden in the firelight. Her breath caught in her throat, but she just could not tear her eyes away from his well–toned body.

Pounding rain blended with the pounding of her heart. As if of its own volition, her hand reached out and she watched as her fingers skimmed across his muscles, gently feathering across his hard, dark nipples. They slipped lower, past the bottom of his ribs, which stood out from the stripes of muscle that played across his stomach. A thin dark line of hair led down from his navel, disappearing into his breeches. She gently traced the line with shaking fingers. His hair was thick and coarse against the soft heat of his skin.

The drumming in her ears grew louder as he stepped closer, and her eyes were drawn up to his. Yellow and orange flames, reflected the fire, dancing in his black eyes. They moved ever closer to her, enveloping her within their deep, dark depths. She sank into those eyes even as her mouth reached up to meet his.

The kiss was gentle at first, but built quickly into a hunger and desperation she had never even imagined possible. Heat seared its way down her body, curling her toes with pleasure. She couldn't get enough of him. She couldn't get close enough.

Thunder rumbled through the cottage, rolling away any remaining thoughts from Adriana's mind. She was pure sensation knowing nothing but soft skin, hard muscles, delicious, hot mouth, and the persistent drumming, pounding, thrumming of the rain.

Vaguely, she was aware of her stays loosening and then slipping down past her hips and to the floor. She pushed them out of her way with her foot. She needed to be closer, to feel him, every inch of him.

His hard muscled chest pressed against hers. His hands slid up and down her back sending shivers along her spine. She warmed from the inside out.

No, not just warm—hot.

His hands finally came to rest on her bottom, as his tongue plunged deeply into her mouth. He tasted fresh, like the wind on a warm summer's day, but it was the heat from his mouth and body that suffused her and made her press closer still. The thunder rolled through them as the rain wove its magic all around them.

And then she was floating, her feet lifted off the floor. She was secure in Morgan's arms. The pounding of her blood, the pounding of his heart, the pounding of the rain—they all swirled together in her mind like watercolors across a page, filling all of her sensations with color.

Morgan gently lowered her onto the rough white sheets of his bed. He shed his wet breeches in one stroke, and lay down beside her, pulling the coarse wool blanket tightly over them.

As Morgan's hard male body press against her most secret feminine parts, another surge of liquid heat shot through her. She ran her hands down his back, marveling at the strength of him, and the contrasting softness of his skin. He pressed ever closer, rubbing himself against her, nuzzling his face into her neck. She could feel his hot breath tickling behind her ear, then moving slowly down to her neck, from where he ran soft little kisses down to her breasts.

A shot of heat ran through her as his tongue lathed a sensitive nipple. She moaned, arching her back, willing him even closer. He pressed his manhood harder against her tender parts, rubbing ever faster as if demanding entry into her most secret place.

"Oh, Adriana," Morgan moaned, his voice deep and husky.

And that's when she heard it.

Silence.

The rain had stopped. A few drips echoed loudly on the roof, and Adriana felt her mind swirling up as if trying to peer through the thick watercolors that were still smeared in front of her eyes.

What was she doing?

With a horrified cry, she realized she was nearly naked in bed with a man who was completely unclothed! Thank God, she still had her shift on, but it was untied and pulled down beneath her breasts.

Morgan's hard length pressed against her again. Rubbing softly, but insistently at her most intimate place.

No! This was wrong! She shouldn't be... The silence washed though her mind cleaning away the pigment and making everything horribly clear.

She should not be here. Oh, God, what had she done!

Stifling a whimper, Adriana jumped away from the burning fire that was Morgan. Scrambling off the bed as quickly as she could, she tied her shift tightly, covering her nudity with shaking hands.

"What? What's happened?" Morgan demanded, sitting up and watching her, confusion pulling his eyebrows down over his eyes.

"This... this..." Adriana could not even get the words out. She bit back a sob of shame, throwing her dress on over her head and slipping her feet into her shoes. She tied together the bodice of her dress so she was decently covered, but thought she might be sick to her stomach.

She pulled open the door and paused, but could not bring herself to even look at him. "I..." she choked. "Oh God!" She picked up her skirts and ran as fast as she could for the abbey.

"Morgan, what do you think you are doing sending Oberon to the abbey? You know your mother will recognize him!" Kat scolded him the moment she walked into the cottage.

Morgan tied another bunch of herbs he and Adriana had picked to the rafters of his cottage. "But what else could I do, Kat? She hasn't come to see me in three days," he said, starting to climb down the ladder. There was no need to say who 'she' was, Kat would know.

"She's left. Didn't Adriana tell you she was leaving?"

Morgan stopped halfway down the ladder. Pain sliced through his gut so that he had to focus for a moment to keep breathing. "No. She didn't tell me."

The pain shifted upward, tightening his throat. He swallowed hard. "She left here rather suddenly the other day, but didn't say why. I might have done something..."

"It is quite possible that you did. She and Lord Devaux left two days ago without a word to anyone other than Aunt Vallentyn."

Morgan dropped down to the floor, ignoring the rest of the rungs on the ladder. "But then... why didn't she tell me? Why didn't she say anything—or come talk to me." He took a deep breath. He had to think about this, to figure it out. If he had hurt her... but, no, he'd been very gentle, hadn't he?

Morgan began to pace back and forth in the confined space of his cottage. The room seemed to shrink around him as he took his long strides across the floor.

Adriana had seemed to be enjoying him as much as he was enjoying her when they had been together. Could he have moved too quickly?

He walked around the ladder that was standing directly in the center of the room.

He knew he was the one who had suggested she remove her dress, but she hadn't seemed to mind, aside from a few blushes.

He could not have kept himself from touching her. She was so beautiful, and her skin so creamy and soft.

He turned and waved a hand absent–mindedly at the ladder as he approached it again.

No, he was certain that if she had not wanted him to touch her, she would have said something. Adriana was not the type to do something she didn't want to do. And she certainly would not have touched him as well.

He turned again and strode across the empty space.

He grew hot with just the thought of how she had touched him. His body stirred with the memory. The fire, burning in the hearth directly in front of him, caught his attention. It was much too hot for it in this small space. He waved an open hand and then closed it into a fist as he turned his back on the fire, willing it to go out.

The way Adriana had touched him had not only made his blood heat, but had filled him with the most delicious sensations—tingles of pleasure and hot crackling energy. He'd wanted her to feel the same way. He'd wanted her in every way—to touch her, smell her, taste her...

"Morgan!"

Kat's voice suddenly jarred him out of his reverie. He stopped pacing directly in front of her. "What? Oh, Kat, I'm sorry, I completely forgot that you were here."

But she didn't seem to be concerned about his lack of manners. She was staring at him, her eyes wider than he had ever seen them before.

She pointed to his hands. "Morgan, look!"

He raised his hands in front of him. Small blue sparks were emanating from his fingertips. Leaping and dancing about between his fingers. But even as he watched, they faded away, and then disappeared altogether.

A shiver ran through him, but whether it was fear or excitement, he did not know.

His eyes met Kat's.

She pointed to the fireplace. "You put it out. With a wave of your hand, you put out the fire! And, and the ladder. You moved it out of your way without touching it—it just slid away."

Morgan spun around, looking at the fireplace, which now had gently smoldering wood sitting in it, but not a hint of the flames that had been there a few moments ago. He then turned to the ladder standing against the wall instead of in the center of the room, as if he had picked it up and moved it.

But he hadn't, had he?

He turned once again back to his cousin. "Did I...?"

She nodded her head dumbly.

"But how?"

"I... I don't know. But I saw you do it."

Morgan looked down at his hands once again. They were tingling, but otherwise looked perfectly normal.

"What were you thinking about?" she asked quietly.

"You don't know?" he narrowed his eyes at her. She had always known what he was thinking. If not his exact thoughts, at least what he was feeling.

But she shook her head once again. "No. I tried to read you, but it was as if there was a wall blocking me from your thoughts and feelings. I couldn't penetrate it." She reached out and touched his shoulder. Staring deep into his eyes she said, "You are... confused and a bit frightened. I can see it now, but I have to touch you to know."

"But you've never had to before."

"I know. Something has changed. And when you were pacing just now, you were so intensely in your own thoughts that I don't think I could have read you even if I had touched you."

And then she paled. Morgan watched, startled, as the color drained from her face. "What is it?" he asked, taking hold of her arm.

"You... it's just like your mother. I can't read her thoughts either. Not even when I touch her. She is the only person whose feelings I can't read. And now, I can barely read yours."

Morgan swallowed hard. He was just like his mother? Did that mean he was finally getting the powers that should have been his his whole life?

"Morgan, have you been practicing your magic?" Kat asked nervously.

"Yes, but it hasn't worked. Nothing has happened, until now."

"But you shouldn't! We talked about this. My goodness, we don't know where this magic is coming from! Don't you see? This could be dangerous. I told you not to..."

"We agreed that you wouldn't tell my mother."

"I haven't!"

"Well, then, what could be so dangerous about me finally gaining the powers that should have been mine my whole life?"

He took another step toward her, his heart was pounding as if he'd run to the far edge of the forest and back. "What are you so frightened of? Not attaining my destiny, or me gaining my powers?

Kat's mouth opened and closed. "I don't want your blasted destiny. I've told you that before."

"Then why shouldn't I practice magic?"

She took a step back away from him, crossing her arms in front of her. She stared back at him for a moment before turning her eyes away. When she looked back at him, he could see her pain in them much too clearly.

"Morgan, please, don't be... I'm only trying to look out for you," she said quietly, almost beseechingly.

The sharp retort he had at the tip of his tongue died, as did his anger.

"You have always looked out for me, Kat. You have always been the one to stand up for me, and to encourage me when no one else in my family would. That's why I don't understand why you've suddenly stopped," he explained as gently as he could. Goodness knows, he didn't want to hurt her.

"I haven't. I just want you to be cautious."

Morgan shook his head, "As always. But the time for caution is over."

"I'm afraid you'll develop these powers only to lose them again on your birthday," Kat blurted out.

Morgan stopped. "What?"

Kat wrapped her arms more tightly across herself. "Your mother said that you would lose your powers on your twenty–first birthday. If that's true and you do, then you're going to be even more upset if you've been working hard to develop these new powers and have gotten used to having them." A tear slowly made its way down her cheek. "I just don't want you hurt, Morgan."

Enveloping his dear, sweet, silly cousin in his arms, he hushed her tears. "It's all right, Kat. It's all right."

"It's not and I don't..." she began, her voice muffled against his chest.

"Yes, it is, because I'm not going to lose my powers."

"But your mother..." she said, pulling away from him.

"My mother said that it I don't develop my full powers by my birthday, *then* I'll lose what powers I have. But I *am* beginning to develop my full powers, and I've got to ensure that they continue to grow."

"But how?"

Morgan gave Kat a sad smile. Immediately she knew what he was thinking and began shaking her head. "No! Oh, no, Morgan."

"Yes, Kat. It is time. It's time I took a page from Adriana's book and did everything, absolutely everything, I can to keep that which is most important to me—my powers and my destiny. Even if it means leaving those I love."

Kat's eyes widened in surprise. "But you cannot leave the forest. You can't break through the curses your mother put up. And what about the suggestions she's put into your mind, are you going to try to break through those as well?"

"I have the power now, Kat. I know I do."

"But..."

"I'm sorry, but I no longer have the time to be careful. I must do this. My birthday is coming in a little more than a month. I must have my full powers before then. Kat. I am running out of time."

He moved away from her, grabbing the bag he used for collecting herbs. Going to his little chest of drawers, he pulled out a change of clothes and stuffed them into the bag.

"Is there nothing I can do to convince you to at least wait a little..."

"No." He placed some dried meat and a loaf of bread in the top of the bag. "Not only do I have to find out where my magical powers are coming from and how I can attain my proper destiny, but I have to find Adriana as well."

"Adriana?"

"She left here without a word to me. I'm going to find out why." He stopped what he was doing and turned back to his cousin. "She's important to me. I cannot just let her go."

Kat nodded slowly, not breaking her eye contact with him. She didn't say anything, but she didn't need to. Morgan could see the sadness in her eyes.

"I love you, Kat, but it is time for me to leave," he said softly, putting his bag over his shoulders so that it lay across his body.

"And the animals? And the forest?" she asked.

He shook his head. "They will have to live without me. Look after Oberon for me, will you?"

"You'll be back. You won't break through the ring of the forest," she said quietly, but without certainty.

"Perhaps I'll see you next in London." He bent and gave her a light kiss on her cheek and then left his cottage.

"Wait! Morgan!" Kat called as she ran out after him. He stopped and turned back. She was tugging at her ears. As she reached him, she put out her hand. He took it, only to find that she was handing him something.

"Here, take these," she said, handing him her gold earrings. She reached around and unclasped her necklace and handed that to him as well. "You'll need money in London. This is all I have."

Her gift touched him—maybe she did believe in him after all. Giving her a hug, he said, "Thank you."

<hr>

Morgan led his horse, Apollo, to the furthest east edge of the forest. It was the direction he would need to take to get to London, so why not start there? It was also the closest to the main road, and furthest from the abbey. He would not ride across the border for fear of harming his horse. No, he would have to walk across and then call for him.

He could just see the road through the thick trees. It beckoned to him, but still his fears crept through his mind. Could he do this? What if he couldn't? He had not been out of the forest—not for six years. And before that he had never been off his brother's estate. Not once in his entire life had he stepped off of Vallentyn property.

Until now.

He boldly stepped toward the edge of the forest, slipping around trees. He continued moving forward until his legs simply refused to go any further. He was only a short distance away from the border—but his feet simply would not move.

His heart began to hammer in his chest.

He would move! He would leave!

Branches blocked his way, surrounding him like bars on a cage. Sweat trickled down his forehead, and prickled at his lower back too.

Life waited for him beyond this forest. The answers to all of his questions. His destiny lay out there, waiting for him. He only needed to go out there and claim it. He only needed to escape.

With great effort, he moved one foot forward a few inches. He stood steadfast, refusing to move back into the forest as his mind kept urging him to do. Taking a deep breath, he slowly moved his other foot forward. It was almost painful making his limbs to move, but he forced himself to stay with it.

Once again, Morgan stopped to catch his breath. He closed his eyes and concentrated. He tried to move his foot. It only moved an inch and that was with a great deal of effort.

Where were those new powers when he needed them?

He had to get out of this forest! He was so close. There was only one last row of trees between him and freedom.

The only way to gain his destiny was to seek it out himself. He had to take control over his own life. His foot moved another few inches.

He was getting closer, but still the edge of the forest might have well been miles away.

He had to be like Adriana. She knew what was important to her. She knew what she wanted more than anything else in this world and would do anything to attain it.

He moved again, but it was getting increasingly harder. He stopped to catch his breath. Never had he moved so slowly in his life and yet he felt as if he were running mile after mile.

He *would* be like her—he moved another inch. He would give up everything to get his powers, to attain his destiny... he stood, breathing heavily. He would do anything to find Adriana and get her back into his life.

His foot moved forward again. He respected Adriana, admired her, and most importantly, she made him happy.

He took another step forward.

She made him happier than he had ever been in his life. She made him feel incredible things he had never experienced before.

He took another step.

He had to find her. He had to be with her again. If he could get to London, he would be able to discover why she had left so suddenly. If he had done anything wrong, anything to have hurt her... he would do whatever was in his power to make it up to her. But he had to see her. Had to talk to her. He couldn't live another day without at least making an effort to be with her.

His legs felt as if they weighed hundreds of pounds each. But he would make it, he told himself again and again. Slowly but surely, he would get out of this forest. Adriana, the woman who had changed his life, would be waiting for him. If only he could get to her.

The moment his foot crossed the tree line onto the verge next to the road, a burst of flames shot from the ground and began to engulf his leg. With a wave of his hand he willed the fire to go out, just as he had done earlier in his cottage. It disappeared, leaving only a blackened singe mark on his boot. He shook his head in amazement as the magic worked so easily once again. How... why? No, that was for later.

He looked behind him at the dense wall of the forest. A shot burst from his lungs. Laughter followed with a happiness he'd never in his life imagined. Only being with Adriana had ever felt this good. He had done it! He had walked out of the forest! He was free!

Apollo joined him a moment later on the road heading east. Heading to London. Heading to Adriana.

Chapter 15

Adriana did not waste a moment lying in bed. This morning she was finally going to get up and get back to work.

Enough was enough. She had moped around Lord Devaux's small London house, allowing the household to run itself with its usual efficiency, for the past three days while she had sat brooding over Morgan.

She had done little else than think about that fateful, wonderful, horrible, embarrassing afternoon with Morgan. How could she... But no. She was not going to go through this yet again. Not today. Today, she was going to get to work, and get that man out of her mind once and for all.

And she was going to be married. The thought still made her seethe with rage. But there had been nothing else she could have done. Lord Vallentyn wasn't going to stand up to his mother, Lord Devaux wasn't going to give up the marriage settlement Lady Vallentyn had promised him.

And she'd had to get away from Morgan.

If she hadn't put a good distance between them, goodness knows what she might have done. She might have gone back, as she had been so very tempted to do. And once there, would she have been able to keep her hands from his hard, muscled body? Would she have not wanted him to touch her and make her feel... No! She must not think such things! There had been no choice. She had had to leave.

And the only way Lord Devaux had agreed to leave quickly was for her to accept Lord Vallentyn's marriage proposal. So she had.

There was no other way, she told herself again, and again. She'd no choice in the matter—the alternative of losing her art was simply unacceptable.

Lord Vallentyn would be kind, if weak, and hopefully wouldn't bother her overmuch with his attentions the way Morgan had. He would certainly never make her feel the way Morgan had. No, she need have no worries about Lord Vallentyn making her feel so incredible, so amazingly...

"Ugh!" Adriana shook her head vigorously, as if doing so would dislodge these unwanted thoughts. Hopping out of bed, she quickly washed and dressed with the assistance of her maid.

There was a lot of work to do in preparation for her wedding. It was time she got started with it.

Her companion, Henrietta, had been wonderfully understanding these past few days. After Adriana had informed her she didn't wanted to talk about her time at Vallentyn, Henrietta had hardly asked her any more questions. Well, yes, she had tried to pry some information from her, but only at odd intervals and only one question at a time. And the moment Adriana had told her to stop, she had done so.

Adriana made her way down to the breakfast parlor noting the sterile good taste of the house. Not a speck of dust littered a surface, not a hint of warmth permeated the walls, no smell dare linger. She had thought, when she was younger, to try to make the house a warmer place, more like the home of her childhood, but Lord Devaux had nipped that in the bud quickly. This was his house and its sole purpose was to further his position in Parliament. That did not lend itself to pretty decorations—not even flower arrangements on the hall table.

As she reached out a hand to open the parlor door, she realized with a start that she hadn't even asked Henrietta once about her time with her family while Adriana had been at Vallentyn. How dreadful! She really should have asked.

Well, that was going to be corrected. In fact, it would be corrected right now.

The sun was making its usual attempt at coming in through the long windows, but, as always, was stopped short by the tree that stood near the back of the house.

Adriana sat down at the table across from Henrietta and gave her companion a big smile. "Good morning, Henrietta. You are looking very pretty today. Is that a new dress?"

Henrietta stopped pouring milk into her tea and narrowed her already small brown eyes at Adriana. "Good morning," she replied warily. She looked down at her plain gray dress, which, unfortunately, accented the gray that was beginning to streak through her brown hair. She then resumed preparing her tea, stealing looks in Adriana's direction every so often.

"No, it is an old dress, although I did add some new lace to it while I was away. Is everything all right this morning?" she asked, suspicion slowing her voice.

"Yes. Perfectly all right. I have decided to stop moping and get to work. If I am going to marry Lord Vallentyn, I imagine I've got quite a lot to do before I can turn over the running of the house entirely to you and Mrs. MacAllister," Adriana said, pouring out her own cup of hot chocolate from the pot the footman had just placed in front of her. She was about to take a sip when she stopped at a thought. "I wonder if Lord Devaux is going to keep Mrs. MacAllister on or require you to do everything?"

Henrietta spread some jam onto her toast, still stealing odd glances at Adriana. "I don't know if Lord Devaux will want me to stay on at all if you are not here. I suppose I shall have to inquire."

"He mentioned to me that he would be counting on you to take my place after I was married. But I hope he doesn't expect you to do everything."

Henrietta carefully cut the toast in half and then asked, "Is there a date set for your wedding, then?"

"No. But I imagine it can't be too far off. Well, a year at most. But we will have to arrange for my trousseau and I don't know what sort of arrangements there will be for the wedding itself. I don't know what Lord Devaux and Lady Vallentyn might have in mind."

Adriana stood up from the table, suddenly feeling awkward sitting still. "I think I will go and see if I can have a word with Lord Devaux right now. Perhaps he can answer some of these questions before he leaves for Parliament today."

As Adriana reached the door, she turned back toward her companion. "Oh, I forgot to ask, how was your visit with your family?"

"It was fine, thank you. My father has passed nearly all of his responsibilities on to my brother—his gout, you know."

Henrietta droned on another few minutes about her family, but Adriana didn't hear a word.

With the mention of responsibility, she remembered how Morgan had made himself responsible for all of the animals in the forest at Vallentyn. He worked so hard to keep them all safe and healthy. She wondered how he was faring with that one foal who still hadn't fully recovered from his bout with the pox.

"...but she seems to be doing remarkably well, considering."

"Good, I am so glad to hear it," Adriana said, cutting into whatever it was Henrietta was saying. "Well, I'd better catch Lord Devaux before he leaves."

She loved Henrietta dearly, but today Adriana just didn't seem to have the patience to listen to even the very little that Henrietta said.

She walked quickly to the library, where her guardian could usually be found when he was home. A knock on the door elicited no response so she questioned the footman at the front door and found that she had indeed missed him, and only by fifteen minutes.

It was all right, she could speak to him later. It certainly couldn't hurt having the maids count the linen and ensure that everything was in good order, even though this had all been done just three months ago during their annual spring cleaning. Mrs. MacAllister took her orders without a word of complaint, and immediately set about turning out all of the linen chests.

As Adriana watched and counted along with the maids, the white sheets reminded her forcefully of the coarse white linen that had covered Morgan's bed. Or perhaps it was the smell. As the sheets were shifted back and forth, that clean smell of sunshine and fresh air filled the room.

The same smell that had filled her senses when she had been laying with him. It was a wonderful fresh smell of the sheets mixed with the sweet musk of his hot, hard body as he had pressed against her. His hands cupping her breasts and playing with... "No!"

"I'm sorry, Miss?" The maid who was sitting on the floor in front of her, stopped counting.

Adriana felt her face heat and knew she must be blushing furiously. "Nothing. Nothing. I'm sorry, I was just thinking of something else."

She turned to Henrietta, who was overseeing another maid's work as she counted out another stack of linens. "Henrietta, could you take over for me here? I... er, I need to attend to something else."

Adriana got up, leaving the room as quickly as possible, ignoring the strange looks she was sure both the maids and Henrietta were giving her. But as soon as she got to her own room, she realized where she needed to go.

She turned and headed to the back stairs that led up to the attic and her painting studio. Here she would find solace. Here she would be able to rid her mind of that man, and the afternoon that would not stop haunting her.

Closing the door behind her, she paused and took a deep breath of the closed, acrid–smelling room. There was no sweet smell of the outdoors here, only turpentine mixed with the smell of her paints, and a musty smell that had accumulated due to the windows not being opened during the weeks she had been away. There was no dappled sunlight struggling to make its way through the trees of the forest—the full sun blared through the window at the far end of the narrow room making the room so bright it was almost blinding.

Yes, this was as far from Morgan as she could possibly get. Her thoughts would be safe from his intrusion here.

After putting on her smock, she took out a fresh canvas and mixed her palette of paints. Each little puddle of color was bright against the plain wooden palette: blue, green, white, black and beige, a touch of yellow and red rounding it out.

Taking her paint brush in hand, she closed her eyes for a moment, clearing her mind of all thoughts. Morgan, Lord Vallentyn, Kat, Lady Vallentyn, and Lord Devaux dissolved away. Her muscles relaxed.

Her mind wandered the broad seas and fields of her imagination. She opened her eyes, dipping her brush into the paint, and allowed her imagination free rein.

Freedom. That was what she longed for more than anything else. Freedom from her guardian. Freedom from having to marry. Freedom from having to play hostess to a bunch of stuffy, foul–smelling old gentlemen. To be free to do as she pleased, paint what and when she liked, not have to worry about running a household that wasn't even hers. Freedom to go where she liked, to travel, to do whatever it was she wanted.

Adriana did not pay any attention to what she painted. All she thought about was the day she would be free. It was a day, she knew in her rational mind, that might never come. But it was a day that lived in her heart, and in her dreams.

She looked down at her palette and noticed she needed some more beige and white. A little more black wouldn't hurt either, she thought, mixing the paints together and putting them onto the board she held in her hand as she painted.

She turned back to her canvas and stopped. Those eyes. Those black, twinkling, merry eyes were staring back at her. Morgan's eyes.

She hadn't even realized what she had been painting, but now, seeing those eyes staring at her she knew—she was painting Morgan.

And not just Morgan as she had seen him so many times in the forest in his white shirt, buckskin breeches and scuffed old boots. No, this was Morgan as she had seen him by the river the day she had discovered him there playing with his dog. This Morgan wasn't wearing his scuffed boots, this Morgan wasn't wearing anything at all.

His back was turned to her, and he was looking at her over his shoulder. Adriana's brush filled in some more details as if it had a mind of its own. The harsh red scars that crossed his muscled back. The dimples just above his buttocks. The curve of his raised eyebrow and the slight smile on his lips as he looked at her with a mixture of happiness and curiosity.

But what caused Adriana's heart to beat faster was that he looked like he was about to turn around. One of his broad shoulders dipped slightly as if he was about to move, about to turn and take a step toward her—to show himself to her in all of his naked glory.

Adriana shifted her weight from one foot to the other. She felt hot and unable to keep still—just as she had when he'd touched her that afternoon. She had squirmed and rubbed herself against him. It had felt so good, and yet it wasn't enough. She had wanted more. She had wanted him to touch her even more intimately as she touched him. So desperate was she in wanting to feel the velvety softness of his skin and the hard pulsing blood underneath that she could feel heat pooling in her most intimate parts.

"Oh my!"

Adriana jumped, pulling her paint brush away from the canvas just in time to save it from smearing a line across Morgan's body.

Henrietta was standing behind her with her hand covering mouth. Her face was bright pink. "Who... who is that? That isn't Lord Vallentyn, is it?"

Adriana couldn't help but laugh, all the tension in her body pouring out as a picture of the slightly paunchy, nearly middle-aged man filled her mind's eye. "No! Lord Vallentyn is much older, and not nearly so fit."

Henrietta advanced slowly into the room and toward Adriana and her painting. "So, who is that?" she asked once again, pointing at the canvas with a slightly shaking finger.

Adriana bit her lip. Would she be able to tell Henrietta about Morgan? The two times she had attempted to speak with Kat about him she'd been unable to do so. She didn't even want to attempt that again.

But, oh, how she wished she could tell her dearest friend all about him!

Instead, Adriana shook her head, gave an embarrassed laugh and moved the painting to the far end of the room to dry near the window.

When she returned, Henrietta was looking very hurt. On impulse, Adriana gave her companion a hug.

"Believe me, Henrietta, if I could tell you, I would," she said quickly. What else could she do?

Henrietta gave her a sad smile, clearly trying hard to be patient.

Adriana sent quick prayer of thanks that Henrietta didn't press her on the issue as a knock sounded on the door interrupting a potentially awkward moment.

"I'm terribly sorry, Miss," Sally, one of the downstairs maids said, as she came into the room at Adriana's bidding. "Lord Devaux gave me this note to give to you this morning and it completely slipped my mind, until now." She gave Adriana a slight curtsey, a very apologetic look, and then the note.

"It's all right, Sally, I understand. We've all been very busy this morning."

The girl gave her a grateful smile, and then left the room.

"Judging by the look on your face, it's not good news," Henrietta said, as Adriana's eyes scanned the note.

"No. He says that Lady Vallentyn wants me to start attending society parties. I am to begin with Lady Collingwood's soiree next Thursday. And he gives me permission to visit the modiste in order to buy one or two appropriate dresses." She frowned at Henrietta. "Lady Vallentyn wishes me to be dressed fashionably."

"Well, it could be worse," Henrietta said, carefully. "And you really could use a few new dresses. I don't believe you've had a new evening gown for over a year."

"I don't need a new evening gown..." Adriana started. She let out a sigh, and sat down heavily on to the sofa. "At least, I don't *want* to need one."

Her companion lowered herself next to her, patting her knee consolingly.

"Lord Devaux has never forced me into society, aside from his own dinner parties. I suppose I've been very lucky that way."

"I believe luck has little to do with it. He wants you available at a moment's notice," Henrietta said honestly. "But it is why you've never met any eligible young men, and now you have to marry this gentleman of Lord Devaux's choosing, instead of one your own."

Adriana heartily wished she could refute Henrietta's words, but she simply could not. She was absolutely right, and it made Adriana sick to her stomach. But there was nothing she could do about it. She really disliked going into society.

"You were fortunate to have been spared this," Adriana said. "All that bowing and curtseying and inane conversation." Turning a pleading look to Henrietta, she asked, "Must I do this?"

Her companion gave her a sad little smile. "I was not given the opportunity to join society because of my family's circumstances. Most girls your age would be devastated not to have such an chance. You are very lucky to be going."

Adriana let out a choked laugh. "I wish I felt that way. And since when have I been like most girls my age?" She stood, pacing to the window and back while Henrietta stayed silent. She had never been like other girls, and there was no denying it.

"I suppose I'll have to go no matter what," Adriana said crossing her arms in front of her chest. "Lord Devaux said I must, so I will. But I will not play the proper miss. I'll... I'll stand in the corner and not speak to anyone."

"Adriana," Henrietta said, as if she were speaking to a recalcitrant child.

Adriana dropped her arms, knowing that she deserved that full well. "But there must be something that I can do in protest. I cannot simply lie down and let Lady Vallentyn determine what I do for the rest of my life. It has been bad enough that I've had to dance to Lord Devaux's tune since I was six years old."

Henrietta stood up and took her hand, giving it a little pat. "My poor dear, you will learn that it is the female's lot in life. There really is nothing you can do about it until you get children of your own whom you can command about in the same way." She paused for a moment as a mischievous smile grew on her lips. "However, I am certain you will think of some way of showing Lord Devaux your dissatisfaction with this latest development."

Chapter 16

Morgan's eyes grew wide, and he just could not contain the smile on his face as the fire sprung to life in front of him. It was amazing! How could this have happened? Why were his powers suddenly working? It was a mystery he hoped to solve, but first he had to get to Adriana.

That thought wiped the grin right off of his face. He had been thinking about it all day as he had traveled toward London, and he still could not figure out why she had left him so suddenly. Nor why she had left Vallentyn without even saying goodbye.

He had gone over that night again and again in his mind—and it had made riding on his horse, Apollo, extremely uncomfortable. How could he not react when he thought about how she had pressed her nearly naked body against his? How she had felt, like a burning, writhing fire of soft velvet underneath his hands. He could still feel her feather–light touch skipping over his skin and it nearly made him want to groan with pleasure all over again.

"Good evening, friend!" a voice called out, interrupting Morgan's more than pleasant thoughts.

Morgan nearly jumped. He hadn't anticipated encountering anyone here in this little clearing off the side of the road. Although he was bone–weary from traveling all day, Morgan stood up as he knew was the polite thing to do.

"Good evening."

Three men approached him, coming out of the woods. They carried nothing with them, nor did they have any mounts—at least, not that Morgan could see. For a moment Morgan worried that he was trespassing on their land, and they were going to send him on his way. The thought just made his limbs feel all the more leaden with exhaustion. He was too tired to go another step, and he was certain Apollo felt the same way.

"Are you a traveler on this road?" the second man asked through a thick black beard.

"Yes," Morgan answered. "But I will be gone by morning. Please, I don't mean to trespass, I just need a place to rest for the night."

The men looked at each other, and then laughed. "Oh, no. We do not own this land," the first said, his voice thick with an accent Morgan couldn't identify.

"We are traveling too," the second put in.

"Oh." That was odd, they didn't have a thing with them. No bags, no blankets, nothing.

"Would you mind if we shared your fire? The night is getting cold."

"No. Not at all. Please, come." Morgan gestured toward the warmth of the fire and seated himself on the far side, closest to the road.

The third man stopped to stroke Apollo's velvet nose as the horse stood underneath a large oak nibbling at the sweet grass. "'Tis a fine horse," the man commented, his deep voice very soft.

"Apollo has been with me for many years. He is a good friend and a fine animal," Morgan said.

"A good friend?" the man laughed.

"Of course! Apollo is my friend. We communicate and look after each other. Is that not what friends do?"

"You converse with your horse?" the second one said mockingly.

Morgan was not used to being in the company of strangers. Perhaps he was saying something wrong that made these men laugh at him. For a moment, he missed his safe little cottage where the only cruelty came from his mother. He knew how to respond to her.

"All right, Marko," the first man interrupted. "If he says he speaks to his horse, who are we to argue? Where do you travel to, friend?"

"To London," Morgan answered turning back to the first man, who had now seated himself to Morgan's left. The three men must be brothers, Morgan thought. They all had the same dark, swarthy features, and the same accent.

"Ah. 'Tis a fine city. Have you friends you will be visiting?"

"I am going to meet a young lady. A friend of mine," Morgan added quickly when the men exchanged knowing looks between them.

"Ah ha. Well, I hope you have brought her some fine gifts," he said, nodding toward Morgan's bag that was sitting next to him on the ground. "You know how the ladies like such things."

No. He didn't know. And, in fact, he hadn't even given it a thought. But now that he did think of it, that didn't sound like a bad idea, especially if she were unhappy with him. Morgan thought for a moment about what he might give her. He had nothing, but a change of clothes and a bit of food.

"I have the earrings my cousin gave me!" he exclaimed out loud as he thought of it.

"Earrings? Are they fine gold. Only the finest will do. And stones of good quality, of course," the man said.

Morgan hadn't even taken a good look at what Kat had given him. He fished them out of his bag now. The man leaned over as Morgan looked at them in the fire light.

"May I see them?" he asked.

Morgan handed the earrings to him. He took one and handed the other to the second man who was on his other side. The red garnet flashed in the fire light as Morgan caught the second man putting the earring to his mouth to test the softness of the gold.

They handed Morgan back the earrings. "Yes, I suppose they might do. They are small, but pretty enough. You'll have to buy her more and perhaps some fine fabrics as well if you are to catch her fancy."

Morgan nearly let his mouth fall open. "But I don't have money to buy such things."

"None at all?" the second man asked.

Morgan shook his head. "All I have is the gold necklace my cousin gave me with her earrings. I'll need to sell that in order to buy food and lodging."

"May I see it?" the man asked.

Morgan fished that out as well, after dropping Kat's earrings back into his bag. The necklace was duly inspected as the earrings had been.

The second man, upon handing it back to the first, gave him a nod. "Yes, that will do," he said.

"I wish you the best of luck," the first man said, handing the necklace back to Morgan.

"You wouldn't happen to have any food in that bag of yours, would you?" the third man asked in his gruff voice.

Morgan nodded and pulled out the dried meat and his water skin. There was barely enough to go around, but each man had enough at least to stave off their hunger for the night.

After they had eaten, the men settled themselves down on the ground to sleep. Morgan stuffed his bag under his head to use as a pillow, and felt bad that he had nothing to offer the other men for any comfort. He was so exhausted, however, that he didn't worry about it for long.

Before he knew it, Morgan was being tugged awake by something slipping out from underneath his head. He couldn't fathom why Oberon might be plaguing him this early in the morning. He rolled over to press his face into his bed, but instead found the cold hard ground.

Apollo's whinny of fright woke him completely. As he moved to sit up his head was snapped back and pain exploded across his cheek. He tried to open his eyes, but all he saw was the blurry outline of one of the men whom he had met the night before, and black spots dancing in front of his eyes. A fist was coming at him a second time, but Morgan moved fast enough to avoid it hitting him in the face.

He kicked to get the man away from him, and landed a good blow in his stomach, but that didn't deter the fellow for more than a moment. Instead of moving away, the man jumped on top of him instead, straddling him and pinning him to the ground.

Apollo gave another cry of alarm, this time further away, as if he were moving deeper into the woods.

The man took a second to look up toward the horse, and Morgan used his inattention to his advantage. He flipped the man over and got the upper hand. That lasted for all of a minute when he was flipped onto his own back again. With all the strength he had, he shot his fist upward into the man's nose.

The man fell off to the side, clutching at his face, blood dripping from between his fingers.

Morgan jumped to Apollo's aid, but was stopped by a fist to his stomach by the second man who must have been standing off to the side. Morgan fell back to the ground, doubled over in pain. The man jumped on Morgan's back and shoved his face down into the ground. The rich smell of the earth filled Morgan's nose as the rough dirt scraped at his face.

"Let the boy go!" a woman's sharp voice called out from behind his head.

Morgan struggled to move hoping that the man would be distracted by this newcomer, but only found his face pressed harder into the solid earth.

"I said, let him go." The woman's voice was closer now.

Morgan tried to turn his head to see who his would–be rescuer was, but the man on top of him pulled his head up by his hair and then smashed it back down onto the ground again. Morgan managed to turn his head just enough to keep his nose from being broken, but the pain to his already sore cheek was excruciating.

"Leave this be, Cosmina!" the man on top of Morgan said in a rough, commanding voice.

"No! I cannot let you harm him." She was right next to Morgan now, but still the man held his face down.

"Return to the camp, now!"

"I will not! Leave him be."

Suddenly Morgan felt the pressure holding him down being released. He lifted his head just enough to see a middle–aged woman in a brilliantly colored dress of blue and yellow grabbing the man's arm and pulling it back.

The man jumped off Morgan and smashed his hand against the woman's face sending her flying to the ground. "How dare you touch me, woman! It is unforgivable!"

Fury filled Morgan in a rush and the man who had dared to lay his hand against the woman was suddenly lifted off the ground thrown against the oak tree on the other side of the clearing. Morgan rushed to the woman's side, gingerly running his hands down her face.

She looked up at him with a touch a fear in her eyes. "It's all right." Morgan said, gently. "He won't touch you again."

She struggled to sit up, but nearly collapsed again in pain, cradling her left arm to her body. Morgan touched her arm. It must have broken when she tried to stop her fall.

He would have fixed it immediately, but Apollo's whinny reminded him that this fight wasn't over yet.

He turned to see his horse rear up on his hind legs, forcing the man who was holding him to let go.

"Good Apollo!" Morgan called in encouragement.

The man took one look at Morgan and then at his fallen comrades, and bolted for the forest The man with the broken nose hobbled off in his wake.

Morgan turned back to the woman sitting beside him. Very carefully he took her arm in his hands. Summoning his magic, he mended the bone quickly and easily.

Her mouth was hanging open and her dusky complexioned face was already beginning to show signs of a large black and blue mark along her high cheekbone. Ignoring these, he asked, "Are you well enough to stand?"

She closed her mouth and nodded.

Gently, he helped her to her feet. "You know those men. Do you need to follow them? Do you stay with them?"

The woman shook her head. Then, in a quiet, unsteady voice she said softly, "I cannot go back with them, they would, would..."

"You need not go with them. You may come with me instead. I go to London."

Her dark eyes filled with fear as she looked back toward the woods where the men had disappeared. Turning back once again to Morgan, she nodded, "If you would be so kind as to take me with you. I... I can never return to my clan."

Morgan did not understand exactly what she meant by her clan, but he understood she would accompany him. Retrieving his bag that the men had left lying on the ground, he helped the woman up onto Apollo's back. She settled herself on the horse, pulling her long black hair behind her and fixing her headscarf back into its proper position on her head. When she was ready, Morgan led Apollo back on to the road before mounting behind the woman.

Without a backward glance, they set off for London.

After they had traveled a safe distance from the wood, Morgan finally ventured to ask the questions burning through his mind, "Where do you come from? How did you know those men?"

The woman kept her head turned toward the road ahead. But answered him softly. "We... I am a gypsy. Those men are members of my clan. We travel together, going from town to town, selling our wares and services. Those men you met earn extra money by stealing from unwary travelers such as yourself."

Morgan nodded, now understanding what a fool he had been. They had managed to trick him into showing them all of his wealth and then, when he was unaware, had nearly got away with stealing everything, including his beloved horse.

The woman turned around to look at Morgan for a moment. "Please, do not blame me. I have told them they should not do such things, but they will not listen to a woman."

Deliberately softening his features, Morgan realized he must have been looking stern. He patted the woman on the back awkwardly. "It is all right. I don't blame you. In fact, if it were not for you, I would be in a very sorry state right now." He paused, and took a deep breath, fully realizing just how much he owed this kind woman. "Thank you. You saved my life."

The woman shook her head. "No. I merely did what I felt was right."

"Why *did* you do it?" Morgan could not help but ask. He would have hoped that anyone would do the same thing, but from what Kat had told him of the outside world, he knew that was not always true.

The woman turned to look back at Morgan once again, a small smile playing on her lips. "You remind me of my son. He would have been about your age if he had not died three winters ago."

"I am sorry," Morgan said quietly.

The woman turned back toward the road, and gave a little shrug. "He was a good boy, although he too let his hair grow too long."

Morgan laughed. Kat had often complained he didn't cut his hair often enough, but he liked it long.

"He was strong and kind," the woman went on quietly. "And he would never have used his strength against another unless forced to do so."

Morgan nodded, understanding.

They rode on in silence for some time and then the woman turned back and asked, "How, how did you... you sent Petsha flying from me without laying a hand on him. And my arm..." her voice faded off in confusion as she absentmindedly rubbed her arm where it had broken.

Morgan thought about this for a few moments. How much could he tell this woman? Once again he had done magic in front of a stranger—though this time, his mother wasn't here to punish him.

He wondered if the woman would run screaming in fright from him if he told her he was Vallen. He wondered if she would know what that meant. He knew that ordinary people sometimes got them confused with witches and because of that, his people had been persecuted and wrongfully executed for centuries.

Would this woman tell others that he had magic? Would she have him killed as so many others had been? How could he know if he could trust her?

"There are stories told by our elders that tell of those with magnificent strength, but you did not even touch him."

"I... I can move things with my mind," Morgan said hesitantly.

The woman nodded. "And you can heal with your hands."

"Yes," Morgan nodded, "And with potions which I make."

"We have potions too. We sell them to the townspeople who do not have the knowledge to make them themselves. But I have never met someone who could heal the way you do."

Morgan shifted a little on Apollo's back. "It is my greatest strength. And until recently, my only strength."

"Have you only recently learned to move things? Is it something you can teach me?"

Laughing, Morgan said, "No. It is nothing I have learned. It is a power that is developing inside of me. But I do not know how or why. That is one reason why I am going to London. I hope to learn more there."

The woman turned around and looked at him for a moment and then asked, "One reason? What is the other?"

Morgan saw her raised eyebrows and couldn't hide his own smile. "There is a young lady..."

"Ah ha. I knew it. There is always a young lady," she said, turning back around to face the road.

Morgan laughed. "She is a friend, but I think I may have hurt her feelings the last time I saw her, so I'm eager to see her and apologize if necessary."

The woman nodded her head. "That is very wise. I shall help you to find her," she stated matter–of–factly, but with a smile that said so much more.

Morgan couldn't help but smile too. He didn't see how this gypsy woman could help him in his search for Adriana, but she certainly seemed determined to do so.

He gave Apollo a little nudge to move faster. The sooner they got to London, the sooner he could find Adriana, and the sooner he could be happy again.

He did have to admit the woman before him was very pleasant company—in her kindly fashion. Without Oberon or Kat with him, he had feared he would become very lonely. But now he had...

"I do not know your name," he said suddenly.

The woman turned back to face him. "Cosmina. My name is Cosmina Nomid. And yours?"

"Morgan Vallentyn."

"I am pleased to meet you, Morgan Vallentyn."

"And I you. Have you ever been to London, Cosmina?" he asked.

"No. Have you?"

"No. This will be an adventure for both of us," he said, passing by a cart laden with fresh vegetables. All of a sudden the road had become much more crowded with traffic, and Morgan had a strong suspicion it would only become more so as they neared the city.

People seemed to close in on them from all directions as they moved further into the teeming streets of London.

Morgan had never seen so many people before—not even when all of the tenants and their families came for the annual harvest festival at Vallentyn.

"Have no fear, Morgan Vallentyn, we will find your young lady, even among these crowded streets," Cosmina's voice was soft but sure.

Chapter 17

Kat didn't even raise her eyes as she entered the sitting room.

"You called for me, Aunt Vallentyn?" the girl asked, her eyes staying annoyingly, discreetly lowered.

"Yes, my dear. Do come and sit here on the sofa, next to me," Tatiana said in her sweetest voice. Could the girl know why she had been called? But how could she?

Tatiana patted the white brocade sofa next to where she sat, and tried her hardest to contain the growing annoyance within her. Not only did Kat's reticence indicate that Tatiana's fears might be very well founded, but it also negated all that she had ever taught that girl.

After Kat had sat down at the far end of the sofa, Tatiana reached over and lifted the girl's chin with the tip of her finger. "I thought I had taught you better than that, Katrina. You do not lower your eyes for anyone. You are a powerful Vallen. Be proud of what you are, and who you are. You are better than all the rest—better than any other Vallen and certainly better than any ordinary person." The last words she spat out as if it were some sort of disgusting disease.

And that's what they were, were they not? Those filthy, weak little creatures. Their lives, their world, their society was built entirely through the work of the Vallen, and those pitiful ordinary people didn't even know it.

If Tatiana had her way, she wouldn't hide away her identity like some scared thief. She would announce it to the world. She was Vallen and she was proud of it. She was better, stronger, more powerful than any ordinary person could possibly be. Never had she lowered her eyes to anyone, nor would she ever.

Kat was her heir. And, although not nearly as powerful, she was certainly more powerful than any other Vallen Tatiana had ever met. She should hold her head up high and stare anyone in the eye who dared to look into hers.

Tatiana said as much, but still the girl stared at her hands clasped tightly in her lap. Her fingers were nearly as white as the sofa on which they sat.

Which led Tatiana to be certain that the girl had information. Information that she, Tatiana, wanted. How ridiculous Kat was being, thinking that she could avoid divulging everything she knew just because she kept her eyes down.

She would give up what she knew. No one ever said no to Tatiana.

"Would you care for some tea?" Tatiana indicated the tea service that sat on the white marble–topped table in front of them. Every time she looked at that table, she couldn't help but look up at Merlin's cup as it sat in its protective nook above the black marble fireplace. It was beautiful. It was power.

It was that power that Tatiana planned to give Katrina— the power of the Merlin's cup. But looking at the girl now, with her eyes downcast and a slight tremble to her hands Tatiana seriously wondered if she would be able to handle it.

"No, thank you."

"Are you sure? Cook has made her lovely cream cakes. I know they are your favorite," Tatiana said, trying to entice the girl into something other than just sitting there with her eyes down.

Kat just shook her head.

Tatiana didn't even try to hide her scowl. Very cautious, this one. Clearly, Tatiana had trained her too well. Whatever secret she had, she was going to guard well.

This was good news and bad. Certainly, Katrina could be counted on to keep Tatiana's own secrets, and that was good. But it also meant that more force than normal would be necessary in prying out this secret. She would have it, naturally. She would simply have to move a little more carefully, that was all.

"Very well," Tatiana said, stirring her tea. "Tell me, how are your potions coming along? Have you managed to make the tincture of belladonna and hawthorn in the correct strength?"

Kat relaxed a little bit. "Yes, ma'am. When I fed it to the dog…"

"Oberon, Morgan's dog?"

"Yes, ma'am. I did as you told me. When I fed it to Oberon, he became rather lethargic and his heart slowed considerably."

"Excellent. In an even stronger dose…" The girl flinched. "Well, I'm sure you can guess what might happen," Tatiana concluded quickly. She knew that Kat had an inordinate fondness for animals and she didn't want her to become upset. Tatiana needed her relaxed and comfortable in order to extract the information she wanted.

"Next, I would like you to try a combination of linden and calendula. Do you know what sort of result you might attain?"

Kat thought about it for a moment. "Linden will calm the mind and calendula the stomach."

Tatiana nodded. "Very good. They work very well together for stomach ailments, along with licorice and chamomile. And in stronger doses, along with a touch of opium, they allow magical energy to flow more easily."

Kat looked at her quizzically, finally making eye contact. "Could it help in strengthening your magical abilities?"

Tatiana widened her eyes, catching and holding on to Kat's gaze while she had it. "No, nothing but innate ability and practice will strengthen magical powers. You know that you must use your magic to keep it strong, like a muscle. The more you use it, the easier it is to use. But if you don't have the muscle or the predilection for strong muscles, there is nothing you can do—you will always be weak and powerless. This is the reason you are my heir and not any of my own daughters. Being the sixth child of the sixth child of the descendents of the great Morgan le Fey, you have that predilection. If any Vallen could increase their magical powers through the use of a potion, why, everyone would want to do so, wouldn't they?"

Tatiana felt the girl try to pull away, but she strengthened her hold.

She reached out for Kat's hands. As they touched, she said in her most soothing, powerful voice, "You have knowledge I want, Katrina. You will answer all the questions I ask with honesty and without hesitation."

"No!" Kat began to struggle more earnestly, fighting both Tatiana's eyes and her hands.

Tatiana could hardly believe the girl's nerve, but she did admire it. Her strength was impressive as well, Tatiana admitted with a touch of pride, but no one could resist her when she had both eye and hand contact. And neither would Kat.

"You will do as I say!" Tatiana's voice grew deeper and stronger as she filled it with magical energy, willing it to infiltrate the girl's mind. "Just relax, Kat, you know you cannot fight me."

Like tentacles, her magical energy wound its way into the girl's mind and grasped a hold of her conscious will. She *would* do as Tatiana asked.

The girl still struggled, trying to break free of Tatiana's hold, but it was useless. Soon she would know it too.

"It is all right," Tatiana said, looking deeply into the girl's frightened eyes. "Just relax, there is nothing to fear." She filled her voice with a calming fog and blew it over Kat's mind.

"Relax, Kat. You see only a pleasant haze as the world slowly slips away." Tatiana made sure her voice was soft and soothing. She infused calm and good feelings into it to relax the girl.

Kat's eyes began to glaze over, and she slowly stopped struggling.

"Very good, Kat, very good. Clear your mind. It is all just a lovely cloud."

Kat's body relaxed against the back of the sofa as she fell completely under Tatiana's spell.

"Now, tell me where Morgan is," Tatiana demanded gently.

Kat gave one last weak effort to break free of Tatiana's hold on her mind.

"That is enough, Katrina," she said gently. "You *will* answer my questions. Just relax. You know you cannot fight me." Tatiana filled her voice with even more energy. "Shh, be at ease and open your mind to me. Where is Morgan?" she asked again.

Kat released her breath and gave in to the fog that Tatiana had over her mind. "He is gone."

"Gone where? To the other side of the forest?"

"No. He has left Vallentyn."

"But he cannot leave. It is impossible!" Tatiana could feel her anger rising.

This is what she had heard from that fool nurse, Maryellen, but she had not believed it. It simply was not possible, not with the ideas she had placed in Morgan's mind or the curses she had in place all around the perimeter of the forest, just in case. One step out and Morgan would be engulfed in flame. She had long ago commanded this.

"He has grown stronger. He has powers now he did not have before," Kat said, her voice beginning to maintain the monotone of one whose mind was deeply enshrouded in a magical fog.

"What powers?"

"He can move things and put out a fire. I do not know what else, but that is what I saw him do."

Tatiana knit her brows. She did not like the sound of this.

"How did he get these powers? When?"

Kat gave a little shrug. "I don't know how. We discovered them the last time I went to the forest to visit him."

That meant that two days had passed since he had left. Tatiana had always been aware of who visited Morgan and when, but Kat had not been giving her regular reports recently, and Tatiana had been too busy to notice.

"Where has he gone, Kat?" Tatiana asked, trying hard to keep her voice soft and calm.

"To London," the girl replied listlessly.

Tatiana saw red. London! He had escaped and gone to London. She could barely hold on to her temper, but she knew that if she lost it, she would lose her control over the girl. She pulled back and tried to calm herself. She would need to go and fetch him back before he became too strong for her to control.

Ha! As if he ever could!

But in the back of her mind was a nagging worry. Perhaps he was getting stronger, gaining powers... but no, that was impossible. He was male and he had never shown any promise whatsoever toward becoming a powerful Vallen. He could not.

But still it would be best if he were brought back here. She would reinforce her curses. Set the trees to hold him fast if he ever tried to escape again. Yes, that would keep him.

But first she had to go to London and find him.

Kat blinked. Tatiana was beginning to lose her hold on the girl.

"You shall remember nothing of this. Now, wake up," Tatiana said, releasing the girl's hands and turning abruptly back to her tea.

The girl sagged next to her for a moment, blinking and rubbing her forehead and eyes.

"Are you sure you wouldn't like a little tea?" Tatiana said as sweetly as she could, behaving as if nothing had happened.

"Er, no. No, thank you, ma'am. I... I think I just need a little fresh air to clear my head. I have a slight headache. If you would excuse me?"

"Yes, of course, my dear, of course."

Tatiana refilled her own cup and took a sip.

She would go to London and fetch Morgan back. He could not be allowed to roam free. She would not allow this child, the bane of her existence, to attain the destiny she had set out for Kat. She had worked too hard for Morgan to suddenly rise up and destroy everything.

No, she would find and punish him in such a way that he would never dare disobey her again. Never would he even try to escape from Vallentyn again, for if he did...

She put down her tea with such force that the delicate cup shattered and the saucer cracked in two. She watched dispassionately as the brown liquid pooled on the table and then slowly dripped onto the floor.

No means would be too strong to ensure he stayed at Vallentyn, forever.

Morgan looked around, appreciating the relative quiet of the street. In just the few hours he and Cosmina had been in the city, he already felt as if his ears would never stop ringing from the constant noise. Everywhere there were people rushing to and fro, hawkers crying out, carriages and horses moving in a constant stream of traffic up and down every street. His head was spinning.

Finally, as he and Cosmina settled themselves into the quiet of Mrs. Lunden's parlor, he could think again.

"It is good of you to meet us right away, Mrs. Lunden," Cosmina said, smiling brightly at the older lady.

The lady nodded, but did not return the smile. "You are looking for rooms?"

"Yes," Cosmina answered, keeping the smile on her face despite the lady's cool reception.

She seemed to be handling this expertly, Morgan thought, as he allowed his mind to wander away from the conversation.

The room was pleasant in a shabby, genteel manner. The carpet on the floor looked as good as those at Vallentyn Abbey, but was threadbare in places. The same was the case with the chairs and sofas that decorated the cozy, little room.

He wondered what Adriana's home was like. Did she live in a pleasant little house like this one, or in one of the grander homes he and Cosmina had passed on their way here? He suspected the latter, based on what Adriana had told him about her guardian.

"I am so sorry, Mrs. Lunden, I didn't realize you had guests," a male voice interrupted Morgan's thoughts.

A very tall, thin man with a hawk–like nose stood in the doorway. He was dressed all in black and, by his stiff bearing, looked rather like the butler at Vallentyn.

"It is all right, Mr. Nestor, you may come in. Mrs. Nomid and Mr. Vallentyn are here enquiring about rooms," Mrs. Lunden said. She then turned back to Cosmina and said, "Mr. Nestor is also a boarder here."

Mr. Nestor's eyes had snapped to Morgan the moment Mrs. Lunden had said his name. Even as he entered the room and closed the door behind him, he still did not look away. Morgan shifted uncomfortably under the man's scrutiny, and then chastised himself for a show of weakness. He must still be jittery from his encounter with the gypsy men.

"Mr. Vallentyn? You wouldn't happen to be related to Lady Vallentyn of Berkshire?" he asked.

Morgan stood up, immediately wary of the man. On the other hand...

"I am Robert Nestor. You've never heard of me, I'm sure, but it is an honor to meet you, Mr. Vallentyn." He approached Morgan with his hand held out.

Tentatively, Morgan grasped the man's hand. He was right, Morgan had never heard of him, but he didn't like that this stranger knew who he was.

"You are...?" Mrs. Lunden asked, hesitating.

Mr. Nestor jumped in, finally taking his eyes off of Morgan. "Lady Vallentyn is a very important member of society, Mrs. Lunden."

"Oh! Why didn't you tell me that to begin with, sir?"

"I didn't know that it was significant," Morgan said, realizing, as he did so, that he was acknowledging his relationship with his mother. He also didn't mention his mother's position in society because, until Mr. Nestor had said so, he hadn't known of it himself.

"Why, yes, of course it is significant," the woman laughed, now suddenly all smiles and warmth.

"Then perhaps you could see to lowering the rent we were discussing?" Cosmina asked hopefully.

"Oh, well," Mrs. Lunden hesitated for a moment, "yes. Yes, of course. There is a Lord Vallentyn, I assume? And your family's estate is in Berkshire?" she asked, turning back to Morgan.

"Yes, ma'am. My brother is Lord Vallentyn. He manages the estate—Vallentyn Abbey and the farms surrounding it."

"There are other properties?" she asked hopefully.

Morgan nodded, not entirely certain why she was so interested.

"Oh, well, that is all right. Yes, that's just fine," she said, fanning her hand in front of her face. "For the brother of a..." she paused, and looked expectantly at Morgan.

"A viscount," Mr. Nestor supplied helpfully.

"Yes," Mrs. Lunden nodded and smiled again. "For the brother of a viscount, I suppose we could lower the rent, to begin with. Just until you find your feet, Mr. Vallentyn, or perhaps apply to your brother for more funds?"

Morgan opened his mouth to say he would never ask his brother for money, when Cosmina laughed gaily and said, "Oh, yes, of course. It will be no problem, no problem at all, Mrs. Lunden."

The lady stood up. "Very good, then. I will just see to your rooms. Perhaps Mr. Nestor could tell you the house rules while I do so?"

Mr. Nestor gave her a little bow. "My pleasure." He then held the door open for her, and closed it firmly behind her.

"What do you know of my family, sir?" Morgan asked, turning to face Mr. Nestor.

He supposed that his expression had become one of suspicion, because Mr. Nestor took a step back and began to wring his hands nervously. "Nothing! Nothing. Well, reputation, you know. Only what is generally known in the er... well among those..."

"Among whom?" Morgan asked sharply, taking a step toward the slender man.

"Well," Mr. Nestor began and then looked meaningfully at Cosmina.

"You may speak freely in front of Cosmina," Morgan said, following his eyes.

Mr. Nestor released his breath.

"Among whom?" Morgan asked again, when he didn't begin speaking immediately.

"Well, among the gifted, shall we say?" Mr. Nestor said quietly, still glancing toward Cosmina.

"There are others who can heal as Morgan can?" Cosmina asked, quite surprised.

Morgan gave Cosmina a hard look. "Cosmina!" He had trusted her not to disclose his abilities to anyone, but he had not expressly forbidden her to do so. That might have been a serious mistake.

"It is all right, Mr. Vallentyn. I know," Mr. Nestor said quietly, bringing a nervous smile to his lips.

If the smile was supposed to be reassuring, Morgan thought to himself, it turned out to be just the opposite. "What do you know?" Morgan asked.

"I know you are Vallen," Mr. Nestor said very quietly. "And judging by your parents, I would say you are a very powerful one. It does not surprise me to learn that you can heal people."

"I don't know what you are talking about," Morgan said, trying to look as innocent as he could.

Mr. Nestor gave him a sly look, a sort of half smile that plainly said, *you don't have to play the innocent, you and I both know what I'm talking about.*

"There is no need to hide it from me, Mr. Vallentyn," he said. "I am Vallen too," he added in a whisper that, although very quiet, could be heard quite clearly.

Morgan turned away from Mr. Nestor and Cosmina. It was not possible. There were no other Vallen besides his family—were there? No! If there had been, then why would he have been told expressly never to reveal his powers to anyone? And why would Kat have never told him?

Morgan laughed out loud as he turned around again. "I do not know what sort of game you are playing, Mr. Nestor..."

"I am playing no game, sir," he said in a normal tone of voice. Indeed, the man looked very serious, if a bit twitchy.

A chill ran up Morgan's arms. "Did my mother send you here? How did she find out so quickly?" Morgan moved to the window and looked out onto the small street on which the house was situated.

There was no one there. The street was reassuringly empty, the sky above clouded over, pale white. Morgan wondered if his face was the same color.

"I... I do not know your mother personally." Mr. Nestor's voice shook. "I don't know what she knows or does not know."

"Do not lie to me, sir!" Morgan said, swinging around and advancing on the man. He was beginning to lose his patience, and could feel his anger coiling up within him.

"I assure you, Mr. Vallentyn..." Mr. Nestor quickly took two steps back away from him.

"Morgan, how could he have been sent by your mother? He says he doesn't know her," Cosmina said, as if she were cajoling a child into behaving properly.

Morgan looked over at her. She, too, was looking a little frightened, but her eyes were pleading with him to calm down. He took a deep breath, and moved back toward the window.

He heard Mr. Nestor heave a sigh of relief. "I assure you, Mr. Vallentyn, all I know of your mother is what I have heard from other Vallen. That she is extremely powerful and the High Priestess of the Coven of England. That is all."

"Coven? You are witches, then?" Cosmina asked, looking from one man to the other.

"No—" Morgan started to say.

"Not at all, ma'am!" Nestor said in disgusted tones. "Witches and warlocks are frauds, fakes. They have been attempting to copy us and our ways for centuries, and have only managed to get many true Vallen killed. We *help* mankind. We bring science, art and music to this world. We lead, entertain and invent. That is why we are here, that is what we do," he ended with a flourish of his voice.

"And witches?" Cosmina prompted.

Mr. Nestor sneered. "Witches pretend to have power— they have none. They scare people, cavort with the devil, and give the Vallen a bad name."

Cosmina looked impressed. Even Morgan hadn't known all that Mr. Nestor had just said. In fact, Morgan was beginning to understand just how much he didn't know.

"I didn't realize there were others," Morgan admitted. "My mother is the high priestess, you said?"

"You did not know?" Mr. Nestor asked, turning and looking completely dumbfounded at Morgan.

"No. But then, I have never been taught anything about... about this."

"Your mother has never taken you to a coven meeting?"

"No."

Mr. Nestor shook his head sadly. "Even I was brought to coven meetings even though I'm a very weak Vallen." He paused for a moment. "You can heal?" he asked.

Morgan nodded hesitantly.

"And move things with his mind," Cosmina added helpfully.

Morgan scowled at her. He was really going to have to speak with her about confidences.

Mr. Nestor waved off that comment, "Even the weakest of us can do that."

"Oh, but Morgan only just learned, and he threw a man four feet or more without even touching him."

That peaked Mr. Nestor's interest. "How is that?"

Morgan shrugged as nonchalantly as he could. "I just imagined him flying through the air away from me..."

"No, no," Mr. Nestor interrupted. "What does she mean, you just learned?"

"Oh," Morgan shrugged again. "My powers are only beginning to show themselves. I suppose I'm just a little slow in my development for some reason." He tried to mask his embarrassment, but there was nothing he could do about the pink stain he noticed in his cheeks when he caught his reflection in the mirror above the fire place.

Mr. Nestor shook his head. "I do not understand. Powers do not develop, we have what we have from birth."

"Yes, but for some reason I have not had my full powers until now. It is one reason why I'm here in London, to see what I can learn about this, and how I can speed up the process of attaining all the powers that I should have—if that's possible."

Mr. Nestor seemed to be at a loss. He had clearly never heard of such a thing—but then he, himself said, that he wasn't a very powerful Vallen. Maybe this was something only the powerful knew about.

Morgan tried his best to stay positive, to keep his hopes up.

Chapter 18

I wish I could help you," Mr. Nestor said, spreading his hands open.

"Do you know of any other Vallen who might be able to help?" Cosmina asked, taking the words right from Morgan's mouth.

The man shook his head sadly. "You would need to consult with someone very powerful..." he paused and thought for a moment. "The only person who might know would be... your mother."

"No!" It nearly came out as a shout. With the word, Morgan's locked onto Mr. Nestor's. "You will not inform my mother or anyone that I am here. No one is to know you have even met me. Do you understand?" The heat of anger mixed with his magical energy to flow like lava through his body.

Mr. Nestor's blinked once and then shook his head. "No, I will never say a word to anyone." He then shook his head and blinked again, this time looking down at the thread-bare carpet.

His eyes then flipped up to meet Morgan's once again. "My God, you... I heard it. I heard your voice in my head. It was as if I was thinking what you said."

"You did? I put a suggestion into your mind?" Morgan was thrilled, but his heart was still pounding at the thought that this man might still be able to tell his mother where he was.

"Yes," Mr. Nestor said, and then gave an awed smile. "I've never met anyone who could do that."

"But it is working?" Morgan asked. He didn't know strong his suggestion might be—strong enough, he hoped. He could not afford for his mother to find out he was here.

"Oh yes, I can most definitely feel it there."

"Good." Morgan relaxed. "I've only done it once before."

"Well, you seem to have done a good job of it."

"You don't know any other powerful Vallen?" Cosmina asked, clearly not grasping the importance of what Morgan had just done. In fact, he was a little awed by it himself. Putting suggestions into someone's mind strong enough that they heard it as their own thoughts was pretty powerful magic.

A tinge of excitement thrummed through him.

He could do powerful magic. He could do it at will. Was he actually getting his true powers? Did he have them already? How did this happen? Well, he was almost too scared to ask that. He was just so grateful that it was—and just in time too. He had to have his full powers within the month!

Something Mr. Nestor was saying caught his attention. "There are different covens for Vallen of differing abilities?" Morgan asked.

Mr. Nestor turned to him. "Well, not different covens, exactly. More like different meetings of the same coven. And it is just in London, and I suppose other big cities that they do this—where the Vallen population is large. It would simply be too unwieldy to have that many Vallen at one meeting. And it would certainly attract a great deal of attention. It's tricky enough as it is with the number of people at each meeting."

"How many are there at your meeting?" Cosmina asked.

"About twenty–five," he answered. "That is at the West–end coven. There would be more, I suppose, but it's really only the most involved Vallen who even go to the meetings."

There was a silent moment as Morgan digested this. Over twenty–five Vallen in just this part of London, and they were the weaker ones. "How many Vallen do you suppose there are?"

"In this area or all of London?"

"All of London?" Morgan asked.

"Oh, at least a thousand, probably many, many more. I honestly don't know."

The number was staggering. This was an entire people that Morgan had never known about. And to think, he thought that his family were the only ones in the world! He nearly laughed at his own naiveté.

"What about this girl, Morgan? The one you were coming here to meet?" Cosmina asked.

That jolted Morgan right out of his reverie. He had completely forgotten about Adriana. "She's not Vallen," Morgan answered quickly.

"But you still need to find her as well."

"Who is she?" Mr. Nestor asked.

"A young lady of my acquaintance, Miss Adriana Hayden. Her guardian is Lord Devaux," Morgan answered with no hope whatsoever that Mr. Nestor would have heard of him. Considering the number of people there seemed to be in London, it would be unusual if he had.

But Mr. Nestor was looking very thoughtful. "Devaux. Isn't he a prominent member of Parliament?"

Morgan perked up. "Yes, he is. Do you know him or know of him?"

"I heard... where was it?" Mr. Nestor snapped his fingers. "Oh, yes, I remember, it was my friend Charlie. He's valet to Lord Bantham. He was mentioning to me the other day that there was a Lord Devaux going about trying to wangle invitations from society's top hostesses. I believe he was quite successful, considering his position."

"Oh."

"This young lady is his ward?"

"Yes."

"And you need to find her."

Morgan nodded.

"Well, in that case, you probably would want to... well, but how would you get an invitation?"

Morgan and Cosmina both looked at him, waiting for him to clarify.

"The best way for you to meet this girl would be at a ball or soiree. But I don't know how you could get an invitation. Do you think your brother, Lord Vallentyn, might help you?"

"No. I told you, my mother cannot find out I am here. And I don't believe my brother is in town."

"Ah, right. Well, then..."

"What if he didn't go as a guest, but was hired to work at the party?" Cosmina asked.

Mr. Nestor shook his head. "It would take quite a lot of time, not to mention experience, for Mr. Vallentyn to learn how to be a footman and obtain a position in one of the better households."

"I wasn't thinking about a footman, but rather a fortune–teller," she smiled at the two men.

Morgan burst out laughing. "Cosmina, that is wonderful. But I don't know how to tell fortunes. Foretelling the future is not one of my powers."

Cosmina shook her head. "You do not need any special powers for this. I assure you my cousin did not. You just make up something that sounds plausible. And with your ability to put ideas into someone's head, you could do that and they would believe what you told them, no matter what you told them."

"But that is unethical," Mr. Nestor protested.

"It is a brilliant idea!" Morgan said, rubbing his hands together and moving to sit down again on the sofa next to Cosmina, ready for his first lesson in fortune telling.

Chapter 19

"Well, I have done my duty. I have attended the soiree. I have sat here for nearly forty–five minutes, bored beyond belief. Do you think we can go home soon?" Adriana asked, looking around at all of the beautiful people who stood about or danced their way through Lady Collingwood's overcrowded ball room. At least, at this moment, there was a parting of people and she could see around the ball room. More often than not, her view was obstructed by people standing directly in front of her.

"You have not been bored the entire time. You did dance twice," Henrietta pointed out.

"Yes, and my toes are still aching from that last one," Adriana scowled as she wriggled her sore toes inside of her slippers. She didn't know why some form of more sturdy shoe wasn't worn to these dances, that way it wouldn't hurt so much when your dancing partner stepped on your toes.

Henrietta smiled consolingly. "No, I'm sorry, but it is not yet time to go." She indicated with her head the gentleman who was bearing down on them rather purposefully.

Adriana sighed a little too loudly as Lord Vallentyn approached them.

"Ah, here you are, Miss Hayden. I've been looking all over for you."

"Good evening, Lord Vallentyn," Adriana said, standing up.

Despite the splendor of his evening clothes, Lord Vallentyn was looking older. Somehow, he also seemed to give the impression of being even more meek than the last time she had seen him. No, Adriana realized, he was simply not meeting her eyes with his own. How odd.

"May I introduce you to my companion, Miss Henrietta Britworth?" Adriana said, looking directly at him and trying to catch his gaze.

Lord Vallentyn briefly nodded his head in Henrietta's direction before turning back to Adriana. He turned his lips up into a smile, while his eyes darted around the room.

"Were you forced to attend this dreadful party too?" she asked, as he opened his mouth to speak.

"Er, uh, you are looking very pretty tonight," he said, deliberately ignoring her comment.

Adriana nearly groaned. "Please, my lord, there is no need for that."

"No need for what, Miss Hayden?" Lord Vallentyn asked looking very confused, and very nearly meeting her eyes. His gaze hovered somewhere in the vicinity of her nose. It was very disconcerting.

"No need to make inane small talk and ridiculous compliments."

"I did not believe my compliment to be ridiculous. You *do* look very pretty." He was now beginning to look a little hurt. Adriana just wanted to shake him.

She refrained, however, and instead decided to make things easy for him. She gave him a little smile and said, "I thought we were good enough friends not to have to exchange empty compliments, that's all."

"Oh." He thought about this for a moment. "I didn't realize that telling a girl she looked nice was an empty compliment. My sisters always seem to enjoy being told they look nice, particularly when they have a new bonnet or dress or some such thing."

Adriana couldn't help but smile. Kat had told her that her cousins were rather empty–headed. "But I am not at all like your sisters, am I?"

Lord Vallentyn frowned at this. "No. No, you are not." A smile then lit up his face. "That must be why I like you so very much."

Adriana felt the heat rise in her cheeks,but could think of nothing to say to this.

Lord Vallentyn too seemed a little embarrassed by his admission, and quickly covered it up by asking if she'd like to accompany him to the refreshments.

"Thank you, I could use something to drink," she answered, tucking her arm into the crook of his elbow, which he had held out to her.

"I do hope you've been enjoying yourself this evening. Mother especially wants you to be an active member of society. She thinks that will help with my career," Lord Vallentyn said, leading her to a table laden with a punch bowl and glasses.

"You are still set on following your mother's wishes, and taking your seat in Parliament?" she asked, accepting the glass of lemonade he'd poured for her.

"Oh, yes, naturally. My mother truly has my best interests at heart in this. I'm certain she's correct and I should try my best to become active in politics."

Adriana sighed, and nodded her head. There was nothing she could do. "Well, I suppose I'm not one to argue with you, since I have also agreed to go along with this scheme, albeit reluctantly."

"I am happy you've decided to marry me. I think we're going to rub along together very well."

Adriana gave him a little smile, and could almost hear the bolt being thrown on the door to her freedom. Her heart suddenly began to pound in her chest. She needed fresh air— alone.

Pulling her hand away from his arm, she handed him her glass saying, "I'm sorry, my lord, you must excuse me."

"Is everything all right?"

"Oh yes. I... er, just need to visit the ladies' retiring room."

"Oh, yes, of course," he said, turning slightly pink.

Adriana turned and walked away as quickly as she could.

Morgan was at a loss. He looked down at the palm in his hand, staring at all of the lines that criss–crossed it, trying so hard to remember what Cosmina had told him. Was this the line of the heart or life, he wondered as he ran his finger across the woman's hand.

Even though this was probably the six or seventh woman who had asked him to read her palm, he still was unsure of himself. He wasn't entirely certain how he had bumbled through the others. He only knew that somehow he had to make it through this one as well, and then another and another, all evening long.

He gave the woman a little smile, and then let his eyes wander around the room. The hostess, Lady Collingwood, had placed him in a small parlor off the main ball room. There were a few candles here, but not enough to fully illuminate the space. Swathes of colorful fabric hung all around, even hanging from the ceiling creating a rather exotic, claustrophobic feel to the room. "To give the room atmosphere," the lady had tittered after leading Morgan in earlier that evening. He had nodded, smiled, and thanked her for her thoughtful arrangements. It wasn't as bad as the forest, he reminded himself. And he could leave any time—as soon as he found Adriana.

He sincerely hoped the atmosphere was convincing the guests he knew what he was doing, since his performance probably wasn't. There were, oddly enough, a good number of people in the room, all talking quietly and enjoying the refreshments Lady Collingwood's servants made sure were always at hand. Some were waiting their turn with Morgan, the gypsy fortune–teller, while others just seemed to be enjoying the atmosphere. There were also a number of younger ladies who must have been taking a break from the dancing. Many of them stood about giggling to one another, but Adriana was not among them.

"What do you see in my palm?" the plain−faced middle−aged woman prompted him, bringing his mind back to what he was supposed to be doing.

He tried to use the tricks Nestor taught him on how to tell a woman's station, and thereby what she would probably be interested in hearing. This lady was dressed rather more plainly than many of the others, so Morgan guessed she must be one of the chaperones.

"You have not have had a very easy life," Morgan began hesitantly.

The lady sighed. "No, but it *will* improve, will it not? Oh, I know that it is too late to hope for a husband or children, but at least an easier time with my charges would be welcome?" Her voice rose hopefully.

Morgan gave the woman a little smile, and was quietly thrilled with himself for having guessed correctly. He then ran his finger along one of the longer lines that crossed her palm. "Yes, indeed, you shall have an easier time. See, here, where this line intersects with this other one," he pointed vaguely at her palm and she bent her head to peer into it. "This signifies that a gentleman will come into your life."

Morgan looked up and caught the woman's eyes with his own. He held them and focused his energy so she could not look away. "Look for him in the places you go to in your ordinary life. He shall change everything for you. Do not be in a hurry, however, change comes with time. Now go and be happy with your life and know it *will* become easier in time."

The woman blinked a few times and looked at Morgan with a slightly confused expression on her face. She then nodded slightly, and with a small smile flitting on and off her narrow lips she got up and meandered away through the crowded room.

Morgan shook his head. When all else failed, putting a suggestion into the woman's mind always worked.

He started to look around once again for Adriana. Surely she should be here by now. He wondered if he could get up from the heavily draped table where he was seated and go looking for her. Nestor had assured him she would be here. She must simply have not ventured into this side room as yet.

Before he could stand up, however, another lady sat down in the seat opposite him. As she leaned her ample bosom toward him, she held out her heavily be–ringed hand to him. The candlelight caught the fire of the diamonds and rubies in her rings that sparkled at him menacingly. This was a woman of wealth and power, there was no mistaking that. From the jewels on her hand and at her throat, to her ornately designed dress with many ruffles and frills, to the high plumage that waved gently from her intricately coiffed hair—everything about her spoke of money. Her bearing said she knew it, and expected to be treated appropriately.

Morgan nodded a small bow to her, and then gently turned her hand over, holding it in his own.

"You are..." Morgan began.

He was interrupted immediately by the lady, "A woman of passion."

Morgan looked up. She was looking at him through her partially veiled eyes with an intensity that made his skin crawl.

"Indeed," he said. "You search..."

"...for a gypsy man of equal passion," she interrupted again. "I have heard that gypsies are talented lovers," she said, her voice low and husky.

This time, Morgan did not dare to look up. He knew precisely what he would see, and he did not wish to give this woman any indication he was interested in her shocking proposition.

Morgan cleared his throat and started once again. "You are searching for love, but it is not where you would think to find it."

"Oh, I think I know where to find it," she said, suggestively. Morgan felt a hand running up his thigh. Resisting the urge to jump from his chair, Morgan crossed his legs in an effort to remove himself from her reach.

"You will find it in your home," Morgan continued with as much magical power and conviction as he could put into his voice without making eye contact, "where your *husband* is waiting for you to return to him."

The woman huffed in disbelief. The hand pulled away from his own and Morgan heard the chair she had been sitting on scrape back on the wood floor as she left the table.

Morgan sighed with relief, dropping his head into his hand for a moment.

Another palm appeared on the table in front of him. This one wore no rings, but the heel and side of the hand was stained with blue and black paint or ink—and it was shaking ever so slightly. Without looking up, Morgan took the hand gingerly in his own and brushed the palm with the tips of his fingers. Minute sparks of electricity jumped from her hand to his as intense tingles and heat went rushing up his arm and through his body.

A smile was beginning to grow on his face as he looked up into the deep, soothing green of Adriana's eyes.

Without a thought Morgan stood, still holding tightly onto her hand.

"Morgan!" She then turned, and, with a quick look back at him, silently invited him to follow her out of the partially open doors into the garden just outside of the parlor. She did not stop there, however, but continued on, away from the sounds of the party, and into the darkness of evening.

Adriana's heart was beating hard.

She almost hadn't believed her eyes when she had entered the side parlor searching for the way out to the garden—and saw Morgan there dressed as a gypsy and reading palms.

There was no mistaking him. She could feel his presence as easily as she could recognize his long dark hair, broad shoulders, and the tilt of his head. She watched with amazement and, she reluctantly admitted, growing pique, as one lady went over and nearly threw herself at him. A thrill went through her, however, when the woman got up in a huff and stalked off.

Now she turned to face him in the soft light of the moon reflected in his dark eyes. The cool, fresh air sent tingles over her bare arms.

"Why?" the question was wrenched out of her before she could even gather her wits. "Why are you here?"

Adriana had worked so hard over the past week to drive him from her mind. She had put away the painting of him her traitorous hand had painted without meaning to, and focused her mind on preparing for her wedding. Shopping, cleaning, preparing menus, making lists of who to invite to the wedding and the ball that would be held in her honor—she made sure all these things, with all of their little details, took up every moment of her time.

And now, just when she thought she had finally won the battle, and managed to go nearly the whole day without thinking about him, here he was again. She felt... well, she didn't know what to feel. Her emotions were all in a turmoil, each clambering for dominance—anger, shock, joy, elation and, yes, desire.

Morgan took her hand again. "I came to see you. You left so suddenly. You didn't even say goodbye." His voice was low, and filled with sorrow. Adriana's eyes stung with unshed tears.

She shook her head, pulling her hand away. She would not give in. She would be strong.

Taking a step away from him, she blinked rapidly a few times to clear her eyes, hoping he hadn't noticed. "I had to."

"Was it your guardian? Did he force you to leave?"

"No." It came out as a croak. Adriana's cleared her throat, and said more strongly. "No. It was me. I asked to leave."

Morgan shook his head slowly. "I don't understand. Why?"

Why? Adriana took a deep breath. How could she do this? Explain this to him?

He was so simple, so earnest, and so hurt. Seeing him here in London, in his shirt sleeves and colorful gypsy vest—looking so sweet and handsome, and completely out of place among the glitter of society... How could she explain to him the mores, the rules of society that had been drilled into her ever since she was a little girl?

She made the attempt. "It was wrong, Morgan, what we did together."

"No. It was beautiful. You are beautiful." He took another step closer and reached for her again, but she backed up, keeping her distance.

She still didn't trust herself to stand too close to him. The threat that she would throw herself into his arms and beg for him to kiss her and hold her was there, at the very edge of her self control. She had to keep her distance. Luckily, the beautifully landscaped garden allowed her to do that.

"Please, Morgan," she begged. "Please try to understand."

"I am trying. What was wrong in what we did?"

Adriana took a shaky breath and tried again. "We... people who are not married should not, *cannot* be so... so intimate as we were. It isn't right."

"Adriana, you are so beautiful. Just looking at you makes me feel good. But touching you like I did, and having you touch me..."

"No. It was wrong. I still don't know how I ever allowed you..."

"Because it wasn't wrong. Nothing has ever been so right." He reached out and took her hand, but she snatched it away again.

"Morgan, we cannot do such things," she said as firmly as she could. Oh, but how I wish we could, her rebellious heart cried. "I'd like us to be friends," she said, before she even had time to think it through. "Friends, but nothing more," she quickly amended.

"Friends." Morgan's bright, happy eyes dulled, and his smile disappeared.

"Yes." Adriana couldn't help wringing her hands together. It was all she could do not to reach out and hold him to her— to bury her face in his broad shoulders and cry out that she wanted to be close to him again too. "Just friends."

He stood staring at some point over her shoulder, his arms hanging uselessly at his sides. She desperately wished he wouldn't look so sad and vulnerable.

She looked up into the star–strewn sky. How could the night be so still and lovely when her heart beat like a horse at full gallop, and her mind so very upset and confused?

"I need you, Adriana. I need to be with you." His voice was quiet and low.

A flash of lightning suddenly rent the sky, and a wave of heat hotter than the hottest summer day suddenly engulfed them. For a moment Adriana struggled breathe, the heat was so intense. Clouds shifted in quickly covering the stars and moon that had been shining so brightly just moments before.

And then as if an unseen hand suddenly shoved her, a gust of wind pushed Adriana away from Morgan, knocking her to the ground a few feet away.

"How dare you!" A quiet, angry, menacing voice came from the direction of the house.

Chapter 20

Adriana's breath whooshed out of her lungs as she landed hard on the ground. She struggled to catch her breath, but then lost it again when she saw Lady Vallentyn lit by a flash of lightning. Her long, pale face was filled with such hatred, Adriana had never seen the like before, and she hoped she never would again.

"What?" The word formed on Adriana's lips, but she didn't have the breath to speak it out loud, nor the voice as her heart hammered in her throat.

"Mother!" Morgan said, spinning around to face her.

Mother? Lady Vallentyn was Morgan's mother?

"Well, well, Morgan. I heard you had escaped, but I simply could not believe it. I just had to see for myself." Lady Vallentyn's voice oozed malice.

Adriana's stomach clutched with fear, but words kept screaming out in her mind—she was his mother? He had escaped? Escaped from what, why, how? Whatever could it mean?

Morgan paled, his face hardening into a look as terrifying as his mother's. He took a step backwards, moving away from Adriana.

"You puny little boy, how did you do it? How did you manage to get past my barriers? Did your cousin help you? I know your brother could not have. He doesn't have the ability."

His brother, that would be Lord Vallentyn? Adriana quickly worked it out in her mind. And his cousin...

Morgan flinched putting up his arm as if to ward off her harsh words. Yet he continued to stand up to his mother. "Kat had nothing to do with it, and neither did Vallentyn," he said.

"Yet you managed somehow, even with your feeble little abilities. You know you are nothing, Morgan," Lady Vallentyn hissed, advancing slowly.

Adriana gasped. She had always had bad feelings about Lady Vallentyn, but that was unnecessarily cruel.

Morgan's arm stayed raised while he briefly turned his shoulder to Lady Vallentyn as she spoke, but just as quickly, he turned back to face the onslaught of her anger. As he turned, Adriana noticed the arm of his shirt flap open as if it had been sliced with a knife.

"You are nothing, and you will always be nothing," she spat at him. "Soon you will be less than nothing, just an ordinary man. And you will never escape me again."

Adriana watched as Morgan flinched and quickly turned his shoulder toward his mother once again. A gash appeared on his chest near the shoulder he had turned towards Lady Vallentyn. Adriana could see something dark beginning to stain his shirt—surely it wasn't... blood?

"You may have worked some kind of trick, but you will never become powerful. Do not even dare to hold out any hope, it will not come. You... stupid... weak... little... boy!"

"How dare you!" Adriana finally said, gathering her wits, and trying to stand up. "How could you..."

"Quiet!" Lady Vallentyn said, raising her arm. As she did so, Adriana was thrown backwards once again. This time her head hit the tree behind her. White spots danced in front of her eyes with the pain.

She blinked her vision clear. Morgan took a step toward her, but then stopped. His shirt was now soaked with blood from his lacerated arm and shoulder. It was almost as if an invisible whip were thrashing him, descending again and again with each harsh word Lady Vallentyn spoke. But that was impossible—but so was being pushed backwards without being touched.

An unnatural heat began to surround Adriana as if she were sitting in the bowels of hell. It stirred the air as Lady Vallentyn said, "Now get yourself back to Vallentyn before I become truly angry. And if you ever try this again, Morgan..." Lady Vallentyn took a menacing step forward.

Morgan, however, would not be cowed. With sweat glistening on his face, he took a quick look over at Adriana. Shaking his head, he stood up taller, squaring his shoulders. "No, Mother."

A bolt of lightning cracked loudly, making Adriana jump. A horse whinnied in fright, but Adriana held onto her cries. She wrapped her arms around herself as the hot wind grew stronger.

"What do you mean, no?" Lady Vallentyn's voice became lower and even more frightening.

But Morgan showed no fear. "I mean, no. I will not return to the forest. And I will not listen to you anymore." Morgan's voice carried like a cool breeze, cutting through the stifling heat, and over the howling of the wind.

"How dare you contradict my orders!" The trees swayed dangerously, as the wind grew even stronger all around them. Looking up, Adriana prayed that nothing would fall on top of her. She would have moved away from the tree she was under, but fear of being thrown back once again kept her still.

"I will do as I please. You have no hold over me anymore, Mother." Morgan waved his hand. Immediately, the wind died down.

Slowly Adriana began to unfurled herself.

"I am not a little boy. I am a man, and I am stronger than you realize," Morgan said, taking a step forward.

"We'll just see about that!" Lady Vallentyn began to raise her arms, but Morgan stretched out his hands in front of him and she froze. "No, Mother. You will do nothing more here tonight."

"But..." Lady Vallentyn lowered her arms and then tried to raise them again, but once again they were stopped about halfway up her body. "How did you do that? What has happened?"

Adriana resisted the sudden urge to laugh at Lady Vallentyn's chagrin at her inability to move. Clearly, if she couldn't move, she couldn't do anything.

"I have learned, Mother. I have learned to use my powers, and they are growing. Soon I will become even more powerful than you."

"Never!" she spat, her face darkening with rage.

"We'll see about that," he said quietly.

Without another word, Morgan turned and held out his hand to Adriana. It was cool, and tingles shot into her wherever he touched her.

"Come, let's go," he said. He put his arm around her waist protectively, and began to lead her past Lady Vallentyn and toward the house once again.

As they passed her, Lady Vallentyn caught Adriana's eye. "Adriana, stop! You will not go with him."

The voice sounded both inside and outside Adriana's head. Her feet stopped moving, and suddenly she was rooted to the spot, unable to move.

"No! You *will not* control her," Morgan's angry voice cut through whatever it was that was holding her in place. Gently he led her forward, "Do not listen to her, and do not look at her. I will protect you. Come now."

The trembling throughout Adriana's body increased as she allowed Morgan to lead her away from a stunned Lady Vallentyn. Her tremors diminished as they moved further away from Lady Vallentyn, although all of her muscles ached from being tense for so long.

The further away they moved, the stronger was the small voice that whispered in the back of Adriana's mind. *It is all right. There is nothing to fear. Morgan will take care of you.*

It made no sense, but somehow, she was able to heed the voice and continue on.

Could your mother have somehow transferred some of her powers to you?" Nestor asked the following morning as he, Morgan and Cosmina were discussing the events of the previous evening.

"Is that possible? I didn't know powers were transferable," Morgan said, taking another bite of his hearty breakfast.

The hopeful light in Nestor's eyes faded. "I've heard myths, but they were probably just that. I'm simply looking for some explanation for how you became so powerful suddenly."

"Well, no matter how you got the powers, Morgan, I am very happy you were able to defend yourself and Adriana," Cosmina said, giving Morgan's arm a pat.

He gave her a little smile. "Thank you, Cosmina. I only wish I could stop worrying."

"What is there for you to worry about?"

"The fact that my mother knows I'm here in London. And she knows I have become powerful..."

"But she doesn't know just *how* powerful you are," Nestor pointed out.

Morgan nodded slowly. "That's true, but neither do I. And I am still worried about what she might do next."

"What could she do? You have beaten her. You are more powerful than she. Now, you need to go and meet Adriana once more and convince her..."

"We don't know that Morgan is more powerful than Lady Vallentyn," Nestor said, putting down his tea cup with the smallest of tinks. "Even if you are, Morgan, what about the other consequences? People noticed the odd weather last night. Did anyone see you leaving the garden? Could anyone associate you with it?"

Morgan sighed, and rubbed his hand over his eyes. He was quickly losing his appetite with this conversation. "No. I don't believe anyone did. I slipped out the back and stayed away from the road, taking the alleyways as far as I could."

"Perhaps someone noticed Lady Vallentyn coming from the garden? Could someone associate her with the odd happenings?" Cosmina asked, hopefully.

"It is unlikely. Why would anyone associate an odd patch of weather with a woman who is well respected in society?" Nestor asked.

"I don't know. Why would anyone associate it with Morgan?" Cosmina asked in the same scornful tone of voice.

"Because he is thought to be a gypsy," Nestor answered.

"And what have gypsies got to do with odd weather?" Cosmina's face flushed.

"Please!" Morgan interrupted their quarrel. "No one will associate the odd weather with anyone. That is not what I am worrying about."

There was silence for a moment while Nestor and Cosmina cooled their tempers.

"What is it you are worrying about, Morgan?" Cosmina asked. "Is it Adriana? I am certain she will admire you even more now that she has seen how strong you are. She will certainly want to be more than just friends, perhaps even..."

"I was thinking about my mother," Morgan interrupted. He hadn't even begun to think about his relationship with Adriana, and didn't have the luxury to do so just now. "I told you, my mother is a very powerful Vallen. She is not used to being thwarted. She will find some way of punishing me for this. I'm just afraid..."

"Afraid of what?" Nestor asked.

"I am afraid she might hurt Adriana."

Cosmina gasped. "She wouldn't!"

"Yes, she would," Morgan sat back and tried to relax his tightening muscles. "That is the way she punishes people, by hurting that which they love most."

No one said anything as they digested this information.

A knock sounded on the door, and the maid peeked her head in. "A young lady to see you, Mr. Vallentyn," she said, giggling. "I've shown her into the drawing room."

Morgan stood up at once. "A *young* lady, you say?"

Nestor too stood. "Did she give her name?"

The maid lost her smile. "No, and I didn't think to ask, Mr. Nestor," she said, closing the door with a snap.

Morgan looked at Nestor and then Cosmina.

"It could be Adriana," Cosmina ventured.

Morgan nodded his head slowly. "It could be, but I..." A smile came to his face as a familiar, warm feeling came over him. "It is Kat." He strode out the door and across the hall to the drawing room.

Indeed, his cousin was sitting looking nervously around at the shabby furnishings when Morgan entered the room. Close on his heels was Cosmina, followed at a more dignified pace by Nestor.

"Kat!" Morgan embraced his cousin warmly. "It is so good to see you!"

"It is good to see you," she said, giving a little laugh. "You act as if we haven't seen each other for a year. It's only been one week, Morgan."

"It feels more like a year."

A gentle cough came from behind him.

"Oh, Cosmina, Nestor, this is my cousin, Kat...er, Katrina Havelock," Morgan said awkwardly.

Cosmina gave her a little curtsey, while Nestor bowed.

Morgan ignored the odd look she gave him—obviously wondering who Cosmina and Nestor were—and instead took her hand, leading her back to the sofa. Sitting down with her, he asked, "Did you hear about last night? You are staying with my mother? Has she said anything? Done anything?"

Kat looked from Morgan to Cosmina and Nestor and then back again to Morgan. Morgan could sense her unease, as well as a touch of fear.

"It is all right. Nestor and Cosmina are friends. I told them what happened, and Nestor is Vallen."

Kat's discomfort lessened a bit, but not entirely. She gave a little nod, and then said, "Your mother has not spoken to anyone. She has not even come from her room yet today, and you know how early she is up and about normally. I knew something was wrong, which is why I came to see you."

"I beg your pardon, but how did you know where to find Mr. Vallentyn?" Nestor asked.

"It was not easy. I've been walking around the area for the past hour trying to get a sense of where he might be. Luckily, you have a very strong aura," she said, turning back to Morgan.

Morgan gave her hand a squeeze. "You've always been able to find me, no matter where I was."

"What an interesting talent," Cosmina said, in awe. "I do hope you didn't get too wet."

"I can only sense people I am very close to," Kat explained. "And I, er, managed not to get too wet."

"By using your magic?" Morgan asked laughing a little.

Kat gave him a guilty little smile and a shrug. She then turned serious and added, "But Aunt Vallentyn…"

"Must be furious," Morgan finished for her, also losing his smile.

"Beyond furious, Morgan. I'm scared for you. I don't know what she might be planning." She looked down at their hands, still interlocked. "Can you tell me what happened last night?"

"Let's just say, my powers have increased again," Morgan said briefly.

"He was magnificent, Miss Havelock. He proved himself to be Lady Vallentyn's equal, defending himself and…"

"Cosmina," Morgan said, warningly. He desperately wished she was more discreet. He didn't want to have to watch what he said in her presence.

Kat looked at Morgan, her eyes wide.

"It is not what it sounds like. I was able to stop my mother from harming anyone, that's all."

"That's all? That's quite a lot." Her eyes narrowed again. "What do you mean, anyone? Who else was there?"

"Just Adriana," Morgan said as nonchalantly as possible.

"Morgan! You met her? What... no, wait. Let's deal with Aunt Vallentyn first. She is much more of a threat than Adriana."

"Adriana isn't a threat at all," Morgan said, smiling at the thought.

"No. Of course, she isn't. But your mother definitely is."

Morgan sobered up immediately. "You don't know what she might do, do you?"

"No. I wish I did."

"I'm certain she will not let this go unpunished," Morgan said quietly.

"But she may also be wary of you now," Nestor put in. "Now that she knows how powerful you've become."

Morgan gave a little shrug, "It's but a drop in the pail compared to her powers, I'm sure."

"You don't know that, Morgan," Kat said. "You know what the proph..."

"Yes, yes, I know," Morgan said, cutting her off. He hadn't told either Cosmina or Nestor about the prophecy pertaining to him. He wasn't entirely sure he wanted to share so much information with them just yet. "The point is that no matter what my powers are now, she will be planning something. She wants me to return to Vallentyn, and I have no doubt she will do anything to ensure that I do."

"You will need to be very careful," Cosmina put in.

"Yes, Morgan. You don't know when, where or how she will strike."

"It is not for myself that I'm worried, Kat. She'll hurt Adriana. I just know she will."

Kat bit her lip. Morgan could see her eyes become glassy with unshed tears. "Oh, Morgan, you are right."

"I must go and warn her. I've got to... to protect her somehow."

"But how? You can't be with her day and night," Kat protested.

"I know," Morgan said, getting up and moving to the window. He looked out at the rain—soaked morning. "It is imperative that you find out anything you can about what she is planning." If she couldn't, and Adriana came to any harm because of him...

He came back to the sofa, and took Kat's hands in his own. "We need to know what she is going to do so that I can protect Adriana."

Kat nodded slowly. "I will do my best." She frowned at him, suddenly upset. "You needn't have put a suggestion into my mind. I would have done it anyway."

Morgan sat back, dropping her hands. "I am so sorry, I didn't mean to. I..."

"You just don't know your powers. You've got to be careful!"

"I know. I am trying to control them, but sometimes, when I feel very strongly about something, it just happens." He sat back against the sofa, feeling bad. She was absolutely right, he had to learn to control his magic better.

She sat back and thought about this for a moment. "What you need is someone to teach you how to control them."

Morgan sat forward again. "Yes! That's just what I need. Could you...?"

She shook her head. "If Aunt Vallentyn ever found out, we'd both be sunk." She paused, "But do, please, remove the suggestion you just gave me."

Where have you been?" Tatiana kept her voice low and quiet, despite the anger simmering in her breast.

"I just went out for a walk," Kat answered, removing her hat and gloves, and putting them, along with her umbrella, into the hands of her maid. She gave the woman a nod, turning back to Tatiana as the maid closed the drawing room door behind her.

Tatiana took a deep breath and let it out slowly. If she played her cards right, she would have the information she needed from Kat with no trouble at all.

"I do hope Morgan is well?" she asked, casually putting aside the book she had been reading.

"I don't know what you mean. Morgan is at Vallentyn," Kat answered a little too smoothly.

Of course, Kat would not remember she had already revealed Morgan's whereabouts. And now she thought to play with her? It wasn't easy, but Tatiana kept a strong hold on her temper. Narrowing her eyes at her niece, she said, "There is no use in lying to me, Katrina. You know I can always tell when you are lying. You know as well as I do that Morgan is here in London, and you are even aware of what happened last evening."

She stood up and moved toward the fireplace. Keeping her back turned so that Kat could not see the fury in her eyes, she asked, "Did he tell you all of the details? Did he gloat and tell you how he managed to best me?"

Kat didn't answer right away. Tatiana veiled her eyes before turning back around. The girl was standing with her hands clutching her arms, her knuckles white with tension. But Tatiana didn't need to see her protective stance to see how scared she was—she could feel it. It radiated from her like heat from a fire. Poor, dear Katrina knew everything and was terrified of her own knowledge.

And so she should be, Tatiana thought.

"He, he didn't tell me anything." Kat grimaced as soon as she had finished speaking, knowing full well what she had just accidentally revealed.

So she had met with him! This was too easy. Tatiana gave a little nod of her head, and then sat down, apparently at her ease, but with all of her senses ready to pick up the smallest bit of information.

"I don't suppose it is a pleasant day for a walk."

Kat drew her eyebrows down in confusion. "No, not very. It is raining."

"And you were not too obvious using your magic not to get wet."

"Oh no, Morgan's not..." Kat stopped speaking before she gave away any more information.

All right, he was clearly living within easy walking distance. Now to find out where, exactly.

Tatiana smiled and encouraging smile. "He's not what?"

"Nothing. I wasn't going to say anything important."

Tatiana gave a little nod of her head, as if to say it was fine for Kat to stay quiet. "I believe I may visit him today, as well. Won't he be surprised by two visits in one day? Of course, I will combine my visit with a stop in Bond Street—I need some new feathers for one of my hats." It was not a smooth ploy, but perhaps it might work.

Kat kept quiet, however, not revealing which direction she would need to go to find Morgan and whether she would pass by Bond Street on her way. Very well, she would find out where he was another way.

Tatiana thought for a moment. Where would the boy have found lodging close to Mayfair?

"He didn't mention whether or not he was in need of funds, did he?" she asked.

"No, he didn't."

"Well, perhaps I should take him some anyway. He'll need to pay his room and board, for certain."

"I believe he has money, or at least he didn't mention the need for any."

So he was not staying with friends—not that he had any.

"But where would he have obtained money? Unless he applied directly to Vallentyn—but Jonathan would have told me," Tatiana said, as if thinking aloud.

Kat once again kept silent. She was becoming altogether too clever.

"Enough of these games, Katrina," Tatiana said, standing and coming toward her niece. "My patience has come to an end. Tell me where Morgan is staying."

"N—n—no," Kat said, taking a step backwards, and firmly keeping her eyes on the floor.

"You know I will find out from you either way. Make this easier on both of us and cooperate."

"I won't...ma'am."

Tatiana could feel the girl putting up her weak mental barriers. They were pitiful, but she supposed it was to her own advantage, and the girl was quite powerful in many other ways.

Tatiana raised the girl's chin with a flick of her finger, but still she wouldn't raise her eyes. "Did we not have a little talk about this show of weakness?"

"It is not weakness, ma'am, it is..."

"What?"

"Defense," Kat said quietly.

Tatiana laughed. "You can't defend yourself against me. Don't even try. You may be a strong Vallen, Kat, and hopefully by the time you attain your destiny you will become even more powerful, but know that you are no match for me. Now be reasonable. Tell me what I want to know, and I will leave you alone."

"No! I won't. I won't jeopardize Morgan in that way."

"Very well," Tatiana said, before infusing her voice with a great deal of power. She would need quite a bit to put a suggestion into Kat's mind without eye contact—even though her barriers were meager, they still required Tatiana to use more power on her than she ordinarily would. With her voice saturated with magic she said, "Tell me the address where Morgan is staying,"

Kat bit her lip so hard it turned deep red. Her face turned deathly pale as she fought the suggestion.

It was such a simple little piece of information, Tatiana thought to herself. She didn't want to have to befuddle the girl just for this.

"Tell me where he is staying," Tatiana said again, her powers reaching out to the girl, willing her to speak the information that she needed.

Kat closed her eyes, fighting the suggestion with everything she had, but it wasn't enough. Finally, her teeth let go of her lip and the words came out choked, "Dartmouth Street."

Tatiana backed off. That was all she needed. She didn't know where this Dartmouth Street was, but it didn't matter. Her driver would know it, and she would be able to discern which house once she was there. She gave Kat a little pat on her arm. "There now, that wasn't too difficult. Hopefully, next time when I ask you something, you will be more forthcoming."

Chapter 21

Adriana stood up, her suddenly limp fingers letting her embroidery fall to the floor. "Morgan!"

"Adriana! Please tell this man..."

"Miss Hayden, this man is insisting on seeing you, but he bears no card, nor..." Jackson, Lord Devaux's butler, and Morgan said at the same time as they both entered the room. Jackson stepped in front of Morgan, deliberately barring his way. They both stopped speaking in mid–sentence as Adriana held up her hand.

"It is all right, Jackson. I know the gentleman," Adriana said with as much authority as she could command considering her sudden trembling. Whether it was from fear, anger, excitement or simply the fact that Morgan's dominating presence was in her drawing room, she didn't know. She just knew she had to clasp her hands together to keep it from being too obvious.

Jackson looked from her to Morgan, and back again. He gave Henrietta a significant nod before turning on his heel, and walking from the room.

In two long strides, Morgan was by her side. He placed his hands on her arms, making tingles and heat rush through her, and a strange calm stopped her heart from beating so quickly. "Adriana, are you all right?"

She was about to say yes, just from habit, but she stopped herself. "No. No, Morgan, I am not all right."

There was a discreet cough nearby, and Adriana realized she had completely forgotten Henrietta's presence.

Morgan dropped his hands, taking a step away from her.

"Henrietta Britworth, may I introduce you to..." And then she had to stop. Adriana's voice suddenly disappeared. It was gone. Her throat had closed up and she could no longer speak. Adriana put her hand to her throat and turned to look at Morgan, panic beginning to lace its way through her chest.

He looked blankly at her for the briefest moment, and then took a deep breath in with realization. Catching her eyes with his own, he placed his hand on her shoulder and said, "I release my hold."

Immediately, the tightness in her throat was gone. She had to take a step to catch her balance, and was grateful for Morgan's hand on her elbow.

"What...?" she said, completely confused, and not a little scared.

"I'm sorry. It's all right now," Morgan said, his deep baritone voice soothing and calming her once again.

"Adriana?" Henrietta said, looking just as confused as Adriana had felt.

"I'm sorry, Henrietta. This is Morgan... er," she turned back to him. She didn't know his last name.

"Vallentyn. I am Morgan Vallentyn. Adriana and I met when she was visiting my family last week," he finished for her.

"Oh!" Henrietta said, giving Morgan a curtsey and Adriana an odd look. She then looked up at him again and her small brown eyes widened. "Oh! You're that man! The man in Adriana's painting!"

Adriana felt her face heat with embarrassment, and then grow even hotter as Morgan turned to look at her, a little smile playing on his lips. "You painted a picture of me?"

"Uh, well, yes," she admitted reluctantly before giving Henrietta a meaningful look. She wished her companion hadn't mentioned the painting—he might want to see it, and she couldn't bear being so embarrassed yet again. Henrietta gave a little shrug and a small apologetic smile, but the twinkle in her eye told Adriana she remembered the painting quite well.

"But that's not why you came to visit," Adriana said, getting away from the subject as quickly as she could.

"No." The expression on Morgan's faced changed immediately. "No." Once again he was looking worried and concerned. He turned his eyes to Henrietta and then back to her. "We need to speak—about last night."

"Yes, we most certainly do!" All of the anger and confusion Adriana had struggled with all night long came rushing back to her. She hadn't been able to sleep a wink for thinking about all she had witnessed the night before. None of it—not from the moment she had encountered Morgan telling fortunes in Lady Collingswood's side parlor, to the time he had left her at the door to the ballroom—had made any sense to her at all. She didn't know what to think about any of it.

But she did know it was not something that either she or Morgan would feel comfortable discussing in front of Henrietta. So far, Adriana hadn't told her companion anything, and she wasn't entirely sure she should—mainly because it was all too bizarre to even put into words, let alone any that made sense.

Adriana turned to Henrietta and looked at her pleadingly. "Would you mind, Henrietta, I need to speak with Morgan alone."

The twinkle immediately disappeared from her companion's eyes. "I don't know, Adriana." She continued to look more and more worried as she thought about it. "I don't think that would be a good idea, especially considering that paint..."

"Henrietta, I promise to tell you everything—later. Right now, I would appreciate just a few moments... please?" She tried to give Henrietta a reassuring smile.

Adriana knew how much Henrietta loved to be daring, to live at the margin of acceptable behavior—and she desperately hoped her companion wouldn't decide to change now.

Hesitantly, Henrietta began to move toward the door. "Well, all right. But just for a few minutes. And I am going to leave the door open," she warned.

"Yes. That's fine." And, in fact, it was absolutely fine with Adriana when she thought about all she had witnessed between Morgan and Lady Vallentyn the night before.

As soon as her companion was gone, she turned to Morgan. She could hardly believe he was here—taking up so much space in her little drawing room. It wasn't just his size, but his whole being that took up all of the space. It was odd, but she didn't remember him being this way—being so large.

But his eyes were the same. Dark as the deepest night, and just now looking at her with such concern. She nearly melted at his look—and it made it extremely hard to continue to be angry with him. But she steeled herself, remembering an entire night spent tossing and turning on her bed.

"You are all right?" he asked again, taking her hands.

"No, I am not. I want to know what happened last night. No matter how I think of it, it doesn't make any sense," she said, shades of anger beginning to blend inside of her. Her head started to ache again just from the memory of the night.

"I'm sorry." He softly rubbed his thumb against her right temple as if he was aware that her head hurt and knew that this would help. It did. It felt wonderful—warm, caring, and soothing. Adriana couldn't help it, she closed her eyes and just allowed Morgan to massage away the pain. Her anger faded under his deft fingers.

"Please don't be upset," he said after a moment, his voice as soothing as his fingers. "I promise to explain everything to you, just... first tell me that you haven't seen my mother today or received anything from her."

"No. Why would I?" Adriana asked, blinking her eyes open again. Her headache had completely disappeared.

He shook his head. "I... I'm just afraid she may try to hurt me through you. Just as she did with the animals in my barn."

The room around Adriana lost all of its color. "The pox?" she whispered.

Morgan tried to give her a reassuring smile. "I'm certain she wouldn't give you the pox, but she knows that I care about you, and I don't want you to be hurt. Please, stay away from her, and I will do everything in my power to keep you safe. Kat has promised to help as well."

Kat would protect her? Was she like him? But what... "What are you?" she asked before she realized she was speaking out loud.

Morgan gave her an apologetic little smile. "I'm Vallen."

"What?"

"Vallen." He paused and then frowned. "Some people confuse us with witches," he explained.

Adriana laughed. Her shoulders dropped as the tension slipped out of her. "Please be serious."

But Morgan hardly cracked a smile. "It's true. I, my mother, Kat, even my brother, Vallentyn, to some extent. We are all Vallen."

Adriana could feel the smile fade from her lips. He was serious. "But witches are the stuff of fairytales. They aren't real."

Morgan gave a little shrug. "Even fairytales have some grain of truth in them."

Adriana shook her head. She just could not believe that Morgan was a witch. It was ridiculous. It was silly! Witches didn't really exist. People couldn't do magic.

Morgan frowned, clearly hurt by her skepticism. "You don't believe me. I'll prove it to you, then."

Adriana tried to pull her hand away from his, suddenly frightened again. He was so serious, and horrible flashes of what she'd seen last night kept flitting through her mind.

"No, it's all right, come." Once again his voice was soft and soothing.

Gently, he pulled her to the French doors behind them leading into the back garden, but she stopped as he was about to go outside into the rain.

"We'll get wet!"

"No, we won't. Watch." He let go of her hand and took a step out the door. Adriana watched in fascination as Morgan stood outside in the rain without one drop falling on him. It all just seemed to bend around him, as if he were holding up an umbrella—only he wasn't.

He took her hand and pulled her outside to join him under his non—existent umbrella. Laughing at her expression, and then said, "You know, I don't think it was supposed to rain at all today." With a wave of his hand, the rain stopped.

Adriana's world faded once again as she watched the deep gray clouds just skitter away with the wave of his hand. A brilliant blue sky appeared, the dazzling sun shining down on them, warm and full of the expectation of flowers and lovely walks in the park. She was grateful that Morgan was keeping a firm hold on her elbow. In the sudden shimmering heat of the sun—drenched garden, the fresh scent of the earth enveloped them making her feel light—headed.

Morgan bent down to a rose bush next to the door that had not yet bloomed, but was filled with the promise of many deep red blossoms. As he gently cupped his hand under one bud, it burst into bloom, unfolding its petals even as she watched. He then plucked it off the bush.

He handed it to Adriana. Their fingers touched as she took the bloom from him. Small pinpricks shot from his fingers into hers, leaving her hand tingling.

Holding the rose delicately in her shaking hand, she tried to steady her breathing. There was no logical explanation for what he had done.

"Then you really are... you truly are a witch?" she managed to whisper not lifting her eyes from the flower—it all seemed so impossible.

"We prefer the term Vallen. Witches are ordinary people who dabble with potions, but they are not truly magical."

Morgan watched as Adriana's green eyes widened with wonder when she finally she lifted them to look him. The gold and red in her auburn hair glinted in the brilliant sunlight. "But, yes, truly. I am Vallen. I am a Vallen who cares for you a great deal."

He couldn't resist reaching out and touching her. She was so beautiful even in her awe, and amid her fears. She was strong and brave in a way he couldn't have expected from anyone else. He ran his hand gently up her cheek and then feathered his lips across hers, leaving a trail of tingles.

A rush of heat went pulsing through his veins as she took a step closer to him. He wrapped his hands around her delicate waist and pulled her close. He needed to feel her, all of her. His lips descended upon hers, pressing his desire into her.

Fire licked at his blood as Adriana opened her mouth and allowed their tongues to dance together. He could feel her arms moving around his neck, as she relaxed and accepted him for who he truly was.

Happiness and joy coursed through him. Now, finally, he could be completely honest with her. How long had he wanted to be able to share his life, his feelings and his problems with her—to show her just how much they had in common. And now, finally, *finally*, he could.

Reluctantly, he pulled away from her. He wanted to tell her everything, to share everything with her.

"Adriana, I am so happy. Happy to be with you, and to be able to speak with you openly and honestly," he began.

A frown marred her beautiful face. "You haven't been honest with me up until now?"

"I haven't been able to be. But I've wanted to."

"So, why haven't you?" she said, taking a step away from him.

"I couldn't. I couldn't risk telling you."

"Why? I don't understand."

"It's too dangerous. I wouldn't have told you now, except you witnessed the fight with my mother. It is very dangerous for people to know I'm Vallen. What if you accidentally tell someone and it gets out? I could be killed. It's not common any more, but witches are still drowned or burned at the stake, and we are commonly mistaken for them. People are not kind to us, Adriana."

Adriana focused her eyes on the ground, clearly thinking about this. Slowly she nodded her head. Thank goodness, she understood—but still, the fear that she might tell someone was sharp in his gut.

"You can never tell anyone what we are—my mother, Kat and I—that we have powers," Morgan said vehemently, adding a touch of magic to his voice.

"I will never tell..." She stopped speaking and raised her eyes up to meet his. "You... what did you do?" she asked, with a tremor in her voice.

"I'm sorry. I put a suggestion into your mind. If you try to tell anyone I'm Vallen, you won't be able to—just as you couldn't tell your companion my name until I released my hold."

"Why did you do that? Don't you trust me?"

"Of course I do, I just.... This is so important, Adriana," He hated using his magic on her.

"You don't trust me not to tell anyone." She was beginning to get angry again. He could feel it sparking out of her, pricking him like tiny little needles.

He didn't do anything for a full minute, hoping she would calm down. He wanted to trust her. He wanted to so very much, but there was just the slightest hesitation, the little voice in the back of his head telling him to be cautious.

But when he saw tears well in her eyes, they were like a blow to his heart, a knife in his chest.

Placing his hand on her shoulder, he whispered, "I'm sorry, Adriana. I release my hold. You're right, I should trust you, and I do." He reached down within himself to see if he was doing the right thing. The voice inside of him still made its warning sounds, but drowning it out was the feeling that this was important. It was a big step, but a significant one—he had to be able to trust Adriana completely, and she needed to know that he did.

"You shouldn't just force your will onto others. It's not right," she said, crossing her arms in front of her.

Morgan nodded. "You're right. I'm still getting used to having the power to put a suggestion into someone's mind. I don't always think about whether I should use it or not."

"What do you mean, you're just getting used to having this power?" she asked, clearly confused again.

"I mean, I've only recently developed this ability. Somehow, my powers have begun to increase."

"But how is that possible? Where do your powers come from?"

Morgan gave a little laugh. "I don't know. Most Vallen are born with whatever power they have. As they use them, their powers get stronger. But for me, I was born only with the power to heal. Now, within the past few weeks, I have been able to do things I never could before. I need to find out how and why, and I need to find someone to teach me to control these abilities. I don't even know how powerful I am."

"You don't?"

"No, and I need to find out, quickly."

"You're afraid you'll hurt someone?"

"No." He stopped and stared into her eyes, searching once again to be sure he was doing the right thing before he answered her with complete honesty. Trust, he reminded himself. "There was a prophecy. It was foretold I would be the most powerful Vallen of our time, and that I have a great destiny."

He turned away from her and stepped over to the old oak tree that dominated the garden. "My mother has always said that because I'm male I'm magically weak and I'll never attain this destiny. She chose Kat to take my place." He paused and ran his hand down the trunk of the tree, taking comfort in its familiarity. "I've spent my whole life trying to increase my powers, without success. But now they *are* increasing. I don't know why, or how, but if I can do anything to help them, to make them grow faster, I need to do that. You see, if I don't attain my full powers by my twenty–first birthday, I'll lose everything and become an ordinary man."

"Would that be so bad?" Adriana asked, joining him under the tree.

Morgan nodded somberly. "When you've been expecting to be so much more? Yes, I'm afraid it would." Just the thought of it turned his stomach.

Adriana nodded, her eyes filled with understanding.

"Well, do you know anyone who can help you? Who you can ask about your powers?"

Morgan shook his head. "I don't know anyone, aside from my mother."

"You don't know any other... Vallen?" She said the new word awkwardly.

"Only one, but he doesn't know how to help me." Morgan reached up and toyed with a leaf that was hanging down from the tree. "I can't exactly walk up to people and ask if they are a Vallen, can I?"

Adriana laughed at the thought. "But surely there is someplace where they get together? Like a society party, only it would be... a Vallen party, I suppose?" she asked.

Morgan smiled at her. "Actually, there are Vallen in society. I just don't know who they might be."

"Really? Members of the beau monde?"

"So I've been told."

"Then why don't you go to a society party and see if you can meet one, and ask if they'll help you?"

"I'm not invited to society parties," he said with a shrug, and he wasn't about to try the same fortune telling trick he had before. That had been an utter failure.

Adriana seemed to be thinking this through. "If I could get you an invitation, perhaps you could attend a ball with me."

Morgan turned to look at her, the muscles in his stomach beginning to loosen. She was willing to help him? "Could you do that? Would you?"

"If it would help you, of course."

He took her hands in his. "Adriana, I can't tell you how much that would mean to me." His voice dropped into a quieter, more intimate tone. "How much it means to me that you are willing to help."

He pulled her into his arms and gave her a strong hug.

But then her soft curves were pressing into his body. Heat shot through him like a lightning bolt. He loosened his grip on her, and kissed her with all of the hunger and passion that resided within him.

But then she wiggled and pulled herself away. "No, Morgan! This is wrong. We've got to stop doing this."

Chapter 22

How can you stand to live in a place such as this?" Tatiana said, looking around at the shabby furnishings of Mrs. Lunden's drawing room.

"It's much nicer than my cottage in the woods at Vallentyn."

Morgan stood with his arms crossed in front of his chest. If he was trying to look powerful, he was doing a very good job of it, Tatiana admitted reluctantly to herself.

In fact, she'd been extremely surprised when he'd walked into the room. The entire feel of the room had changed. Somehow it had gone from being a small room to being a tiny room, as her son—and she could hardly believe that he was indeed her son, took up so much of the air in the room.

It wasn't that he was particularly large, although he certainly took after his father in the impressive breadth of his shoulders and his height. No, it was more the feel of him.

When Morgan had walked into the room, immediately, Tatiana knew that this was a man to be reckoned with—which was ridiculous. This was Morgan after all. Her measly, powerless little boy. When did he become... no!

She refused to believe what her own well-honed senses told her. He certainly could not be the powerful Vallen he seemed. It was impossible!

She wouldn't allow it!

Tamping down the anger that had begun to simmer inside of her, she asked, "Well, won't you ask me to sit down at least?" A brief look around at the shabby furnishings almost had Tatiana take back her words. If any one of her other children had dared to live in such squalor she would have removed them at once. For Morgan, this seemed almost fitting.

"No. This interview is not going to last long enough for you to get comfortable. Please, just say what you have to say, Mother."

Tatiana's eyes snapped to his and he met hers with equal force.

How dare he? It was beyond rude—it was disrespectful. The nerve of this boy!

But she grudgingly had to admit he did not lower his eyes the way Kat did. She had to respect him...

No! She did not have to respect him for anything!

She ground her teeth together, but then took a deep, calming breath.

Walking over to the window, she kept her back to him so he could not see the fury in her eyes. "You know very well why I am here," she said, beginning to gather together the force of her magic, calling on it from all around and within her. It would have been better had there been a fire in the hearth, for then she could have called on her element to assist her, but she would have to make do with what she had. On the other hand, perhaps it was better the way it was, after all. If she wasn't mistaken, Morgan too was tied to the element of fire, as were all the seventh children in her family.

"I am not returning to Vallentyn."

"Why? What is it you want here in London? If it is Miss Hayden, you can simply remove that thought from your mind. She is already engaged to your brother."

She sensed Morgan twitch at that. Ah, so he hadn't know that little piece of information. Tatiana supposed Miss Hayden had conveniently forgotten to mention it during their assignation the night before. Now was the time to hit him with her magic. Now, when he wasn't expecting it. When he was thinking about Adriana.

She gathered her energy together quickly. She wasn't sure how powerful he was, but she would hit him with all she had the first time. There was very little likelihood that she would get a second chance.

Putting it all into her voice, she spun around and made direct eye contact with him. "There is nothing for you here. Return to Vallentyn!"

He took an involuntary step backwards, but then smiled as he shook his head slowly from side to side. "It's not going to work anymore, Mother. I've grown too powerful for you."

Tatiana stifled her gasp. There had been so much power in that suggestion she was a little weakened from it. How could he have blocked that? When had he become so strong? Where was his magic coming from? It just didn't make sense—he'd never had any powers. This simply wasn't possible.

The heat of her anger boiled within her, but she kept a strong rein on it. She would not allow him to see how he affected her. If she did, he would surely take advantage of it—she knew she would if she were in his place.

No, she would simply have to use something else to convince him to go back. If sheer brute force of magic didn't work, there were other ways to get what she wanted.

Oh yes, he was confident now. But what about when she mentioned Miss Hayden? He didn't seem to be quite so sure of himself.

"Very well, Morgan. If you will not go back, then stay. Enjoy yourself and your new—found freedom." She eyed the parlor, it's shabby gentility and sneered, "Enjoy your new home. Enjoy it now, for you *will* be spending the rest of your life at Vallentyn. After Miss Hayden marries your brother, there will be nothing else for you here, will there?"

"She won't be marrying him," he said, trying to put on a good show of bravado. But she could sense his uncertainty.

Tatiana could see right through him. He was scared she was right. "Oh no? Do you think she'll marry you instead?"

Tatiana gave a little laugh and congratulated herself on finding his weak point.

Morgan remained silent.

"My dear boy, Miss Hayden is too intelligent for that. She knows marrying Vallentyn is in her best interests. She will do as she is told."

"Only because you have put the suggestion into her mind."

"I? Oh no, I assure you, I have done no such thing," Tatiana said in all honesty.

Morgan could sense this, she could tell. He frowned at her.

"No," Tatiana continued, "Miss Hayden is marrying Jonathan because she knows just what she will get from marriage to him. Does she really know you, Morgan? Trust you? Does she know what marriage with you will be like? Do *you* even know what you'll be doing for the rest of your life? How do you expect Miss Hayden to give up a certainty like the Viscount Vallentyn—a title, wealth and a position in society— to be with you, Morgan?"

Worry lines creased her son's forehead. His shoulders slumped a little and his eyes dropped to the floor.

Tatiana kept the smile of triumph from her face. There was always more than one way to win a war—and she always won.

She walked to the door. "Enjoy your time here in London, Morgan. I will see you back at Vallentyn."

With her parting shot, Morgan's eyes met hers once more, and then she turned and walked out the door. She had given him enough to think about, and she had no fear that her words would come true, very soon.

Adriana fiddled with the tassel of the pillow next to her. It was a beautiful pillow, covered in dusty rose silk perfectly matching the striped chair on which she sat and the others surrounding the rose marble fireplace.

She hated what she was about to do, but it simply had to be done. She had no choice.

Lord Vallentyn was seated across from her in the lovely drawing room of Vallentyn House. His face was that of an innocent man, and indeed, he was. It was Adriana who was guilty.

She looked around her once again and wondered if Lady Vallentyn had decorated the room herself. Somehow she just couldn't see that woman in a shop picking out such pretty fabrics.

"I am so sorry, my lord."

"Sorry about what, Miss Hayden?" Lord Vallentyn gave her a little smile. She guessed it was supposed to be reassuring, but it wasn't. "If this is about your disappearance the other night from Lady Collingswood's soiree, I completely understand. Your companion explained to me that you've been excessively tired of late. All the planning and preparations for our wedding, I suppose?"

"I have been doing quite a bit of planning for our wedding, but I'm afraid it has been for nothing." Adriana took a deep breath and continued, "I'm afraid I cannot marry you after all, my lord. I am terribly sorry."

Lord Vallentyn lost his easy smile. Scowling heavily, he looked, well, almost frightening. "That is impossible. It is unacceptable. No. I am sorry, Miss Hayden. You promised to marry me, and you will."

"No. I cannot." The tassel popped off the pillow, its fragile string toyed with beyond endurance.

Lord Vallentyn sat forward in his chair, now beginning to look a little scared himself. "You must. My mother is expecting us to marry. She has planned out my future, and you are the key to it. She will accept nothing less."

Adriana shook her head. "I honestly do not wish to make Lady Vallentyn any angrier with me than she is already, but I simply cannot marry you. Not with what I have learned about her and... and your family."

Lord Vallentyn's pale blue eyes widened. "What have you learned?" he asked in a hollow voice.

Adriana took a few deep breaths and remembered that Morgan had told her that his brother had very few powers of his own. She lowered her voice just in case there were any servants lingering in the hall. "I know you are Vallen, and that your mother is too, and very powerful."

"But you are..."

"No, my lord. I have seen her powers, I have seen what she is capable of doing and I will not, I cannot, subject myself to living under the same roof as her or putting myself under her power. I will not do it."

Lord Vallentyn sat back once again, his mouth and eyes drooping with defeat. Slowly he nodded his head. "You are very wise, Miss Hayden. Either that or very stupid. I'm not entirely sure which one. It is wise of you to not want to put yourself into this position—as you say, under my mother's power. On the other hand, I don't want to see what she will do when she learns that you are refusing to marry me." He shook his head slowly. "Oh, no. I don't believe I even want to be in the city when she finds this out."

A chill ran up Adriana's spine. She wasn't sure she wanted to be here either. Perhaps she could... but no, there was nowhere for her to go.

"You aren't actually leaving the city?" she asked.

He gave a little laugh. "Actually, I will be next week. I have plans to visit my estate in Wiltshire, why?"

"Oh, no reason," Adriana said, thinking hard. This was how she was going to be able to get Morgan to a society function! If Lord Vallentyn would be away for Lady Cowper's ball next week, then perhaps Morgan could attend with her. She just needed to write a note to Lady Cowper—and hope their friendship was strong enough that she could impose on her in this way.

Lord Vallentyn broke Adriana out of her thought when he stood up, "Well, Miss Hayden, I beg you to think about our marriage some more. You must not make this decision in haste."

Adriana, too, stood and looked around one more time. How nice it was to be surrounded by such elegant beauty. She gave a sigh. "I assure you, my lord, I have thought about it. I am terribly sorry, but my answer will not change."

He took her hands, returning her sad smile. "No, I have confidence in you. I know you will do the right thing—the intelligent thing—and marry me." Giving her hands one last squeeze, he said, "We will be very happy together. And don't worry about Mother. As long as you do as she says, she can be very pleasant, even kind."

Morgan clasped his hands together in a desperate attempt to keep himself from fiddling with his neck cloth. Nestor had tied it just so, and not five minutes later was scolding Morgan for having touched it and ruined the effect he had managed to attain with the starched cloth. Now all Morgan wanted to do was run his finger around the inside of the tight linen binding his throat, but he did not dare.

He envied the ladies with their low–cut, flowing dresses. They did not have to squeeze themselves into tight fitting coats and pantaloons, and then nearly choke themselves to death with a piece of starched linen. He wished Nestor had not been able to obtain for him such perfectly fitting clothes.

Adriana looked so relaxed, walking next to him with her fingertips resting gently on his arm. She was looking even more beautiful than she had when he had seen her at the soiree, and he hadn't thought that anyone could look prettier than that. But somehow, she managed it. Perhaps it was the color of her dress, which managed to bring out the red in her hair, the green of her eyes, and set off the pink blush of her cheeks. Or perhaps it was the gentle swells of flesh that her décolletage managed to just not hide from view, and which Morgan yearned to reach out and touch—with his lips and tongue.

They entered the main salon where most of the guests wandered about chatting here and there, greeting people, and sipping from glasses of wine and lemonade. Morgan nearly stopped in mid–stride. "My God, there are so many people!"

Adriana gave a nervous little laugh. "Welcome to the beau monde," she said quietly, so that only he could hear. A shiver went down his spine at the intimacy of her voice, but instead of reveling in it, he had to steel himself for the onslaught of humanity.

At least a hundred people crowded into the large room, and there were probably many more in the other rooms about the house. All of the ladies' dresses were as low, or lower cut, than Adriana's, with glittering jewels gently resting on their pale white skin and dangling from their ears. Many of the gentlemen looked to be wearing clothes even tighter than Morgan's. He marveled at how they moved with ease, without the slightest hint their clothes were in the least bit restricting.

Adriana pulled Morgan's attention to the man and woman who were standing just inside the door.

"Lady Cowper, how wonderful to see you again," Adriana said, curtseying. "My lord," she added to the gentleman.

The lovely raven–haired woman greeted Adriana warmly, "Miss Hayden, how wonderful it is to see you getting out, finally. I have been telling Lord Devaux for the past two years that he must insist you attend *ton* functions."

"Thank you, ma'am." She indicated Morgan next to her and said, "May I introduce Mr. Morgan Vallentyn, to whom you were so kind as to extend an invitation?" Turning to him, she said, "This is Lord and Lady Cowper, Mr. Vallentyn."

Morgan quickly placed a grateful smile on his face. "It is an honor, ma'am, sir. And thank you so very much for the invitation."

"Not at all. When Adriana told me you were in town, I was very happy to send an invitation. I know so many members of your family, you are most welcome, Mr. Vallentyn."

"Thank you," Morgan bowed again before leading Adriana off, and allowing the couple behind them a chance to speak with their hosts.

"That was well done," Adriana said quietly.

Morgan gave a little shrug. He noticed quite a few people were looking their way. He supposed it was Adriana they were looking at—she looked so lovely tonight.

"Do you see anyone who might... you know," Adriana whispered, leaning closer on his arm.

Morgan looked around, and then shook his head. "I don't know how I'm ever going to find someone among all of these people."

"How will you know if they are the right person?"

"My friend, Mr. Nestor told me of a stout gentleman with a rolling voice who led a coven meeting he attended not too long ago. Nestor was certain that the man was both a member of the aristocracy and a powerful Vallen. He thought the gentleman was very knowledgeable and would, most probably, be able to help me."

Adriana looked up at him with a gleam of hope in her eyes. "But that is wonderful. What is his name?"

"He didn't know."

"Oh." Her face fell and she knitted her brows in thought. "Stout with a rolling voice. My goodness, that could be anyone of—oh, of a hundred men."

"Yes. Well, at least it is something to start with," Morgan said, trying to look on the bright side of things, even as he looked around the room once again. He had noticed on his first glance around that there were, indeed, quite a few stout gentlemen who could fit the description Nestor had given him.

Adriana took a deep breath. "Well, I suppose you will just have to meet every gentlemen of that description."

"Me?" Morgan said, his voice suddenly a bit hoarse. He cleared his throat and tried again. "You mean us, don't you?"

Adriana shook her head. "No, I'm afraid I mean you. I cannot simply walk up to a strange gentleman and introduce myself. It's not done. However, you can because you are a man."

Morgan thought about this for a moment. "Society's rules are very restricting for women."

"Yes, they are. And I would be more than happy to be able to turn my back on it all and disappear into some village to spend the rest of my life painting. Unfortunately, I can't do that," she said with a heavy sigh.

"Why not?"

Adriana smiled up at him a little sadly. "Well, first of all, I am not a woman of independent means—I don't have the money."

Morgan did not get a chance to respond, for a handsome blond gentleman strolled up to them just at that moment.

"Good evening, Miss Hayden," he said, bowing to Adriana.

"Oh, good evening, my lord. How nice to see you this evening. May I present Mr. Morgan Vallentyn? Mr. Vallentyn, this is Lord Freeston who has worked with Lord Devaux in Parliament for many years."

Morgan bowed. This must be one of the men Adriana had told him about when they had been together in the forest. Morgan worked hard to keep his smile small and innocent— was this one of the pompous men who thought the country would fall to ruin without them, or one of those who belittled her with his comments, he wondered.

Lord Freeston then said, "I am surprised to see you here, Miss Hayden. It is so rare we are graced with your presence at a *ton* party. Is Lord Devaux here this evening?"

Adriana gave a little laugh. "You mean you *never* see me at *ton* parties. No, Lord Devaux could not make it this evening. You know how little he likes these sorts of things."

"I have heard the same of you, and yet here you are," Lord Freeston said, with a small smile playing on his lips.

"Indeed." She gave a little shrug of her shoulders as if to say she couldn't help but be there.

The gentleman laughed, but before he could say anything more Adriana asked, "Perhaps you can help us, my lord?"

"Of course, Miss Hayden. For you, I would do nearly anything," he said, giving her a warm smile.

Morgan bristled, but held his tongue firmly between his teeth.

"Mr. Vallentyn was particularly desirous of meeting a gentleman who made a very favorable impression on him the other day when he was out riding. I promised I would help him find the gentleman in question, but now I find I may not be able to live up to my word."

"Oh?" Lord Freeston turned to look at Morgan.

"Er, yes. I was out riding the other day and a rather stout gentleman with a wonderful rolling voice, er," Morgan thought quickly—something admirable... "The gentleman saved my dog from getting hit in the street." Morgan ignored the tickle of sweat that was making its way down his back. He just wasn't good at lying, and yet, he'd needed to do so disturbingly often since he'd come to London. "I wanted to thank him, but he drove off before I could do so. Adr... er, Miss Hayden suggested I might find the gentleman here, this evening."

Adriana nodded approvingly, and then turned to Lord Freeston and gave him a most beguiling smile. "Do you think you might be able to introduce Mr. Vallentyn to a few gentlemen who fit that description? He so desperately wants to thank the kind gentleman."

Lord Freeston gave Adriana a look that made Morgan's blood boil. He bit down harder on his tongue. Taking her hand, Lord Freeston placed a kiss on the back of it, and then continued to hold it in a most intimate way while he said, "Miss Hayden, for you, I would be happy to be of service to Mr. Vallentyn."

And then Adriana did something that made Morgan feel he was about to explode with fury—she giggled! And not only that, she batted her eyelashes at the damned popinjay!

"That is so good of you, my lord. Thank you."

Morgan tasted blood in his mouth.

Reluctantly letting go of Adriana's hand, the fool then turned to Morgan and asked, "What does the gentleman look like?"

Morgan unclenched his jaw and said in clipped tones, "I'm not entirely certain, since I only got a glimpse of him. But I know that he is quite stout and has dark hair."

Lord Freeston frowned. "Well, that is not very helpful. There are quite a number of large dark–haired gentlemen present here this evening."

"Yes, I know."

"Well, perhaps you could introduce Mr. Vallentyn to a few of them, my lord? And maybe one would remember the incident."

Lord Freeston shrugged. "Yes, all right, very well." He moved off toward the closest stout gentleman present.

Adriana hung back a bit with Morgan and whispered, "How are you going to tell?"

"I don't know. The only other Vallen I know recognized me by my name, so perhaps this person will too." Morgan wished he could call Adriana to task for giggling and batting her eyelashes at Freeston, but before he could say anything she stepped ahead of him and walked up to a large man with whom Freeston was speaking.

Five gentlemen later, they were no closer to finding the Vallen. None of the men reacted in any way to the Vallentyn name, and short of asking them straight out, Morgan really had no idea how to tell if someone was a Vallen or not. His positive attitude was fading fast. If they didn't meet someone soon, he was nearly ready to give up this idea and try something else.

And he was becoming extremely self–conscious. Every time he looked around, someone—or at times, quite a few people at once—were staring at him. He wondered if he had inadvertently untied his neck cloth or was committing some sort of faux pas.

They were speaking with a Lord Merseywell, a portly gentleman with a very high squeaky voice—definitely not rolling at all—when Morgan had a horrible creeping sensation slowly walk up his spine.

Chapter 23

Morgan knew that sensation too well. He spun around and found his oldest sister, Mary, staring at him malevolently from across the room. She was standing next to two more of his sisters, Elizabeth and Caroline, although Caroline was turned and looking in another direction. They blended in so well with the other party–goers, he almost hadn't seen them. This was definitely their element, he thought with a little inward laugh.

"I am terribly sorry, I see someone I must speak with," Morgan said, cutting the man off from telling a long and involved tale of how he once saved a goat from being run over by a curricle in the middle of Hyde Park. "Please excuse me."

He couldn't remember the last time he'd seen his sisters— it had to be two years at least. Yes, it must have been that. It was two years ago that Caroline, the youngest of his five sisters was married. He had watched the wedding through the chapel window since his mother hadn't allowed him to attend. At least she'd allowed him out of the forest for the day. It was the last time he'd been out of the Vallentyn forest—until only a week ago.

"What are *you* doing here?" Mary hissed, after he had bowed formally to the three of them.

"Does Mama know you are in London?" Elizabeth asked with enough venom in her voice to kill a horse.

"Oh, Morgan, what a surprise!" Caroline said, vacantly. Morgan stifled a laugh—his sisters never changed!

"Morgan?" Adriana had joined them, and was now looking curiously at him. He gave her an apologetic smile.

"Miss Adriana Hayden, may I present three of my sisters, Mary, Lady Broughtworth; Elizabeth, Lady Fenton; and Caroline, the Duchess of Stirling."

Adriana curtsied, her eyes wide with curiosity. "How do you do?"

His sisters each nodded to her in turn, and then turned back to him for some explanation. Morgan took a deep breath. "Yes, our mother is aware I'm here in London," he said to Elizabeth. "But I do not believe I need to account to you for my whereabouts," he directed to Mary. It was a shame that Mary tried to be an exact replica of their mother—especially when she didn't have the power to back up the arrogance.

"But I thought you couldn't leave Vallentyn," Caroline said airily.

He gave her a little smile, Caro had always been his favorite sister. "I managed to break through Mother's curse."

Mary and Elizabeth gave Adriana a look, but she looked more concerned than shocked at the mention of the curse.

"Really?" Caroline replied, not noticing what her sisters were doing right away, and giving him a little smile of encouragement.

Mary shrugged, and turned her scowl back to Morgan. Elizabeth too, clearly decided to ignore Adriana, and narrowed her eyes as she turned back toward him. Noticing her sister's expressions, Caroline quickly adopted an angry, disbelieving stance as well. Morgan had to stifle another laugh.

"I don't believe you. You are not strong enough!" Elizabeth said, with a lift of her chin.

"Believe what you will," Morgan shrugged.

"It was Kat wasn't it? That little traitor..." Mary hissed.

Morgan turned on her. "Kat had nothing to do with it."

"She is always taking your side, and sticking her nose in where it doesn't belong," Mary said through clenched teeth. "She had no right to live with us at all. I cannot see why Mother took her in the way she did."

Morgan gave a little laugh. "You know very well why she did so. If any of you had shown the least inclination you might be harboring magical powers... but none of you did." Morgan knew that Kat's special place in the family's birth order had to do with it as well, but he just wanted to goad his sisters. After a lifetime of dealing with their teasing of him, it was nice to have an opportunity to do a little teasing of his own.

"I have powers!" Mary said, indignantly.

"As do I," Elizabeth added. "I'm more powerful than..."

"Not more powerful than Kat," Morgan reminded her.

There was nothing she could say to that, for they all knew it was the truth.

"So it was she who let you out of the forest. Does Mother know?" Mary asked, crossing her arms and giving Morgan a mean little smile.

He looked at her in silent contempt for a moment. "No. I told you. I broke through Mother's curse on my own."

"But you are the least powerful of any of us. You couldn't have," Elizabeth sneered.

"Morgan's powers are growing," Adriana said with open honesty. Morgan was warmed by her tone, which, of course, held not a drop of anger or bitterness with which his two oldest sisters imbued everything they said.

The three women turned to look at her. Elizabeth pursed her lips together before turning them up into a sneer. "And what would you know of it?"

Adriana gave a little shrug. "Not much, only that he was able to protect both himself and me from his mother the other night." She gave a little shudder.

"You didn't!" Mary hissed, her pale blue eyes going wide with shock and disbelief.

Morgan had not wanted to tell his sisters so much, but now that it was out, there was nothing he could do but to confirm what Adriana said. He nodded.

"Where did you get the power, Morgan?" Caroline asked, innocently.

He gave her a little smile. Her vacantly pretty face looked up at him so innocently that he couldn't help but tell her the truth. "I don't know. I've just suddenly been able to do things I couldn't do before. I am trying to find out how and why this is happening, but so far I haven't had any luck."

"Just like that, your powers have increased," Mary asked, folding her arms across her narrow chest.

"Yes."

Elizabeth narrowed her eyes at him. He could tell that she was fighting the urge to copy Mary's stance. Her arms twitched, but she held them firmly at her sides. "I don't believe you. That can't happen."

"You must have done something," Mary added.

"No. I assure you..."

"Tell me what you did, Morgan, or I'll..."

"What? What are you going to do, Mary? Tell Mother? She already knows. And you aren't powerful enough to do anything to me, I assure you."

Mary flushed bright red. "Just you wait, Morgan Vallentyn, I *will* have my revenge on both you and that usurper, Kat! I'll find out how you increased your powers and when I do, you will both be very sorry. I will become the most powerful..."

"Keep your voice down!" Elizabeth whispered fiercely to her sister, who clearly had completely forgotten that they were standing in the middle of a public party.

"Mary, you will do nothing of the sort, and you know it," Morgan said softly, willing his sister to calm herself.

Mary silently raged at him, but slowly she did calm down.

Morgan gave a nod of approval. "I do hope you enjoy the rest of your evening." He then turned and, taking Adriana's elbow, led her away.

He needed a break. He felt like a cat with its fur ruffled the wrong way. He just wanted to shake the image of his three sisters out of his mind.

But Adriana wasn't going to let him. "So those are three of your sisters" she said, thoughtfully as they walked away.

"I actually have five."

"Yes, Kat told me that once. Well, she told me Lord Vallentyn had five sisters, but as you are his brother, I assumed the same of you. Do you have more brothers?"

Morgan sighed. "No, there are just the seven of us. I am the youngest," he said, anticipating her next question.

"I'm surprised you weren't doted upon."

Morgan had to laugh at that. "Quite the opposite."

"Yes, I could see that," she said quietly.

They found the dining room where refreshments were laid out for guests to help themselves.

"Having been an only child, I always envied children who came from large families," she said, helping herself to some sort of savory cakes. "But now that I've seen you with your sisters, I almost wonder if I didn't have an easier time without any siblings."

Morgan laughed, and helped himself to some food as well. "I did my best to avoid my brother and sisters when I was growing up, so in a way I was an only child as well."

"How could you not meet them? Did you grow up living in your little cottage in the woods?"

"No, but I had my own room which was apart from the rest of the family's rooms. I didn't move out of the abbey until I was sixteen."

"Why did you move out?" Adriana asked, picking up a glass of lemonade, and moving toward a table in order to sit down.

"My mother insisted upon it," Morgan said, following her. "It was more comfortable for everyone once I was living in the woods." He deliberately did not mention the unpleasant incident with his mother and second youngest sister, Susan, which led to his being banished from the abbey.

A rather stout gentleman with a booming voice sat down at the table next to where they were seated. Immediately,

Morgan's attention was caught. Could this be his Vallen? He certainly had what could be classified as a rolling voice.

Morgan looked at Adriana, who was also looking at the gentleman—in fact, he was so loud that he had caught the attention of many of the other guests in the room.

"Excuse me for a moment," Morgan said. Adriana nodded and gave him a hopeful smile.

Morgan's excitement level rose as he approached this gentleman. For the first time all evening, he thought he might actually have a hope of finding out where his powers came from, and where his destiny might lie. Surely, this must be the man he'd been looking for. He was a large man, with an equally large voice who moved and spoke with great self–assurance as if he were someone very important.

"I beg your pardon," Morgan said, as he approached the other table. The man had just taken a large bite of his fish cake, but he looked up enquiringly at Morgan.

"My name is Vallentyn, Morgan Vallentyn," Morgan said with great meaning.

The man looked at him blankly.

"Have you, possibly, heard of my family?" Morgan asked a little hesitantly.

The man finished swallowing, wiped the corners of his mouth delicately with a napkin, and then shook his head, sending his many chins wobbling. "No. Should I?"

"Er, I had hoped that you would. You see, I am looking for a gentleman who matches your description."

"Oh?"

"Yes. He was seen at a meeting a few weeks ago near London Fields."

The man shook his head again. "Haven't been to any meetings out there." He then leaned closer to Morgan who bent down to hear what he said. "Wasn't a secret sort of meeting, was it?" the man whispered.

"Yes!" Morgan whispered back, becoming very excited. Maybe this was his man, after all.

"Lots of young females? Virgins? I've heard of those meetings. Didn't know they held 'em out in the fields though. Somehow thought they were in basements and cellars and such." The man whispered to him, giggling a little.

Morgan feeling his stomach begin to churn a little, sighed and straightened up. "No, I'm sorry, it wasn't that sort of meeting."

"Oh." The gentleman was clearly very disappointed. He too straightened up in his seat, and turned his attention back to his food, Morgan clearly forgotten.

"Thank you for your time," Morgan said, giving him a slight bow and turning to leave. The man grunted in response, but didn't look up from his plate.

Morgan went back and sat down opposite Adriana once more.

"Not the right gentleman?" she asked.

Morgan just shook his head. He was too crestfallen to say anything just at the moment. For a minute there, he thought he had found his man. For a minute, he had allowed his hopes to soar, but now...

"I don't think I'm ever going to find him, Adriana. I'm sorry," Morgan said, rolling the bottom edge of his glass around on the table.

"Oh, no, Morgan. You can't give up. You *will* meet him. There are many more stout gentlemen here who you haven't met yet, and probably many more in society who may not even be here this evening. I'm certain you will find him."

Morgan gave Adriana a little smile. He appreciated her kind words, but no longer did he actually believe them to be true. With a sigh he pushed himself up from the table. "Please excuse me, Adriana, I need a moment."

Chapter 24

Morgan stepped into the darkened room. Although there was an acrid smell of tobacco, there didn't seem to be anyone there.

He went in, but did not close the door all the way behind him, needing the little bit of light provided by the wall sconces in the hall way. Moving toward the fireplace, he pointed at the stack of wood that was laid there. Immediately, a fire burst to life, providing enough light so he could close the door.

He had just turned from doing so when a deep voice came out of the darkness from one of the corners of the room. "Very impressive," it said.

Morgan's blood and body froze. He turned toward the voice. "Who is there?"

The wood floor creaked under a man's weight and there was a shuffling of uneven footsteps. Slowly, into the soft flickering light of the fire, a man appeared. His thin face was startlingly handsome, despite a slightly long nose. His eyes were heavy–lidded, his hair dark and curly. As he approached, he casually removed the cheroot he had been holding between his teeth and blew a cloud of smoke. Morgan recoiled a bit from the smell.

"My name is Byron," the man said. "And you are?"

Morgan had heard of Lord Byron, and had even read some of his poetry, but he had never thought to actually meet the man in person. How exciting to meet a famous poet, he thought as he took a step forward again. "My name is Vallentyn, Morgan Vallentyn."

Lord Byron paused before casually resuming his awkward gait toward the fire. "Well, that explains that, doesn't it?"

Morgan's heart stopped for a moment. "Have you heard of my family?" he asked quickly.

"But, of course. Who hasn't?"

"No one outside of the world of the Vallen," Morgan said, daringly.

The man spun around to face Morgan once again. His face registered shock for a moment and then he threw back his head and laughed a deep, full–bodied laugh. "Indeed, my friend, indeed!"

Morgan breathed a sigh of relief. It was a risk to be so bold and direct when speaking of Vallen. He wasn't quite sure what had made him say such a thing. He just knew he suddenly felt very bold, even adventurous.

At a wave of Lord Byron's hand, a chair slid across the floor toward him. Casually, he sat down again and crossed his legs. He indicated Morgan should pull up a chair as well.

Morgan did, but could hardly sit still. He was too worked up. He wanted to be up and moving about, doing something—and yet just before he had come into the room, he'd wanted nothing more than to sit quietly by himself and think about how he was going to try to find a powerful Vallen. It didn't seem to make a lot of sense that he should feel so energetic now.

"So you are a Vallentyn. Yet another child of Lady Vallentyn's or a more distant relation?"

"I am the youngest of Lady Vallentyn's children," Morgan stated.

Byron perked up at that. "The youngest? The seventh?"

"Yes. Is there something notable about that?" Morgan asked, leaning forward.

"I don't know, you tell me," Byron replied, looking at Morgan warily. He took a few more pulls at the cheroot in his mouth.

"I know nothing except that my mother has never forgiven me for being male."

Byron nodded slowly. "Yes, that is... awkward. But what of your powers? I see that you can control fire. What else? Are you very powerful like your mother, or are you more like your esteemed brother and sisters?"

Morgan side–stepped his question for the moment, not sure if this was the time or place to try and get his questions answered. "Are you a powerful Vallen?" he asked.

Byron raised one eyebrow. "I suppose it depends on who you ask. Some of my friends believe me to be quite powerful, but I have known others who are much more powerful than I."

"Where does your power lie? What can you do?" Morgan asked, unable to sit still any longer. He stood up and moved to the fire place.

"Let's just say that I inspire others, and help them to reach out for what they want."

"Oh. And you do that with magic?" Morgan asked.

"Yes. And I have some small ability to craft words."

Morgan laughed. "Small ability? Sir, you are a master poet!"

Byron spread his hands out. "I do my best."

"There are so many different types of Vallen," Morgan marveled aloud, "with such varying powers."

"Indeed, as individual as the person who wields them," Byron agreed.

Morgan wondered if he dared to ask Lord Byron to help him in his quest for his powers. Did he have the knowledge to become the mentor he'd been looking for? He hardly hesitated a moment before deciding that it couldn't hurt to ask—why not take the risk? If he didn't ask, he would never learn the answer.

"I have been looking for someone," Morgan began, quelling his need to move. "A powerful Vallen who might know the answers to... to some questions I have regarding magic and the world of the Vallen. And I am looking for a tutor to help me control my powers."

Byron sat back in his chair. "I am not certain I can help you. Why don't you ask your mother? She would surely be much more capable of helping you than I."

Morgan slumped back against the mantel piece. "No. I can't do that."

"Can't?"

"Absolutely cannot," Morgan stated firmly.

Byron nodded slowly, stroking his chin in thought. Even in the quiet of the room, the sounds of the party still going on above them could be heard.

"If I agree to help you—assuming I can—is it possible that Lady Vallentyn may not be happy I have done so? I'd rather not risk the wrath of the high priestess."

Morgan hadn't thought about that. He certainly didn't want to put anyone else in danger—it was bad enough Adriana might be in his mother's sights.

Morgan stood up again. "I swear, no word of your assistance will reach my mother's ears." He was too desperate for help to give up this one possible chance at finding it.

Byron thought about this for a moment, then sat up. "Very well. I will do what I can, but not here, and certainly not tonight." He took a last draw on his cigarillo, and flicked the butt of it into the fire. "Meet me tomorrow, at my home." He stood, and with a wave of his hand, moved the chair back to where it had originally sat. "Three o'clock." He limped from the room, not waiting for Morgan to respond.

Morgan finally felt free to walk about the room as he'd been eager to do for so long. The sensation was not quite as strong now, and was growing less and less by the minute, but it was still there—this recklessness, a restless need to be out and doing something.

He stopped suddenly, realizing what it was. It was Lord Byron. He himself had said that this was his magic—he inspired people to do things. Morgan nearly laughed. He had been caught up in the man's magic and hadn't even realized it!

Well, but just look at the outcome—he was invited to Lord Byron's home, and hopefully would get all the answers he needed.

Adriana stifled a yawn, but it was certain she was not going to get to sleep anytime soon. Morgan's usual calming presence was anything but. He was agitated and excited. He could hardly keep still—his leg was bouncing, and for the fifth time in two minutes he leaned forward and peered out of the carriage window.

"Mr. Vallentyn, is there something wrong?" Henrietta asked.

He stopped moving and turned toward her. "No, not at all, why?"

"It is clear you are anxious about something," Adriana said, laughing at how oblivious he was to his own actions.

"It is? But I'm not." He paused. "I'm not anxious about anything." He looked out of the window again and then, turning back to Adriana, added, "Well, I suppose I am a little anxious, but it's more that I'm excited."

Even Henrietta had to laugh at this disjointed speech. "And what is it you are so excited about?"

Morgan was looking out of the window again. His knee continued to bounce, adding a jiggle to the movement of the carriage.

"What? Oh. Did I not mention? I met Lord Byron."

"Lord Byron?" Henrietta sighed. She had read and reread all of his works aloud to Adriana, quite a few times.

"That is exciting. Have you read his poetry?" Adriana asked. Somehow she just couldn't imagine Morgan being a great fan of the poet's works—or, indeed, of any other. He didn't seem to be the type who read a lot.

"I've read some. Kat gave me one of his books once," Morgan admitted, calming his bouncing knee.

"Isn't it wonderful?" Henrietta sighed once again.

"Well, to be honest, it's not quite what I enjoy, but I'm not a great judge of these things."

"Oh, but his Childe Harold..."

The carriage rolled gently to a stop, and Henrietta was interrupted by the footman opening the door.

Morgan quickly got out first then turned to help the two ladies out of the carriage. Following Adriana up the stairs and into the house, he placed his hand on her arm when she turned to say goodnight.

"Do you think I could have a word with you for a moment... alone?" he asked quietly.

Adriana could not resist the look in his eyes. He seemed to be so eager to speak with her, and he clearly needed to tell her something—he had ever since he had rejoined her at the ball. Henrietta had joined her, though, and he hadn't been able to speak freely.

She gave a little nod, and led him up to her drawing room. When Henrietta followed them, Adriana said, "It's all right, Henrietta. We're only going to have a very brief word, and then Mr. Vallentyn will be leaving."

Henrietta paused, before giving Adriana a very sly little smile and leaving the room. The door was left mostly open for propriety's sake, but Morgan closed it further, leaving it open only a crack.

He took two long strides to reach Adriana's side. Taking her hands in his own he declared in a quiet voice that was no less full of enthusiasm for its volume, "Lord Byron is Vallen! He is a powerful Vallen, and he's agreed to speak with me tomorrow." Morgan was radiating excitement.

All of Adriana's exhaustion evaporated in his fervor. "Morgan, that's wonderful. It's wonderful you managed to find a Vallen to help you. Oh, I am so happy for you!" Adriana gave his hands a squeeze.

"You've got to come with me," he said, leaning toward her, his face alight with happiness.

That stopped her. "What?"

"I need you there. I want you to be with me when I find out about my powers and, hopefully, he'll even know about my destiny. He seems to be a very knowledgeable man."

"I...I don't know."

He took another step closer to her so that their toes were nearly touching. He placed his hand on her cheek, his deep black eyes looking into her own. "Please, Adriana, I need you there. I don't want to go alone."

Adriana's her heart stopped momentarily at the sweet, earnestness of his plea. His eyes sent chills of warmth skimming through her. How could she deny this man? How could she deny him anything when he asked her like that? He didn't try to force her into it by placing a suggestion into her mind. He simply asked, with all of his heart. She could feel it, and it touched her.

Adriana swallowed hard and nodded. "If you need me, I'll be there for you," she said, her voice not working quite right.

The smile that slowly spread across his face was all that she needed to know that she had made the right decision. The kiss that followed just reinforced it, tenfold.

"Thank you, Adriana," Morgan said, gently nuzzling her cheek. His voice, deep and husky, made Adriana's knees weak. She leaned against his strength and was rewarded with sweet little nibbles across her cheek and down her neck. She buried her fingers into his soft black hair. She was so glad he hadn't cut it short as so many men did. Instead, he kept it tied back in a queue from which she could easily free it to splay all over his broad shoulders. She was tempted to do so now.

A sigh escaped from her lips as she moved so she could capture his lips with her own once again. But it must have been a more chaste kiss than he had hoped because as she pulled back he still reached for more.

She smiled and put her finger to his lips. "You should go before Henrietta comes in to check on me," she said softly.

Morgan kissed her finger, but then withdrew, sighing, "I suppose you're right."

"I'll pick you up a little before three," Morgan said, as Adriana showed him to the door.

She gave a brief nod, but her mind was now whirling with panic—how was she going to get out of the house without Lord Devaux's permission, or his knowledge?

Chapter 25

It's Adriana," Tatiana said, sitting forward on the sofa.

"How could it be? How could she be giving Morgan these powers?" Mary asked, her tea cup clattering into its saucer.

"I don't know. But they've got to be coming from her. Nothing else in his life has changed."

"Perhaps there is something or someone else you don't know about?" Mary asked, and then began stuttering, "I...I mean... certainly there isn't...well, you know everything..."

"I know everything that goes on at Vallentyn, do not think for a moment I don't," Tatiana said with dangerous quiet. She had always liked her eldest daughter, but sometimes she spoke without thinking.

"Yes, of course you do, but couldn't there be something..."

"Do not prove yourself the idiot, Mary," Tatiana said, not even bothering to become angry. Her daughter just wasn't worth losing her temper over.

"No, of course not, Mother," Mary said, actually beginning to show some intelligence. "It must be Adriana, then." She paused. "Is she Vallen? Could she be transferring some of her powers...?"

"No." Tatiana rubbed her hand over her eyes. "Mary, please, please try not to be so very stupid?" she said, swallowing the anger that threatened her equilibrium.

Mary set down her tea cup again and folded her hands into her lap. "I am sorry, Mother. I'm just trying to help."

Tatiana sighed, "Yes. I know you are. But until you actually have an intelligent thought in your head, the only way you can help is by being quiet and letting me think."

Tatiana bent her mind once more to the puzzle of her youngest child's newfound powers. There were so many reasons why this was wrong that she was nearly baffled by it.

It had been obvious to her soon after Morgan's birth that there had been a mistake. Somehow, on the same day, her twin sister had had the child destined for Tatiana—a girl, born on the night of the summer solstice, of magnificent powers. Katrina was obviously the one meant to inherit this great destiny. Morgan was just an anomaly. A child that should never have happened.

And yet, here he was developing powers he surely was never meant to have. It was impossible. It was wrong.

Kat hadn't been born the most powerful Vallen, but with Tatiana's guidance she was learning to make the most of what she had. Naturally, she would never be as powerful as Tatiana, but no one could be. No one!

No, it was Kat who was her true daughter. Kat who would care for her as she grew older. Kat who would treat her with respect when she had given over her position to the next generation—to Kat.

Morgan would never do that. And she shouldn't have to rely on him to do so— *he would not inherit this destiny!* A man could not become the high priestess.

She focused on the chalice, which she had brought with her to London. It stood in an ornate nook over the fire place very similar to the one at Vallentyn Abbey. It calmed her just to look at it, and inspired her. It's magical energy filled her. Closing her eyes, she felt it's pulse like a life all its own.

With its energy thrumming through her, she cleared her mind. Morgan had to return to Vallentyn. Adriana was set to marry Jonathan. It was inconceivable that Adriana and Morgan could...

"I need a woman," she said, opening her eyes and turning back to Mary.

"I'm sorry?" Mary asked, lowering the piece of cake she had been about to bite into.

"I need a woman to distract Morgan," Tatiana said, a plan beginning to form in her head. "He is a man after all," she continued. "Any woman would do. But I need him to stay away from Adriana. I told you, she is the key to his powers."

"Oh, yes. But what woman? How?" Mary frowned, clearly trying to think this through. But before Tatiana had time to berate her, she snapped her fingers. "I'll follow him."

"What?" Suddenly, Tatiana was interested. Perhaps the girl did have a brain. She sat back down on the sofa, across from her daughter.

"I'll follow him. See where he goes."

A slow smile grew on Tatiana's face. "Yes, you follow him. There is certain to be a woman wherever it is he goes. Then, you will simply convince her to distract him." She looked sharply at her daughter. "You can do that, can't you?"

Mary looked slightly offended. "Of course I can!"

"Good."

"But what good will be done by distracting him?" Mary asked.

Tatiana closed her eyes and prayed for patience. "With Morgan distracted, Adriana will be married to Vallentyn by special license and packed off to the Abbey. Morgan will follow her, naturally, and then..." Tatiana snapped her fingers, "we have him. He will return to his forest, and the spells I have already put into place will keep him there—forever."

Mary smiled and clapped her hands together in appreciation.

Tatiana gave a small nod of acknowledgment before standing up and giving the bell a sharp tug. "I shall make your job easier."

A maid servant answered the summons.

"Tell Miss Havelock I wish to see her," she said to the maid, and then watched with satisfaction as the young woman practically ran out of the room on her errand.

Tatiana was helping herself to another cup of tea when Kat entered the room.

"My dear, would you care for some tea?" Tatiana asked sweetly.

"No, thank you, Aunt Vallentyn. Good afternoon, Mary."

Mary nodded coldly to her cousin, and then sat back to watch the proceedings.

"Is there something you wished to see me about?" Kat asked, hesitantly coming a little further into the room.

"Yes. Come and sit by me," Tatiana said, patting the sofa next to her.

"I'd just as soon stay here, if you don't mind, ma'am," Kat answered.

"But I do mind," Tatiana said, trying very hard to keep her voice soft and easy.

Kat came forward slowly and sat down at the edge of the sofa. And then she made the mistake of lifting her eyes toward Tatiana for just a moment as she sat down. Immediately, Tatiana had her.

"That's right, Katrina," Tatiana said soothingly. "You are learning, my girl. It makes me so happy when you cooperate."

Kat struggled to tear her eyes away from Tatiana's but there wasn't a chance she would succeed.

Tatiana's eyes held hers firmly as she gently took Katrina's hand. "I need information, Kat," she said lacing her words with magic. "Will you tell me what I need to know?"

Kat struggled to pull her eyes away. Tatiana could feel the girl's magic building as she tried desperately to shield her mind from Tatiana's magical fog–laced words. "Do not resist, my dear. It is quite all right."

Tatiana added more magic to her voice, magic that would weave its way into the girl's mind, making it nimble. "You remember the last time you and I spoke like this, I told you not to resist and to give me whatever information I required. Now calm yourself, Kat, and do as I say."

Her voice had the desired effect, and the girl began to calm rather quickly. Tatiana smiled, exuding calm and tranquility. Out of the corner of her eye she could see Mary relaxing against the cushions of the chair in which she was sitting.

"Tell me, Kat," Tatiana said gently, "have you been to see Morgan recently?" She let her words slide and slither their way into her niece's mind.

Kat gave one last effort to repel Tatiana's magic, but the fight was already lost. Slowly, Kat shook her head. "I haven't seen him for a few days," she said quietly.

Tatiana nodded. "Very well, then. I want you to go and see him tomorrow. I want to know his plans—where he is going and with whom. I want to know what my dearest son is up to." Tatiana gave her niece a soothing smile. "When you find out, you are to come and tell me. Do you understand, Kat?"

"Yes, ma'am," Kat said, in the monotone that came with the befuddlement Tatiana had placed over her mind.

"Very good. Now go and enjoy your rest before this evening's amusement. You shall not remember this exchange, but you will tell me Morgan's plans as soon as you learn them."

Kat's head dropped to her chest for a moment and then she rubbed at her eyes.

"You look very tired, my dear," Tatiana said, gently letting go of Kat's hand. She laced her words with just a touch of magic to set them into her niece's mind. "Why don't you go up to your room and rest for a little while before dinner?"

Kat nodded and slowly made her way from the room.

Mary gave a little giggle. "It is amazing how you do that, Mother!"

Tatiana narrowed her eyes at her daughter. The young woman stopped laughing right away and cleared her throat.

After taking a sip of her luke–warm tea, Tatiana said, "I will pass on the information when I receive it. And then you will play your part, Mary."

The summons to Lord Devaux's study was not a welcome one. She had yet to finish her morning chocolate and had only taken a bite of toast when the maid had come in.

Henrietta gave Adriana a startled look. It was never a good sign when Lord Devaux asked you to his study.

Adriana gave her companion a reassuring smile as she stood up. "I needed to ask him about going out to the modiste's today anyway. I'm glad he called for me," she said with more confidence than she felt.

Henrietta nodded, and then whispered "Good luck" so the maid, who was still in the room, wouldn't hear.

Adriana braced herself for a potentially difficult interview as she knocked before entering the study.

Lord Devaux was sitting at his desk, going over some papers. He didn't pause or look up as she entered, so she was forced to stand in front of his desk until he was ready to speak with her.

It was probably her imagination, but her guardian's study seemed to be harsher today. Every piece of paper on his desk was perfectly squared off, every book on the shelf stood perfectly at attention. There wasn't any touch of comfort or personality to the room at all. Not one painting graced a wall. Over the fireplace was a framed map of Britain denoting the counties—it was the brightest object in the room as each county was outlined in a different color. Everything else—from the books, to the chairs, to the desk was a plain, ordinary brown. It was as if her guardian didn't believe in beauty.

Finally, setting aside the papers, he frowned at her and then steepled his fingers together. "I ran into Lord Vallentyn at my club last evening," he began.

Adriana shivered. This was going to be worse than she had expected.

"Yes, you should pale at that. He told me you didn't wish to marry him—that you were trying to back out of the engagement."

Adriana stayed silent—she truly didn't have anything to say.

"Do you know what would happen if you did that?" Lord Devaux's voice went high with his irritation. "Do you know how society would look upon that?" He paused, waiting for her response.

"I knew what I was doing when I spoke with Lord Vallentyn," Adriana replied, her voice as steady as her nerves were taut.

"Did you? Did you *fully* know what you were doing? Did you think about *all* of the implications of your actions?"

"Yes. I did," Adriana answered. She wasn't certain, but her heart may have stopped. It was that brief moment, that stop in time, just before it burst into a thousand tiny pieces.

Lord Devaux tapped his fingers together. "I see. Then you want me to destroy all of your paintings, do you? You don't ever want to be allowed to paint or sketch..." he left his words hanging.

It exploded. The pain seared its way down into her stomach, and up into her head. Adriana blinked back her tears, but kept her head held high, her back straight despite the urge to double over with pain. "I cannot marry him."

"Cannot or will not?"

"Will not. Cannot," she answered with more bravado than she felt. She would not put herself at Lady Vallentyn's mercy, no matter what. She would rather deal with this—a broken heart, a shattered world.

Lord Devaux threw himself back in his chair. "Why must you persist with this nonsense?" A small, cruel smile flitted across his face. "I will not hesitate to carry out my threat. I will personally burn all of those pictures. And your paints and paintbrushes. You will never lift a pencil again except to make notes as to who to invite to my next political dinner."

Adriana blinked again. She would not allow this man to see her pain. She had tried to prepare herself for this. Naturally, it hadn't worked. Nothing could prepare someone for losing the only thing they had ever lived for. But it was the gleeful menace he used to describe destroying her life that was making it so she couldn't breathe. She wished he didn't have this effect on her. But he had to rub the salt into her wound.

"Now, listen to me well, Adriana. You will do as I say and call Lord Vallentyn here. And you will tell him you've changed your mind," Lord Devaux's voice was now coarse with anger. But Adriana didn't move. She didn't dare breathe.

She managed a small shake of her head. "I cannot."

"Cannot! Cannot!" His fist banged the table to emphasize the words. "You *will* and you will do so immediately!" Lord Devaux was up out of his chair, screaming at her in a way she had never seen before.

Adriana's hands were clasped together so tightly, her fingers beginning to prickle with pins and needles, but she held her ground. "I cannot and I will not, my lord."

"How dare you!" Lord Devaux stopped, took a deep breath and then tried another tack. In a moderately calm voice he asked, "What is this? What has happened to you? You used to be so obedient, Adriana. Suddenly you've begun to assert yourself in a way that is most unbecoming."

"I am sorry, my lord, but you have never before asked me to do anything so repugnant. I have made up my mind. I will arrange your parties and take care of your house, but I will not..."

"That is enough!" he shouted. "You are the most stubborn girl. You always have been."

Adriana stood in silence, staring straight ahead at her guardian.

He took a deep breath.

It *was* enough. In fact, it was more than enough, she thought. She had nothing more to say. Her heart was broken, and she was certain the dam of tears inside of her was about to burst open. But still, she stood.

"If that is all, my lord?" she finally asked.

Lord Devaux looked up at her with a look of fury in his eyes that made Adriana shiver. Only Lady Vallentyn scared her more than her guardian—and that fear was enough to keep herself in check and go through with what she had begun.

"No, that is not all," he said, a terrifying grin growing on his face. "This evening, when I return from Parliament, I will personally burn all of your paintings. One by one, you will watch all of your precious work destroyed until you agree to marry Vallentyn."

Adriana's hands begin to shake. No matter how tightly she held them together. She knew that it wouldn't be long before it spread to other parts of her.

Abruptly, she turned her back on her guardian and walked to the door. As she opened it, she paused and said without turning around, "I will be going out this afternoon, my lord. I have an appointment at the modiste's for a fitting for the last of my new dresses. I think it will be perfect to wear to your next dinner party. Please inform the footman that I may go before you leave for Parliament."

Adriana made it as far as the first landing before she lost control. She didn't know how she managed to stumble all the way up to her studio.

The shaking, the tears, and eventually the headache didn't leave her all morning. She looked through each and every one of her paintings. From the time she was six years old and her parents had died in that horrible fire, she had not thrown away a single one of her drawings and paintings. She marveled over the slightly awkward yet powerful paintings of burnt buildings she had painted when she'd been young, and then at her increasing deftness with the brush and colors as she slowly taught herself to represent the world. And if, perhaps, she lingered a little too long over her most recent work—the painting of Morgan by the stream—who would know? Henrietta came by to check on her only once. Adriana had locked the door so that she wouldn't be disturbed. She was too busy. Too busy mourning her own life.

It was nearly twenty minutes to three, the time that she had arranged to meet Morgan, when she finally stepped outside of her studio. Carefully, she locked the door behind her, and pocketed the only key. Through her sadness, she took perverse pleasure at the thought that at least her guardian would have to break down the door to the studio to get at her creations.

A splash of cold water and a touch of Henrietta's face powder would have to be good enough, she thought eyeing herself in the mirror. There was nothing she could do about her blood–shot eyes, but perhaps if she kept them lowered nobody would notice.

Much to her surprise, Lord Devaux had remembered to tell the footman that she had permission to leave the house that afternoon, so she had no trouble meeting Morgan just outside as they had planned.

Chapter 26

Morgan could sense the power in the room the moment he walked through Byron's door. He had been surprised by Byron's charisma while speaking with him the night before, but what was in this room was so much more potent. There was a sense of being in the presence of greatness, and an irresistible energy that pulled Morgan toward it. He eagerly looked around the room for the source. It was easy to find—leaning casually against the mantle was another gentleman.

Another Vallen, Morgan was sure of it.

Lord Byron came forward to greet them. Out of the corner of his eye, Morgan saw Adriana hanging back, almost as if she were afraid to enter the room.

"Lord Byron, may I present Miss Adriana Hayden," Morgan said, after giving his host a small bow. He could tell by the look on her face that he wasn't the only one affected by the power in the room.

Lord Byron bowed to her. "I am very pleased to meet you, Miss Hayden." He then turned to the other gentleman who was still standing by the fireplace. "I'm sure no introduction is needed, but this is my good friend, Edmund Kean."

Morgan could hear Adriana gasp quietly beside him. He had heard of the famous actor from Kat, but the man baffled him. He was a rather small person, but he gave off the impression of being much larger. Could this be part of his magic? By his size one wouldn't think much of him, but by his bearing it was easy to imagine an entire theatre of people on their feet shouting accolades and praise—as Kat had described to him in one of her meticulous letters that always kept him so well entertained when she was in London.

"It is an honor to meet you," Adriana said quietly, while curtseying to Mr. Kean.

Morgan bowed, then took a moment to take in the room. It looked like an ordinary drawing room. He didn't quite know what he had expected, but he'd thought that a powerful Vallen, and especially one as talented as Lord Byron, would have some outward sign of his impressive abilities. But there was nothing but a well–appointed, if rather masculine, ordinary drawing room. For some reason, he was acutely disappointed.

"Naturally you have seen Kean perform on the stage?" Byron asked, while indicating they should seat themselves.

Morgan put out his hands apologetically. "This is my first visit to London. I'm afraid I haven't had the honor of going to the theatre yet."

Lord Byron nodded and turned to Adriana. She turned a little pink before saying quietly, "My guardian has never allowed me..." her voice faded away as her blush deepened.

Mr. Kean had resumed his pose by the mantle.

"In that case, you must join me one evening. I have a box at the theatre," Lord Byron offered.

"Thank you," Morgan said. "I would enjoy that a great deal. I've heard a great deal about your performance of Macbeth from my cousin." There was an awkward silence for a moment. Adriana didn't say anything, but just stared down at her interlocked fingers.

"I read the play as a boy, and look forward to seeing it enacted. Will the witches be played by Vallen?" Morgan asked, although he was pretty certain what the answer would be.

Mr. Kean burst out laughing. He had a bold, loud laugh, just how Morgan imagined an actor's laugh would be.

"No!" He spread his arms open wide. "Do you really believe we would allow the public to think that witches might be real? No, I say! To do so would be foolhardy." He finished raising one arm and extending one finger up toward the ceiling in another striking pose.

Morgan had felt it as soon as Mr. Kean began speaking—a strong magic interlaced with his words and his motions. What was it that Kean was doing? With hardly a thought, Morgan blocked the magic.

Adriana laughed and shook her head, but then stopped suddenly and gasped. A thrill rolled through Morgan as he saw Adriana recognize the magic the actor had wielded so expertly.

"So there are no other Vallen who are actors?" Morgan asked skeptically, deliberately ignoring the magic still reverberating in the air.

A slow smile spread over Mr. Kean's face. "Ah, I did not say that, did I?"

"No, you simply answered my question."

"And do you not believe me?" Mr. Kean looked sideways at Morgan.

"I do. Although I doubt very much the public would think for a moment that the Vallen on stage were actually magical unless they did something that clearly proved they were."

Mr. Kean seemed to be silently assessing him. He then turned to Byron and bowed slightly. "You were right, my friend, he is a powerful Vallen." Turning back to Morgan he said, "You were able to completely block my mesmer."

Morgan gave a little apologetic smile and a shrug.

"You doubted me?" Byron asked his friend, raising an eyebrow.

"Never again!" Mr. Kean answered firmly.

"But to answer your question, there are other Vallen in the theatre," Mr. Kean went on, turning back to Morgan. "Perhaps you will recognize them when you see them. I shall not tell you who, but we will see if you can discern who they are after you have seen our play."

"But I'm not able to tell who is a Vallen and who isn't. Are you?" Morgan asked.

"At times. But it is just a guess. It is not always correct and certainly not based on any sort of magical ability, I assure you."

"I have heard of Vallen who have that ability, although I, myself, have never met one," Lord Byron said. He turned more fully toward Morgan. Immediately, Morgan was even more aware of the strength of his presence, the energy exuding from him. He shifted to the edge of the sofa as Lord Byron continued, "So you are able to block Kean's enthrall. That is interesting, very interesting. He is quite strong, you know. Although," and here he turned to Mr. Kean, "I don't think you were giving it your all. Try a little harder next time."

Mr. Kean bowed his acquiescence.

"How can you tell who is Vallen?" Adriana asked Mr. Kean, sitting at the edge of her chair. Morgan had never seen her look so demure.

Mr. Kean held out his hands on either side of his body in a large shrug. "They are nearly always prominent people, Miss Hayden. Men and women who are somehow larger than life or who have done fabulous things. Mozart, Wellington, Nelson."

"There's that fellow in America, what was his name? Franklin?" Lord Byron asked.

"Yes, and General Washington I believe must be Vallen as well," Kean agreed.

"Are they mostly men?" Adriana asked.

"Oh no, there are quite a number of very powerful women as well. You don't hear of them so often. Frequently they are the power behind a great man, telling him what to do or making sure what he does is admired or believed. Washington's wife and Abigail Adams probably fall into that category. Very powerful women."

"And, of course, our esteemed leader is always a woman— your mother in this case," Lord Byron said nonchalantly, but looking at Morgan through half–closed eyes to see his reaction.

Morgan froze. He gave a small nod, but pressed his lips together. He didn't know how close Lord Byron or Mr. Kean were to his mother. He thought it best to find out more about them before laying himself open.

"Is the king a Vallen? Or the prince?" Adriana asked, moving the subject away from his mother.

Mr. Kean burst out with his grand laugh once more. "No, Miss Hayden, most definitely not. There are some at court, however, and they guide the king and prince so one might easily be fooled into thinking the royal family is greater than it is."

Lord Byron too laughed at this, although it was just a small shaking of his shoulders. "Our esteemed royal family... well, all I can say is it would be a very different world were they Vallen, I can assure you."

"Well, we wouldn't be hunted, now, would we?" Mr. Kean asked rhetorically.

Morgan nodded at the wisdom of this statement.

"May I ask a rather personal question?" Morgan asked.

Byron raised an eyebrow, but Kean relaxed his back against the mantelpiece, and crossed his arms over his chest, ready for anything.

How close are you to my mother and can I trust you? The words nearly tripped off of Morgan's tongue, and with the feeling of daring that had been coursing through him, it took quite an effort to hold them back. Instead, he consciously tamped down that urge and did his best to close himself off to the magic that seeped from Lord Byron. His mother already knew too much about him. He needed to play his cards close to his chest. If either Byron or Kean reported their meeting back to his mother, he didn't want her finding out what he was seeking. He would have to ask his questions in a round–about way.

"When did you know that you were Vallen and the extent of your powers?" he asked, hoping that one of them would have attained his powers later in life as he was.

"I have always known," Kean replied immediately, much to Morgan's chagrin. "I come from a family of actors, and Vallen."

"And you, my lord?" Morgan asked, looked at the gentleman next to him.

"I've always been able to convince people to do things they otherwise might not have done." He gave a lopsided smile and a little shrug. "I didn't realize it was magic until I was at school and met other Vallen who recognized my powers."

"But you've always had your powers, you just didn't know it?"

"Yes, that's right," Lord Byron nodded.

Morgan worked to control the frustration that was beginning to build up inside of him. Nestor was wrong—even powerful Vallen may not be able to help him.

"You can convince people to do things they don't wish to do?" Adriana asked.

"I can, but I don't—generally. Not unless they truly wish to do whatever it is, but are just too timid or frightened. Then, with just a touch of my magic, their fears disappear and they become less... inhibited."

"Oh..."

Adriana seemed as if she wanted to ask more, but a footman entered the room, carrying a tea tray. He put it on a table and withdrew.

Byron sat up and smiled at Adriana in such a way that made Morgan know why his cousin had gushed in her letter to him after she had met the poet for the first time. He was handsome and charming. Morgan was nearly certain it was part of Byron's magic, but that didn't make Adriana any less susceptible to it. It might have also made Morgan extremely angry if it hadn't been immediately followed up with a twinkling of his eye and the innocent question, "Tea, Miss Hayden?"

"Thank you," Adriana said, turning slightly pink, and stealing a guilty glance over at Morgan.

With a wave of Lord Byron's hand the tea pot rose and tilted itself to pour out the tea into a cup sitting next to it. A lump of sugar then hopped out of the sugar bowl and straight into Adriana's cup. She watched with a smile playing on her beautiful lips as her tea prepared itself and then floated over to rest gently in her outstretched hand.

Parlor tricks, Morgan thought, trying not to laugh.

Byron then did the same for the other cups of tea. He hardly watched the proceedings, only paying attention to it every so often.

"I believe all Vallen can move objects," Byron said, keeping half an eye on the tea pot."Depending on their strength they can move bigger or smaller objects." He paused while a cup passed in front of him on its way to Morgan."What's the biggest object you've moved, Mr. Vallentyn?" he asked casually.

Morgan shrugged as the cup settled into his hand. "I pushed a man who was attacking a friend, but I haven't tried to move anything larger than that," he admitted. He looked down at his tea and swallowed the urge to show off to Adriana just how strong his magic was. This was not a competition— he was here for information.

He fought down his pride when both Lord Byron and Mr. Kean looked very impressed.

"How about you, Mr. Kean?" Morgan asked.

Mr. Kean gave a little chuckle, "Oh, I can only move small objects about, like my Lord Byron here. Most of my power lies in my mesmer."

"I also have the ability to start and put out fires," Byron added. "It comes in handy when things get out of hand, as they have a tendency to do at times. When I was younger..." he paused and looked over at Adriana. "Well, let's just say it took some time for me to learn how to control the strength of my power."

"So you did spend some time learning how to control your powers?" Morgan asked, interested again.

"Oh, yes," Lord Byron said, taking a sip of his tea.

"And how did you learn?"

Lord Byron gave a little shrug. "Trial and error mostly."

"Can you control the elements?" Mr. Kean asked Morgan as he was struggling to control his disappointment at Lord

Byron's answer. He had been hoping he would be able to ask for some guidance in using his own powers, but it seemed as if it was something you were supposed to learn on your own.

"Your mother is especially adept at dramatic entrances, complete with thunder, lightning and wind," Mr. Kean continued, clearly in awe of this ability.

"When have you seen her do this?" Morgan asked, deliberately not answering Mr. Kean's question.

"At coven meetings, naturally," he answered as if this was obvious. "She doesn't preside over them often, but when she does, you know it."

Morgan nodded thoughtfully. "I have never been to a coven meeting. Do you know when the next one will be?"

"They are held once a season. We have yet to have our summer meeting. I imagine it will be some time in July as usual," Byron answered just before taking a sip of his own tea.

"How do you know when and where it will be?" Adriana asked.

"Oh, word gets about," he said with a shrug.

"What other magical powers do you possess?" Kean asked.

Morgan stole a look at Adriana, who gave him an imperceptible nod of encouragement. He supposed if he didn't take a leap of faith and reveal everything to these men, there was no chance they would be able to help him.

Taking a deep breath, he told them his story of his growing powers and the fact that he was trying to learn all he could about them and his destiny.

The men were silent throughout and afterwards.

"Do you think you can help me?" Morgan asked, in case he hadn't made it clear that that was what he was looking for.

"That's quite..."

"I have never in my life heard of someone's powers growing," Mr. Kean said, interrupting Lord Byron.

"Nor have I," Byron asserted. "If that is the case, then why can't others increase their powers through whatever means you have increased yours?"

"That is indeed the question, my friend," Mr. Kean said with growing enthusiasm. "If one could increase the powers he has—not that I would want to do so, of course, I am quite happy with the way that I am," he added quickly, "then who's to say we couldn't all become powerful Vallen with abilities similar to yours—whatever they may be," he added with a slight frown.

Morgan nodded his head slowly, thinking this through. "Then my case must be very special. Different. As you say, otherwise everyone would be trying to increase their powers."

"But that still doesn't answer the question. Even if it is something special to Morgan, where *are* his powers coming from?" Adriana asked, and then turned slightly pink once again as she drew the direct attention of all three men.

Both Lord Byron and Mr. Kean looked blankly back at her. Mr. Kean then raised his arms, saying, "How could we, two humble, ordinary Vallen, know the answer to such a question?"

Morgan's heart sank in his chest and his frustration grew another notch.

"I had hoped that because you are more powerful Vallen, you would know. Or because you are more experienced, that you would have heard of something like this before," Morgan said.

"I am terribly sorry, but we cannot help you."

Morgan tried very hard to keep his mind on the conversation as it turned to the mundane. It wasn't easy. He had sincerely hoped he would come away from this visit with much more information. Although he had learned more about Vallen, he still wasn't close to having his own questions answered.

The clock on the mantelpiece chimed, announcing the hour, and Adriana jumped. Four o'clock! There wasn't much time left!

Her heart lurched. She only had perhaps one more hour before Lord Devaux would slowly start destroying all of her work. She had to get back. She had to spend her last precious hour with her paintings, and perhaps drawing one last sketch before it was forever denied to her.

She put a shaking hand to her mouth and held her breath. She could not afford to lose her composure now.

Morgan stood up and put his hands on her shoulders. "What? What is wrong?"

Adriana shook her head and then took a deep breath to calm herself. "It... it is just that it's so late," she said, working hard to maintain a calm facade. "I am so sorry, I was not paying attention to the time. My guardian..."

"Isn't he at Parliament today?" Morgan asked.

"Yes, but he might be back early... I really should not have stayed away so long." She turned to Lord Byron. "Thank you so much, my lord, for your hospitality. If you wouldn't mind ringing for my maid..."

"What is the hurry? What will happen if you don't return home before your guardian?" Lord Byron asked, also standing up.

Morgan moved to take Adriana's hands into his own. "Calm, Adriana. It will be all right. Whatever it is..."

She wrenched her hands from his grasp. "No. No, it is not all right. I must get back. I don't have much time," she said, her voice starting to break with emotion. She blinked back the tears that came into her eyes as she could feel the pain of her heartbreak begin again. At least now the pain wasn't as intense, but more like a dull ache that was pervading her body and soul.

"My dear Miss Hayden, whatever it is, you know we will assist you in any way possible. I shall see your guardian myself, and tell him you have done nothing wrong," Mr. Kean offered. "You can be sure, he will believe me," he added with a smile.

"Thank you, sir, but it is not that..."

"Then what is it, Adriana?" Morgan asked.

Adriana wrung her hands in indecision for a moment. Should she tell them? There wasn't anything they could do... but Morgan especially looked like he was ready to do anything for her. It made her feel better, stronger, even a little braver at what she was about to face. "It is my work, my paintings."

"You are an artist?" Lord Byron asked.

"An extremely talented one," Morgan answered for her. He then turned back to her. "Why are they in danger? Did you not agree to Vallentyn's suit?"

Adriana nodded at the hopeful look in Morgan's eyes. "I did, at first, but then I went back and told him I couldn't marry him after all. Lord Vallentyn went to Lord Devaux, and asked him to see if he couldn't do anything to change my mind." She hastily wiped away a tear that had slipped from her eye.

Morgan turned to the other two gentlemen and briefly explained the situation. Adriana was grateful, because she wasn't sure she could trust herself to maintain a hold on her emotions if she had to go through the whole explanation herself.

Mr. Kean slowly raised his eyebrows so that by the time Morgan was finished he was looking very startled.

Lord Byron just shook his head sadly, but then said, "Clearly, we cannot allow your artwork to be destroyed."

"But there is nothing that can be done. I will not marry Lord Vallentyn," Adriana said, her voice quiet with emotion.

"There is always something that can be done, Miss Hayden," Lord Byron said, offering her a smile. "And I applaud your tenacity in not allowing yourself to be forced into a distasteful match."

She appreciated his kindness, and was about to say so when he asked, "Where are your paintings now? Are they in your home still?"

"Of course. Lord Devaux said he would burn them one by one in front of me this evening when he returned from Parliament."

"The cad!" Mr. Kean said vehemently.

Lord Byron nodded, but gave Adriana a reassuring smile. "Then I will simply have my footmen go and remove your work from your home," he said, making it sound so simple and obvious a solution.

"Remove them?" Adriana asked. Could he do that?

"Yes. If they aren't there, he can't destroy them, can he?"

"But..."

"Why don't you give them to an art dealer?" Mr. Kean asked.

Lord Byron swung around. "Brilliant idea, Edmund!"

"I know of an excellent art dealer," Lord Byron said, becoming rather animated. "All of the best artists show with him and only the most serious collectors attend his shows."

"If you are speaking of Sir William Agnew, it is no use. He refused to even see me or my work when I applied to him once before. Well," Adriana amended at the surprised look on Lord Byron's face, "it was really his clerk who turned me away. Sir William probably never even learned that I had called."

"I assure you, he will see me when I call," Lord Byron said with the air of a man's assurance.

"But what if he doesn't like them? My guardian calls them emotional hogwash," Adriana argued, trying to hold on to a losing battle.

Lord Byron spread out his hands. "Why don't we let Sir William decide? He is exceptionally knowledgeable when it comes to what will sell."

Adriana didn't have an argument for that. She wasn't entirely sure she liked the idea, but it was certainly better than the alternative, as Lord Byron had pointed out. And wouldn't it be exciting if they did sell?

Chapter 27

So was he able to help?" Cosmina asked as soon as Morgan walked through the parlor door. She, Nestor and Kat were all there, having tea.

"I'm not certain," Morgan answered honestly. He declined the cup offered by his cousin with a casual wave of his hand.

"What did he say?" Nestor asked.

"Edmund Kean was there as well," Morgan said, but before he could go on both Kat and Nestor were exclaiming, "Kean? The actor?" and "Oh, Morgan, how exciting! You met Edmund Kean?"

Morgan stifled a laugh. "Yes, he is very powerful, you know."

"I can imagine!" Nestor agreed with enthusiasm. "I have never seen him myself, but the tales I have heard..."

Cosmina shrugged. "Even I have heard of him. But did he know anything about your powers?"

Morgan tried not to lose his smile, but it was becoming a little forced. "He did not. Nor did Byron. But I did learn some interesting things." He turned to Kat. "Did you know that Wellington was Vallen? And Nelson and Mozart?"

Kat thought about that for a moment and then gave a little shrug. "I didn't know it, but now that you mention it, it makes sense."

Nestor agreed, "Yes, it would make perfect sense. Not surprising at all."

"Nestor, you said that Vallen are always great artists, politicians and scientists," Morgan said.

"Yes, that's right."

"Are they always someone famous? Or someone who does something important like that?"

"Not always. Well, I imagine the most powerful usually become famous because of what they do," he answered, thinking it through. "And then there are those like this, who become infamous." He handed Morgan the newspaper that had been neatly folded on the table next to him.

It was turned to a short article about a robbery.

Lord and Lady Windmere were relieved of their jewels, watch and purse while on their way into London yesterday. No shots were fired, and the couple themselves were completely unharmed, if a bit dazed by the events.

"We aren't quite certain what happened," Lord Windmere admitted to authorities who questioned him about the robbery. "We simply found ourselves handing over all of our most precious possessions to this masked man when he asked for them. I don't believe he even had a weapon."

This is the eighth instance of such an occurrence this month. Authorities believe this to be the work of the notoriously sly criminal, Jack the Lad. Any further information on this nefarious criminal should be directed to Mr. John Cummings, Bow Street.

"But this is terrible!" Morgan said, standing up. "Do you think this Jack the Lad is Vallen?"

Nestor gave a small nod of his head.

"And he's using his powers to rob people of their money? This cannot be allowed! This is wrong. Completely wrong." Morgan began to pace around the room. He wanted to run right out, find this fellow, and stop him. Now. He couldn't let this continue. "Where can I find him?"

"Morgan! Calm down," Kat said, moving over to him. She placed a calming hand on his arm and flowed gentle, calming feelings into him, but Morgan pulled his arm away. He didn't want to be calmed. He wanted to be agitated and upset. This wasn't right.

"No, Kat. Now is not the time to be calm. This Vallen is using his powers to harm people, to take advantage of innocents. Something must be done about this."

"Yes. And I'm certain that it will. Your mother will handle it."

That stopped him. "My mother? My mother is going to face this thief and stop him from using his powers to rob people?"

"Yes," Kat said, leaning into the word. "That is what she does. That's why she is so powerful. It is her job to ensure that Vallen only use their powers for good, to help society, and not for their own personal gain."

"What? My mother?" Morgan didn't believe this. Not for one moment. "My mother is obsessed with using her powers for her own personal gain."

"Oh, Morgan, that is not true," Kat protested.

"She has always taught me that it's important to be powerful," he argued.

"Yes, it is important for her to be powerful because without her power she couldn't stop others from misusing their own."

That made Morgan stop and think. It did make sense. "But then... She has always worked hard to make you powerful. Is it because she wants you to take over her role? Is that my destiny, to ensure that Vallen only use their power for good? Is that why I was supposed to be powerful and why she was upset that I wasn't?"

Kat shrugged. "I don't know. Perhaps."

But it didn't feel right to Morgan. "No, there needs to be more. There is something more that I am destined to do." He walked over to the window. "I definitely think that this Jack the Lad needs to be stopped, and I feel as if I should be the one to stop him, but there must be..." He turned to face the others in the room. "All of these other Vallen—Mozart, Wellington and so on—they all use their powers to better society, and you, Kat, just said that it is my mother's job to see that Vallen only use their powers for that purpose."

"That's right. That's why we have powers," Kat nodded.

"What are you getting at, Morgan?" Cosmina asked.

"I don't know exactly. I feel as if I'm on the edge of something. If I can just reach out and catch hold of it, I'll know what my destiny is." He paused to try to think—to reach out with his mind. "I've always used my own powers to help people and animals. I've always been able to heal."

"And you've always known when someone was in need of your healing powers and have gone to them," Kat added.

"Yes, except when my mother stopped me," Morgan agreed. "I've always felt the desire to help people."

"That sounds perfectly normal to me," Nestor put in. "You are Vallen."

"Yes. But all this time, I've been thinking that I needed to become powerful because it was important to be powerful and for that alone. That's what my mother taught me. But it's not right. I need to be powerful so that I can help people more than just healing them." He turned and faced his friends. "I want to help people."

"This is very good," Cosmina said, nodding her head approvingly.

"But with my increased powers, I no longer know how I can help people. I don't know what I can do, or what I should be doing. When I could only heal, it was easy, that's what I did. But now..."

"It's all intertwined—once we know what you can do, we'll be able to figure out your destiny and once we know your destiny, we'll know if you have all the powers that you need," Kat said.

Morgan shook his head. It was a horribly tangled knot. "Yes. But how do I find out the answers?"

Morgan looked around the room, but no one had an answer for him.

"Maybe Jack the Lad?" Cosmina offered.

Morgan nodded. "Well, I need to find him anyway."

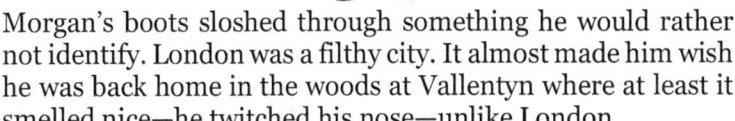

Morgan's boots sloshed through something he would rather not identify. London was a filthy city. It almost made him wish he was back home in the woods at Vallentyn where at least it smelled nice—he twitched his nose—unlike London.

He was grateful for the cover of darkness that hid most of the filth from his sight, if not his nose. On the other hand, it added a level of unease to his walk, especially since he was unfamiliar with this area.

Nestor had called it the Rookeries, and said it was where the poorer elements of society lived—where he was sure to find a thief. Nestor had opened Morgan's eyes to a number of unpleasant aspects of humanity before allowing him to venture here alone—prostitutes, pickpockets and, of course, drunkards.

A hand reached out from a doorway and caught hold of his leg. "Got a ha'penny, govna?" a child's voice reached up to him.

Morgan squatted down next to the filthy child. His heart burned to see one so young like this. "Does your mother know you're out this late?"

"Motha?" the boy asked. "Ain't got one," he added almost proudly.

Morgan closed his eyes for a moment to hide the pity in them. With his eyes closed, he remembered why he was here in this awful place.

"Do you know where I might find Jack the Lad?" Morgan asked. "There'll be a whole penny in it for you if you can lead me to him."

The large blue eyes opened wider and the small bundle of gray rags was gone before Morgan could say another word.

"Wait! Am I to follow...?" Morgan started running after the child, but he disappeared down an alley and was quickly swallowed by the dark.

"'Ere now, whatcher scarin' the child for?" a woman said, poking Morgan in the chest with a bony finger.

He turned to face his accuser. He quickly decided she must be a prostitute. The neckline of her dress was untied and only just barely concealed her small breasts. "I didn't mean to scare him," Morgan said. "I just asked him if he knew where I might find Jack the Lad."

The woman pulled back. "Eh? Ye don't want ta know that. Ye go back on 'ome, back to where ye belong. Ye don't bother with the likes o'Jack."

"But I need to speak with him," Morgan said. "Do you know where I might…"

"No, I don't, nor do I want ta. An' if ye're smart, ye won't either." She then turned her back on him and sauntered away.

Morgan turned and walked in the opposite direction, not entirely sure he was heading the right way. He wandered in and out of streets, asking anyone and everyone he encountered where he might find the notorious criminal. He scared quite a few people and got a number of nervous looks, but no answers.

He also got himself hopelessly lost. He was beginning to miss the quiet, genteel streets near his boarding house.

Nestor had been absolutely right—he could not have brought Adriana here. He wasn't entirely sure he should have come himself. Only his drive for answers buoyed his nerves and set his determination.

A man bumped into Morgan, neither one of them watching where they were going.

"Sorry," the man hiccoughed, reeking of spirits.

"I beg your pardon," Morgan said at the same time and then resisted the urge to cover his nose. He stopped and asked, "Do you know where I might find Jack the Lad?"

The man seemed to lose his balance, but regained it quickly enough. But then, oddly enough, he began to laugh. "Jack the Lad? Ye be wantin' to find Jack the Lad?" He staggered on, laughing as if Morgan had just told him the funniest joke.

Morgan continued on, asking anyone he found, and trying desperately to keep his mind on the task at hand, rather than letting it wander back to Adriana. It was so much more pleasant to think of her than to pay attention to the filth that surrounded him. A chill ran through him at the thought of living in such squalor.

He walked on, down a particularly dark and narrow alleyway, but a creeping sensation made its way under his skin, giving him an abrasive chill.

His boots sounded loudly against the paving of the street, and he noticed it had become oddly quiet. He slowed his walking. And then he heard it. It was no more than a whisper and at first Morgan couldn't make out what it was.

He stopped walking, and tried to peer through the darkness.

"I hear ye're lookin' fer me," the voice said again, deep and slow.

Morgan turned around, but couldn't make out from which direction the voice had come. It bounced off the walls of the buildings that lined the narrow street. Shadows jutted out here and there, but there was no light to speak of, just the waning moon overhead. He could see no one.

"Are you Jack the Lad?" Morgan asked, his voice sounding much too loud amidst the silence. The chill made its way up his spine to sit at the base of his skull as he waited for an answer.

"I might be," the voice said slowly. "Why? What do you want?" The words whispered like death in Morgan's ear.

Morgan shook himself and continued to look around for the source of the voice. "I want to have a word with Jack the Lad. If you are him, I'd appreciate it if you would show yourself."

A step sounded very quietly behind him and Morgan spun around to face a tall thin man with long, pale blond hair pulled back into a queue. His arms hung by his sides, but everything about him told Morgan he was ready for anything. "Here, now, what are ye wantin' with the likes of Jack?"

Morgan eyed the man warily, but somehow a feeling of lethargy stole over him. "I want to speak with him. I think he may have some information I need."

As the man got closer, Morgan could see his eyes were an odd pale brown color, almost gold. They pierced into him as the man said in a soft, almost sing–song voice, "Ye don't want to speak with Jack. Ye don't want anythin' but to get back home to yer comfortable bed."

Morgan took a step back away from the man as he approached. He did just want to go home, he thought, fighting to stifle a yawn. There would be nothing nicer than shucking off his clothes and climbing into his warm, comfortable bed.

"That's right," the deep, voice soothed. "Go on home now. Yer bed is a–callin' to ye."

Morgan took another step backwards. He could almost feel the soft sheets as they caressed him, the soothing softness of the mattress as he sank down...

"No!" Morgan flung his arms out and the man went flying backwards, hitting the wall on the opposite side of the alley.

Morgan's energy began to burn inside of him once more as he strode over to the fellow and picked him up by his coat lapels. "You are Jack the Lad. Now, you are going to give me the answers I want," Morgan said, shaking him violently.

Morgan was furious. He had nearly been caught in the man's mesmer. He couldn't believe he had fallen for that. By God, the fellow was horribly good!

The man threw up his arms, dislodging Morgan's hands and putting him off his balance. He turned and ran.

"Stop!" Morgan called, throwing out his arm and using his magic to enforce it. He'd never stopped something from moving before, it took a great deal of mental and magical strength to do so.

Jack stood frozen for a moment while Morgan ran up, grabbed hold of him and released his magical hold.

"Who in the name of hell are ye?" Jack asked, as Morgan turned him around to face him.

"I am Morgan Vallentyn, and I want answers. You *will* answer my questions," he said, infusing his own voice with magic.

The man pulled his arm free of Morgan's grasp, but didn't attempt to run away again. "Vallentyn? I've heard o'that name."

"My mother is the high priestess of the coven."

"Right. That's right. Never been to one of them meetin's."

"Neither have I," Morgan admitted.

"Whatd'ye want then? I ain't got no answers for ye, whatever it is ye're after."

Morgan's heart began to sink once more, but refused to give up. He'd gone through too much trouble to stop now.

He briefly explained about his growing powers, and then asked, "Have you ever heard of this happening to anyone else? Do you know where my powers might be coming from?"

Jack took a few steps back while he was thinking, and leaned himself against the wall. "Hmmm. That's a tricky one, ain't it? Never heard o'anythin' like that happenin', not that I know a lot of Vallen, mind ye."

He thought for a moment, then said, "I've always thought the power came from within. There must be somethin' changin' within ye. What is it, inside of ye, that's changin'?"

Morgan shook his head, thinking hard. "I don't know."

"Well, when ye figure that one out, then ye'll know where the power's comin' from."

What was changing within him? Morgan stood back and began to think about this. So many things had changed within him recently. It could be his self–confidence, it could be Adriana, it could be his determination not to wait for his destiny to come to him, but to go and seek it out on his own, it could be so many different things.

He looked up suddenly. The calming presence that Jack exuded was gone. Morgan looked down the alley, but it was deserted.

How had he done that? Morgan hadn't even heard him walk away.

He hadn't even gotten a chance to ask him about his destiny, although he had a suspicion the man wouldn't have known anything. And he also didn't warn him to stop using his powers to rob people.

How did his mother do that, he wondered. Did she mesmerize them? Put a suggestion into their minds? Use force? No, he couldn't see her doing that. It had to be done with magic—powerful magic. Magic that Morgan now possessed. Which he now needed to learn how to use.

Chapter 28

For the hundredth time Morgan's eyes slid over the bare wash stand, the dresser, the small window of his bedroom through which the day's feeble muted light shone. He should be happy. He should be feeling light and energetic. He only needed to figure out what it was within him that was changing and then he would know why his powers were increasing. From there, it was just another small step to knowing what his destiny was.

He nearly laughed. What inside him wasn't changing? Never had he experienced so much in his life, never had he known so many people, had so many friends, been so self-confident—and then there was Adriana.

That stopped his train of thought. Adriana. Goodness, she'd been so upset the day before at Lord Byron's. She'd nearly been in tears when she'd told them about her guardian taking away and burning all of her paintings. Morgan couldn't say that he blamed her. He wished there had been something he could have done to help her. Thank goodness, Lord Byron had been able to help.

He wondered if what Lord Byron had proposed had worked, if things were better with her now. Morgan wanted so much for her to be happy. He wanted so much for her to be here, with him.

Well, if she couldn't be here, then he could certainly go to her.

Morgan got himself up and dressed in a flash, and was on his way to Adriana's house within half an hour. But then that damned butler of Devaux's wouldn't let him in. Not at home to callers? He didn't know what that meant, but it didn't sound good. He didn't like that at all.

He was beginning to get a very bad feeling about this. His need to see her grew imperative.

Finding a convenient tree just outside of the back garden wall was perfect. A quick, easy climb and he was over the wall and in the garden. He scanned the windows of the house. Which one was hers? He hoped most fervently it faced the back of the house and not the front. Or maybe she was in the drawing room, it led out into the garden.

He began to approach the back door when Adriana came rushing out of it. "Morgan! What are you doing here?" she said in a loud whisper, as if she was afraid someone within the house could hear her even through the closed doors and windows.

"I had to see you. I had to see that you were all right," he said. As she came nearer, Morgan reached out and took her hands. They were cold.

"No. You shouldn't be here. If anyone sees you, I'll get into trouble."

"Why? That nasty butler of yours said you weren't at home to visitors. I told him that I was certain you would see me, but he still wouldn't let me in."

"I'm not allowed any visitors," she said, blinking a little too fast, as if she were trying to hide tears.

"Didn't Lord Byron get here in time to save your work?" he asked gently, worried of what the answer might be.

Adriana closed her eyes for a moment, and then with a sniff said, "Yes, he did. Lord Devaux was furious when he got home and found all of my work gone before he could destroy it himself. Every pen, pencil and scrap of paper has been removed from the house to ensure that I can't draw. All of my paints and brushes have been disposed of." She stopped abruptly and lowered her head and closed her eyes again. She was trying so hard, so hard not to cry, Morgan could feel it in his own throat. His own anger rose up in her defense.

"That isn't fair. That isn't right," he said, his voice coming out low with anger.

But she, brave thing, just shook her head. "It is only what Lord Devaux said he would do if I refused to marry Vallentyn. I can't fault him for carrying through with his threat. I knew he would."

"But this isn't right, Adriana! You love to paint and draw."

She gave him the saddest little smile—a smile! "It's my life. I feel... I feel as if my right arm has been cut off. The pain... it's almost too much."

In one sweep of his arm, he crushed her against his chest. Fury didn't come close to describing how he felt. This was wrong. How could Lord Devaux do this to her? What sort of man could punish someone in this way?

But Adriana separated herself. "No, Morgan, please."

Never had he seen anyone hurting so much, and trying so hard to be strong. Adriana was an incredible woman.

He wracked his mind for something he could do, something he could say that would help her. Was there nothing with which he could cheer her, at least?

"I have good news," he said, attempting to lighten his voice.

She blinked a few times and looked up, hopefully.

"I have learned that my powers come from something within me, something that has changed. I don't know what it is yet, but I'm trying to figure it out."

Adriana didn't say anything.

"And I've also learned that whatever my destiny is, it involves helping people. I don't know how yet, but I'm determined to find out."

She still said nothing, but the hopeful look in her eyes had faded.

"I'm thinking that perhaps I can find more Vallen, maybe with Lord Byron's help, and question them," he continued.

Her lips began to purse together, as if she was holding something back.

"And you do remember that we are invited to the theatre on Thursday? That's going to be..."

"How can you be so cruel?" she whispered fiercely, finally bursting out with it.

Morgan stopped. "Cruel?"

"Throwing your freedom in my face? Is it not enough that I've had my drawing taken away from me? You have to remind me that I am a prisoner as well? You know that I can't go to the theatre with you. I can't leave this house. I have no freedom to move about as I please. My God, I'm lucky I'm allowed to leave my room at all, and that is only because Lord Devaux still expects me to run his house for him and I can't do that if I'm locked into my room."

Morgan didn't know what to say. He was stunned by her words, but even more so, by her anger. It seemed to be directed at him.

"I don't mean to hurt you, Adriana. I want to help." And then he had a wonderful idea. "I know, I can bring you pencil and paper..."

"No!" She looked away for a moment as if trying to figure out how to speak to this idiot—to him. "If you do that, and I'm discovered with them, Lord Devaux will think Henrietta brought them to me and she'll be sent away. I couldn't do that to her!"

Oh. He hadn't thought of that. "Well, is there nothing...?"

"No. There is nothing that you can do." Adriana's breathing became harder, more labored, as if she had just been walking too quickly. "All that you can do is to go away, Morgan. Take your freedom, and your magic, and get away from me. If it hadn't been for you showing me what you can do—if you had never told me to be careful of your mother, that she might hurt me—I would never have broken off my engagement with Lord Vallentyn. I would be happily living in ignorance. I would, at least, have had some chance at freedom. Now, because of you, I have nothing."

He stood rock still. He wasn't even certain he was breathing or his heart was still beating. She wanted him to leave? She blamed all this on him? But...

"Leave, Morgan," Adriana said, a cold, hard expression in her glaring eyes. "Go away, and never come back!"

He didn't need her. He had Kat, and Cosmina, and Nestor. He certainly didn't need Adriana.

But she had no one, a voice quietly whispered in his ear. And now, she didn't even have her painting.

He could only imagine what she must be going through. No wonder she had lashed out at him. No wonder she was hurt and angry.

But she needn't have hurt him. He'd only wanted to help.

But how could he?

Maybe she was right. Maybe it would be better if he never saw her again.

Morgan leaned his arms on the edge of Lord Byron's theatre box, and tried to pay attention to the play. It wasn't easy. Paying attention to anything hadn't been easy for the past three days. Adriana was all he could think about. The pain inside of her had been intense. He'd never felt anything like that before. And her anger—all of it directed at him, as if it had been he who had taken away her drawing materials, as if he had locked her into that house.

But she shouldn't have treated him the way she had. It wasn't his fault. He had tried to help her, to soothe her, but what had he gotten in response? A slap of angry words.

No, he certainly didn't need that.

Cosmina had said he was better off without someone who would hurt him and who clearly only thought of herself. Nestor had agreed, but only because Adriana couldn't do anything to help with his magic.

He hadn't told Kat. He knew she and Adriana were friends, and although he was sure her loyalties would lie with him, he didn't want to put her into an awkward situation. But

Nestor and Cosmina's reassurances hadn't made him feel any better.

Perhaps nothing would make him feel better—nothing but putting Adriana and her sweet smile behind him. Yes, that's what he would do. He didn't need her, after all.

A gentle slap on his back startled Morgan out of his reverie, and he noticed everyone was standing and applauding. The play must be over. He had dreamed his way through the entire thing.

"Well? Magnificent, isn't he?" Lord Byron was saying.

"Oh, yes. Absolutely," Morgan agreed, just for politeness' sake.

"Had you completely enthralled, I could tell," Lord Byron laughed. "You hardly moved a muscle the entire time."

Morgan gave a noncommittal little shrug of his shoulders and smiled ruefully. He could never admit he hadn't paid the least attention to the play.

"Come, let's meet Kean."

Lord Byron led the way out of the box and down the hallway in the opposite direction from the rest of the crowd. They slipped through a door, and then down a flight of stairs.

The space behind the stage was crowded with actors going here and there, members of the crew carrying pieces of scenery and he didn't know what else.

Lord Byron pulled him away from the hubbub and down a slightly quieter corridor. A knock on a door, and they entered a room that looked very much out of place in a busy theatre. It looked to be more like a comfortable parlor than anything else. Mr. Kean stepped out from behind a screen in the back of the room, partially dressed.

"Ah, Mr. Vallentyn, Byron! Good evening to you! Good evening," Mr. Kean welcomed them warmly, his arms open wide. "Tell me, how did you like our little play?" he clapping his hands together and looking pointedly at Morgan.

"Er, I liked it very much, thank you. Very much, indeed," Morgan lied.

"He didn't move a muscle throughout the entire performance, Edmund," Lord Byron laughed.

Mr. Kean burst into laughter as well. "Good! Good! That's the way I like my audience, paralyzed with rapt attention."

He laughed at his own joke.

A gentle knock on the door interrupted him, and one of the most lovely women Morgan had ever seen walked into the room. She looked a bit shy at first, but stole a glance up at Morgan.

He suddenly felt as if every drop of blood in his body had dried up, but then, just as quickly, it reappeared, churning and rushing through his veins like the stream after a heavy rain.

"Sarah, what a pleasant surprise!" Mr. Kean said warmly to the young woman. "What may I do for you?"

"I'm terribly sorry to interrupt, Mr. Kean," she said in a slow, quiet voice that slid like liquid silver over Morgan's skin. "I couldn't help but notice you had guests this evening," she glanced over at Morgan. "I was wondering if you would honor me with an introduction?"

Mr. Kean raised his eyebrows and gave her a little knowing smile. "I would be happy to." He turned toward Lord Byron saying, "My lord, you have had the pleasure of meeting Miss Jordan, have you not?"

"On many very happy occasions," Lord Byron said with a small bow.

"It is good to see you again, my lord," Miss Jordan said, giving him a little curtsey. She then took a few steps closer to Morgan and the room suddenly seemed to be much too overcrowded for Morgan's taste. "And who is this handsome stranger?" she asked.

"Ah, this is my new friend, Mr. Morgan Vallentyn," Kean said with a sly smile on his face and broad wink to Morgan.

Sarah's eyes widened, showing their deep blue depths, her perfect pink mouth opened to form a perfect O.

"Mr. Vallentyn, Miss Sarah Jordan," Mr. Kean said, finishing the introduction.

Morgan bowed to the woman and she executed a graceful curtsy for him.

She then gave Morgan a most dazzling smile. "Mr. Vallentyn, it is indeed an honor to meet you. I've always wanted to meet a truly powerful Vallen," she said, slowly moving forward so that by the time she finished speaking, she was gently laying her hand on Morgan's chest in the most intimate manner.

Morgan couldn't tear his eyes away from the blond beauty, nor did he think he would ever want to. Oddly enough, he wasn't certain that his mind was working quite the way it normally did. He felt thick and slow—as opposed to another part of his anatomy, which had certainly thickened and was growing harder with each passing moment he was in the presence of this incredibly beautiful woman.

"That, that is very kind of you, Miss, er..."

"Jordan, but please, call me Sarah," she said, her voice becoming just the tiniest bit raspy as if there was a great passion within her she was desperately trying to control.

Morgan nodded. "Sarah. It is a beautiful name. You are Vallen too?" he asked, just beginning to grasp that she knew that he was one.

"Oh, yes. But alas, I am not very powerful at all. I wish I were. I want to be a great actress and have the ability to enthrall my audience the way Mr. Kean does."

"I'm sure if you keep working at it, you'll be able to do very well," Morgan said, encouragingly. He was immediately glad he did, for Sarah, in her pleasure at his words, pressed herself against him and gave him a warm hug.

"Thank you, Mr. Vallentyn. You are so kind to say so—oh!"

This last exclamation, Morgan was certain, came from the fact that she had pressed herself right up against his manhood, which was now straining against the flap of his breeches.

Morgan felt his face burn. "I beg your pardon!" he said, and quickly extracted himself from her embrace.

Her cheeks also turned a pretty shade of pink and her eyes slipped downwards. "That's perfectly all right," she giggled. "I do sometimes have that effect on men."

"Sometimes?" Mr. Kean said, laughing. "Try all the time. You have to be very careful, Mr. Vallentyn. Our Sarah, here, is quite, er..."

"Intoxicating," Lord Byron finished for him.

"Excellent word! Yes, intoxicating." He gave Morgan a knowing smile.

Morgan looked back at Sarah, but she didn't seem to mind the turn in conversation at all—she seemed to revel in it.

"Well, if you'd like to taste some more, Mr. Vallentyn, you need only to come knock on my door. I live just around the corner. It is the house with blue shutters, number 64." She gave him a broad smile and a wink, before gracefully flowing from the room.

"I'm terribly sorry about that, Mr. Vallentyn," Mr. Kean said. "I certainly did not inform Sarah you would be here, nor did I intend for you to meet... well, Miss Hayden is a lovely young lady," he finished weakly, which was very unusual for him. It caught Morgan's attention.

He was still staring at the closed door, but he quickly called himself to order, especially upon hearing Adriana's name. "Er, thank you, but she and I, well, we aren't... It was very nice to meet Miss, er, Sarah."

"Oh? I do apologize, I had thought..."

"No apology necessary. Your assumption would have been correct, except that Adriana informed me a few days ago that she no longer wished to see me," he said, finding it didn't hurt quite as much now as it had even earlier that evening.

"I am terribly sorry," Mr. Kean said, looking concerned.

"Well, I am not going to continue to brood over it," Morgan said forcefully, for himself as much as his new found friends.

"Certainly not," Mr. Kean said.

"Perhaps you should take Sarah up on her offer, in that case. You will not regret it, I assure you," Lord Byron said, with a small smile playing on his lips.

Morgan frowned, wondering just how well Lord Byron knew the young lady. The heat of anger began to build up within him when Kean put a calming hand on his arm.

"Here, now, Mr. Vallentyn, you are still under Sarah's enthrall. Just calm yourself down."

He pulled his eyes away from Lord Byron with some difficulty, and turned towards Mr. Kean. "Sarah's enthrall?"

"Why, yes, didn't you realize? That's how her magic works—she enthralls men. Gets them all riled up, hot and aching for her. I can't tell you how many men have fought duels over the girl. But it is her magic, that is all."

Morgan shook his head. He couldn't believe he hadn't been aware that Sarah had used magic on him. He hadn't sensed it at all. He'd only felt... as Mr. Kean said, all riled up.

"That is why I hadn't intended for you to meet, but now I suppose there was no harm done. And there is certainly nothing wrong with a little, er, riling every so often, now is there?" Mr. Kean said, laughing. "But for now, what say you to a nice dinner and a bottle of wine?" he continued, quickly moving toward finishing dressing.

"Ah, yes," Lord Byron said, "I've just the place in mind."

Chapter 29

Very well done, Mary," Tatiana said, impressed. "I almost despaired of your ability to handle this, but you have done very well, my dear, very well."

Mary frowned, and said in a testy tone, "Of course I was able to handle this. It was not so very difficult after all."

"Oh, no? Tell me all," Tatiana said, settling herself on her sofa.

"Well, I followed him, as we agreed I should," Mary began. "He sat in Lord Byron's box, which is very close to my own, so it was not so easy to see him during the show. But during the intermission and afterwards, I waited for him just outside. He didn't leave the box during the intermission, as some people came to visit with Lord Byron, but after the show, they went backstage, just as you thought they would."

Tatiana handed Mary a cup of tea.

She stirred it quietly for a moment, then continued, "The rest was very easy. I simply found Miss Jordan in her dressing room and gave her your note. She had no problem going into Mr. Kean's dressing room and when she came out she gave me a smile and a wink, so I knew that everything was all set."

"Very good. Very good!" Tatiana helped herself to a cream cake. "No man can resist Sarah. She is a talented Vallen," she laughed.

Mary gave her a little smile. "What is it that Miss Jordan does? What is her power?"

Tatiana smiled at her daughter. "She is a seductress. No man can say no to her, whatever she asks of them."

Mary's eyes grew wide. "That's quite a skill to have."

"It is a very useful one," Tatiana agreed.

Mary sipped at her tea. "So what have you asked her to do to Morgan?"

Tatiana scowled at her thick headed daughter. "I told her to do whatever is necessary to turn his eyes away from Adriana. What did you think, fool?"

Mary flinched at the careless insult that whipped from Tatiana's tongue. Someday, Tatiana prayed, someday she wished just one of her children would show some semblance of intelligence.

"So when will Vallentyn wed? Do you already have everything arranged?" Mary asked, rubbing at her arm.

The remnants of Tatiana's rage began to burn once more. "No," she hissed. "Your brother was unable to convince Adriana to marry him. Even that imbecile Devaux couldn't force the chit to the altar."

She stood up and walked to the fireplace. With a careless wave of her hand, she made a blazing fire appear. "I am surrounded by incompetent men!"

Mary was watching the fire with wide eyes that she then turned to Tatiana. "So what are you going to do? How will you get Morgan back to the forest?"

Tatiana picked up the poker and tapped it against her hand, thinking. "Sarah will use her delicious wiles on our dear boy. There is no way he cannot be entranced by her. So all we need to do..." Tatiana could feel the heat of her anger turn into a warmth of satisfaction, "...is make certain that Adriana is kept informed of her lover's whereabouts. Who he has seen, and exactly what he was doing."

"How will that help?" Mary asked, looking completely baffled.

Tatiana sighed and explained it all in painstaking detail for her daughter, and then wondered how she'd managed to have seven children without one of them inheriting her intelligence.

Mr. Vallentyn! What a very pleasant surprise," Sarah said, moving from the pale pink sofa to greet him.

"Good evening. I hope I'm not disturbing you," he said, suddenly feeling a little shy.

"Oh, no, not at all. In fact, I was hoping you would come," she said, taking his hand, and gently pulling him further into her flower–scented drawing room. It was all very pink and feminine, Morgan thought, feeling overly large and ungainly amidst her delicate furniture. Everything was built on spindly legs that looked as if they might break if he did so much as look at them too hard.

Surprisingly, the sofa took both his and Sarah's weight.

"It was quite thrilling to have met you yesterday evening," Sarah began in her soft, slightly husky voice. "As I said then, I've never met a Vallen as powerful as you. I still can hardly imagine all that magic dwelling inside one person, even such a large, strong, handsome man like you." She ran her fingers up Morgan's arm, sending chills chasing through his body.

He swallowed and tried to control his heart, which was suddenly pounding in his chest. "Well, I, er, I understand you are a seductress," he said, and then cringed with embarrassment.

But Sarah only laughed. "Ah, did Mr. Kean tell you, then? Yes, that is my meager little power." She then sat back to look at him, meeting his eyes with her own eyes. "You don't mind, do you?" she asked, fluttering her thick, black eyelashes at him.

"No," Morgan tried to say, but somehow his voice didn't seem to be working so well. He cleared his throat and tried again. "No, I don't mind at all. It is why... well, I thought..."

"You thought you might like to learn about my powers for yourself? To, shall we say, experience them first hand?"

"Er, yes." A trickle of sweat rolled down Morgan's back. "If you don't mind," he added hastily.

"How could I possibly mind? Even if you weren't so incredibly handsome," she said, looking into his eyes, "and powerfully built. My goodness, look at the size of you," she whispered pushing his coat back, off of his shoulders. "Oh, Mr. Vallentyn, just looking at you, just being with you..." She pulled back as he shrugged out of his coat, and ran her hands suggestively down her bosom, which was spilling out from her very low cut dress. "You give me the tingles."

And indeed, Morgan could see the points of her nipples straining against the material of her dress. Oddly enough, he couldn't seem to pull his eyes away from her breasts. He knew that he shouldn't stare, but something, her magic perhaps, kept him focused right there. His mouth watered at the sight of them—so full and beautiful. He wanted to taste them, and explore them.

"It's all right, Mr. Vallentyn, go ahead," she whispered, pulling her bodice down to reveal her beautiful body.

He did not need to be told twice, but immediately buried his face in between them, caressing them with his hands and his lips. His tongue swirled over and around the luscious tips of rose. But there was an odd taste to her.

He vividly remembered tasting Adriana and thinking there couldn't be a sweeter wine in all the heavens. But Sarah, although soft, and much more round and generously proportioned than Adriana, didn't elicit the same feelings Adriana had.

He closed his eyes, remembering the most wonderful afternoon of his life when he and Adriana had spent that all too brief thunderstorm in his cottage. He groaned with the taste and feel of Adriana in his mind.

He could feel his breeches, which had become unbearably tight, loosen as if they were being unbuttoned. And then he realized that they were. Sarah was smiling at him wickedly as she released his manhood.

She looked down at him for only a moment and then back up into his eyes. "Oh, Mr. Vallentyn, I should have known you would be so big and thick," she purred, stroking him and sending the most delicious sensations through his body. It was all Morgan could do to keep from exploding right then and there.

Sarah slipped down onto her knees in front of him as he sat back on the sofa. With a smile as sweet as an angel's, she gave the tip of him a lick with a quick flick of her tongue, nearly making him scream with delight as she took him into her hot, wet mouth.

Never in his life had he felt such a sensation! My God, he was in ecstasy. He could barely think because of all of the sensations running through his body and the blood which was pounding in his ears as Sarah moved her mouth up and down his shaft. Faster and faster she went, bringing him ever closer to the brink. But even as he teetered at the edge he knew that something wasn't right.

He opened his eyes to see not Adriana's auburn hair, but Sarah's pale yellow tresses.

He couldn't do this. Not to himself, and not to Adriana.

"No!" The word tore at him. It was literally painful, but he pushed her away. "No, this isn't right. You must not." She sat back, looking up at him with an expression of absolute shock on her face.

Morgan stood up and moved away from her, hastily buttoning his breeches and trying desperately to calm himself. He took two long deep breaths and thought of Adriana.

No, thinking of Adriana didn't help. He would think... he would think of Kat and Cosmina. Yes, that helped. Nestor and his mother helped even more. Finally, he was able to finish buttoning his breeches comfortably.

He turned back around to face a quiet and demure woman.

"I'm sorry if you didn't like..." Sarah began quietly.

"Oh, no. I liked what you were doing. I liked it very much. It was amazing, but..." Morgan took another deep breath, "but it wasn't right."

He turned and took a step toward the window that looked out onto the street. The drapes were drawn, but he could hear the rattle of carriages as they rolled past Sarah's house. "I'm terribly sorry. I shouldn't have come. I thought that I'd wanted to... to understand your magic better, but I was wrong."

"I don't understand."

Morgan leaned against the cool window frame. How could he explain to her what he himself didn't understand? "I... there is a young woman."

"Ah, I see."

Morgan turned back toward Sarah. "No, you don't. I want to be with her—with all my soul, I want to be with her to, to share my life and to share in hers..." He expelled his breath and ran his hand through his hair, pulling it out of the neat queue. "But she has told me that she doesn't want to be with me."

"But you love her," Sarah said simply. "You want her. You need her," she said, her voice growing quieter. Morgan could feel the sensation of longing in her voice. "You can't imagine your life without her."

"Yes! Yes, that's it exactly!" Morgan strode over to her as she sat on her pretty pink sofa gazing out at nothing.

"Sometimes you need her so much, it hurts," she whispered.

"Yes," Morgan said quietly, dropping down next to her.

"You want to make love to her and show her just how much she means to you. Your two bodies joining as one," Sarah continued, her voice weaving a beautiful picture in Morgan's mind. "Touching her, tasting her—you want to make her entirely yours, because she is yours to cherish and care for. To love and be with for the rest of your life because you can't possibly imagine your life without her."

"Yes." The word was wrenched from deep within his soul. This was right. This was how he felt about Adriana. He could never imagine not being with her, and he could certainly never, ever be with another.

Morgan dropped his face into his hands, pain slashing through his body as he remembered Adriana's face when he last saw her. Tears burned his eyes, and he could barely breathe. When he managed to regain control over himself, he said, "But she doesn't feel that way. She doesn't want me."

Sarah stroked his back. "I'm certain she does. She would be a fool not to want you."

But Morgan shook his head, but didn't raise it from his hands. "No. She said so."

"Oh, Mr. Vallentyn. I'm sure she was just upset over something. But I assure you, and I know about these things, if you go back to her, she will welcome you with open arms. You simply need to tell her how you feel. You will find that she feels the same way."

Morgan took out his handkerchief and wiped his face with it. "She must. She has to. We were meant to be together. I know it. I feel it."

"Then it is that way. And you will be together."

Chapter 30

Adriana's grip on Lord Byron's arm tightened.

He patted it gently and gave her a reassuring smile before leading her from his carriage toward the gallery for the opening night of the exhibition and sale of her paintings.

The fact that Henrietta followed at a discreet distance behind did nothing for her nerves, which had been on edge all evening.

"No, wait," she said, pulling him to a stop before they began to climb the steps to the door. "I can't do this. I can't go in."

"Of course you can. Don't, please, don't become missish now," he said, sounding a little exasperated.

"No, I'm not, I just..."

"Miss Hayden, you are just nervous, that is all. But truly, everything will be fine."

She pulled her hand away from his arm. "I'm not just nervous, my lord, I'm nauseous." She turned back toward the curb, seriously wondering whether the very little she had managed to eat for dinner wouldn't soon be at her feet.

Henrietta was no help at all. She kept a proper distance, wringing her own hands, and looking as anxious as Adriana felt.

Lord Byron came up next to her. "Just take a few deep breaths, Miss Hayden, and you will be fine," he encouraged her gently, his voice becoming more resonant.

Adriana did as she was told, and indeed, her stomach did settle itself down. She didn't think he'd used his magic, yet, but he seemed ready to do so should she need it.

"Better? Good, now, please, let us remove ourselves from the street. There is nothing more gauche than standing about on the footpath."

Lord Byron had done so much for her that she certainly didn't wish to put him out any more than was absolutely necessary. He had not only taken all of her paintings to the art dealer and had arranged for this exhibition, but he had even somehow convinced her guardian to allow her to attend, as well. If it hadn't been for him, she certainly would not have been here tonight.

She swallowed her fear, bit back her bile, and placed her hand once more on his outstretched arm.

"All right?" he asked gently.

She gave a little nod, not entirely certain she could trust her voice not to give away her fears.

"Very good, then, in we go."

Just as the footman reached for the handle, she shied back one again, "Oh, no, my lord..."

This time Lord Byron turned and looked Adriana in the eye. "Miss Hayden..." he began, his voice becoming even more resonant than before. But Adriana stopped him, holding up a hand. She didn't want him to use his magic. She didn't need it, she told herself firmly.

"It is all right, my lord. You don't need to do that," She said, knowing he would understand full well she was referring to his magical power without having to risk saying so in public.

He stopped and looked at her closely, but with a little smile playing on his lips. "Are you certain?"

Adriana took a deep breath and straightened her back. "Yes." She turned back to the door. With the knowledge that both Lord Byron and Henrietta were with her, she walked into the gallery.

"Well done," Lord Byron said approvingly as he moved next to her.

A short rotund man with large sideburns approached them, laughing jovially. "Lord Byron, my lord!" He reached out and grasped his hand. "So good to see you, my lord!"

"Sir William, how do you do," Lord Byron said, suffering the gentleman's attentions. "May I introduce Miss Adriana Hayden?"

"Ah! Our artist! How wonderful to meet you, Miss Hayden. Delighted, delighted!" he said too loudly for Adriana's comfort, especially as she noticed that the heads of the few people who were present all turned in her direction.

Thank God, Adriana thought with sigh of relief as she took a quick look around the gallery, there was almost no one there. Perhaps no one would come. Perhaps everything would be all right after all. Out of the corner of her eye, she saw Henrietta take a seat in one of the little gilt chairs set off to the side of the room for chaperones.

She still couldn't imagine how she had come to agree to this. She probably never would have, had Lord Byron not used his magic to convince her.

"Thank you for agreeing to hold this exhibition, Sir William," Adriana said, with only the smallest hint of a quiver to her voice.

"Not at all! My pleasure, my pleasure!" he said, laughing, and giving Lord Byron a wink. Adriana wondered what that was about, but forgot about it almost immediately as Sir William led them forward, further into the room.

Her nausea came back in full force when she saw all of her work displayed on the walls. Quite a few of the pieces had been framed, including...

"Oh, no! Oh, my goodness! No, you cannot sell that. Oh, how did that get here?" Adriana was absolutely distraught. She couldn't breathe! She was going to faint or throw up or both.

She put one hand to her chest, attempting to breathe, while putting another to her red hot cheek.

In front of her, framed and sitting on a stand prominently displayed in the center of the room, was her painting of Morgan.

She turned to the gentlemen next to her. "Oh, Lord Byron, please. Sir William, have that removed at once." She looked desperately around the room, and was grateful once again that there were so few people present—and, most importantly, no one she knew.

But it had to, absolutely had to be removed before anyone else saw it!

How could her painting of a naked Morgan standing by the stream be so prominently displayed? If anyone saw it, she would never be able to show her face in public again! Oh, my goodness, and he truly looked as if he was about to turn around and show himself as God had made him!

She walked straight up to the painting and began to pull it down. Where was a cloth to cover it? Perhaps she could hide it under her skirts—but no, it was too big and her dress just did not have that much material to it. She looked frantically about for something, anything with which to cover the offending piece.

"Miss Hayden, stop!" Sir William said, coming over to her and pulling the painting back onto its stand. "You cannot remove this piece!" To reinforce his point, he forcibly placed himself between her and the painting.

Adriana wanted to cry, and indeed had to furiously blink back the tears that had come to her eyes. She looked desperately at Lord Byron. "Please, my lord, you cannot allow him to display this painting."

Adriana came very close to stamping her foot, preferably on Lord Byron's own, as an expression of mild amusement twitched at his lips. "I could hardly believe you had painted such a portrait, but once I saw it, I knew it would be the *piece de resistance*. " He then leaned down and whispered to her, "I'm not entirely certain I want to know how or when you saw Mr. Vallentyn in such a pose, but perhaps you can tell me later." He gave a chuckle and Adriana was certain she was as close to swooning as she had ever come in her life.

She didn't have time for such an indulgence, however, because a large number of people had just entered the gallery. And they were coming straight towards her—and her painting of Morgan! She looked desperately at Lord Byron, but he just gave a small shrug of his shoulders before turning to greet the newcomers.

Adriana stood back and watched them arrive. There was nothing she could do. Well, she supposed there were two things she could do—she could give way to panic, which was a very enticing option, or she could pull herself together, which was what she needed to do.

Adriana closed her eyes for a moment, took a deep breath, and let it out slowly. When she opened her eyes again, she was staring directly at her painting of Morgan. All of the wonderful feelings she had felt when she had painted the portrait in her studio—just days after she had come back from Vallentyn—came flooding back to her. The longing for him, the happiness, and the desire. It was there, captured in her painting.

But there was more, now—more inside of her because she knew Morgan so much better now than she did the day she had painted his portrait. He had become a part of her life since then—an integral part.

Voices intruded on her thoughts.

"It's incredible!" a man said.

"My goodness! How very provocative!" his companion said, giggling.

"It's brilliant, absolutely brilliant."

Adriana was pushed away from the painting by a surge of people all straining to see it. She slowly moved away while listening to the whispers and exclamations from the people now pouring into the gallery.

Standing next to where Henrietta sat, she could hardly believe the number of people who had come to the exhibition within the last few minutes. There had to be at least two hundred people crowded into the room. But as she watched all of the beautiful people of the beau monde—the women in their glittering jewels, the men with their impeccably tied neck cloths, and even her most beloved companion—she had never felt more alone and out of place.

There was a shuffle of displaced people and she could hear Sir William's overly loud voice. "Excuse me. I beg your pardon. Ah, my lord, so good to see you, so good to see you! Yes, excuse me just a moment." And then he was standing in front of her. "Ah! There you are! Miss Hayden, what in the world are you doing hiding over here?" he nearly shouted.

Adriana momentarily felt a panicked need to run and hide, but there was nowhere for her to go. She locked eyes on Henrietta who just looked at her with a broad smile and that twinkle in her eye, while all of the people surrounding her turned and stared. There was no chance for escape.

"Please, ladies and gentlemen, our artist! Here is the talented Miss Hayden!" Sir William said leading her, with a strong hand on her back, towards the center of the room again.

And just like that, she was suddenly surrounded with gentlemen taking her hand and women murmuring their congratulations.

"Brilliant."

"Absolutely amazing!"

"Where have you been hiding?"

"Your work is incredible!"

The compliments washed over her as she slowly made her way through the crowd.

With tears of wonder and joy, Adriana looked over at her portrait of Morgan and wished with all of her heart he was here to share this moment with her.

She was empty without him.

Tatiana sat and watched her niece sleep. The draught she had given her that evening at dinner had worked exactly as it should have, naturally. Kat was in a very light sleep, one where she was awake enough to hear everything Tatiana would tell her, but deep enough so that she wouldn't fight her.

It was perfect.

"Katrina, I have some sad news which I need you to convey for me."

The girl stirred a little restlessly.

"You can hear me, Katrina, can't you?"

She nodded, but didn't open her eyes.

"Good. Katrina, something terrible has happened. One of the footmen saw Morgan with another woman."

Kat frowned, her brow wrinkling with concern.

"She is Vallen. A rather powerful one, so naturally, he was attracted to her. And, of course, she is very beautiful."

"But Morgan..." the girl's words were slurred as though she were very drunk. "Morgan loves Adriana," she managed to get out.

"Not any longer. His head has been turned by this other woman. He doesn't want to be with Adriana any more. He was heard telling this other woman that he wanted to be with her."

Kat shifted again.

"You must tell Adriana. She will be devastated, but you must tell her. Tell her to forget Morgan. She should marry Vallentyn. He is a good match for her, and he will never stray."

Kat nodded her head. "Good match," she agreed, "but Morgan loves Adriana."

"No, he doesn't love her any more. And Vallentyn is a good match." Tatiana sat back for a moment, giving the girl a few moments to digest her instructions. Kat lay there quietly, but with a frown wrinkling her brow.

Tatiana then moved forward once more. "You must also speak to Morgan, Kat."

"Morgan."

This time, just to be sure, Tatiana added magic to her voice. This was the truly important point, and she would put it into Kat's mind as a suggestion above and beyond the power of the potion.

"Yes, you must speak to Morgan. No matter what Adriana says when you talk to her, you must tell Morgan that Adriana was happy to hear of it. You must tell him she wants nothing more to do with him. She is happy he is lavishing his attentions on someone else because she isn't interested in him anymore. She is through with him, for good."

The girl seemed to have slipped into a deeper sleep, for she was completely silent and still.

"Did you hear me, Kat? Do you know what to tell Morgan?"

The girl nodded, and then turned over on to her side. "Adriana's happy he's with someone else," she slurred.

"Yes," Tatiana hissed quietly. "She wants nothing more to do with him. She's going to marry Vallentyn."

Kat's heavy breathing was the only sound in the room as Tatiana quietly closed the door behind her.

Chapter 31

~~~~~

Kat! How wonderful to see you!" Adriana said, coming into the drawing room. She had been so thrilled to hear her good friend was calling—it was so rare now that she was allowed visitors.

She had so much to tell Kat—she had to share her news about her art exhibition. She just knew Kat would be thrilled.

Her friend was standing by the window looking out. But, oddly enough, she wasn't wearing her usual bright, cheerful smile.

There was something wrong.

Adriana stopped. "What is it? What's happened?" Fears rushed through her mind and body as she rushed to her friend's side and took her hands. "Is it Morgan? Is he hurt? Did his mother do something to him?" Adriana thought her heart might stop beating all together if Kat didn't answer her questions immediately.

But Kat just stood there with tears brimming in her eyes. One finally slipped down her cheek, and she hastily wiped it away. Shaking her head, she said, "Morgan is well. His mother hasn't done anything. It, it is him who has..."

She tore her hands away from Adriana's, turned and walked away.

Adriana swallowed the lump that suddenly had formed in her throat. "What has he done?" she asked quietly.

"He has been with... he is interested in another woman."
She turned back, "Oh, Adriana, I am so sorry. I know that you
and Morgan... well, I thought that maybe... I mean, I was sure
he cared for you. He told me he did, but perhaps being here in
London, and meeting other Vallen has turned his head."

Adriana began breathing again. She wasn't sure when she
had stopped. She opened her mouth, but wasn't certain what
she should say, or what she *could* say. She grasped her hands
together, and found that they were cold and shaking.

Morgan had been with another woman? He wanted to be
with someone else?

She shook her head. "Perhaps she is just a friend. Do you
know who she is?"

"No. I just know she is a Vallen. A rather powerful one."

"Oh, well, then, he must have just been gathering some
information from her. You know, trying to learn more about
his own powers," Adriana said, trying hard to believe her own
words.

But Kat just shook her head. "He was heard telling her
that he cared for her, and... and, he kissed her."

Adriana just stared at Kat for a full minute trying to
accept what she was being told. Morgan had been seen kissing
someone else. He didn't want to be with her any more. The
words kept going through Adriana's mind, but somehow they
weren't registering.

Oddly enough, she didn't feel anything. She didn't feel
anything— it was as if her whole mind and body had gone
numb.

Morgan had been with another woman. He *wanted* to be
with another woman.

"Well, I suppose it is no more than I should have
expected," she finally whispered. "I did tell him to go away and
leave me alone."

"You didn't!"

Adriana gave a laugh, that hiccoughed into a sob as her
numbness disappeared in a rush of anguishing pain. "Yes, I
did."

"Why?"

Adriana shrugged and held her breath, hoping the spasms of her tears would go away. She pressed a shaking hand to her mouth as she tried to regain control. She wouldn't cry in front of Kat.

Blinking rapidly, Adriana looked at Kat, who was looking so lost and upset standing in the middle of the drawing room. "I was upset." She paused to take a deep shuddering breath. "It's all right," Adriana managed to whisper, ignoring the grief that was still boring a hole in her chest. She shook her head trying to dispel the pain, and cleared her throat. "It's all right. I had no right to expect anything else."

Kat moved forward and took her hands. Heat and good feelings moved from Kat's hands to her own. It was very calming. Adriana took a another deep breath.

"Perhaps it would be better if you married Vallentyn after all," Kat said quietly. "You know he would never do anything like..."

Adriana looked at Kat. Did she really believe that. Did Lady Vallentyn tell her to say that? Adriana pulled her hands away. "Are you... have you spoken with your aunt about this?"

"No! Oh no! Adriana, I would never speak with Aunt Vallentyn about you. I promise!"

Adriana wanted to believe her friend. She would believe her. Kat wouldn't lie to her, she wanted Morgan to be happy, and hopefully she wanted to same for Adriana.

But Adriana could never marry Vallentyn, even if Morgan... tears blurred Adriana's vision once more as the pain clamped down hard on her heart.

Morgan, I can't believe you," Kat said, rounding on him the minute he walked into the drawing room.

"You can't believe what?" Morgan asked, completely confused.

"I can't believe, after all you've done, after all you've said, that you would go and be with another woman. I thought you cared for Adriana."

Morgan stopped. "Be with another woman? How...?"

"The footman saw you," she said, lowering her voice. "He saw you kissing some woman last evening," she hissed. Kat was truly angry.

But then, so was he. Had he been followed? Spied upon? He hadn't told anyone he was going to visit Sarah, but he hadn't hid it either.

"And what business is it of yours if I did pay a call to another woman?" he asked, trying hard to contain his own growing anger.

"It is my business when you are clearly trying to both destroy your own life, and the happiness of one of my good friends. Adriana, by the way, wishes you well. But I could tell she was very upset."

"Wait a minute! You *told* her?" Anger exploded in Morgan's head as if he had just been struck by lightning. He had never felt anything like this toward anyone, aside from his mother. Suddenly, he felt as if he was suffocating, and yet a fire sparked to life in the pit of his stomach.

"Yes, of course I told her. She's my friend," Kat said, taking a step away from him. She glanced nervously at the fireplace where the coal there mimicked the burning within him.

"What did you tell her, exactly?" Morgan asked, his voice low, as he pressed down his anger. She wouldn't have, couldn't have...

"I told her exactly what the footman told me," Kat whispered.

"You told her I had kissed another woman?" Flames burst to life both within him and the fireplace.

Kat looked at the fire again. "That's what you did, so that's what I told her."

The fire began to rage within him. "You had no right to tell her that!"

"Morgan! You're going to set the house on fire."

He looked toward the fireplace, but his eyes were caught by the flames that were leaping from his own fingertips. He suppressed the fire, but needed to dispel his anger somehow. With a lift of his arms, all the furniture in the room rose a foot into the air. In one swoop it all flew against the far wall. China smashed and wood cracked.

Kat screamed and ran toward the door as a chair nearly hit her.

"Morgan, calm down!"

"Calm down? How do you expect me to calm down when you have just destroyed my last hope of ever being with Adriana? I love her, Kat! I love her and you told her that I kissed another woman!"

Kat covered her ears and backed away from him. "Please, Morgan, I'm sorry, but..."

"But? But what? What am I supposed to do? I was planning on going over this afternoon to tell her that I loved her, but now..." The chair that had nearly hit Kat rose up in the air and hovered threateningly above the ground.

Kat looked at it with fear in her eyes. "Morgan, put the chair down. Please, I'm sorry I told her, but destroying the house won't help anything."

Morgan looked over at the chair. He wanted to break it. He wanted to burn it, and everything else until there was nothing left but ashes. He flexed his muscles, curling his hands into fists and opening them again. It took all of his control not to set everything on fire.

Just before the chair hit the wall next to him, he stopped it and set it gently down on the floor.

With a moan, he closed his eyes and sat down on the chair—swinging it under himself just in time. His head dropped into his hands. "What am I going to do? Adriana must hate me," he groaned. He had to ask, he had to know, "What did she say?"

Kat was slowly rearranging the furniture, putting it back where it belonged. She stopped what she was doing and turned back to him. "She said she was happy for you."

Morgan looked up. "Happy for me?" Morgan looked down at his chest fully expecting the blade of a knife to be protruding from it.

"Yes, because now you won't be lavishing your unwanted attentions on her anymore."

Morgan winced. There was no knife, but he was certain he could feel his hot blood trickling down to his stomach.

The sobs continued to rack Adriana's body despite her exhaustion. For how long she had lain there crying, she did not know. All she knew was that Henrietta—dear, Henrietta—had sat by her the entire time, softly stroking her back and murmuring words of support mixed with cruel words for Morgan.

But Adriana couldn't stop crying. She didn't think she would ever be able to stop. The pain was too much.

She loved him. He was a part of her life. He meant more to her than even her painting—she hadn't cried this long after all of her art materials had been taken away.

But now, her heart was truly broken. Her dreams were gone. Any hope of freedom destroyed. She would live a very lonely life without Morgan.

How could he? "How could he?" she said aloud, sitting up.

"He is not worth your time, Adriana," Henrietta said, sitting back.

"He is worth more than my time, he is worth everything. But he needn't have been so cruel," she said, wiping her tears.

"You are better off without him, my love. He has encouraged you to..."

"He has encouraged me to live. He has encouraged me to not just sit back and accept the life that Lord Devaux has laid out for me, but to fight for my freedom," Adriana said emphatically.

"But dearest, you are a woman, you have no choice but to do what your guardian..."

"No! I am a woman who has the right to live her life as she chooses. Everyone should have that right!"

"In a perfect world, my dear, but not in this one," Henrietta said sadly.

"I thought he cared about me," Adriana said, sitting back against her pillows. "I thought he... well, I suppose it doesn't matter anymore, does it?"

Chapter 32

The rain started that afternoon. Adriana just stared out the window, her mind and heart empty. The tears had stopped, but only because there was nothing left. The world was gray and colorless.

"I'm terribly sorry, Miss," a maid said after briefly knocking on her door, "but Lord Byron is here and he says it is extremely important that he speak to you."

"Lord Byron?" That jolted her. "Tell him I'll be with him in just a moment," she said, swinging her legs off the chair she had been curled up on. What could be so important to bring Lord Byron out on a day like today? And at this time too—it was past normal visiting hours.

After very quickly tidying her hair and trying to smooth the wrinkles from her gown, she rushed down to the drawing room. Henrietta was standing just outside of the room waiting for her as she came down the stairs.

"It is Lord Byron!" she whispered excitedly.

Adriana managed a small smile at Henrietta's excitement. Her dear friend still hadn't gotten over the thrill of meeting her favorite author. "Yes, let's see what it is he wants," Adriana whispered back, as she opened the door to the drawing room.

It could have been a warm sunny day the way Lord Byron looked. He was dry and dressed as immaculately as always. And quite a change from his usual demeanor of ennui, there was the closest thing Adriana had ever seen to a smile on his face. His eyes were virtually twinkling with glee.

"Ah, Miss Hayden, I am sorry to intrude on your evening. I hope I didn't disturb your toilet? I know I, myself, was about to begin to get dressed when I received a most welcome caller to my home. I simply had to come immediately to see you."

As always when she was with Lord Byron, Adriana was suddenly very awake, full of energy and good feelings. It was such a relief from the emptiness she been consumed by for the past few days. She gave him a true smile. "I thank you for doing so. What was it that you needed to share?"

He pulled a leather pouch from out of his pocket. "It is just this," he said, handing it to her.

It was surprisingly heavy, and made the most delightful chinking noise as he placed it into her hand.

"But what is it?" Adriana asked, honestly bewildered. "And do, please, sit down," she said, suddenly remembering her manners. She then perched on the edge of the chair next to the one he had chosen.

"That is half of your share of the monies earned the other night. A total of twelve paintings sold. I left with your footman materials for another painting that has been commissioned. Sir William said that Lady Bertram would like something bright in tones of amber and blue to match her new drawing room. A landscape or, rather, a seascape, I imagine."

Adriana could hardly breath. Materials? Painting materials? She was going to paint again? Her heart began to flutter within her chest, but then constricted once again as she thought of Lord Devaux. Would he allow her this?

"Sir William has received three more commissions for works from you, including one from a lady who wants a painting of her lover in exactly the same position you painted Mr. Vallentyn." Lord Byron said, his eyes narrowing in amusement.

Adriana gasped with delighted shock. She didn't care what her guardian said, she was going to do these paintings!

"The advances for those paintings and the other half of the money owed to you will be coming forthwith," Lord Byron finished.

Adriana could barely believe it. Her paintings had sold! She had the money in her hand. It was hers to do with whatever she liked. She weighed the bag in her hand—it was very heavy. My goodness, she could... she could leave London, leave her guardian, and move into the country with Henrietta. She could spend the rest of her life painting!

This money was her freedom!

"This is only half?" she asked, the shock beginning descend upon her.

"Yes, certainly. And, of course, there are still many more paintings which Sir William still expects to sell."

Oh, my goodness! She could hardly believe this! Never again was she going to be stopped from doing what she loved. Never.

"I would suggest you keep the money someplace very safe, Miss Hayden. Perhaps you might even consider investing some of it, or ..."

"Indeed, that money will be kept very safely," Lord Devaux said, interrupting Lord Byron.

Adriana jumped. She hadn't even heard him come into the room.

Lord Byron stood. "Lord Devaux, what a pleasant surprise. I was just..."

"Giving my ward the money earned by her paintings?" her guardian finished.

"This is my money," Adriana said, standing.

Lord Devaux snatched the purse out of her hand. "Any money you earn, my dear, is rightfully mine. And it's about time you began to pay me back for the hospitality I've shown you for the past fourteen years." He turned to Lord Byron who looked as dumbfounded as Adriana felt. "My lord," he gave Lord Byron a slight nod of his head. "From now on, all money from Sir William can be delivered directly to me." He turned and started out of the room.

"I say, Lord Devaux, that's not right..." Lord Byron began. His shock now turned to anger on Adriana's behalf.

"I beg your pardon?" Lord Devaux said, slowly turning back around.

"That money belongs to Miss Hayden. She earned it with her work."

Lord Devaux cocked his head to the side just a touch. "I beg your pardon, my lord, but seeing as Miss Hayden is my ward, any money she earns is rightfully, and legally, mine. And I would appreciate you staying out of my business." Once again he gave a slight nod of his head. "Good day to you."

Adriana sank back down onto the sofa as Lord Devaux closed the door as he left the room.

Gone. It was all gone. Her freedom had just been taken out of the room in Lord Devaux's pocket. It had been her last hope. Her only hope. And now it was gone.

There weren't tears for how she felt. She had spent them all on Morgan, anyhow. No, now there was nothing, nothing at all.

The warmth of Lord Byron's hand on her own hardly registered, but she did look up into his intense eyes. "Miss Hayden. I don't know what to say."

Adriana shook her head. "It's not your fault," she said with difficulty.

"But it is. If I had only known he would..."

"No, you couldn't have known. I don't know what I'm going to do now. My work is gone. There is nothing left."

"No, please don't say that. You'll come around. You'll see, it will work out."

"No, my lord. That is exceedingly kind, but I don't think it will. I just don't know..." her voice trailed off and she knew how she sounded, but just as this moment she didn't care. She just wanted to curl up in her bed and stay there.

Morgan was gone from her life, and now her work—all of her beautiful paintings, her life's work—they were all gone and she would get nothing for them.

"Miss Hayden, I am so sorry," Lord Byron said again just before he closed the door behind himself.

Adriana worked feverishly.

For the two nights since Lord Devaux had allowed her to paint again, now in the hopes that she would earn money for him, she hadn't been able to sleep properly. For two nights she had done little else but toss and turn in her bed.

When she did finally sleep, her dreams were too vivid for her to truly get any rest. There were unending images of Morgan, his arms wrapped around another woman, kissing her passionately. Sometimes she would wake up crying. Sometimes she would wake up and just lie there like a stone in her bed, feeling nothing. She didn't know which was worse.

But there was another other dream too—it wasn't so disturbing as the first, but just as vivid. It was this dream she was painting now.

Yes, her conscience pricked her as she used the canvas and paints bought for her so she could complete a work commissioned at the exhibition—but she had no choice. This image from her dream just had to be painted. And she would not rest until it was finished.

Twice this morning, Henrietta tried to cajole her into coming down for a meal, but she would not, she could not. Not until the painting was done.

Her companion now stood beside her, wringing her hands. "But really, Adriana, you can't just stay here the whole day working on this painting."

"Henrietta, please. Lord Devaux has allowed me to paint, so that is what I am doing," Adriana said, not even bothering to put down her paintbrush or even turn away from her painting. There was something about this painting that demanded her complete devotion. "When I am done, I will come down, I promise. Just a few more hours, and then I'll be finished. Just give me a few more hours."

She heard the door click behind her as Henrietta left again with a sigh. Adriana didn't know what this place was that she was painting. She didn't know where it was, or its significance, but it was there in her mind and it had to get out and onto her canvas. That was all she knew. It was all she could do for now.

It was nearing four o'clock when she finally finished. She was dropping with fatigue, but it was done.

Collapsing on to the sofa behind her, she reached for a piece of the bread and meat that Henrietta had left for her to eat hours ago. Nibbling at her food, she examined the painting that had consumed her.

The focus of the painting was a circle of standing stones. Some had horizontal stones perched precariously upon others forming doorways, others stood as sentry forming the curve of the circle. A full moon shone pale in the deep blue of the night, making the stones glow with an almost otherworldly grace. It was a place filled with magic and mystery.

Fear and joy, but most of all awe, filled the picture. It was almost as if you knew that something great was about to happen here. Shadows on the ground gave the impression of people, cloaked and waiting to come out from behind the stones. They were waiting to come through the doorways, to enter the sacred circle. Waiting for just the right moment, when the moon would be at its peak, waiting for the stroke of midnight.

The anticipation of that moment made Adriana lean forward. She knew it was about to happen, she could see it, feel it. She could almost hear the rustling of the grass as the people stood anxiously waiting and yet, and yet... it was a painting. Nothing was really going to happen.

Almost incongruously was a pack of wolves off in the lower right hand corner of the painting. They stood glaring at the standing stones amidst a stand of trees. Some stood with teeth bared. Each was ready to pounce and attack at any moment. The moon—shadows hung around them. The closeness of the trees made it impossible to tell just how many animals there were. No matter—they were menacing. More menacing and frightening than anything, Adriana gave a small shiver as she sat there looking at them.

Sitting back and taking another bite of her bread, she realized what had to be done.

With her mouth still full, she went running from the room. "Henrietta! Henrietta!" she called as she ran down the stairs. Where was she?

Her companion came rushing from the upstairs sitting room. "What is it? Adriana, are you all right? What's wrong?"

Adriana pulled Henrietta back into the sitting room and then took a moment to catch her breath and swallow her food.

"Just calm down, dear, it's all right, just relax," Henrietta said patting her hand comfortingly.

Adriana took a deep breath. "I need you to go out. I need you to deliver that painting to Morgan—to Mr. Vallentyn."

"What? After all that's happened? Didn't you say you never wanted to speak with him or see him ever again?" Henrietta was now the one becoming agitated, and Adriana wished she'd never told her companion all that had happened.

"Yes, but it is vitally important. Please, Henrietta, you must go. If you don't..." Adriana steeled herself, "If you don't go and take it to him, I will. And I truly mean it. This painting has got to be given to him. No matter what he has done. No matter what I have said. *He has to get this painting.*"

Henrietta just stood, looking at her as if she had completely lost her mind, and to be honest, she wasn't entirely certain that she hadn't.

"Please?" she asked again.

Finally, shaking her head sadly, Henrietta said, "Very well, but only to keep you away from him. If he must have it, I will bring it to him."

Adriana pulled her companion into a hug. "Thank you!"

"Morgan, you can't go," Cosmina said, sounding more like a coaxing mother than ever before. "Truly, my dear, it isn't the right thing to do. You know this."

"No really, Mr. Vallentyn. She is right this time, you cannot simply leave," Nestor said, adding his voice to Cosmina's.

"Well, I am glad to see you two finally in agreement on something," Morgan laughed forcibly, hardly pausing in his packing. There was no humor in his laughter, however, no place for happiness in his heart.

"Yes, on this we definitely agree. You cannot allow Miss Hayden to drive you from London. There are many more young ladies. She is not the end of the world, my dear," Cosmina said. "I am certain if you put your mind to it, or perhaps attend another fancy ball, you'll find someone else just as..."

"Cosmina," Morgan said warningly. "There is no one who could ever replace Adriana. There never could be."

"Well, no of course not," she said, quickly retracing her steps. "But there will be others."

"No. Not for me."

"Then don't think about the young lady, sir," Nestor said. "Think about your powers. How are you going to find out what your powers are and where they have come from? You still haven't found a satisfactory answer."

Morgan stopped what he was doing and straightened up. "I don't know about that, Nestor. I don't know if I have found the answer or not."

"What do you mean?"

"Well, I've been thinking a lot about what Jack the Lad said. He told me the powers had to have come from inside of me. And I do believe he is right. I've probably had these magical powers my whole life, but something, somehow, triggered them into coming out."

"But what?"

"I don't know. My growing confidence, maybe? I can tell you, I have a great deal more self-confidence now than I ever had in my life."

"And did you get that confidence first before any of your new powers began to show themselves?"

Morgan sighed. "I don't..."

A knock on the door interrupted him. "There is a lady to see you, Mr. Vallentyn. She's downstairs in the drawing room," the maid announced, after Morgan had opened the door.

"And it's not the young lady who's come to see you before, either. It's someone new, and not so young. And she's got something with her," the girl said, very mysteriously.

Morgan gave Nestor and Cosmina a surprised look, then went downstairs to find out who this new woman was.

Adriana's companion was sitting at the edge of the sofa when Morgan came in, followed immediately by Nestor and Cosmina. She stood up and give him a hint of a curtsey, but no smile.

Picking up a good sized package, she handed it to Morgan. "Miss Hayden asked me to deliver this to you."

Morgan's heart lifted. "Adriana did?"

"Yes," she said, her mouth in a straight disapproving line.

Adriana had thought of him! She had thought to send him a gift? Morgan was so overwhelmed with relief and with happiness, he could hardly move for a minute. She still thought of him. She still cared! His heart soared.

Morgan quickly tore the paper from the package and found the most lovely painting. It was beautiful and magical. As he looked at it, Morgan's heart began to race.

He had dreamed this! Last night, and the night before. He had dreamed of this place, of this very scene. The moonlight and the stones...

"Stonehenge!"

Morgan spun around to face Nestor. "Stonehenge? What is that?"

Nestor pointed at the painting. "That's what that is, in the painting. It's Stonehenge."

Morgan shook his head, not comprehending. Nestor explained. "It's an ancient circle of stones. No one knows who built it. Some say it was the druids. But all I know is that it is..."

"It is a place of magic," Cosmina finished for him.

"Yes," Nestor said, looking a little put out that she had finished his sentence.

"I've been there," Cosmina said.

Morgan turned to look at her, standing beside him. "You know this place?"

"Yes, but that isn't there," she said, pointing at a small copse of trees in the lower corner of the painting. "Stonehenge is in the middle of a large field. There are no trees nearby. And I don't like the look of those wolves," she added as an afterthought.

Morgan looked more closely. There were rather nasty looking wolves there. "Has Adriana ever been here?" he asked Henrietta.

"No!" she answered her eyes widening.

"Are you certain?" Nestor asked.

"Absolutely," the woman responded straightening herself as if affronted by the question.

"Then how did she paint this?" Cosmina asked.

The woman deflated a bit. "I, I don't know."

Morgan knew however. She must have had the same dream he'd been having. It was the only answer. And it made a great deal of sense now that he saw it. This painting was filled with magic. Real magic! Just as there was magic in everything that Adriana drew or painted. He couldn't believe he hadn't seen it before.

Adriana was Vallen! Not only that, but they *were* meant to be together. Morgan knew it with a certainty—and Adriana probably did too, otherwise she wouldn't have sent him the painting.

There was such a rush of good feelings, love and... Morgan searched around in his mind to name this feeling coursing through his veins. It was... magic. Strong, empowering magic.

He turned back to Nestor. "Do you feel it?" he asked, knowing that his friend would know exactly what he was talking about.

Nestor looked at the painting, and then nodded his head. "Yes." He then paused and asked, "Do you think..."

"Yes. She must be!" Morgan turned back to Henrietta. He didn't wish to say anything in front of her, just in case she didn't know anything about the Vallen.

But the thought that Adriana had recognized the magic and the importance in this painting... it made everything, absolutely everything, fit into place.

"Please thank Adriana for me. This is very special. And that she thought of me... well, please tell her I am touched. And..." Morgan thought to choose his words very carefully. "Tell her this painting means as much to me as she does. I think she will understand."

With a harrumph of disbelief or just disgruntlement, Adriana's companion bobbed him a curtsey and left.

Morgan looked back at the painting. Staring deeper into it, he could feel the chill of the night air, smell the fresh grass of the field all around and even sense the age of the stones. It was almost as if he were there, standing in the center of this magnificent structure. He could feel it.

There were others there as well. Standing in the shadows were other Vallen. They all seemed to be excited, happy in their anticipation of the night.

But, even as Morgan looked around and reached out with all of his senses, he knew there was something missing. There was something wrong. *He* needed something more that he just didn't have and without that, the evening would be wasted.

There was something more that he needed before he could attain his destiny.

"... are disturbing," Cosmina was saying when Morgan pulled himself back from the painting.

He didn't know what it was that she found disturbing, but it didn't matter. He knew what he had to do.

Chapter 33

"Morgan!" Vallentyn said, with as much shock at seeing him as Morgan felt at meeting his brother.

"Hello, Vallentyn," Morgan said, taking his brother's hand. He had changed, Morgan thought. He was definitely looking older. It was odd, but he supposed he hadn't seen his brother for a number of years now, despite living on the same estate. Only Vallentyn never came to visit him in the woods, and Morgan had never been able to leave them.

His brother looked around the nearly deserted room nervously. Morgan had never been inside a gentleman's club before, but when Nestor discovered this was where his brother was this, and every, afternoon, they had decided that it was much easier for Morgan to meet Vallentyn here than risk seeing his mother if he had gone to Vallentyn House.

The room they were in was large, but where they were, near the back wall in one of the many small clusters of chairs scattered about the room, there was a feeling of privacy.

"Please sit down," Vallentyn said, gesturing to the chair next to the one he had just vacated. "Would you like some brandy or port?" he asked, raising a finger to call the footman who was hovering nearby, but not so close that he could hear their conversation.

"No, thank you."

"Oh."

The footman placed a tray with two bottles and two glasses on the table at the edge of their little area. Vallentyn walked over and helped himself with a slightly shaking hand.

"Did you go to the house?" he asked, after taking a liberal gulp of his wine.

"No. A friend of mine went for me to see if you were home. He learned you were here," Morgan reassured his brother.

"So she doesn't know that we're meeting?"

"No." Morgan didn't need to ask who 'she' was. He was certain his brother was just as terrified of their mother as he had been until very recently.

Vallentyn gave an almost inaudible sigh of relief before sitting back in his chair and taking another sip of his drink.

"So, how have you been?" Vallentyn asked awkwardly.

"Well, thank you," Morgan answered, just as uncomfortable. They had never really spoken much to each other, even when Morgan lived in the abbey. Vallentyn had always been out, seeing to the estate—or, perhaps, as Morgan had always imagined, avoiding their mother.

"Well, it's quite something to see you here in London. How did you manage to escape the woods and Mother's curses?"

"My powers have increased," Morgan answered simply.

"Ah, yes, so I heard. Mother was quite furious, you know."

"Yes."

A silence fell between them. Morgan cursed Cosmina and her practicality that had driven him to seek out his brother in the first place. "What are you going to do after you tell Adriana you love her?" she had asked—damn her.

He hadn't had an answer. He knew he had to go to this Stonehenge, and that there he would probably attain his destiny whatever that was, but beyond that he hadn't really thought of what he was going to do with his life. He wanted to do good for society, but that, he was certain would be tied up with his destiny.

But Cosmina had been right. He needed to have some place more permanent to live than Mrs. Lunden's boarding house. He certainly couldn't bring Adriana there. He knew he wanted to marry her, but again, if he did so, he would need to find some way of supporting her, and himself.

It was all very disconcerting having to think of such things. He'd never had to before. So here he was, in front of his brother, the head of his family. If anyone would know what Morgan could do, it would be Vallentyn. Once he had this settled, he would be able to turn his attention to his destiny, but not until then. Adriana had to come first.

Morgan swallowed hard, forcing down his pride and said, "I'm in a bit of a fix."

"Oh? Anything I can do to help?" Vallentyn asked, putting down his drink and focusing his full attention on Morgan.

"Well, er, I was hoping you would know..." Morgan paused, and wished he'd accepted that drink. He took another breath and started again. "I'd like to marry."

"Really? Why, that's wonderful! I didn't know you knew any young ladies. Is this someone you met here, in London?"

"Er, well, no, actually. It is... well," Morgan took a deep breath. It would be easier if he just got on with it and said it, he thought to himself. Right. He took another breath and said, "Actually, it is Adriana Hayden."

The smile on Vallentyn's face froze. For a full minute he sat there looking at Morgan. "You do know that Mother wanted her to marry me?"

"Yes. I know. But I love her. And... and I have very good reason to believe she loves me as well. So I... I want to ask her to marry me, but I, er, don't have anywhere to live. I'm staying at a guest house right now, but I can't stay there forever, and I would need a way to support her, and myself. So, I was wondering..." Morgan finally ran out of breath and nerve. He swallowed again and then got up to help himself to the brandy.

Vallentyn just sat there quietly. Steepling his fingers, he tapped his two forefingers together, clearly thinking this over.

Morgan drank down half a glass of brandy and nearly choked on it. He wasn't used to spirits.

"Mother doesn't know about this, does she?"

"No!" he said, a little too vehemently. He then added, more calmly, "Although, she does know that Adriana and I have met."

Suddenly Vallentyn stood up and took a step toward Morgan so quickly that he was worried for a moment that his brother was going to attack him for stealing his fiancé Morgan took a few quick steps back, but Vallentyn went straight to the bottles and poured another drink for himself.

After drinking down nearly a whole glass, he said, "I would help you, really I would. But if I did, and then Mother found out... well..."

"I'll protect you from her. Don't worry about that."

Vallentyn stopped, his drink raised halfway to his lips, and just looked at him. "You can do that?" he asked, lowering his drink again. "You can protect me? Er, stop her?"

"Yes. Oh, yes, most definitely. I'm probably much stronger than her now, although I haven't actually tried out my powers to see just how strong they are. But the last time we met, I was able to stop her rather easily."

"But you don't have any powers to speak of," Vallentyn scoffed, taking a sip from his drink and sitting down again.

Inside of Morgan, all his childhood feelings of inadequacy fought with a new–found anger that he would be dismissed so easily. Pushing aside both, Morgan stood in front of his brother.

Vallentyn looked up, a shadow of uncertainty already clouding his eyes.

"I am stronger than Mother. Do you not believe me? Do I need to prove myself to you?"

"How can you?" he paused and shifted his eyes around the room. Morgan turned, too, to see if they were being observed. The room was still mostly empty except for another group of men at the other end of the room.

"Listen, Morgan," his brother continued, "I appreciate the fact that you've fallen in love with Miss Hayden, really I do. She is a beautiful girl. But it is simply too dangerous from where I'm sitting..."

"You will help me," Morgan said, infusing his voice with magic. "You have the power to help me, and you will. I don't need to prove myself to you." He paused and let the magic fall away. "I am above doing parlor tricks, Vallentyn."

His brother's jaw dropped open, but he quickly caught it and closed his mouth again. "You... you really are powerful now. I could feel that. I could hear it. You put a suggestion into my mind, just like Mother does."

"I'm sorry," Morgan began, but his brother interrupted him. "No, no, it's quite all right. I don't mind. I mean, it wasn't a bad suggestion. It was what I had wanted to do anyway, but still..." A note of awe crept into his voice. "Still, I'm impressed. You truly have become quite powerful, but can you truly stop Mother?" he asked.

"I have before, and I can do so again," Morgan reassured him once again.

Vallentyn looked up at him, clearly lost in indecision for a moment. Finally, he got up and went to the table that held their drinks. He opened a drawer and pulled out a piece of paper, a pen and ink and sat down again.

Using the small side table next to his chair as a desk, he began to write.

"This is a note to the steward at Stoneside, and I'll write another to my solicitor informing him of what I'm doing." He stopped speaking so as to concentrate on his letter.

Morgan finished his drink as he sat quietly while his brother wrote. When the letter was finished, Vallentyn folded it and handed it to Morgan.

"If you give this to Mr. Black, he is the steward there, he will teach you all you need to know about running the estate. It's not so very difficult. I'm sure you'll pick it up quickly."

Morgan took the note and asked, "So, I'm to run the estate for you? This Mr. Black won't be upset that I'm taking over his position?"

"What? No, oh, no!" Vallentyn began to laugh. "You're not taking over Black's position. He'll stay on, unless you'd like to replace him with your own man, of course. No, the estate is yours."

"Mine? The entire thing? You're just giving an estate to me?" Morgan was shocked.

"No. It is yours. It has been ever since our father died. I've just been caring for it since, well, you were only five at the time, and then there was all that nastiness with Mother. When you were old enough she had you confined to the forest and well... But I'm sure you'll find everything in order. The money the estate earned has been kept in a separate account for you—aside from what was needed to keep the estate running, you know, maintain the house and a skeleton staff. Everything's on the up and up, I assure you."

Morgan swallowed hard. "I own an estate? I have money in an account?" he repeated, dumbfounded. "A house and staff?"

"Yes, of course. What, you didn't think our father would leave you destitute, did you? He knew Mother would never allow you to enter the army or the church. The estate has been well taken care of for you. It doesn't earn an enormous living, but you won't starve, and you'll have a good roof over your head, and one that won't leak, I promise you."

"I don't know what to say. This is much more than I expected," Morgan finally said, as all this began to sink in.

"Well, don't thank me. It's Father who provided for you."

"Yes. Well, thank you for taking care of it for me."

"Oh, no problem. No problem at all. Quite enjoy it, actually. If you need any help, don't hesitate to ask."

"Thank you." Morgan stood to go, the letter still clutched in his hand. But then he stopped, and turned back. He gave an embarrassed little laugh, then asked, "Er, where is the estate?"

"What? Oh!" Jonathan laughed. "It's near Stonehenge, in Wiltshire."

With his brother's letter tucked safely in his pocket, Morgan had one more important call he needed to make. He knew that now was the right time to face his mother.

He had no concerns about Adriana, he knew that she loved him and there was now nothing to stop him from taking her away from this horrendous life that she was living. He had the wherewithal to care for her as she should be, and the determination to force Lord Devaux to allow her to marry him.

He had tried every avenue to find the answer to where his powers had come from, and what his destiny was going to be. But there was still that one thing that had been missing when he'd let himself be enthralled by Adriana's painting. There was something he needed that only he could get—but what was it?

All roads seemed to lead him to his mother. She was the only one who knew the answers he needed. And so he followed that path and walked through the city to Vallentyn House.

Somehow his mother wasn't surprised to see him. In fact, she was practically purring when he was shown into the drawing room. She sat back like a satisfied cat after a big meal and practically licked her lips. "Morgan, I was wondering when you'd come by."

"Good afternoon, Mother," Morgan bowed formally.

She extended her arm, indicating that he be seated.

As he settled himself in the chair across from her, she said, "So, you've finally given up, have you? I knew it was only a matter of time before you realized that there was nothing for you here. When do you leave for Vallentyn?"

Morgan was silent for a moment wondering if he should let his mother continue on in her beautiful daydream. But no, that would be cruel, better to get right to the point, he decided.

He sat forward and gave his mother smile. "I am sorry to disappoint you, Mother. But I'm not here to tell you that I'm returning to Vallentyn. Quite the opposite. I'm looking forward to joining you at Stonehenge on the summer solstice."

Lady Vallentyn's face lost all trace of emotion for a moment, before it turned dark. "Who told you?" she hissed.

"No one needed to tell me. I know." It was a lie, but he wasn't about to tell his mother about Adriana's painting. "Now, I want to know what I need to attain my destiny." He inlaid strong magic into his voice. He was certain that she wouldn't tell him unless she were compelled to do so. He just didn't know how much magic would be necessary to get her to do what he wanted.

His mother's eyes widened as she realized what he was doing. "Don't even try," she said unpleasantly. "Your magic wouldn't work on me anyway."

"Oh, I'm not too certain of that."

She brushed his words aside with her hand. "All I know is that you need your full powers."

"There is nothing else?"

"Not that I know of," she said, shrugging her shoulders as if she didn't care.

"Oh, come now, Mother, you don't really expect me to believe..."

"The knowledge is closed to her," a voice said from near the fireplace.

Morgan started. He was on his feet within seconds, looking for the source of the voice, but there was no one there. His mother was by his side faster than he had thought she could move.

"Who said that?" Morgan asked, his eyes darting everywhere a man could hide.

There was no answer right away.

"The chalice," his mother whispered.

And indeed, the stone chalice, which always sat above his mother's fireplace no matter where she was, was glowing. Morgan sensed his mother leave the room, but he didn't take his eyes from the cup. He wasn't certain he could.

Drawn to it, he moved closer. Slowly, carefully he lowered the cup from its special stand above the mantle.

A jolt of magic shot through his body as he touched the chalice. He almost dropped it. Never had he experienced anything like this! The power within the stone was incredible.

His mother was back by his side, panting. Where ever she had gone, she must have run. She touched his arm so that he lowered to chalice to a more comfortable height for her, and then she poured a clear liquid into the cup from a leather wine skin.

He would have said it was water, but he'd never smelled any water like this before. It smelled crisp and clear, like a bright summer's day. The scent of fresh flowers, and the sweetness of fruit tickled his senses. It smelled like the most wonderful place on earth, someplace he'd never been before, and yet it was home. Yes, the liquid smelled like home— comfortable, happy, joyous even. Warm and, even when it was dark and rainy, beautiful. Morgan just closed his eyes and inhaled this lovely, comforting smell.

When he opened his eyes again, he was looking down into the chalice and looking back at him was the face of an old man. Moving his eyes from the length of the man's white beard, Morgan saw a happy mouth surrounded by deep creases from too much smiling. His nose was long and thin and ever so slightly crooked. His deep blue eyes twinkled with good cheer and something else... wisdom, Morgan realized after a moment.

"Who are you?" Morgan whispered, not certain the man could hear him.

"I am Merlin," the man answered, his voice sounding hollow as if it was coming through a long tunnel.

"Oh," Lady Vallentyn breathed. She sounded as if she was going to cry, but, although her brows were drawn together, her eyes were clear.

"Merlin?"

"I do hope you have heard of me. I was wizard to the great king, Arthur, lover to Nimuë, and dear friend to the high priestess of Avalon after whom you are named, Morgan."

Morgan's hands began to tremble with the enormity of who he was speaking with. It wasn't possible. It just wasn't possible, his mind screamed out to him. The words nearly left his mouth, but he closed it tight against them. If this was the famed Merlin, he certainly didn't want to offend the man.

"How... where..." Morgan stopped. He wasn't able to form even a simple question!

Merlin chuckled. "Yes, yes, I'm certain you are quite shocked, but at least you haven't dropped the chalice. When I visited the last Vallen to hold your position, she did. Nearly broke it too! Thank goodness I made it well." The old man's eyes became mere slits as he laughed.

"Maybe you had better put it down, Morgan," his mother said, resting her trembling hand on his arm. She didn't seem to be any steadier than he.

He nodded and together they moved to the sofa where his mother had been sitting earlier. Carefully, Morgan placed the chalice on the low table in front of them.

"Actually, what I've got to say won't take a great deal of your time," Merlin said after they had settled the cup safely on the table. "You were asking about your destiny, Morgan."

"Yes. Do you know what it is? What I need to attain it?"

"Naturally. I'm not certain if you'd heard, but I am also a bit of a prophet." The old man smiled up at them, but then became serious as his focus toward inward. "Listen carefully for this is the prophecy which I gave to your ancestor, Bridget, many, many years ago when she defeated the most powerful, the Vallen Nimuë. Within it you will find your answers.

The seventh child of the victor's kin
Will lead the people away from sin
Guide them through the Wind and Fire
Through difficulties cold and dire
The Magic's seventh child shall keep
The laws intact or penalties they'll reap
To the Seventh of Seven shall be assigned
A task of soul, of will, of mind
To re–empower the world with love
From east to west, below, above
Our work is to move progress along
Seventh of Seven will keep us strong."

As the voice faded away, so too did Merlin's image.

Morgan sat back thinking about this, trying to make sense of it. He was certain that it would make sense and it would tell him all that he needed to know. He just needed to think about and put the pieces together.

What he needed was Adriana.

Chapter 34

Thank you Mrs. MacAllister," Adriana said, dismissing the housekeeper.

That would be the end of it. Three menus chosen for the three dinner parties Lord Devaux would host—which meant that Adriana would organize them, send out the invitations, and act as hostess at each. It was a lot of work, but it was what she did, what he expected of her, what she had always done ever since she was old enough.

She turned to Henrietta who was writing out the invitations to the first of the dinner parties. "Henrietta, you never did tell me what Mr. Vallentyn said when you gave him the painting."

Actually, since Henrietta hadn't volunteered the information the minute she'd returned, Adriana had been too nervous to ask. Now, she was desperate enough. She had to know.

But Henrietta was silent, clearly thinking over her answer. Finally, she took a deep breath, gave Adriana a nervous little smile and said, "You shouldn't think about him, Adriana. He's not right for you. Why don't you go to more parties? There are so many eligible young men out there. You would have so much fun dancing and flirting. I just don't see why you avoid all that."

Adriana pulled her shawl closer around her body. "He didn't say anything?"

Henrietta pursed her lips together and then shook her head. "Nothing of consequence."

"Did he even open it? Look at the painting?" Adriana hated herself, but she had to know.

"He glanced at it and then set it aside, uninterested."

"Oh." She whispered, unable to make her voice do more than that. The pale world shimmered around her for a moment until she blinked her eyes clear. Perhaps Henrietta was right. Perhaps she should go to parties, if Lord Devaux ever allowed her that privilege.

"You do want to continue being Vallen, do you not?" Tatiana said in her sweetest voice. She didn't think it would sit very well with the man who was slouching against the wall next to her if she used a threatening tone. Jack the Lad wasn't the type to be scared or intimidated by anyone. She had to respect that. What she didn't like was the dark, dirty ally where she had finally run him to the ground.

"What do ye want? I know ye're not going to just let me go with a rap on my wrist and tell me not to do it again."

"I have a job for you and your... cronies," she admitted.

"Won't get caught? I'm adverse to spending any sort of time as a guest o'the crown."

Tatiana couldn't help but smile. "You won't get caught, I can absolutely assure you of that."

Jack raised one eyebrow. "Ye sound awfully certain."

"I am. Now you run along and bring back as many men as you can to help you—ten or fifteen should do the trick. I'll wait right here." Not happily, but she would do what must be done.

Jack stood up. "Ten or fifteen? Where do ye think I'm going to find that many blokes to help me out?"

"I'm certain you have at least twice that many you could rally around you at a moment's notice."

Jack slouched back against the wall, a small smile played momentarily on his lips. "They're gonna have to get paid."

Tatiana hadn't considered that. Well, she didn't care. It would be worth it—this was her future security she was planning for. "I will take care of that once the job is done."

"An' just what job is it that ye want done?"

"I need someone killed."

She paused to let that sink in, but Jack didn't even flinch.

"A powerful Vallen so it may take a number of you to overwhelm him."

Jack thought about this for a moment. "An' we won't get caught? A group o'ten men attacking one bloke and beating him to death, and ye think we won't get caught?"

The unspoken question that hovered on Jack's lips was when she was going to be taken off to Bedlam. But Tatiana just laughed. "Who said anything about ten men. I was thinking a pack of wolves—hungry, blood–thirsty wolves. Who knew they roamed through Hyde park at night?"

Jack's eyes narrowed, and then one side of his mouth quirked up, just a little. "Ye can do that?"

Tatiana simply inclined her head with a knowing smile.

With a laugh and a mutter of "I've gotta see this", Jack pushed himself off the wall and went to fetch his men.

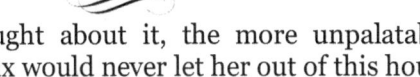

The more she thought about it, the more unpalatable it became. Lord Devaux would never let her out of this house to attend parties. Who was she kidding? And even if he did, how could she ever forget Morgan?

As her mind wandered the past few weeks the pain clutching at Adriana's heart hurt so much she could barely breath.

What was she going to do? How could she live with this? Without him?

A quiet knock at her door interrupted her thoughts. Hastily, she wiped away the tears. "Come in," she called.

Henrietta slipped through the door. Her eyes were red, as if she had been crying too.

Adriana hopped out of her chair. "What is wrong? Henrietta?"

Her dearest companion sniffed, dabbing at her eyes with a sodden handkerchief. "I can't do it, Adriana. I am so sorry!"

"Can't do what? Henrietta, what is wrong?" She pulled her friend to her bed where they could both sit, side by side.

Henrietta took a moment to compose herself and then said. "I lied to you, Adriana, and I just can't live with myself for doing so. I must tell you the truth."

Adriana stopped and waited.

After another deep breath, Henrietta continued. "Mr. Vallentyn. He didn't set aside your painting as I told you."

Still Adriana waited, her heart beginning to beat faster in her chest.

"He looked at it and he, he loved it. He was thrilled that you had thought of him. He said that the painting meant as much to him as you did." Henrietta paused and looked down at her hands. "I'm so sorry I lied to you. It's just that I love you, and I don't want you to leave." Bringing her eyes back up to Adriana's again she said, "You are going to leave now, aren't you?"

Adriana took the breath she hadn't realized she'd been holding. With a start, she realized that her companion was absolutely right. She was going to leave now. She had to. There was nothing for her here and she needed Morgan. Like air, she needed him to live.

She reached out and gave Henrietta's hands a squeeze. "Yes, but I will send for you. As soon as I am settled—I don't know where or how, whether I'm going to be with Morgan or on my own, but as soon as I can, I will write and you'll come join me."

Henrietta broke down again, sobbing and shaking her head. "You are too good, Adriana. After I lied to you..."

"But you came and told me the truth, Henrietta. It's all right. You told me and it was exactly what I needed to hear. Thank you."

"Adriana?" Morgan began to rush down the path the few yards that separated him from the young woman coming toward him.

She stopped as he approached. "Morgan!"

"Adriana, I was just coming to see you."

"You were?"

Was that a hopeful note in her voice? Morgan glanced around them. There was no one else about.

It was a beautiful summer night. The nearly full moon shone brightly overhead and the fresh scent of the park all around them made Morgan feel secure—it was almost like being at home in the woods at Vallentyn. All in all, it really wasn't such a bad place to propose marriage, he thought after considering it for hardly a moment.

But now that it came to the sticking point, could he actually propose? It didn't even take a heartbeat to decide. Absolutely, yes! He loved Adriana. He wanted to spend the rest of his life with her, no matter what was coming his way.

He dropped down onto one knee and took her free hand in both of his. "Adriana, would you do me the honor of becoming my wife?" he said without preamble.

The words were barely out of his mouth, the surprise at what he was saying barely registering on her face when he heard a snarl. Pain exploded in his shoulder. Adriana screamed and let go of his hand, staggering backwards. Morgan hardly knew what was happening.

Pain came from every part of his body, as if it was being torn apart. He forced his eyes open again. All around him wolves were tearing, biting and circling him.

He was completely surrounded, but it was his terror for Adriana's safety that rushed through him. "Run, Adriana, run!" he screamed out, even as he began to struggle against the beasts that circled him.

They were trying to rip and shred every part of him. Morgan was overwhelmed by the pain in his own body, and the anger and hunger for blood coming from the animals. He could barely think. He fought the instinct to blast them all with a shot of magic. He could hurt them, possibly kill them—he didn't want to do that. There had to be a reasonable explanation for the sudden attack.

He'd always had some ability to communicate with animals, but trying to concentrate now was nearly impossible. Morgan reached inside of himself, forcing the pain aside to concentrate enough to communicate with the wolves.

Reaching out with his mind, he said "Stop! Why are you hurting me?"

"Kill! Die!" was the only response he got back.

They were single minded in their goal. There was no worry of territory or harm being done to them. They all just had the one idea in their minds—to kill him.

The animal on his right bit down harder on his arm, making it impossible to defend himself. Another latched on to his left shoulder while a third attacked his body. Wolves were everywhere. For a moment all Morgan could do was to keep his own panic at bay so that he could think of a way out of this.

As he lay there, something whizzed by his head and the wolf attached to his shoulder let go with a whine. The other pulling at his arm did the same as Morgan caught sight of Adriana wielding a large stick.

"No!" he tried to yell out, but it was too late. She was knocked to the ground as three wolves piled on to her, snarling and biting.

Adriana's screams snapped something inside of him and Morgan let go of the burst of power he'd been holding back. The wolves attacking him all flew backwards. Taking only a moment to regain his feet, he sent those attacking Adriana tearing off into the bushes. Standing over Adriana, he dared the animals to come back and try attacking them again.

A few of them slunk around, eyeing them hungrily, but not one dared to approach.

Blood dripped along his arm as he reached down to help Adriana up. Shaking, but amazingly not in tears, Adriana stood up and clung to him. A quick calculation of exactly where they were in the park and what their reception would be depending on where they went, Morgan turned around and headed back toward his boarding house, his arm tightly holding Adriana to his uninjured side.

As they limped along slowly, Morgan could hear the animals following them. He stopped. Releasing Adriana, he turned around sending out a message to the animals, "Do not dare to attack again. I can kill you, easily."

They stopped following them after that.

Slowly, Adriana became aware of her surroundings. She felt as if she had been asleep and had had the most terrible nightmare. She knew she hadn't, and she knew that it hadn't been a dream. The pain was much too real.

A man was just finishing up binding the wound on her arm. "There you go, Miss, you're going to be just fine, now."

She didn't know who he was. Had she been introduced to him? Was he Morgan's valet? He had the look of one.

"Thank you, Mr...?"

"Nestor, Miss. Just Nestor is fine."

"Thank you, Nestor. You are Mr. Vallentyn's man servant?"

"What? No, Adriana, Nestor's my friend." Morgan said through clenched teeth.

Adriana twisted to see Morgan sitting on the bed behind her. While she was sitting in a worn, but comfortable chair by the fire with Nestor on a small stool at her feet. Morgan was on the bed just a few feet behind her with an older woman focusing intently on his bare shoulder.

Was she? Oh, yes, she was! Adriana swallowed a sudden rush of bile in her throat. The woman was sewing his skin back together.

"Oh," she said, and quickly turned back to face the fire. It wasn't that she didn't want to see Morgan's naked torso. As she had discovered a while ago, it was very pleasant to look at, but just now a good part of it was covered with bloodied bandages and she didn't think she could bear to watch his shoulder being sewn back together. The deep red blood trickling from the wound down his arm... ugh! A shiver shot through her.

"No, no, Miss, you shouldn't look. It is not at all pleasant," Nestor said, giving her hand a comforting pat.

"I'm sorry. I suppose I should be stronger than that."

"Not at all," Nestor reassured her.

"It is almost done," the older woman said. "Just one more..."

Nestor got up and retrieved a decanter of brandy from the dressing table next to the fireplace and poured out two glasses. "You'll feel better with this inside of you," he said, handing a glass to her and then, she supposed gave the other to Morgan.

The liquor burned all the way down her throat and pooled like liquid heat in her stomach, but it did make her feel better. At least, she stopped trembling.

Taking a deep breath, she asked, "I don't understand. Why did those wolves attack like that? Where did they come from? Were they sent by your mother?"

Morgan was silent. Everyone in the room was. Adriana was about to turn around again when Morgan said quietly, "I don't know. I hadn't thought of that. I hope you're wrong, but..."

"She wouldn't have!" the older woman said.

"I suppose she could have," Nestor replied, although he didn't sound happy about it.

Morgan didn't say anything more about it. Adriana heard him move about and then he came around and stood by the fire. He'd put on a fresh shirt, but his breeches were still the same ones he'd had on earlier. There were splatters of blood on them, but they didn't seem torn.

"Are you legs all right?" Adriana asked, looking at the dark red stains.

Morgan looked down at his legs and bare feet. "Yes. Thank goodness they only went for my lower legs, which were safely encased in my boots."

"The boots are destroyed, but your legs are whole," Nestor put in.

Morgan gave the man a smile. "I can buy new boots. It's harder to buy new legs."

The man laughed and shook his head. He hoisted himself up off of the low stool. "Come along Cosmina, these two young people have some talking to do, I imagine."

The older woman was gathering together the bloodied cloths and unused bandages, but she stopped at Nestor's words. "You want me to leave them alone? A proper young lady and an unmarried gentleman? And you claim to have been the servant of, what was it, a viscount?"

Nestor straightened up to his full height. "A marquis." But then he lost some of his stiffness and added, "But I suppose you are right. It wouldn't be proper. They aren't married yet."

Adriana choked on the word "yet" and nearly started coughing, but Morgan didn't say a word. He looked as if he were desperately trying to hide a smile.

"Miss Hayden can share my room with me tonight," Cosmina said, meaningfully.

"Well, then, I suppose we should all retire for the night. Tomorrow is going to be a long and busy day," Nestor said.

"And tomorrow night even more exciting for Morgan and Miss Hayden," added Cosmina.

Adriana wasn't quite certain she knew what the older woman was referring to, but felt as if she could fall asleep right then and there. A bed would be most welcome. "I would appreciate retiring, I'm still a little shaken," Adriana admitted and stood up. As if to prove her exhaustion, her knees nearly gave out, and her head felt woozy as soon as she'd regained her feet.

Morgan reached out and caught her before she made a fool of herself by falling to the floor.

"Thank you," she said, looking up into his deep black eyes. They were full of the one thing that could stop Adriana's heart—love. There was a touch of concern there as well, but mostly, there was unabashed love.

Heat seared its way through her but before she could react, Cosmina had taken her arm from Morgan and began leading her from the room.

"Good night," Morgan said softly as the door closed behind her.

Chapter 35

It was beautiful. It was even more beautiful and magical than it had been in her painting.

Morgan just stood staring at the stones before them, still some distance away. "Can you feel it? Can you feel the magic?" he asked, his voice quiet with awe.

And to Adriana's amazement, she could. It practically hummed with magic. It was the oddest sensation she had ever experienced. A frission of excitement rolled through her.

Even though it was past nine in the evening, the sky was just turning a dusky rose. Purple clouds streaked across the horizon where the sun was slipping away. The power of the night was on the rise, growing stronger with each passing minute.

"This is it," he said, looking around as they approached the outer circle of stones. He paused just outside.

Adriana could feel his indecisiveness as he hovered outside of the circle. He turned toward her, uncertainty wavering in his eyes and face. "What is it, Morgan?" Adriana asked, reaching out and taking hold of his hand.

"What if this isn't right? What if I'm not the one? I am a man. Only women have ever been made high priestess. Only women have ever inherited this destiny. What if my mother is right, and this destiny belongs to Kat and not to me."

His hand grew cold and sweaty in her own, and for a moment his doubts assailed her too. But then she realized that it was just him, pushing his feelings into her.

She pushed them right back out again, saying firmly, "No, Morgan. Your mother was not right. This is your destiny. It doesn't matter that you will be the first man to take on this role, it is yours. You were born to it." She pushed her own emotions, her certainty that this was the right thing, into him giving his hand a squeeze of reassurance.

He relaxed, his hand growing warmer again. "Yes, you're right." He released his breath. "Merlin surely would have said something to me if I wasn't the one, right?"

"Merlin?" Now Adriana was confused. Who was Merlin? Surely he didn't mean the wizard from the stories of King Arthur.

But that was exactly whom he meant.

They sat outside the circle and laid out a blanket to eat the small supper that had been packed for them at Stoneside, Morgan's new estate. As they did so, he related to her the whole story of how he met that famous wizard, and even recounted for her the prophecy he spoke. Adriana was truly in awe after that. "I can hardly believe you've met the most famous wizard in history!"

Morgan laughed, "Me neither! I must say, I have met the most amazing people on this journey to find my destiny— Nestor, Cosmina, Lord Byron and Mr. Kean, Jack the Lad—" He paused, "—and you."

Adriana felt heat rise in her cheeks. Her mind shifted to his proposal the night before just before the wolves had attacked them. "And what about that woman?" she asked, knowing that the heat in her face had faded and been replaced by a deep cold.

But Morgan smiled and shook his head. "Which woman?"

"The one Kat said you had been seen kissing," she said, looking directly into his eyes even though she didn't want to look at him at all, the thought was so painful.

Morgan lost his smile. "I don't regret meeting Sarah. She was the one who pointed out an obvious truth to me. She told me that I loved you, and she was right." He shifted himself so that he sat cross legged in front of her. "Adriana, I won't lie to you and tell you that I didn't kiss her. I did. And as soon as I did, I knew it was wrong. She knew it too because she immediately asked me who it was that I was in love with. I told her all about you." He gave a little laugh. "She was very understanding. Very kind."

Adriana didn't know what to say. She didn't exactly know what to feel. She was both hurt that he'd kissed this other woman, and elated that it meant nothing to him—that it had only made him realize how much he loved her. She supposed she should be happy.

He reached out and took her hand. "Adriana, I love you."

She just looked into his eyes. Deeply into his eyes. Yes. It was there. His love for her shone out of him like a beam of sunshine, and she was warmed by it. "I love you too, Morgan."

"You complete me," he said quietly, as a flash of lightening arched overhead.

Adriana's heart lurched, but she knew he was right. She felt it too.

He raised himself onto his knees in front of her and gently cupped her face in his hands. Running his thumbs down her cheeks, he looked deeply into Adriana's eyes. "Complete me, Adriana. Love me, and let me love you."

"Yes, I love you," she whispered as the ground began to rumble with thunder. The rich scent of grass and earth filled Adriana as rain began to fall all around them.

It was odd, only a short time ago the sky had been clear with just a few clouds skittering overhead, and now rain pattered down all around them. It didn't make sense, but then, when did the weather ever do anything predictable? Adriana laughed as Morgan looked up, smiling at the clouds, letting the rain wash his face.

This was right. Her with him, here, at this time, on this night—amidst the storm.

Gingerly, Morgan ran his hand down her cheek and then her body. His eyes followed his hand. "You are so beautiful," he whispered as his hand flowed lightly over her breasts.

Adriana felt everything with a heightened awareness—the way his hand paused ever so slightly as it passed over the tip of her breast, the heat of it as he gently cupped her and then slowly moved on, sliding down her abdomen and then lower to her hips and legs.

And with his open admiration, she felt beautiful. She felt special and beloved. But she would not allow this to be a one–way loving, she decided. She would not be shy. She wanted to show Morgan she felt the very same way he did.

Taking a deep breath, she raised herself up onto her knees, and then let her hands roam freely over his body—touching his broad shoulders and running her hands down his strong arms. She pushed aside his soaking wet coat and running her hands down his chest, and then she became truly bold and unbuttoned his waistcoat so she could feel him even more closely through his shirt. It clung to him as the warm rain soaked through the thin material. She supposed that he'd healed his wounds with magic, because he no longer wore any bandages under his shirt.

And he clearly had no problem with her explorations, quickly divesting himself of both articles of clothing, and even pulling his shirt off over his head.

His tawny skin hadn't lost its glow even after weeks in London. In the cool of the breeze that accompanied the storm, his nipples stood out tight and small from the strong muscles of his chest. She ran her fingers over them lightly, delighting in the soft purring sound he made in response.

Morgan's lips came down to taste the swell of Adriana's breast, and soon he was helping her from her wet, restraining clothing.

The cold air hit Adriana's heated body, but Morgan's proximity quickly dispelled any chill she might feel.

She arched involuntarily as Morgan began to suckle at her breast. Shocks of heat rushed through her and tingles of excitement gathered at her core. Heat pooled there, made even more luscious when Morgan touched her ever so gently. His fingers teased her, dipping in and out and around her soft sensitive flesh. A shudder rushed through her as he wove his magic in and around her body. It was all she could do not to press herself against him and rub against his strong, hard body.

But she restrained herself. Consoling herself by running her hand and then her lips over his chest. She tasted his sweet skin, suckling at his nipple as he had done to her. But then she became truly bold. She wanted to taste him, all of him.

She sat up, and pressed him onto his back, while she licked and kissed her way down the center of his stomach and then nipped at the sweet soft skin of his side, carefully avoiding the places where Cosmina had stitched him together the previous night. He giggled and his hand pushed her lips away from his ticklish flesh. She reached out for his breeches and slowly began to unbutton them, exposing the coarse, soft hair near his sex.

With a moan he lifted his hips and pushed his breeches off, revealing his manhood to her. It was long, and hard, and thick, but his skin was softer than anything she had ever touched before. Gently, she explored the length of him with her finger tips, and then spurred on by his moans of delight, she became even more bold and tasted him. His body spasmed, and she pulled away, afraid she had hurt him somehow. But he reached out, and brushed back the tendrils of hair that had fallen into her face.

"Did I hurt you?" she asked.

"No, oh no. It felt good. Never have I felt anything so wonderful," he said, his voice hoarse with passion.

"Oh, good," she smiled, and then went back to tasting his sweet saltiness. She ran her tongue along the length of his shaft, delighting in his moans as her hand followed her tongue back up to the tip. His hand came around hers, and he showed her how to stroke him even as she sucked gently at the head of his manhood.

But he didn't allow her to continue this pleasure for very long. Too soon, he was pulling her up to him, and capturing her lips with his own. He switched positions with her. Licking and kissing his way down her body, he performed his own magic on her making her writhe in ecstasy. Never had she felt anything so good as his tongue flicking in and out and all around her sensitive flesh. She couldn't contain her moans as the intensity within her built. He continued his assault until she couldn't bear it anymore and she called out his name when she thought she would explode with pleasure. He rushed up to her and cradled her face in his hands. "Did I hurt you?"

"No. Oh no, it felt, oh, Morgan, please!" Adriana couldn't help herself, she wanted more. She needed him deep inside of her.

He gently moved himself on top of her, supporting most of his weight on his arms and spreading her legs with his own.

"Become a part of me, Adriana. Let me love you, let me make love to you," he whispered into her ear.

He pressed himself up on his arms and looked down at her with such love in his eyes. "With the two of us together…"

"As one…" she said, reaching out and pushing his dripping hair out of his face.

He pressed into her then. Moving slowly, he pushed himself into her body. The pressure of him was uncomfortable at first, but he continued to move slowly in and out.

Adriana shifted as pleasure began to replace the discomfort and Morgan slowly moved himself further inside of her. He moaned and closed his eyes. Adriana hoped it was with pleasure.

As he moved himself out once more, he opened his eyes again, pausing before swiftly pressing himself in to the hilt before coming to a stop once again. A flash of intense pain gripped her, but then eased again as he waited patiently for her. He moved slightly, rubbing himself against her womanhood, and suddenly she didn't want him to stay still any longer. She moved her hips. He followed her lead, pulling himself almost all the way out before pressing himself deep inside of her once again. Again and again he did this, quickening his pace each time, sending shivers of delight through her.

More, more… she wanted… she needed… she writhed and moaned, pressing him deeper and then, delighting in his withdrawal only when he would come surging back in again. Faster and faster, until she could bear it no more and her whole body shuddered with a passion and release. He, too, began to shudder, calling out her name as he arched his back and pressed himself as far into her body as he could. Lightning flashed over head as he gave a few more quick thrusts, and then laid still.

The rumble of the thunder slowly moved away and a flash of lightning lit the world beyond Adriana's closed eyelids—only it stayed. Adriana opened them to see small sparks of light swirling around them. The wind swirled around the stones, weaving between and among them. The rain had stopped. Clouds flittered across the full moon. Slowly, the sparks died away with the wind and everything was left in stillness with nothing but the naked moon hanging over them.

Morgan pushed himself up off of her, where he had collapsed after his passion. "Adriana," he began.

But a strong emotion welled up inside of her, and she couldn't wait for him to say whatever it was he had to say. Cradling his face in her hands, she placed her thumbs over his lips to still them.

"I love you, Morgan. I love you with all my heart."

But he was looking at her oddly. "You're glowing," he said.

Adriana blinked. It wasn't the response she was expecting. "I'm glowing?"

He smiled, then laughed lightly. "Yes. I mean it, literally. There is a bright halo of light surrounding you."

He backed away from her onto his knees. It was cold without his warmth. She too sat up and looked at him. "You're not glowing, but, but there is definitely something..." It was as if he was giving off some sort of feeling—an aura, she had heard Kat call it—which made her feel good. It made her happy. And in another way, it made her keenly aware that she was in the presence of a great Vallen.

"I can feel your power. I can feel that you are powerful," she said, trying to explain it to him.

"Is it bad?" he asked, frowning with concern.

"No. It's good. It makes me feel happy and secure." She reached out for him and ran her hand down his arm. His skin was warm and soft, just as it had been before, but she could feel a tingle there as well. He took her hand in his, interlocking their fingers. Small blue sparks began to dance around their fingers.

Morgan's eyes widened. "It's you."

"What's me? Not this magic."

"Yes. This magic. It's you. It's been you all along." He threw his head back and laughed right out loud. "Oh, what a fool I am!" He swung back towards her. "You are the reason. You are the one who gave me my powers!"

"What? How could that be?" This was too confusing.

"You are Vallen Adriana, and you are the one who has given me my powers."

Adriana stood and pulled on her chemise and then her dress as she thought about this. "I don't understand. How could I be Vallen? Wouldn't I have known it? Wouldn't I have been able to feel it or something?"

Morgan reached for his breeches. "I don't know. But I realized it the minute I saw your painting of Stonehenge. It was filled with such magic! Like all of your work, I could feel everything about the place—the way it smelled, the air, and even how you felt as you'd painted it. It's magic, Adriana, your art is your magic."

Somehow this made sense to Adriana. More sense than anything else anyone had ever said about her work. It felt right. "But even if I am Vallen, how could I have possibly given you such incredible powers. I don't have powers like that, surely."

Morgan pulled his shirt on and then began to pace back and forth in front of the stones. "No, but it makes sense. The more I've gotten to know you, the more I've loved you, the more powerful I've become," he said, thinking this through.

"But I'm not powerful..."

He stopped and turned toward her. "Yes, Adriana, you are, but that's not the point." He stood directly in front of her and cradled her face in his hands. "The point is your love for me and mine for you. It was that—our love—which has caused my powers to increase."

The rumble of carriage wheels interrupted them. Morgan jumped away to finish dressing while Adriana quickly packed up what was left of their picnic.

Chapter 36

Soon enough, the carriage pulled up to where Morgan and Adriana were standing. Morgan took a step forward and was very pleasantly surprised when Mr. Kean, followed by Lord Byron, climbed down.

It was amazing to see that they glowed softly just like Adriana. He'd thought it was just Adriana because she was special to him, but now that he saw Byron and Kean, he understood it was their magic that made them all glow in this way.

"Vallentyn," Lord Byron said, as if it was no great surprise to see him here, "good to see you. And Miss Hayden." He took Adriana's hand and lifted it to his lips.

"Lord Byron! Mr. Kean! What a pleasant surprise," Adriana said.

"Shouldn't be too much of a surprise," Byron said, giving her a smile. "I am certainly not surprised to see you here."

"You're not?" she asked.

"It was clear as daylight that you were one of us," Mr. Kean said, making a grand gesture with his hands.

"We didn't know if anyone else would be here," Morgan said.

"But of course others are coming!" Mr. Kean said, expansively. "It is the summer solstice, after all."

"Is this a common thing, to come to Stonehenge on the solstice?" Morgan asked.

"Not really," Lord Byron answered. "First time I'm here. How about you, Edmund?" he asked, turning to Mr. Kean.

"Yes, absolutely, first time. But we were called here, were we not?"

"Called here?" Adriana asked.

"By the dream," he explained.

"You had the same dream Adriana and I had?" Morgan asked, amazed that such a thing could happen. He had thought only Adriana and he had shared this dream. But now he began to wonder how many others had had it too.

"That's how we knew to come," Lord Byron answered.

"How many do you think will be here?" Adriana asked.

"I honestly don't know." Byron turned to look down the road from the direction he had come. "But it looks as if others are beginning to arrive, so we should soon find out. If you will excuse me?" he said, turning to his driver. He gave the man some instructions, then moved out of the way as the coach turned around and headed back the way it had come.

Two more people arrived on horseback from the other direction, and then the coach they had seen approaching arrived. Some came alone, others in pairs like Byron and Kean. Some were cloaked to hide their identities, but others showed themselves boldly as Adriana and Morgan did. Each one had their own particular glow, some stronger than others, each in varying colors as individual as the people themselves.

Morgan was surprised to recognize Jack the Lad among those who arrived on horseback. He seemed to be moving about more slowly, as if he were stiff or in pain. Most of the others he didn't know. No one introduced themselves. Eleven people had arrived as it came closer to midnight.

Some had already started for the standing stones, milling about just outside of the circle. Morgan, Adriana, Byron and Kean were about to move in that direction when one last coach approached. Out of curiosity, they stayed closer to the road to see who the last arrivals might be.

Kat was the first to descend from the coach. Morgan noticed she glowed a beautiful soft pink, and realized the color a Vallen glowed must have something to do with their powers, although, so far, no two Vallen he had yet seen, glowed exactly the same color.

As soon as Kat's feet were on the ground, she went straight to him. "Oh, Morgan! I'm so glad to see you here!" she said, grasping his hands.

Conflicting anger and love waged a silent battle in Morgan's heart and mind. Kat had been the one to tell Adriana about Sarah Jordan. She had attached the strings that had pulled them apart, but he began to think that it wasn't she who was operating them. He set aside his hurt for now. "It's good to see you too, Kat."

There was a deep rumble of thunder followed immediately by a flash of lightning that lit the night sky. More lightning and thunder followed as his mother stepped regally from her carriage.

"Morgan!" his mother hissed. Her eyes flipped to Jack the Lad who was standing with his arms crossed and his legs in an aggressive wide stance behind Adriana. His mother glowed the brightest of anyone Morgan had yet seen, but her color was an unpleasant stark white.

"Good evening, Mother," Morgan said, bowing his head.

"And Miss Hayden," she said, with unmistakable malice.

Adriana took a step closer to Morgan before bobbing her a small curtsey. "Good evening, Lady Vallentyn." She turned to his cousin, and gave her a smile. "Hello, Kat."

"Are you surprised to see me?" Morgan asked his mother.

"No, why should I be?" she asked, raising her chin.

"Because you tried to have me killed last night," he said loudly enough for everyone nearby to hear.

Kat gasped.

"Morgan! How could you even say such a thing?" Suddenly his mother was the gentle, caring mother she had never been to him. "You're my son, why would I..."

"Who did you get to do it?" Morgan turned and faced Jack. "Was it you? And who else?"

Jack just shifted his weight from one foot to the other, but said nothing.

"Morgan, you are talking nonsense," his mother began again.

"You wanted me dead so that Kat could take my place here tonight. You will be brought to justice," he said before turning and walking into the center of the circle.

The others joined him, standing silently around, some closer, others farther away in the shadows of the stones. For a moment, Morgan stood there and knew that this was Adriana's painting.

The silence of the night, the cool air shifting softly around him and the deep feeling of magic. Morgan glanced at Adriana standing nearby, but not directly at his side and he knew exactly what it was he had been missing in Adriana's painting.

It was Adriana herself. And it was their love. That's what he had needed. Without both of those, he would not be ready to attain his destiny. It wasn't pure magical power that gave him the right to be here, it was love and the wholeness that it brought him.

Taking a deep breath, he turned to the one who should have loved him. A mother's unconditional love was the one thing that had been lacking his whole life. It had been the hole in his soul. It had been what had kept him from developing his full powers from childhood.

And yet, he had no choice but to face his mother now.

She approached him in great solemnity, holding out Merlin's chalice in front of her. There was no love in her heart for him. There was only disappointment, touched with anger. It saddened Morgan, but it couldn't be helped.

The night became absolutely still as they all stood about the circle of stones. Not even a cricket or the hooting of an owl could be heard as they formed a broadly spaced circle with Morgan and his mother in the center. The moon glowed full and bright directly overhead, bathing the scene with an ethereal light. In absolute silence, his mother approached.

Raising the chalice to the night, she began to intone:

'Neath the moon's warm silvery cloak,
We, Thy true coven, Thee do invoke
This midsummer night, please give Thy grace
For our blest rite, in hallowed place.

Come all to bear witness this night
As you watch this sacred rite
It is to him allegiance is owed
Time, strength and bloodline all have showed.

Like the North wind born from frozen floes,
And lightning torn from stormy throes,
As green stalks fill then burst with grain
Let this one child be born again.

Slowly she lowered her arms, and then, with a wistful glance to Kat, she held the chalice to Morgan's lips.

He placed his hands over hers and stared down into the cup. Once again filled with that sweet scented water, Merlin's face smiled up at him as he took a sip.

The taste was as clean as a spring day, warm and yet refreshing. But then his blood began to burn. Fire flowed through his veins, scorching him from the inside out and the horrid thought that his mother had poisoned him flashed through his mind. But no, as soon as the hot pain had begun, it was immediately followed by the cold of ice. That too spread through his body making him shiver violently. Then slowly, his temperature returned to normal.

And that was when he could feel it. A power like no other coursed through his veins. It was white hot and burning cold. It doused him with fire and brought a wholesome breath of earth and air to his lungs. He was all of the elements and more.

He turned and looked at Adriana. Her eyes shone with love for him and he felt that same love for her deep within him, mixing and blending in with his magic making him stronger.

He held out his hands to her. She took them and as she did so, her eyes widened. She seemed to swell with magic at his touch, the glow around her brightened perceptively.

"It is you who has given me what I needed to come here tonight," he said.

Her smile radiated from her face, even as she shook her head. "It is your strength, Morgan. The love you feel, not only for me, but for others. The desire you have to care for those in need. You are truly good."

The thought of good and evil made him turn back to his mother. She was still standing there, holding the chalice looking forlorn.

"You did wrong, Mother," he said. The sadness inside of him was nearly as painful as the love he felt for Adriana was wonderful. "You should not have used your magic to try to stop this. You know that."

"It is not for you to judge and punish her, Morgan," Merlin's voice said, from within the cup.

Morgan looked at the chalice. His mother held it away from herself and Morgan wondered if he should take it.

"Then who should? Is it you?" Morgan asked.

"No. Normally, it is the job of the high priest or priestess to meet out such punishments and make such judgments. But you are the Seventh, so for your time, that job will fall to the Sixth."

"The sixth? Do you mean my sister, Caroline?" Morgan couldn't believe it. "Sir, Caroline is a sweet and gentle person, but she's, well, a little simple, shall we say?" Morgan said as gently as he could.

"Caroline's not simple!" his mother argued.

Morgan gave her a look. "Caroline's never had a thought of her own."

"No, but that doesn't make her simple."

Merlin's laughter broke into their conversation. "It is not your sister of whom I speak, but your cousin. The sixth child of the sixth child of the seventh generation. Katrina."

Morgan, and everyone else, turned to look at Kat. She took a step backward away from Morgan and the chalice.

"Me? But I don't want..."

"It is not what you want, Katrina, it is what you are meant to do," Merlin's voice sounded like that of a stern father. "Morgan take the chalice. Katrina, do what you know must be done."

Morgan did as he was told, and took the chalice from his mother's grasp. For a moment, he thought she wouldn't give it up, but with a pursing of lips and a lift of her chin she turned toward Kat, prepared to face her punishment.

Nervously, Kat stepped forward. Taking her aunt's hands in her own, she looked deeply into her eyes. "I'm so sorry." And then very gently she touched her lips to her aunt's.

A brilliant flash of light broke them apart and both women staggered backward. Adriana caught Kat before she fell, and Jack the Lad made a lunge for his mother.

"I'm sorry that was painful," Merlin's voice sounded old and weary. "But it will get easier for you, Katrina. As with all magic, it gets easier the more you use it."

"I will have to do that again? To others?" Kat asked, her voice hoarse with fatigue. Lord Byron stepped up and took her weight from Adriana, who was having difficulty holding her up.

"I'm afraid so."

"My power, it's gone!" his mother cried. "All gone." Her knees began to buckle from under her, but Jack caught her and then slowly led her away from the gathering.

There was a silence everyone still present retreated into his or her own thoughts. But Morgan's eyes fixed on Adriana, drawn to her as if beyond his control.

"Let us not end this night in sadness," he said, determined to be cheerful.

He took a step forward, taking Adriana's hand with his free one. "Before all of these witnesses I would like to pledge myself to you, Adriana. I think now is the perfect time for us to marry."

A smile spread slowly across her face, brightening it into joy.

"An excellent idea!" Mr. Kean said. Other voices chimed in, and everyone seemed to be relieved of the oppressive sadness that had blanketed them all.

"May I?" Mr. Kean asked, reaching for the chalice.

Morgan turned it over to him and then turned back to Adriana.

"Tonight is the start of something new," he said quietly, but in a clear voice that carried around the circle. He held his hands out palms facing up

"Tonight we leave our old lives behind and forge a new life together," Adriana replied, placing her hands gently upon his.

"Tonight I devote my life to you, for you are my life," he said.

"Tonight I devote my soul to you, for you are what makes it complete."

"Tonight I devote my body to you, so that we may join as one."

"Together we shall live, breathe, and be as one."

"Together we will create, work and die."

"We join our lives, our souls, and our minds."

"We are one in our love," Morgan said with finality.

If you enjoyed this book, please write a review and recommend it to a friend.

Love getting free stories in you inbox? Join Meredith's **Magical Romance Newsletter**! Sign up here:
http://meredithbond.com/subscribe/

Excerpt From

Through the Storm.

The next book in the Storm Series

Some plans are made to be broken...

Being judge, jury and executioner for the magical Vallen people is Kat Havelock's hereditary duty, but she's desperate to live a normal life. Sometimes even just a few minutes for herself would be amazing. Her plan is to enter Regency society, fall in love, and live happily ever after.

Jack the Lad, the notorious smuggler, has a single-minded quest to destroy his wealthy, intolerant father, who drove Jack's late mother to penury and despair. It has taken him ten years, but now the powerful Vallen is finally ready to put his plan into action.

When Jack tries to use his magic for revenge, Kat is obliged to stop him. He convinces her to give him another chance, entangling her into his vengeful scheme. Can Jack and Kat carryout their dreams? Or does destiny have a better plan to steer them together through the storm?

Chapter 1

K AT COULD HEAR the hysterical tears all the way from the library. With a sigh, she stood up from the table where she'd been attempting to read through the cramped handwriting of one of her ancestors and prepared herself for the inevitable knock. It came faster than she expected.

"I beg your pardon, Miss Havelock," said Michael, the footman, his voice shaking slightly. Kat couldn't understand why he sounded so upset when they had been dealing with these magical problems almost non-stop for the past nine months. They'd started out with as many as twenty visitors per day, but more recently it had trickled down to no more than five, thank goodness. Ever since last summer, when her cousin Morgan had been elevated to high priest and took on the role of the Seventh—as the seventh child of the seventh child in the seventh generation, he was tasked to re-empower all the Vallen—people hadn't been able to control this increase in their magical abilities.

Normally it would have been his job, as high priest, to help with magical mishaps, but since he was off empowering people throughout the country and enjoying being newly married, Kat was left to deal with problems in London and the surrounding area.

It was almost her job.

When Morgan had been made the Seventh, Kat, as the sixth child of the sixth child in the family, was tasked with being the Sixth, keeping the laws of their people. They were pretty simple laws—do no harm to others and don't profit illegally through the use of magic. But now she also had to deal with this...

"What is it, Michael?" she asked the footman.

"A woman, Miss. Her hands are on fire," he said, holding the door for her as she started down the hall.

Kat paused and half turned back to him. "Did you say on fire?"

"Yes, Miss."

Kat spun back toward the front of the house and walked more quickly. "Oh dear," she breathed. As she approached the drawing room, she could smell the heat of fire.

The woman was dressed in scullery maid's clothing, covered with soot and singed in a number of places.

"Help," the woman cried as soon as Kat walked into the front parlor where all visitors, regardless of rank, were to be brought. "Oh please, help."

The woman held up her hands from which brilliant yellow flames writhed and danced.

Kat approached the woman with a confidence that had grown remarkably over the past few months. Taking her elbow, Kat tried to encourage her to sit next to her.

The woman looked down at the beautiful rose brocade sofa as if it were going to attack her if she dared to sit on it. "No, oh no, I couldn't."

"You can, and I need you to do so. Now, please." Kat kept her voice firm and yet gentle enough so as not to scare the young woman.

Reluctantly, she sat at the very edge. Her crying had quieted to a gentle whimper.

"Good. Now, close your eyes, if you would..." Kat let the word hang in the air.

"Peggy," the woman supplied.

"Excellent, Peggy. Now close your eyes." She waited a moment while the woman complied, her tears calming further.

"Now I want you to picture your hands as they normally are—not on fire," Kat said, infusing her words with calming magic. She made sure to keep a hand on the woman's arm to keep the connection between them, and strengthen the impact of her magic, but did her best to stay away from the fire licking Peggy's hands.

The flames began to flicker and die.

"That's good. Now, take a deep breath and keep seeing your hands in your mind's eye. They look perfectly normal to you, don't they?"

The woman nodded after taking a deep breath, her crying now completely stopped.

The flames went out altogether, leaving the woman's hands filthy but otherwise perfectly normal.

"Well done, Peggy! You can open your eyes now."

She did so with a gasp as she beheld her flame-free hands.

"Oh, thank you!" Peggy said, throwing her arms around Kat's shoulders. "Thank you, thank you."

Kat laughed and gave her a squeeze back.

"Oh, I beg your pardon, ma'am," Peggy said, suddenly remembering her position.

Kat laughed. "It's perfectly all right. But that's all you need to do, Peggy. If you accidentally set something on fire, just calm yourself and imagine it without the flames."

Peggy sniffed and nodded.

Kat took one the woman's hands and looked at it. "I'm glad you weren't hurt."

"Oh, no, Miss, I never get burnt."

"How excellent! What a special ability." Kat gave her a smile.

The woman returned it and then stood to leave. "How can I thank you," she said. "I... I ain't... I don't have—"

"Oh, no! There is no need for you to do anything. I'm just doing my job." Kat gave her a bright smile that she wished she felt deep inside and waved Peggy out the door before things got awkward.

"Thank you. Thank you again, Miss," Peggy said, giving her a curtsey before being shepherded out the door by Michael.

Kat dropped back down onto the sofa once she was alone again. She just couldn't go on like this. She truly liked helping people, but it had gotten to be too much. Yes, the visits had become less frequent, but this wasn't what Kat wanted to do with the rest of her life. She had to do something to free herself.

It was Morgan's responsibility to see to these people, not hers. She wanted nothing more than to have a normal life, be brought out into society, and find a man she could love and marry. Morgan had fallen in love and married last summer; surely, it was only fair that Kat have the chance to do so as well?

It had been long enough since he and his wife, Adriana, had left on their combined honeymoon and trip for Morgan to reinvigorate the Vallen. If Kat wasn't mistaken, he and Adriana were now back from their wanderings and settling into their new home, but there was no reason why they couldn't settle into married life here instead.

That was it. She would write to her cousin and get him to come and deal with these people and their magical problems.

She strode back to the library where she pulled out a piece of paper, her pen, and ink. Twenty minutes later, she had what she believed was a well-worded letter—not accusing him of neglecting his duty, not pleading for him to come and help her—requesting him to come to London. She carefully folded and sealed it, and then checked the time.

Just barely eleven. Perfect. Now to put the rest of her plan in motion and visit her cousin Caroline quickly before another problem came through the door.

She took no more than a moment to grab her coat before heading out into the fine spring weather. Happily, her cousin lived very nearby, so there was no need to call for her carriage and await its arrival. She escaped from the house before anyone could stop her.

About the Author

Meredith Bond's books straddle that beautiful line between historical romance and fantasy. An award-winning author, she writes fun traditional Regency romances, medieval Arthurian romances, and Regency romances with a touch of magic. Known for her characters "who slip readily into one's heart," Meredith loves to take her readers on a journey they won't soon forget.

Merry has two adult children and a loving, supportive husband. She is currently living in Europe enjoying the Bohemian life.

Merry loves connecting with readers. Be sure to find her:

Website: http://www.meredithbond.com

Facebook: https://www.facebook.com/meredith bondauthor

Pinterest: http://www.pinterest.com/merrybond/

Goodreads:
https://www.goodreads.com/author/show/847484.Meredith_Bond

Amazon: http://www.amazon.com/Meredith-Bond/e/B001KI1SNE

BookBub: https://www.bookbub.com/authors/ meredith-bond

Newsletter: http://meredithbond.com/subscribe/